BOUND FOR PERDITION

MYSTERIOUS ARTS
BOOK ONE

CELIA LAKE

BOUND FOR PERDITION

New magic brings new challenges.

Charged with creating a magical journal that would allow rapid communication during the Great War, Lynet has worked with a papermaker to overcome the technical challenges.

But brilliant magical innovation isn't enough. When she returns from a leave after the death of her father, Lynet is told they have to make more journals, cheaper and faster. The last thing she needs is a set of unskilled hands assigned to help her at this impossible task, and she's dubious that a man will be more of a help than a hindrance given her ongoing problems with most of the men of the research department.

Reggie is recently invalided out of the Army but has no relevant skills other than being a magically trained Schola man. When he's assigned to help Lynet, he's not sure how much use he'll be. He's soon swept up in Lynet's ambitious project and fascinated by her skills and knowledge.

Together, Reggie and Lynet must figure out how to get the magical materials they need for the project and move forward despite unexpected obstacles. Their mission is quickly complicated by odd goings on with other research in the department, something that might change the War itself!

Bound For Perdition is the first book in the Mysterious Arts series. A cosy historical fantasy romance set in 1917 in the magical city of Albion, Britain's magical community, it is a great entry to Celia Lake's Albion books. *Bound for Perdition* is full of bookbinding, coming to grips with injury, navigating class differences, and making a new future in a rapidly changing world.

CHAPTER 1

Lynet frowned as she looked at the workshop. As spaces went, it had more than adequate lighting, a sufficient lack of leaks, and plenty of storage space; that was not the problem she had with it. She simply, or not so simply, wasn't sure how to arrange the space she had. Not in a sensible way. It was not something Papa had taught her, not like this. It wasn't something her teachers at Alethorpe had taught her. And it certainly wasn't a problem she'd ever faced before.

Lynet knew it had been a risk taking the Ministry's offer. But she had been desperate last year, and truth to tell, she was still desperate. And she had wanted to do her part for the War, of course. Only now she'd ended up on the wrong side of a fairy tale. Rather like Rumplestiltskin, only first, this was rag paper, not straw, and second, she absolutely had no time for princes, and certainly not pregnancy.

She had created a triumph in the third week of March.

1

They'd figured out how to create a set of journals that would communicate with each other without needing to be made from the same batch of materials. She and Ellis had created seven rounds, a total of 23 journals, and she was sure the charms would hold.

Lynet had presented the initial set, bar the ones she and Ellis had kept for themselves, to Master Brand. He had hmmed and hawed, saying it would be at least a few days before he had an answer from the Ministry about it.

In the end, it had been more than a few days. That night, Papa had taken ill, or rather had become far more seriously ill than he had been before. The final descent had been rapid, and two days later, he had died. At home, at least, as the Healers had said there was nothing they could do for him.

The powers that be had granted Lynet a fortnight's leave to see to Papa's funeral and finishing those items he'd had in the workshop. Mind, that was to their advantage. She was sure her lords and masters had wanted her well away from questions from the Ministry about the real challenges of making their new invention in mass quantities. The Schola men had no use for practical Alethorpe considerations making a hash of their airy promises of results, so it was certainly convenient for them that she couldn't be there to try to set expectations.

Making a bound blank book, charmed and enchanted in every flick of paper, stitch, and drop of paste, so it could communicate with books made the same way, was complicated enough. But that was manageable. She had, in fact, managed it. Not by herself, of course. She'd relied on other people's research, and Papa's help, all the way through. But she was the one who'd perfected the methods. She was the one who'd done the painstaking testing of which papers and thread and all the other materials worked best with Ellis.

Now, he at least wasn't difficult to work with. For one thing, he'd been a couple of years behind her in school. Enough that he didn't try to take over, like most people did. He knew what she could do, and what he couldn't. And he knew that a proper magical book needed the best paper, but also a binder who could handle it properly.

Lynet had honestly expected it would take more than a fortnight for whoever it was in the Ministry to make a decision. She knew the costs were high on the materials, but she also understood that sometimes that was what was needed for a particular bit of work. It would make sense that the Ministry might need to figure out funding and materia and everything else that was needed.

In the meantime, the research projects had moved buildings. Ellis had overseen it at least, so things were stored more or less sensibly, but she'd have to figure out the actual layout now. Quickly, too.

She assumed there was some sort of urgency, because she'd had a very brusque message from Master Brand last night, to present herself at his office at half-nine this morning. As she'd been trained to do, she'd turned up a few minutes early. Being on time - never mind being late - wasn't the sort of thing people like her could get away with. Besides the fact it made people like Master Brand irritated, and that didn't do any good for anyone either. At least she'd had that instruction, both at school and from Papa.

Master Brand had a beautiful office at the end of the ground floor. The whole place was given over to their work now, not the previous hallway they'd had in the old building. Well, not just hers, not just the journals, but all the research projects that were supporting the War effort.

She'd been shown down a long row of offices on the ground floor. Master Harold's, Mistress Ockley's, Lord Carillon's. There had been a Mistress Williams and a Mistress Aylett, side by side. Half a dozen names that were new that she couldn't even catch from the nameplates. They were written in that ridiculous calligraphy that wasn't at all readable at speed, a horrible choice.

Not that it mattered. Those people wouldn't know who she was unless they were angry with her. And she wouldn't be allowed down in those dainty panelled halls unless there was some emergency. She spent her life in smocks, with blotches of paste or bits of ink or dye or whatever she'd been working with. Her hands, right now, were still a deep indigo along the finger pads from the book she'd been glueing last night.

She'd dressed well this morning, at least. Tressy, the publican's wife across the street from Papa's workshop, had dyed the frock for her for the funeral. Not the best sort of cloth, but it didn't look too poorly, at least not since she'd mended a couple of worn spots in the cuffs. Her sewing was certainly up to that much, even if she hated working on clothing.

The meeting was over almost before it began; Master Brand had been very brief. Crisp, even, the way men of his class were, as if she were some cog in a great factory machine. The Ministry had funded them to figure out how many journals they could produce at a given price point. He'd laid out the limits, told her it was for the book as a whole. He didn't care whether the savings came from the materials, who did the work, or some other part of the process, as long as they came in under budget.

That budget, though, was going to be a problem. It was near a quarter what had been involved in the original set, on a book-by-book basis. Lynet didn't see a way to cut the costs that far at all. It wasn't as if she could give up her salary, but that wasn't the bulk of the expense anyway, it was the materials and the materia that were. Lynet had kept the books for Papa for a decade now. She knew how to squeeze the most out of materials.

But Master Brand made it clear the Ministry - and the Army - wanted more speed. That would mean more help, and that sort of budget wouldn't allow for it. At best she'd get someone who got dumped on their doorstep needing a place to work; someone like that would be no real help at all. Certainly not familiar with her art and craft and the magic she made.

Not that Master Brand was either. She'd swallowed, trying to find a way to tell him that what they wanted was impossible. She could make the books, certainly, with Ellis to do the paper. But the method they'd sorted out, it cost three or four times what was permitted. And it was vastly slower, as well. She could speed up some of it by working in stages. Paper had a process. Paste had to have time to dry under weight.

But that only went so far. Book presses didn't grow on trees, for magic's sake. Even cobbling something together that would work would take space and materials that were going to be hard to come by. Metal was going to the War, and so was stone and wood and a whole host of other things she might otherwise have used. That didn't even get into the costs for the materia, the herbs and stones and all that made the magic of the journals work.

Master Brand hadn't permitted an argument. He'd just waved his hand. He'd told her she could have the use of the building porters over the next few days to move the heavier things into the workshop in the attic. When they weren't busy with other duties, of course. Then he'd had one of the clerks show her up to this room. Half the attic of the building, and no idea what to do with it. At least it felt more like a working space, not somewhere she'd smudge polish or scuff something, just in the ordinary processes of the day.

She was still standing there, overwhelmed, when she heard a knock on the door. She'd closed it behind her, thankfully, so no one would see her looking like a ninny.

Lynet rubbed her face. "Yes?" She tried to keep the sharpness out of her voice, and she was sure she had failed.

The door opened anyway, and there was Ellis, with curly brown hair framing his face. "Heard you were back. Or rather, Everson told me I should come up."

Lynet grimaced. "Close the door, come in. Can't offer you tea, the kettle's downstairs. Where do they have you?"

"A building out back here." The equipment he needed was not only bulky and heavy but also often odoriferous. "There's a hoist out the back stair there. To bring the paper up without going up the stairs."

"Well, that's going to be a joy, isn't it? Not that we're going to be working in that kind of quantity just yet." Lynet held up a hand when Ellis would have cut in. "I know that's the goal. I just got told, give me half an hour to catch up."

"Look, hop up on the counter. You think better that way. Let me see if I can sweet-talk someone out of some tea and biscuits. There's a tea lady somewhere. She doesn't come up this far, but if I can find her, I can get something."

Trust them to have a tea lady. She nodded, and Ellis went out the door, closing it behind him. A moment later, she found a kick stool, brought her satchel with her, and found her perch on one of the long workbenches, facing the door. That way, no one else could surprise her.

It took Ellis a good fifteen minutes to come back. By

that point, she'd started half a dozen lists. Questions about the paper, what he would be using, how he wanted to approach it. And then everything else. Linen thread would be vastly cheaper than silk, but she hadn't liked the way it reacted in the experimental versions. And then there was the paste. She couldn't alter the fundamental recipe too far, but there was a far too long list of what might help anchor the charmwork and enchantments. There'd need to be bookcloth and endpapers, and if they were making journals in bulk, surely people would want some choice. They'd gone with blue, for now.

Even if it were like a uniform, surely people would want different covers to tell their journal from someone else's. Well, they would when there were more than a couple of dozen of the books in existence. She could understand why people wanted the things so much. Being able to write back and forth freely, not waiting for the post to go through the portals. Well. It had made a world of difference for her and Papa at the end.

Ellis knocked, then nudged the door open only when she called out, "Come in," which she did only after she'd seen his head through the smudged glass window. A good cleaning would be high on her list to start, once she figured out who had supplies, and whether there was anyone who could help. Ellis, somehow, had a tray with a pot of tea, two teacups, and a plate of biscuits. "Mrs Evers, that's the tea lady, took a liking to me. Said I need feeding up."

Ellis did. He'd been quite ill as a kid. He'd told her that much. Rheumatic fever or something like that. It meant his heart wasn't steady enough to go into the Army, and then he'd had skills they needed here. He didn't talk about it, and she didn't push. No good could come of that. He'd treat her differently, at the least, and not in a way that would help her keep her own head above water.

"Lists?" He nodded at the notebook lying flat next to her. One of her own, of course, made to a size that was comfortable in her hands.

"Always." Lynet took the cup of tea Ellis poured for her. "How long have you known?"

He ran a hand through his hair. "A week. Or they asked me to start getting things ready then. I think they only got approval on Thursday, and then there were forms and requisitions and all that. They told you not much chance of other staff?"

"Certainly not anyone with training." She grimaced. "I mean. I suppose someone to fetch and carry and help mix the paste would be a help, but not even that? And they want speed."

"They want us to figure out how to get speed." Ellis pointed out. "Maybe if we work it out, and then explain what we need to keep things running."

"You had the sequencing class, same as I did." Most of Alethorpe's finest ended up in positions where those above them didn't understand the basic concepts of 'paste needs time to dry' and 'tinctures need time to steep'. So they'd had courses on how to explain the basic limitations of time to people who apparently thought they could bend that to their will as readily as anything else.

Lynet knew there were chronological magics, but she assumed - like any sensible person - that they had functional limits. And that you couldn't just stop or speed up time, especially not when making something that had a process, with a dozen or more steps. On the other hand, the people who thought that were men who had meals appear from behind green baize doors in a matter of moments, with no idea how much went on behind the scenes. They had no knowledge of making stock or letting bread rise, or the way something cooked down from toughness to tenderness in the stew pot.

"All right. Tea first, plan second. First, do you know how to track down the porters? All my things are still in the workshop I was using." That had been a cramped little room with awful ventilation, a block away, and this space was certainly better than that. She'd have to figure out how to bring in a few things from Papa's workshop, too. If she were going to be making things at speed, she wanted her proper bookpress, her own, where she knew all its little preferences.

CHAPTER 2

Lynet was given a bare four days' time before she was summoned downstairs again. By a note in her own journal, one of the early successful trials. It made her eye the thing warily when it chimed.

Of course, she went downstairs at the appointed time, half two on Friday afternoon. She was cranky, not stupid. There was a war on, she had obligations to service, that had been made very clear. And the salary here was generous enough she could keep the lease on Papa's shop, long enough to figure out what to do with it, even if going back and forth to London was a bother and a half. She was mostly sleeping in one of the Guard training barracks in a tiny room barely big enough for a bed, and eating in their dining hall at a lonely table by herself.

Lynet had at least made progress with Ellis. They had put their heads together, and figured out how to run half a dozen parallel lines of exploration as efficiently as possible. He was working on the paper for that, while she had been gathering up materia for glue and bindings and endpapers. She was waiting on one last requisition to arrive, but next week she'd be able to start into that properly.

She'd spent the rest of the week cajoling the porters into bringing her various tools upstairs. And she'd talked one of the Guard quartermasters into putting together a few more book presses for her. They just needed vises and some solid boards, nothing complicated. Enough so she could have a dozen books in a press at once, which would do to be getting on with. Not that it would suffice if they wanted to turn out dozens of books a week, or hundreds, but she had to start somewhere.

She'd also managed two batches of marbled papers, the simplest of the components in some ways, while also the most artistic. Lynet had, on the whole, been quite pleased with the effect. It was a mingled green and blue print with hints of white and dots of red anchoring the green magic of Albion with the blue, red, and white of the flag.

It would do nicely to start with. Her own journal was much plainer, a simple brown bookcloth with a beige and brown and green endpaper. Like a bird, really, a female bird who didn't need flash to attract attention. She'd thought about adding something to the front. She certainly had tools and stencils for it, but she hadn't decided what yet. Thinking about something just for show wasn't in her right now. It hadn't been for three weeks, since Papa had taken ill the last time.

It was no use dwelling on that, it wasn't as if it would change anything. She'd done what she could, and she had to keep going. Anything else was even more hopeless. At least right now, she had work to keep her busy, it might do some good, and she had the skills they needed.

Which is why she'd turned up at Master Brand's door

precisely on time. She'd checked on Papa's pocket watch - she knocked on the door. There were two people in there. She could hear them talking before Master Brand's voice became more audible. "Come."

Like a servant or a dog. Not that either were bad or shameful things, Papa had drilled that into her about people in service. But she was neither. She forced a smile on her face, the pleasant one she'd practised, and went in.

Master Brand was sitting at his desk, with a man facing him. The second man twisted around in his chair, half-bobbing upwards at her arrival, the way men of a certain type did with women before they realised she wasn't their sort of woman. Master Brand waved a hand at it. "Sit, sit. Mistress Alder."

He had at least given her the proper title this time, and that made her wonder why. Last time, he'd simply avoided the title altogether. Finding a chair, the other corner of the desk, nearer the door, gave her a chance to get a look at the other man. Tall enough, dark-haired. Early thirties, maybe, though his face had some lines of pain or tiredness that made it a bit hard to tell. Five years older than she was, give or take. That meant he'd feel free to take over whenever they were thrown together. She was sure of it.

She was also suddenly very aware that her dress had a faded spot or three - it really needed to be dyed again. And her cuffs were grubby. Lynet had been cleaning upstairs to make sure the paper would get stored somewhere spic and span. She really should have found some sleeve covers. She could run some up this weekend, adding to an increasingly long list.

"Sir." Lynet nodded at Master Brand as she settled.

"You said you could use some help, yes? Hollis here, he's

willing." Master Brand waved a hand at the other man. "At something of loose ends at the moment."

Lynet blinked several times, unsure what to say to this first. "Trained help?"

"Not in your field, no, but he's a quick learner. He did well at Schola." As if that actually answered any sort of useful question. She didn't need a treatise on the theory of magic. She needed someone with good hands, whose fingers did what he told them, over and over and over again.

"In?" She turned to Hollis - no first name provided, of course not - and added, "Pardon, but do you even know what I'm up to?"

He, oddly, looked rather abashed. "I gather you're working on expanding a project for wider use. I do have a bit of knowledge of that sort of thing. I did quite well in Materia though it's not a speciality, and I'm a quick learner. Lifting's no problem." Though the way he said that made her suddenly suspect there was some other limitation he wasn't mentioning.

Master Brand smiled serenely at her. "Give him a try for a fortnight. Can't promise you anyone else, so, well. See how he gets on." Which was to say, it was this Hollis or no one. He could presumably at least be a help lining things up and closing the presses, or prepping materials for her to work on. With some training and careful oversight.

Lynet didn't have it in her to fight. She nodded. "Sir." Best not to say too much more, or she might say things he wouldn't approve of. More things. Even if they did need her particular skills or something close to them for a while yet, there was no point in being difficult simply for the sake of difficulty.

"Where are you so far?"

She'd turned in her weekly report promptly yesterday afternoon. Of course he hadn't read it yet. "Ellis is working on the paper. The first batches will be ready for testing on Monday." That was a slow part of the work, too. It had taken him a week to get enough paper to do a dozen sample books. If he could get an assistant, it would go faster. Or if they could figure out how to apply the materia to one of the machines for making paper, but that seemed a lost cause so far.

"Grand, grand. We expect to see some results next week, of your tests. Take Reggie off with you, then."

"Master Brand." Lynet stood, nodding, then waited for Hollis to join her. "This way. We're up at the top of the building."

It wasn't until they were out in the hallway with the door behind her that she realised he walked oddly. Not quite a limp, he didn't seem in pain as he walked, but there was an unevenness. He opened his mouth as if to ask something, then he heard a sound from one of the other offices, and pressed his lips together. "Stairs, I assume?"

Lynet nodded. "This way." His lungs were in decent shape, he wasn't gasping for breath by the time they were three flights up, but he was moving more unevenly in the last flight, leaning on the rail hard. She unlocked the workshop with the press of her hand on the charmed metal plate, and added, "Touch there, please." It would - somehow, she didn't understand the specifics - recognise him, but not allow him entrance without either her or Ellis being in the room.

Given how much materia would likely be up here inside the next week, well. That was just good sense. Even if she was supposed to be keeping costs down, she needed some of it in quantity for the testing and refinements. "Sorry, don't have much in the way of chairs, but take that one?" There was a desk with a rather scarred chair in one corner, and Lynet swung herself up onto the workbench via a stepstool as he pulled the chair out. It gave her the advantage of both height and of informality. She'd see what this man did with that.

It turned out that the first thing he did was blink. "Beg pardon?" It was the sort of phrase that meant a score of things, everything from a request to something just short of an insult. Here, she thought it more the former, but who knew.

"What did they tell you about the project? Let's start there." Lynet at least knew what she was doing there, and the longer this man stayed off-kilter, the more control she'd have over the situation.

He folded his hands, then cleared his throat. "Um. Pardon. Can I have a minute? The stairs..." She raised an eyebrow, but he didn't explain. "And is there a chance of some tea?" That last had a plaintive note, as if tea would make a difference to him.

Lynet did in fact have a kettle now. It was near the first thing she'd unpacked. "Nothing fancy, black." She swung down from the workbench without waiting for a response from him and went and turned on the kettle. She added over her shoulder. "No biscuits or anything like that. Just tea." He might as well get a sense of the state of the resources provided.

He said nothing, just staring off at her, his mouth set in a straight line. Not giving much away, either, was he? When she brought the tray back with the pot and two cups, he nodded. "Show me how to make it next time?"

Lynet raised an eyebrow. This did not seem the sort of

man who made his own tea. "Perhaps." She nodded at him once. "The project?"

"Well." The interval had at least given him a chance to gather his thoughts. This time he didn't duck the question. Lynet poured herself a cup, leaving him to pour his own, and set it on the workbench to settle there, peering down at him. She preferred higher seats. Papa had always said it suited her being named for a bird. "The people in this building are all doing various projects related to research and development, for the War effort."

She nodded. Lynet knew of at least a dozen. Also, seeing which groups of people went out for lunches together. "And?"

"And you are working on one related to journals that allow you to communicate with other journals. A complex combination of enchantments, I gather. That's certainly out of my sphere of expertise."

What was he good for, then? Honestly. If she couldn't select her own help - all right, not that Master Brand would admit she could - they might at least have given her a precis of his skills. "Which is? Start there."

He swallowed. "I was at the front until three months ago. Invalided out." He didn't specify why. "Nothing that should interfere with this kind of work."

"How," she asked, keeping her voice mild, "can you be sure of that, if you've never done this kind of work?"

CHAPTER 3

Reggie sucked in a breath. He was in over his head, far over his head, and he had the sense to know it. It wasn't just this woman in front of him. Mistress Alder. She was small-boned, with deft hands gesturing here and there, but always with a precision that his teachers would have praised. No wasted motion, no jerkiness. Just efficiency and flow.

That wouldn't help either. He needed to understand this better, not just the project, but the odd unsteadiness of the ground between Mistress Alder and Brand.

He swallowed, then cleared his throat. "My hands work well, mistress. My feet work well enough, so long as you don't need me to dance at any speed. And I don't believe your occupation has much to do with dancing. The rest of me, also reasonably sturdy."

She looked him up and down from her perch on the workbench. She'd hopped up there as freely as Reggie had mounted a horse a couple of years ago, or climbed a stile on a long ramble. It made her seem very active, given her work apparently had to do with fine handcrafts. Books. Book binding. Whatever the word was. She opened her mouth, as if to press him on the nature of the injury, and he tried to muster a quelling expression.

To be fair, he had never managed anything that would quell more than a slightly dubious and nervous dog. It did well enough in the moment, though, because she tilted her chin, and then asked an easier question for him to answer.

"What do you know about this project? Let us start there. Why have you been assigned to help me, if you have any knowledge or theory on the matter?"

Reggie paused to sip his tea and gather his thoughts. Master Brand had used the moderately formal title for her, Mistress Alder. That meant she'd apprenticed to some master or mistress of whatever her arts were. But her accent, that was London, and more Spitalfields than Bedford Square. Certainly not the way most of his fellows at Schola sounded, whether they were men or women. Though she sounded more like the men, really, in the edge to her sentences, the way they ended firmly.

"I am recently invalided out, and they do not have a need for my other skills at the moment. Protective magics."

That got another tilt of her head, the other direction now. "I would have thought there was a great deal of that to be done, one way or another."

"Mostly, um. In the trenches and along the front. And that's where I'm no use now." He did not want to explain why, the indignities of losing three toes to trench foot. And a fair bit of the flexibility along the outer side, too, which was rather more challenging to manage. His magic hadn't been enough to protect him from that, it turned out. Not nearly enough.

He straightened his shoulders. "My impression was that this office needed more hands, even if they're untrained. From what Master Brand said, someone who could help set things up under instruction. Manage paperwork, perhaps. Keep an eye on a timer and alert you when it was time for the next stage. Fetch the tea."

She looked him up and down, and now she was no bird, but a most disdainful cat, the way they looked right through people they found wanting. "You'd fetch tea? For me?"

Reggie shrugged. "If your skills were needed doing other things, certainly." He had, perhaps, discarded most of his sense of shame somewhere in Belgium. Along with a lot of things besides his toes.

Mistress Alder clearly didn't believe him. She certainly didn't bother arguing with him, and Reggie had no idea what to make of that. The women of his acquaintance might duck an argument to keep things pleasant, or they might demand things their own way. This refusal to engage was entirely different. He forged on, because he had not yet answered her questions, and whatever else he did, he could at least attempt that.

"I gather from Master Brand that there are a dozen different research projects going in this building. Some with one or two people working on them, some with a dozen or so. From what he said, you and a Master Ellis Stromer, who makes paper?" He had at least filed the relevant names correctly, because she nodded once, with that same efficient movement.

Reggie paused for another sip of tea. "Your project is making books that allow someone writing in one book to have the message passed to another book. Not just two books made at the same time, from the same paper and the enchantments cast all at once, but books made at different times. And to many books." He hesitated. "Is that true?"

He could think of a dozen ways it would change the world. The War, first and foremost, to have accurate messages that didn't have to cut through lines of attack. But also the human nature of the War. Censoring the things would be damnably hard, and people would say the most horrendous things in letters. He'd learned that, as an officer doing his part of the censoring. All sorts of military details, but also things that would horrify people at home, destroy morale, share news of deaths before the proper announcements were made back in Albion. And that was before you got to the actual information that would tell the enemy just where they were, if they ever saw it.

On the other hand, it might be a comfort. To know what was going on, that loved ones were well. Reggie thought fleetingly of the girls he'd known in the distant land before the War. Maybe if he'd had an easy way to write, that would have gone differently. Or his parents would have worried more about the right things. Or he'd have been able to talk about something else, literature or music or something beautiful that might survive the grinding awfulness.

Mistress Alder nodded slowly. "It is. We have made twenty-three samples. The most recent batch, we made six, at three different times, with six distinct batches of materials, and they communicate properly. The next portion of our assignment is to find ways to reduce the cost per volume and speed up the time of production. As well as determine how many steps could be handled by people who are not trained bookbinders."

Reggie looked up at that. "Well, I can help with that, at least. I appreciate a book, but I know nothing of how they go together, except that the pages are sewed in, and there's glue involved."

"In the style we are making, yes." He must have looked blank, because Mistress Alder sighed and hopped off the workbench again. She came back a minute later with half a dozen objects, including three bound books, on a rimmed wooden tray. "Tea away, please. We won't risk spills."

Her voice was curt, as if she expected him to argue, but he just nodded. It was sensible. And if a lot of handwork, never mind magic, went into these, he wasn't going to be the one to spoil it.

"You've only used books? Never made them, or mended them?"

He shook his head. "Isn't that rather delicate? Isinglass, or do I remember that right?"

Mistress Alder looked surprised. Pleasantly surprised, perhaps. "Isinglass. It comes from fish bladders, it's one of the ways to make a delicate glue." She added, a bit repressively. "One of many ways to make glue."

Clearly, glue was a thing she had mastered. Was mistress of. However the wording went. Equally clearly, he was going to be learning a fair bit about glue and quite possibly stirring it at length. Mistress Alder leaned forward, tapping the books. "It is Friday afternoon. I am not starting the proper explanation now. You can learn it as we go along. But this is a signature, folded paper. It is worked into the binding as a unit. This is a signature block." She tapped a stack of pages, sewn together with a bright blue thread, with fabric tapes sewn across in three places. "Do you follow?"

"Those are the insides of the book." There must be specific preparations there, somehow. For one thing, they had a Master making the paper, so presumably it wasn't just ordinary stuff you could get anywhere. And it made sense that the materials for what someone wrote on would be of particular interest. Perhaps the inks too. He'd have to ask about that at some point. He'd been good at Materia in school, but he'd not spent a lot of time with it in the past decade. And more to a point, a fair bit of it had been theory, and he suspected the applications were a different sort of thing altogether. Warding did and didn't care about Materia, that was the rub of it, and it wasn't as if he could turn his hand to the warding work right now. He could at least follow that much, though, and he nodded.

"Then you attach things, step by step. And of course, whatever such things as ribbon bookmarks or embossing of the cover or what have you." Those were clearly not details she bothered much with, at least not as a matter of course.

Reggie leaned forward, peering at the books. "But there are different styles?" One of the books, he could see the stitching was left visible. Another one seemed to be sewn directly through a leather cover.

Mistress Alder glanced at him again, and then put her hand on one, the one where he could see the stitching. "This is Coptic binding. Not as sturdy for long-term use, because there's no protection for the spine. It's a tad easier for the thread to work loose, too. If you're not careful. Or for it to get cut on a sharp edge in a bag, possibly." Clearly, her books did not have that weakness.

"And the leather?" Reggie rather liked the look of that, honestly. Leather had a solidness that had always appealed to him. The smell, too, and there was a hint of that here, the same as a horse's tack or good outside walking boots, or a falconer's glove.

"Long stitch binding. Again, less support for the signature block. We considered an option like this, but in our early testing, we found that using the paste and endpapers and bookcloth to anchor related enchantments was rather better." She glanced down at the leatherwork, then back up. "If I lent you a book, would you read it by Monday?"

Reggie swallowed. "About making books?"

"Just so." She stood, taking the tray away with her, before he could get a closer look at the books on it. She came back with a single volume, bound in plain brown bookcloth. "You can keep that, if you find it useful."

Reggie looked up and blinked. "Pardon?"

"I'll give you a trial. If you can't pick up something useful by the end of next Friday, I'll tell Master Brand to find you something else."

It was more generous than he deserved, really. She clearly hadn't expected to have an entirely untrained assistant dumped in her workroom. "Thank you, Mistress Alder." He kept his voice even.

"And you are Reggie Hollis. Is there a proper title that goes with that?"

"I was Captain Hollis." He shrugged. "I earned my mastery, but that doesn't really apply here, does it?"

She leaned back against the workbench. She should have looked small or unimposing, somehow. Her hair was coming a bit loose from the bun, and her frock didn't offer any colour or even much shape. "I am Lynet. And you are Reggie. Otherwise, we'll be forever asking for help."

It seemed like a particular concession from her, one where Reggie couldn't begin to sort out what it meant to her. "As you wish. Linnet?" He spelled it out, and she shook her head.

"L-y-n-e-t. Named for the bird, but an older form."

Reggie wanted to ask, all of a sudden, if the mourning dress, such as it was, was for a husband or a fiance or someone else. He didn't know how to ask that without putting a foot in it. Instead, he cleared his throat again. "And Master Stromer?"

"I'll introduce you to Ellis on Monday morning." Again, that little twist of her head. "I'll meet you in the back court-yard at nine on the dot. Don't come up here before then. I'll need to set some things up."

Reggie didn't argue. "Nine on Monday, in the back courtyard. Wearing things that can get, I don't know. Stained or smudged?"

"Good boots, you want to protect your toes." Reggie barely managed to repress the flinch at that. He did, and he hadn't. Point taken, though. "Clothes you don't mind getting a bit dirty. Paste's the biggest risk. I'll bring a spare smock, but if you have one you prefer, bring that. I bring my luncheon. You are welcome to take a break for it and go to one of the shops or the Ministry canteen." Clearly, she was not going to spend more time with him than necessary. "We work eight to six, normally, with an hour for lunch."

"Thank you." Reggie let out a long breath. Somehow, the expectations settling into place were more of a help than he'd thought they'd be. "Nine, Monday. I'll get out of your hair now. I'm sure you have things you were hoping to finish this afternoon." She seemed like a woman who had a precise timetable in her head at all times.

Certainly, she didn't argue, just showed him to the door and out of it. He heard the soft click of a lock as he turned away.

CHAPTER 4

An hour later, Reggie was settled in a chair in the bar at Bourne's, nursing a drink and listening to the gossip ebb and flow around him. He hadn't yet really thought about supper. In the unlikely chance someone invited him to join, he would do that. If no one had by half-seven, he'd see what the club could rustle up.

He'd thought about going along to the Arthur and hadn't been able to face it. He didn't belong there anymore. Certainly, people would wonder why he was out of uniform. And it was the sort of club that bragged over wounds and scars. Half the older men had some sort of duelling scar they trotted out, whether caused by a duelling blade, among the non-magical or by some hex or curse or impact in a magical duel.

Once upon a time, a few months ago, that had been Reggie. Reggie, with the scar on the edge of his cheek, just hidden by his hair. The mark of a burn skittered along his upper arm, from a strand of fire that had nearly snared him. He glanced, just for a moment, at his boots, and how they hid that set of scars. In there, invisible, were the remnants of his foot, the way the tendons and muscle twisted just enough. Easy enough to manage with sturdy boots and an insole that filled the space as needed. But also, always a reminder, one he couldn't run from. He grimaced at the bleak pun, but it was true enough.

One group passed by, what sounded like men on leave. No one he knew particularly well, a couple of whom must have been brothers to people he'd known in school. Either that or every man in uniform gained a certain similarity.

The company in the room turned over, and turned over again, but around half-six a knot of people came in that he recognised. No one he'd known well, but a couple more distant. Reggie twisted slightly in his chair, thinking about where the light would hit. He moved his fingers under the table in the form that would call the light to illuminate him that much more. His apprentice master had drilled the subtleties into him, as well as the loud dramatic magics.

It worked. Reggie didn't have time to crow about it, but one of the men waved. "Join us, Hollis? Didn't expect you back here. Weren't your orders for Belgium?"

Reggie stood, moving to join them at their table, careful to hide the slight jerk of his foot, the way it rolled differently. "Invalided out. M'foot. Back in Trellech for the duration, or maybe London, depending on what's needed."

Klover looked him up and down, catching the slight shift of his foot. "Bad luck." Mind, he wasn't in uniform, neither were any of the others. "You were keen on being there. Doing all you could, I'm sure."

It had a hint of mockery in it, the sort Reggie wasn't used to hearing these days. The Army valued stubborn bravery, or at least unthinking bravery. Reggie had a reputation, he knew, for digging in and getting the job done. Holding his place, whatever came his way. He'd been proud of it before.

Now he just shrugged. "The world goes on." Or at least he hoped it did. Down in the trenches, he'd been entirely unsure about that prospect. Even now, with his head - and his feet - out of the mud and the dust and the blood, he was none too sure any of the rest of the world were real. Not some days, at any rate.

"And you, Klover? And, erm. I'm Reggie Hollis. You're Drawer." Reggie nodded at a man a bit older, with ruddy lights to his dark hair. "And Perks." That, to a man with sharp black hair, decidedly longer than military length.

"And I'm Hopkins." That last from a cheerful looking blond, who seemed more relaxed than the rest of them. "Schola man, I assume?"

"Bear. A couple of years behind Klover here. I apprenticed with Master Wilton, same as Perks, but of course a fair few years later." That was the calling card of their kind, which house, which apprenticeship, which family. His own family was impeccable. Threaded through the Gold Book listings, back to the Conquest, with their share of Lords and Council Members and every other prestige. Though admittedly, neither he nor his father had particular honours. Not at the moment. Nor his sisters. "Anything interesting you've been up to?"

"Oh, start with yourself, old chap. You always wanted to keep busy. You must be reassigned somewhere."

"Just today. I spent four days warming a bench in the Ministry while they decided where to send me. There might be something for me in warding work, down the road." Reggie shrugged. "Research and development. Lending a strong arm, at the moment. Not anything I've got training in."

Master Brand had been careful to impress on him the need for secrecy. But he had also conveyed those code words that might confirm others working in the same department. 'lending a strong arm', in this case.

Reggie saw Hopkins react for just a moment, a slight widening of the eyes. Then, deftly, he encouraged the others to talk about what they were doing. Perks was developing some new approaches to warding, likely to go overseas in a few months. That sort of thing that could help keep a trench up, or shore up a hospital or field headquarters. Useful enough, and the sort of thing Master Wilton would approve of extensively.

Klover was on escort duty, showing senior staff from place to place and being handy. Being charming, clearly, and he let it continue to pour out. He peppered the conversation with jokes that drew a few uncomfortable looks from other corners of the room, as if that much laughter were unseemly.

In due course, they migrated into one of the supper rooms, a table just big enough for six, and a bit more protection from other conversations. Hopkins didn't say much about his own work until the others were gathering up their bits and bobs. "One more drink, Hollis? There's something you said about Belgium I'd like to ask more about."

Reggie settled back in his chair. "Sure. A brandy?" Hopkins nodded, and ordered another round for them both.

It wasn't until the protections were up and they were alone again that Hopkins raised his fingers then gave a quick roll of them on the table. First a tap of all four fingers, then a roll from pinkie to index, then the thumb and index together. It made him wonder what men did who were missing fingers rather than toes.

Reggie repeated the counter, two taps of index and middle, then the three inner fingers. Those were the codes that Master Brand had showed him, yes, and not likely to be done idly. "Good time to have a chat." An utterly ordinary phrase, to conceal so much.

Hopkins burst into a smile. "Quick learner. Good, that's what we like to see. I knew you were joining us, Brand told me this afternoon." He wrinkled his nose. "All the way up in the attic, though, that's no fun."

Reggie shrugged. "Mistress Alder needs a hand. And it's a ... that could change the War. A dozen ways."

"Oh, everything in the building could change the War a dozen ways. And I'm sure there are other buildings. Country houses, maybe, somewhere. Every little corner, doing its part." Mind, neither of them had mentioned anything directly. "I'm by way of being a welcome. Obviously, you're not going to go out and socialise with Alder, are you?"

There was something decidedly dismissive in the comment, and Reggie wasn't sure why. That she was a woman, possibly, though plenty of Schola women were holding their own when it came to Ministry projects.

Then again, he was fairly sure she wasn't a Schola woman. The accent was London, certainly, but the pace of it was the thing. Perhaps it was how she spoke to him that was the clue, as if she expected him to take over at any moment. A Schola woman went about that differently. She'd had years of practice before her apprenticeship.

He spread his hands. "Now we've given our bona fides. I admit, I'm curious about what sorts of things are going on. The different projects."

"We might be able to swap you around in a bit. If you can stand the glue and paper for a while." Hopkins wrinkled his nose. "I'm on a project about magical traps and snares. The sort of things you could throw out into No-man's-land, or shoot into a trench, with enchantments. Bogging someone in the mud, paralysing their leg."

It would be a slaughter if it worked. And likely on both sides, it wasn't as if people could keep track of a trap like that in gas mist and fog and explosions. Reggie kept his face calm. On the other hand, he knew well enough that the Germans must be working on similar things. Knowing how to make them would teach how to defend against them. "Might be a use. Better than gas, I suppose, in some ways."

"Did you face it?" Hopkins leaned forward. "There's a whole division working on that, but it's chemists, mostly, not our sort."

"Not terribly near us. It still doesn't - well. Gas doesn't go where you tell it. Something of a problem. Friendly fire and all that." Not that he wanted to talk about the bits he'd seen. He'd been assigned behind the lines for one of the last attacks, and seeing the men gasping and dying - or gasping and living a little longer - had both been horrible. There hadn't been much that helped, in far too many cases.

If magic brought death, couldn't it at least be a kinder death, one with less pain and terror? It was a thought he'd never have had three years ago, and now it was the one that woke him up regularly at night. Not the sort of thing he could tell anyone. They'd look at him like he was mad.

Hopkins brushed right on. "You know who you ought to get in good with. Lord Carillon."

Reggie frowned. "Lord Carillon?" The one he knew was the age of Reggie's parents, a bit older. Distinguished socially, and a book collector, but not someone he'd have expected Master Brand to attract.

"Temple Carillon. Inherited the title last year. He's, mmm. A decade older than you, perhaps? He and I overlapped by two years, both in Fox, of course." He nodded at Reggie. "Not that Bear's bad for this sort of work. And of course we've got our set of Owls. The swots have to be good for something."

"I'm sorry for his loss, then." Reggie contemplated. "His younger brother was two years ahead of me. Good bohort player, and pavo." An Owl, actually, Reggie remembered, but he decided he wasn't going to comment on that. Either Hopkins knew it, or he didn't.

"Oh, him. Off somewhere on special assignment. One of them had to be somewhere safe, and that's Lord Temple. Let me see about an introduction, sometime. A fair number of us take a long lunch. You should come out with us some day."

Reggie considered. He could just imagine what Lynet might say. "Not this next week - I'll be learning my tasks for the moment. And Mistress Alder seems prickly enough, honestly. Also, it's a big task on her shoulders."

"Chivalry won't work with her. And why would you want it to, anyway?" Hopkins utterly dismissed the prospect that courtesy might be worthwhile, even for someone who couldn't benefit him.

Reggie, though, kept thinking about the way her fingers had brushed the books. She knew things he had no idea about, and they might change the War.

After a moment, Hopkins added, "Mind, if you pick up a bit of how the project's going, a number of us might be interested. Lord Temple's got one of the early journals, I know that much. Alder doesn't share well with anyone, and Master Brand doesn't gossip. Not with us, at least."

Reggie spread his hands. "Not as if I know much right now. I suspect I'll be fetching and carrying, and holding things in place or whatever. Stirring glue and such. But we can see about a drink next week, for certain."

"Where are you staying? In Trellech?"

Reggie nodded. "I've a small flat, one of the side streets. A rather finicky landlady, but the food's quite a good standard so far." It ran to roasts and veg, but with a remarkably unstodgy Yorkshire pudding and better gravy, and that did well enough. They chatted for a few more minutes about which restaurants to try, if he wanted a change. Then Hopkins walked him out to the street, disappearing in the other direction into the dark.

CHAPTER 5

On Monday morning, Lynet had already been in the attic workshop for a good ninety minutes when it was time to meet Reggie in the court-yard. She'd woken earlier than she'd wanted after a fitful night's sleep. On the other hand, she'd been up early enough to get through the Southwark portal without waiting in line for long.

It wasn't the waiting that bothered her as much as people wanting to chat, who knew her or who remembered Papa. Or, worse, hadn't known he'd died. Telling people was the worst, the way they were caught between sorrow and grindingly awful questions she never wanted to answer again.

So on the whole, she had been glad to retreat up four flights of stairs to her own aerie, where no one would bother her. She'd closed the door behind her. She spent the time until she was due to meet Reggie in laying out materials for the week. Ellis would have paper for her. They could get the porters to bring that up. She had folded signatures until her hands ached. Aching hands at least felt like they'd done something useful, unlike her equally aching heart.

They'd settled on Council octavo size. That would make a book of about six inches by nine, comfortable to carry and write in, even if someone were balancing it on a knee or against a convenient wall. The signatures, those had to be seven sheets each for the charms to take best, so she'd had to cut the sheets to size, then stack and fold them properly. Now, she counted out folded signatures into stacks of fourteen.

Just under two hundred pages per book. Nearly two hundred possible conversations. If you wanted to talk to more people than that, you'd need a new journal, but that was a problem for a different time. She suspected there'd be conventions for addressing, too. Right now, you just had to hit on enough to differentiate from everyone else who had a journal, and first name might do there. If the project succeeded, that wouldn't last long, but there were plenty of ways to identify someone that magical folk knew. Full name, affiliations like school or house, family relationships, where someone was from. Papa had made sure that bit of the design work was solid.

She finished just in time to wash her hands. At least they had multiple sinks up here, that would be handy in the near future. Lynet chose the back stairs. She wouldn't run into anyone besides the porters and tea ladies, not like the front staircase, where people lingered and gossiped, especially in the morning.

Reggie was waiting in the yard, not quite leaning on the stone of the building. He nodded at her once, touching his cap in an automatic gesture at either etiquette or a salute, and she had no idea which or why he was doing that. She nodded, briskly. "Morning." She wasn't at all sure it was good yet, and she didn't want to encourage him into needless social pleasantries. "This way."

They went through the yard, taking a sharp left into the outbuilding at the back, and immediately the scent hit her. Rag paper had a particular aroma, never mind the various herbs and concoctions that went into the mix for the necessary enchantments. Vervain, which didn't have the strongest scent, but others as well, and that was part of what he was testing.

She could smell the greenness of the nettle today. That was the latest batch he'd wanted to try. It was certainly easy to grow in abundance, far less fussy than the irises and lilies they'd been working with. That particular aspect wasn't her area of focus, but of course the entire book had to work together, magically speaking.

Reggie had followed behind her, keeping up easily, and now she gestured at a place along the short wall, where Ellis had his desk and some smaller storage. Ellis was just finishing laying out pages to dry, and he turned around, lifting a hand to indicate he'd wash up first. Well, wash up and shrug out of his smock, hanging it on a peg. He wiped his face with a clean cloth and then came over. "Lynet." He nodded at Reggie.

"Ellis, this is Reggie Hollis. Master Brand assigned him to help me." Now that she thought about it, why hadn't he assigned Reggie to Ellis, who actually had more awkward lifting? Damp paper was decidedly heavy. But Master Brand had been very clear with her. By journal, as well as in the meeting, laying out the expectations. "Reggie, I asked Ellis to show you the process of making paper start to finish tomorrow. He's finishing a batch right now. You can help him clean and prepare the tank, and go from there."

Reggie nodded and then ventured, "Hence the smock?"

"The smock, yes." She flicked her fingers. "Suits don't do well with the damp." Ellis was in shirtsleeves, suspenders, and trousers. Ellis also took his cue well, walking Reggie through the various stations briefly, emphasising the time needed between steps. When he was done, Ellis brought him back to where Lynet was perching on his desk. "All yours, Lynet. Come down here at eight tomorrow, Reggie. We'll have a full day's work."

Reggie just nodded. At least the man didn't argue or complain. That was a blessing of sorts. Lynet would have no patience for whining. She hadn't before, and she had even less now. That done, she nodded. "Back upstairs. Would you see if you can collect some tea and biscuits on the way by while I set up the next part of your education?"

She said it as a challenge, to see if he'd defer about being the tea boy in front of Ellis. Reggie just nodded. "Of course. Be up in a few." Granted, it meant he could take the stairs in his own time, and he might appreciate it. Lynet wasn't sure if she'd meant to do that part as well, but she certainly could use a cuppa by this point in the day. Going short on sleep was catching up with her a bit, and she'd put in a long day yesterday, sorting out Papa's records a bit more.

It turned out he was perhaps ten minutes behind her with the tea, suggesting he'd had to wait for the kettle. By that point, she'd laid out items at each of the workstations she'd set up. Reggie set the tray down carefully on the desk, as she had done on Friday. She came back over, her hands empty, which always felt odd. Most of the time, in a working space, she had a book or bone folder or needle or thread or cloth or paper in hand, plus various other comforting items weighing down the pockets of her smock.

Reggie let her take her cup first, and this time she perched on the stool by the desk, gesturing for him to take the chair. "Do you have questions?"

"I think, Mistress. Um. Lynet. I would like to understand what it is you are doing. The idea of the journals, I grasp. But not how they go together, what that means. Was it you who came up with the process?"

Her shoulders went tight for a moment, and perhaps he wouldn't notice. "Yes, and no. Ellis and I worked together on it, and I consulted some others. Not available now. Once we worked out the layers of charms, then - well. Making the physical objects is the tricky part, it turns out."

"How do they work? I mean, how long can your notes be? How much space do they take up?"

Lynet found herself grinning, because honestly, this had been a bit of brilliance. Mostly Papa, in asking the right questions, until she could chivvy one of the researchers, the ones who revelled in the most esoteric details, to figure out the charmwork. "One page for each conversation - a person or more than one. There are charms to make an index, so the first few pages are for that. By person, generally, but someone could index by topic, I suppose, with a little cajoling of the charms. Each conversation has - you open the book and lay it flat, and the conversation appears on the left side, the verso of the sheet. And then on the right side, the recto. You can see two pages at a time, your writing and their response, both."

He nodded slowly. "And that - scrolls, as you work through the text?"

"Just so. The charm works rather like unrolling a scroll,

actually. You can brush the top or bottom of the page to move it. Some people find that easier than others."

"And does it take a particular magical skill to use it?"

Lynet grinned more broadly. "Enough to make the Pact. But that's not much magic in the scheme of things. It doesn't need to be trained. So a fisherman who rarely touches their magic could have one. A child of twelve, once they've made the oath. Mind, we won't have enough books to spread around for anything other than the War effort for a very long time. They're terribly time-consuming to make. And expensive."

"And that's the part you're supposed to sort now." Reggie leaned back, frowning slightly. "Making the thing, the way you describe it, that's a miracle, isn't it? But now you have to produce another."

Lynet was caught, suddenly, by her feeling like she was in Rumpelstiltskin, just last Friday, before she'd met this man. She hoped her face didn't show it. "I want to do my part for the War effort, of course. And parts of this have been common. We've been able to make pairs of books, or sometimes a small group of them, for a while now. Expensive, but not out of the reach of the Council or Lords and Ladies and all that if they wanted them."

"Like an automobile?"

"About like that." The kind of thing ordinary people like her didn't own routinely. But you saw them about, other people owned them, they weren't impossible objects of pure fantasy.

Reggie considered. "And so the trick was making them - um, is the word talk? - to other journals. The paired ones, that's because they're made of the same batch of materials throughout, yes?"

Lynet was impressed by him putting that together. "A

number of tricks. Right now, though, they take quite a lot of materia. Some in the water and paper itself - that's Ellis's doing. Some in the thread, part of the dye. Some in the paste, and the endpapers, and the bookcloth. Not the book boards themselves. I think that's the only part we didn't touch with magic." She then gestured. "If you're done with your tea, I'll show you."

He nodded, setting his cup aside. He was, in fact, mostly done, just a swirl of brown liquid in the base. "Here, these are the signatures, stacked. They'll be sewn together, with these tapes, those help stabilise the book when it's glued to the book boards. They're woven for us specially." That part wasn't hard work, exactly, but the enchantments on it had to be done precisely. "We're working up sets with different paper components, then we'll test pastes, and so on. See which ones work best, and most quickly, and at the lowest cost."

"Quite a lot of stitching, then." He frowned, looking at the pencil marks along the folds of the signatures. "There's eight marks, here. I'd have expected seven?"

"Most of the book components are in sevens, but the stitching has to be an even number. And better eight than six. It lets us get four sets of tapes." Four was not so wonderful a number as seven, magically speaking. Three would likely have worked fine, but three tended more to the Fatae magics in some odd ways, and it had been decided the elemental four was more stable.

"And then there's ... oh, that's rather a lot." The next station had the mull, the fine canvas material that stabilised the spine.

"We glue the mull on, and that dries. The press helps keep it under pressure. Then here," she moved to the next workstation. "We glue the book boards together. Here, we're using a piece of paper, because it has some of the sigils that make the enchantments hold." They'd experimented twenty ways with that, at least. "Adds a step, but it makes some of the later work a little easier. Everything stays in place."

Reggie just nodded, without questions here, and Lynet moved on. "Once that has dried, we add bookcloth, paste that, and wait for it to dry. Then this station here, we'd insert the signatures, paste the first and last page in, to hold, let that dry, and then add the decorative endpapers. The rest of it is mostly cosmetic, adding in ribbon bookmarks or whatever other decoration might be desired."

Reggie stepped back for a moment, leaning against the end of one of the empty workbenches in the centre of the room, after a glance to make sure he wasn't going to upset something. "So there's the issue of materials, but also of the glueing time, for everything to dry. And the fact that all of this must be done by hand? You can't automate it? However it is they make ordinary bound books these days."

"All by hand. We might automate cutting the paper, we can standardise on the size of the book boards - we have - but the magical components need to be done by hand."

"You should have dozens of people. For each step, certainly. And so much more storage, ventilation, perhaps some gentle heat, so the glue would dry evenly."

Lynet blinked at him. Whatever she'd expected from him, it hadn't been that. She hadn't thought he'd produce a list of what she'd asked for and already been denied.

He must have seen something in her face, because all he said was, "Is there a piece of this I may learn to help with now? Without taking more of your time at the moment?"

She nodded, considering her options. Cutting the bookcloth would do well, and the endpapers, while she worked on sewing the signatures. If he did well with the cutting, she might show him how to mark the intervals on the signatures and pierce them with the awl, ready for her to sew.

"Come here, and I'll show you how to cut the bookcloth. Do you know how to - no, you probably don't. Let me start with how you handle good scissors so you don't dull the blade before time."

CHAPTER 6

TUESDAY, APRIL 24TH

"Good work, so far." Ellis handed over a mug of tea, something sturdy and rugged. Rustic country crockery, Reggie's mother would have said with a sneer. Right now, Reggie thought it was soothing. Not bone china that might snap in his hands. They'd been working since eight. Now it was half-ten, time for a cuppa while the great vats came up to temperature to boil the rags with the potions that would make the magic work.

That was the outline. Reggie still didn't understand the details, though Ellis had said it would make somewhat more sense by the end of the day.

"You should have a helper, too." Reggie gestured. "Lots of these tasks, easier with two hands."

Ellis shrugged. "I'm not the sort who gets priority for help."

That made Reggie pause and glance up in the direction of Lynet's attic. "And she is?"

"Ladies first, right?" Ellis chuckled over it, not offended.

Then he shrugged, a certain resignation in the movement. "They see bookbinding as more of a skilled trade than papermaking. She and I disagree, mind. She's the first to point out that paper's at the heart of her work. Well, paper and cloth. But she's got a proper earned mastery, and I'm a journeyman yet."

Reggie cupped his hands around the mug. His fingers had got chilled, stirring up the vats before they got the fire going under them, and the heat from the mug was entirely welcome and necessary. "Young for it, isn't she?" It was one more thing that didn't add up right here, though this one didn't seem to be about that vague sense of discomfort he kept feeling.

Ellis was, he thought, a bit older of the two, maybe Reggie's age. Though he found it hard to tell these days, the War aged people unevenly.

"I'm twenty-four. I was a couple of years behind her, at school." So much for his ability to estimate, then. Ellis hesitated. "Bad heart, and I can at least do something worthwhile here."

"Alethorpe?" Reggie considered that. It would be the school that made sense with the crafting.

Ellis nodded once. "Same house. They don't do it like Schola does. We live all the same place at first, and then they put us into houses based on our interests. Aiming for complementary ones. Paper and books, you see? And we had someone in with us who did dyes, and someone who did leatherwork. Someone else who spun the finest threads."

Reggie considered that. "And that actually works?" He couldn't quite keep the disbelief out of his voice. "Schola - I learned a lot from the others in my house, and we get on well enough at the club, but I'm only close to a handful."

"We don't exactly have the luxury of ignoring each other, most of us. We'll be relying on each other's skills the rest of our lives, seeing each other at the Crafter Guild meetings, at the pubs in Crafter's Row. Learning how to get on, even if we don't like each other, that's as much a skill we need as any we do with our hands or our magic."

Reggie nodded slowly. "And she's still young for a mastery."

"Ah, that's her father." Ellis's voice caught. "He died. Three weeks ago now. T'wasn't unexpected, exactly. He'd been poorly for a year or so."

Oh. The black. "She didn't say. Just the dress." Reggie frowned. "Would she be upset you told me? I mean, should I not let her know I know?"

"She doesn't want to talk about it much. I didn't know him well as a person, just professional. He was a grand bookbinder. Shop in Southwark, in London. She's going back there a fair number of nights, I'm pretty sure." Ellis shrugged slightly. "But he was - he was a real master of the craft. Skills, and decades of experience. And she grew up at his knee. Been helping him since she was eight or so, properly. Her Mum died around then, and he'd have her in the workshop, where he could keep an eye."

Reggie grimaced. "You sure I should be hearing this?"

"Not telling you anything you wouldn't hear if you went round the pub across the street from their workshop." Ellis clearly had a deeply pragmatic view of gossip.

"And I don't know where that is." Reggie held up his hand. "I - part of me appreciates the information. Part of me doesn't want to overstep. Not overstepping is mostly winning."

Ellis sipped from his mug several times before peering

over it. "How'd you end up here, then? You're not as much like the rest of them as might be."

"I was in the trenches, an officer. Got invalided out, the sort of thing won't heal up enough. And I'm not soldier enough to—" Well, he'd been hoping to be reassigned behind the lines, doing warding work. There were all sorts of people he could have helped. Mistress Gospatrick's lot, for one, but for all he'd asked around about that, they apparently didn't have any open space. "I'm on half a dozen lists, in case there's something I can turn my hands to, but they sent me here."

"And a Schola man. Which house?"

"Bear. Some focus on Materia. I did well with Professor Trembley. Some protective magics work, that's part of what Bear does." He felt queer talking about it. It wasn't something much discussed outside the House itself. And then he realised that of course Ellis wouldn't know Professor Trembley, and he tried to find a new topic. "Lynet walked me through the details of the books yesterday. Well, not the details, but each step. You came up with that, yourselves? Most of what I know is thinking about things, not making them happen."

"Yes and no." Ellis waved a hand at the ground floor offices. "Lord Carillon he is now. His family has a tradition of magical books. They don't make them all themselves, but they help with the process, with a bookbinder. No one here in England, he went to Italy for his. He thought some of the techniques might apply. They gave us some supplies and told us to work it out from a day or so talking to him about it, adding in what we knew afterwards. Not that anyone really asked about that part."

Reggie let out a low whistle. "And you've got something that works at all? That's impressive."

"Took the better part of two and a half years. And now they want us to make it - cheaper, faster, easier to produce in quantity. And they don't..." Ellis caught himself about to say something risky, and Reggie was glad he had enough sense to hold his tongue. "People not in your line of work don't understand the details, that's part of the point, innit?"

That was something Reggie could agree with, and he nodded several times. "Right. And it's not exactly like you're dripping with supplies. Lynet said you've got - I don't know, a score of tests to try out, see if you can cut down the time and materia?"

"Like that. We might manage to job out the paper-making to a larger producer. Do it in sheets. But they can't usually add the materia the same way. Or they'd need a lot more of it, bigger tanks. Even if you get more paper out, it's not entirely proportional."

Reggie looked around, thinking about what Ellis had shown him already. "And the process just takes a certain amount of time. For the paper to dry, you can't really rush that."

"We could speed it up a little - a drying room, with ventilation and gentle heat. We could set up an outbuilding for it. But it's tricky. And the paper's real fragile, until it dries, it tears if it shifts. So carrying it is a trick."

"That's a problem. All right. And so then there's the materia, how much you need, how easy it is to get. How much of it's, I don't know, a crocus stamen, saffron, plucked in a three-day window at the height of the bloom. Or how much is, I don't know, mint, which you can grow in a window pot most of the time and have more than you need."

"Like that. Lynet wants to test dill, dill's pretty easy to

come by, and dried works as well magically as fresh for what we need. Better, sometimes. Cinnamon. Lavender. Thyme. But all of those have some amount of scent, and we don't know what people would think of books with a smell. And there are the different components, too, to consider. The paste and the marbled paper, and the bookcloth."

"These books - they could change the War. Being able to get word out and back, quickly. Even if it wasn't to every unit, even if it weren't easy to explain. Just - more information than we could send by radio or runners."

Ellis shrugged. "Problem if they fell into the wrong hands. And we haven't figured out how to solve that yet. Lock it to one person's use. We tried a few blood locks, but it's not something either of us knows a lot about."

"Wouldn't that be a help in making them work more smoothly for someone?" Reggie thought through the implications. It wasn't that blood locks and the like were a big part of the curriculum at Schola, but likely more than they were at Alethorpe. Or maybe he was wrong.

"Some items people make, they work like that. A drop of blood, a bit of hair woven in. That sort of thing. But people get odd about it. And it's a bit tricky to do, so either we'd have to have somewhere people could have it done - doesn't work for the Army in the field. Or we needed a method anyone could do. The one we settled on involved licking a stamp for the back of the book. It goes on the last page."

"Ah, that's clever, isn't it? Enough of a person's essence in the spit." Reggie nodded at that. "I don't mean to tell you your work. Either of you. You've been at this for more than two years, you've likely thought of it all, anyway."

Ellis tilted his head, looking at Reggie now, up and down. "You're not like the rest of them. The ground floor men, the first floor men." Reggie already knew that those were where the better offices were. The second floor had a number of swots, who spent their days nose down in their research and the numbers. Wain and Norton and Phipps, he'd been introduced to them in passing. People like Lynet and Ellis and, he acknowledged, himself, had to make do with whatever was left, even if it meant a further haul for supplies.

"Hopkins and all?" he offered.

Ellis's face was very informative all of a sudden. "He thinks he knows best about a lot of things. And I hope I'm not speaking out of turn, sir."

"None of that." Reggie did his best to make it not an order, but an expectation. "You know far more than I about this work at hand. I know it, you know it. Lynet certainly knows it."

"Put you in your place, did she?" Ellis leaned back. "She wasn't sure how you were taking it."

Reggie shrugged. "She's the expert. You're the expert. I'm a spare pair of hands. And I'm brand new here." He hesitated. "Out at the front, taking over when you were new was a way to get killed."

Ellis hesitated. "Saw it?"

"Four times." Reggie looked away after that, unable to bear the look Ellis gave him. It wasn't exactly sympathy, though it had some of that. But it also was as if Ellis had figured something out, something Reggie hadn't sorted for himself.

There was a long silence, then Ellis cleared his throat. "Done with the tea? Let's get back to it, the vats are steaming."

CHAPTER 7

L ynet had been grimacing over the report for an hour when Reggie came back upstairs. He'd been down helping Ellis set the trays for the last round of paper pulp for the week, and he came bearing tea.

She still wasn't sure what to think of Reggie and tea. He had claimed it as his task, without commentary. By now she had learned to listen for his slightly uneven step on the stairs, coming up from the last landing. He always brought a pot, enough for two cups each, and biscuits.

Lynet had been missing biscuits. She was a barely competent cook, and her skills didn't run to baking. Tressy, in the pub, had said her sense of timing was all for glue. And living in London, she hadn't needed to bake. She could run down to one of the bakeries while something was set up to dry.

Here, she didn't dare take the time. More to the point, it would mean running the gauntlet through the ground and first floor staff to the tea lady's lair at the end of the ground

49

floor next to the porters. The men would ask where she was going. She was sure they'd imply to Master Brand that she wasn't doing her work, if he didn't notice it himself, and hiding things from him was clearly not terribly likely.

Lunch wasn't as much of a problem. She went home, got two pies or pasties or sandwiches from Tressy at the pub, and kept one in stasis for lunch the next day. And some rolls and cheese for breakfast, or she could get something from one of the stalls on the way in. It was a boring diet, but not bad. But biscuits, or anything else like that, that came from a bakery, that wasn't an option.

None of this solved her problem with the report, either. For the moment, she ran her hand through her hair, absent-mindedly, until it tangled in the braid coiled around the crown of her head. She dropped her hand on the desk as Reggie came through the door. "Tea, Lynet. And there's shortbread."

The shortbread was, admittedly, one of her favourites. Whoever made it, they had a knack for it, getting the crumb and the sweetness balanced just right, and a good dash of vanilla. "Here." She made space on the desk, tidying off the papers. "I'm still working on the report."

"You do one every week?"

"Mmhmm." Lynet glanced away, and when she looked back, Reggie was pouring her a cup and sliding the biscuit plate between them. Two each. He must have charmed the tea lady again. "Two biscuits?"

"Mrs Hodge likes me." Reggie grinned. "Or likes that I'm reasonable about what we ask for, I suspect. Hopkins lost a bet, and he was being - well. Tetchy, when he was fetching theirs."

The men downstairs had their own groups, certainly their

own hierarchy. She not only didn't fit into that, she didn't much want to. And she certainly fit even less with the few women she'd seen down there. They appeared to come in two varieties, sharp battle-axe and sharply decorative. Lynet might aspire to the first, but not for decades yet. But she could still feel the ebbs and flows. Several of the groups had been visibly cranky the last day or two, as if something was going wrong in their research.

Reggie seemed to know more of their names than she did, no matter how much longer she'd been here. Though he'd gone out to lunch with a group of them yesterday. He'd been back, full of apologies, fifteen minutes late, and promised it wouldn't happen again. She'd believe it when she saw it. But one couldn't build a consistent pattern on four days, two of which had odd schedules on his part.

Lynet just nodded, focusing on her biscuit. Reggie was quiet until she finished the first one. "What sort of things go in the report? I mean, if it's inventory of materials or something of the kind, I could do that for you?"

"You still don't know the difference between the finish-es." She looked up. "Or the materia."

"Not how to tell when it's in the paper, no," he agreed. "But aren't most of them labelled now?"

She had to admit they were. "Well." Lynet let out a slow breath. "I suppose that would be a help. Give me a count, and if there's anything you're not certain of, mark that instead."

"Will do." Reggie finished up his biscuit and then took himself off to count the stacks of waiting paper. When he saw her looking up, he asked. "We count sets of seven, right? For the big sheets?"

"That would be the most help." There would be some wastage, probably, here and there. Paper did tear unexpectedly, or she'd come across some piece that had a stain that wouldn't do for a book for fine gentlemen.

"This one's very smooth, isn't it?" She didn't have to look up to figure out which he was referring to.

"Silk couching. Well, silk and wool felt, but the silk makes it smooth. It needs a charm for that. Ask Ellis to show you next time." Then she bent her head over the report again, and Reggie didn't say anything else.

It was a good hour later when she looked up. He had slipped a scrap of paper with the inventory numbers onto the other side of the desk, held down by a small brass paperweight. He was at the other end of the room, silently counting out book boards. Lynet added the numbers to her report and grimaced. "You can come back. Or go for lunch, isn't it about time?"

He came back across the room with another scrap of paper. "I think you want more book boards, but check my numbers?" Lynet knew they did, but she held out her hand for the slip.

"We'll need to order them. I'll do that tonight. They come from a shop in London."

Reggie nodded. "You go back there every night?" He must have seen something daunting in her expression, because he swallowed hard. "Pardon."

It was, on the whole, an innocuous comment. But she didn't know why he was asking, and she particularly didn't know what he might pass on to the men and women downstairs. Mostly men, and the more she thought about that, the odder it was.

She could understand Reggie being invalided out, and Ellis couldn't have gone. But two-thirds of the offices downstairs were inhabited - during the majority of working hours - by men who had no obvious reason not to be fighting. This deep into the War, two and a half years, the Army needed more and more men. Fighting men.

The women - except for Lynet herself and a couple of other specialists - were secretaries, clerks, set to running to and fro. She didn't know how to talk to them. They wore dresses that weren't practical for anything other than office work. And shoes, too, the sort that were a menace on ladders and steps and damp floors. Anyway. She didn't want to talk about being in London.

"The others. You could go to lunch with them." It was a terrible deflection into a new topic, but it was what had come out in the moment.

"They - no. Drinks after work, maybe. But not lunch, again. You need my hands, right?" He gestured at the report, changing the subject abruptly himself. "What sort of things do you need to report besides the stock?"

"Well, today, I'm reporting that we're set up to run a set of test volumes. It's not just making them, of course, it's seeing how well they communicate with each other. How securely. We did a batch where only parts of words came through, and one where only the top halves of the letters did. Neither of those is any good at all. We need to test one out of each revised batch against the existing journals. If it works, grand. If not, those journals will talk to each other, but nothing else."

"It must have taken a lot of trial and error." Reggie settled back in his chair. "And Master Brand is the one who oversees all the projects?"

"Mmmhm." Lynet ran her fingers down the numbers one more time to make sure they were both accurate and legible. "He gets direction on some projects from someone else. I've never met him. More than one, I think. Someone associated with the Army. Someone from the Ministry."

Reggie went quiet, as Lynet wrote a bit more, as if he were thinking. When she glanced up after a couple of minutes, he cleared his throat. "What's your report trying to convince Master Brand of?"

"Convince?" She glanced down at it.

"Do you report anything in person regularly? Or does he just demand a command performance?" Reggie was leaning forward now, his elbows on his knees.

Lynet went quiet. She didn't know how to deal with this, the way he was. It wasn't angry; it wasn't yelling, but there was something intense there. And she knew what Papa was intense about. Not what Reggie was.

He must have seen something, because he stood up, and did a slow circuit of the room, as if giving her space to sort herself out. That was mortifying, honestly. He took his time, too, lingering at the far end of the attic, where she'd laid out half a dozen end papers to choose from. When he came back, she looked up, refusing to let him see that she was unsettled.

"Pardon, Lynet." He settled down. "I'm still trying to figure out how they're setting priorities. Mind, that's been a problem throughout the War, don't know why it would be different here."

He said it almost diffidently, as if he didn't expect to find trouble chasing him down for saying that sort of thing. It wasn't treason, not exactly, but it certainly wasn't patriotic. Or optimistic. Lynet wondered if it was a trap of some kind. She thought for a good minute, then looked up again, meeting his eyes.

"I got the impression that while they'd like the books to be a thing that could be spread out widely, they don't know much about what that means. In terms of materials, labour, all of that."

"Or what it means in terms of implications, I suspect." Reggie nodded. "Do you put the labour in your report? Explicitly?"

Lynet shook her head. "Not explicitly. They've never asked."

"Well, you have an excellent excuse this week. I'm a new - what's the maths term? Variable in the equation. Could you talk about what's going faster because I'm available to help, even though I can't offer skilled help? Yet, at any rate."

She snorted once. "Not doing badly at lifting or tightening the bookpresses, and that is a help. And the paper." Then she glanced down at the paper and put the top sheet aside. "That's an idea, though. I'll need to work through lunch to get it done. You, um. See to cutting the paper, use the measurements I showed you yesterday, would you? And go to lunch when it's time."

Reggie nodded slowly. "Can I bring you something back?"

She thought of her meat pie, how she half wanted something lighter - it wasn't as if her appetite had been much the past few weeks. Lynet shook her head. "Thanks, I brought mine."

CHAPTER 8

Friday afternoon, Reggie was still chewing on the conversation with Lynet the day before. She'd sent him off to lunch without further comment. When he'd come back, precisely on time, the report was gone from her desk, and she was pointedly cutting bookcloth with some wickedly long scissors. He had sensibly left her to it, working on setting out the pieces for future use as he'd been shown.

The stitching itself was apparently not terribly difficult, at least not once one got a sense of how tight to pull. However, needle and thread were not one of his better skills, and the magical aspects of it were apparently more complex. So that was Lynet's for the time being. He could probably be doing the cutting, but he wasn't going to interfere.

That morning, she'd at least handed some of the glueing over to him, once she'd prepared several books with sigils underneath the endpapers. He had applied himself diligently and carefully to the work, doing his best to paint the paste within the bounds he'd been given, and doing a decent job at it. Lynet had looked over his work at half-three and said, "That's a good stopping place for you today. See you on Monday."

He frowned. "I can help clean up?" He gestured at the glue pot still sitting beside the small warmer. She'd been testing a different kind of glue, made from wheat paste with different materia added in, for much of this week. It had meant endless pots and jars of the stuff, carefully labelled by what was in it, small batches. He'd been deemed competent to whisk them, at least.

"I've some more work to do. Monday." There was something absolute in Lynet's voice, and Reggie didn't argue. He wasn't sure how he could, anyway. He could stop downstairs and see if Ellis needed a hand with anything.

"Monday." He washed his hands, properly. She'd already drilled that necessity into him. "I - um. Good night?"

"Good night, Reggie." Lynet had already turned back to her work.

Ellis had, in fact, had something useful he could be doing. Reggie had been working for nearly half an hour before Ellis said, carefully. "She in a mood, then?"

Reggie shrugged. He wasn't going to speak against her. Besides, a person had a right to their moods. She hadn't been nasty to him, just clear. "She wanted me to be done for the day up there, so I was."

Ellis opened his mouth, then closed it. Then he turned to face Reggie. "Has she talked about her dad at all?"

"Sparingly. Barely." He shrugged. "No reason she should, as things are."

"Your parents still alive?" Ellis turned away again,

busying himself in carefully lifting layers of paper from the felt that had cushioned them.

"Yes." He'd been back there to convalesce, not that he'd seen very much of either of them. Pater was dealing with various matters at the Ministry, supply chains, and his mother was deep in a flurry of charitable activities. Genteel nursing, bandage rolling, knitting for the fine young men in the trenches. Her knitting was, honestly, only slightly more competent than his bookbinding so far. She didn't leave holes in her work, like some of the pieces he'd seen. But not all of what she made had the give it ought to, the way proper knitting flowed.

Ellis grunted. "Mine don't understand the crafting entirely. But they know it's solid work, and - well. No one's sent me a white feather in a bit." He glanced up at Reggie as he said it.

"Lynet explained you couldn't. Me, I did, and I can't go back." Reggie hesitated. "May I ask a question? About … " He jerked his chin at the building, but flat across, hoping to indicate the lower floors.

Ellis hesitated, turning back to face him, then glancing at his pocket watch. "Make it quick. They'll be out for a smoke in the courtyard in ten, before they go off to wherever."

"Bourne's and Wishton's. I ran into some of them at the former, last week."

Ellis nodded. "G'head. You've earned a question or two. Not promising answers, y'mind."

"Of course not." Reggie turned to face him a bit better, keeping his voice low. But the chance to ask something that had been nagging at him, that was worth a lot. "That's an awful lot of men, of fighting age, here and not there. D'you know if there's a reason for that?"

"Skills. Connections. Sometimes for good reasons, like Lord Carillon inherited, just last year, still sorting his land obligations, they can't send him abroad. And his younger brother's fighting." Ellis turned his palm up, down, then up again, in a gesture of 'you know how it is.'

"One rule for most, another rule for them." Reggie nodded. "Is there - is there anything it might be useful to get someone talking about?"

Ellis's eyes went a bit wide, and then he gathered himself in. "Won't ask you to do that." Reggie suspected it was more like couldn't. That the idea was too far beyond what Ellis was comfortable with.

"Right. Let me help with this last bit, and then - well. Might see about a drink." They finished the last batch of setting paper to dry, and Ellis waved him off just as a gaggle of men came out of the door into the courtyard. Reggie rinsed his hands, drying them with a cloth, then strolled out in time to share out a cigarette or two and get invited out for drinks and dinner.

Mostly, he let the stream of conversation flow around him. Part of him, back in a bit of his head that still could manage that sort of thing, kept track of the eddies. The places one or the other of them changed the subject. This lot was all from Research and Development. They'd taken a private dining room at Bourne's, so the conversation was at least more applicable to his current life than last week's had been.

It wasn't until they were to the tail of the main course that Reggie asked, "This thing Lord Carillon's working on, you know anything about that?"

"Why, what've you heard?"

Jenks leaned over and elbowed Hopkins, who was across the table from Reggie. "Can't have heard much, up in the aerie. Miss Cold Fish say more than two words to you all week?" Jenks was working with Master Harold, something about explosives. They weren't testing that in the building, thankfully, just doing the theory.

Reggie held his face in place, the agreeable expression he'd been wearing all evening. They'd made another comment or two like that. "Well. Not our sort, old chap. Pretty sure she's as aware of it as we all are. She does her work though, and from what I've picked up, she's damnably good at it."

That got the rather predictable guffaws from the other four at the table, but Hopkins waved a hand after a moment and they settled. "The man's got to work with her. And you're the sort to get along, aren't you, Hollis, not make a fuss."

Reggie spread his own hands out. "Generally not, no. Don't want the bother." He wanted to point out that a woman who'd lost her father might not be in the most social of moods. But of course, the mood clearly predated that, by at least some months. Though Ellis had said her father had been ill for a year. He certainly had not asked.

He wondered, suddenly, which of them had assumed she'd come to their call, however briefly they were interested. The comments hadn't made that clear, but they'd had that note to them. These were men whose passions rose and fell, who dallied as they liked, without thinking too much about the consequences.

"Hah." Hopkins said it like he'd won an argument, though what it was, Reggie had no idea. "Look, I suppose it's reasonable enough, you wanting onto a better project. Anything other than fetching the tea and - what else?"

"Stirring glue. Setting up paper to dry." Reggie shrugged. He didn't find it demeaning. His definitions of what was actually demeaning had changed dramatically in the trenches and that was certainly nothing he knew how to explain to these men. They'd never had more inconvenience, so far as he could tell, than a late tea break.

"All right." Hopkins nodded at Jenks. "We might find you something better. You're a Materia man, but not Fauna, right?"

"Not more than horse and hound and all that. More warding than Materia, until recently of course, though I did well enough with it at school." Reggie agreed.

"There's a knot of people - not here, they're at some gods-awful island off the coast of Scotland. An island to keep whatever they're working on in one place. Couldn't pay me enough for that, but some swots like that sort of challenge, I guess."

"Not the sort of thing someone would pick me for. Besides, 'm not supposed to sleep out in the cold again." It wouldn't do his feet any favours, but they'd probably think it was his lungs that were the problem, which was nominally better. Less shame in lungs.

Hopkins waved a hand. "Lord Carillon's working on something new. He did his bit with the books, getting them started, and then other people took over." People who were actually experts in books, Reggie had to assume. Hopkins went on, without a pause. "They had specialists in, someone from the Portal Keepers, an old man. He barely talked to Master Brand. Even less to Miss Priss upstairs."

Reggie considered keeping a mental list of the nasty nicknames, and doing something nice for Lynet each time they used one. She'd never know why, and she shouldn't, but if it meant a deluge of biscuits, well, he could probably make that happen. It would at least amuse him a tad.

Instead, outwardly, he nodded. "Well, complicated magic. And now he's onto something else? Lord Carillon?"

"Something about the land. He had a thought, I guess. Something about the land magics. Struck him more, because he'd just inherited. You know how it is. Some new perspective shakes a bit of genius loose?"

Reggie had some idea of that, though it had been an absurdly long time since anything like genius had come his way. Or been shaken out of his head. If it had ever been there, anyway. He was rather more made for steady consistency built on other people's brilliance. His parents had said so, his teachers had said so. All slightly disapproving, except for the fact that his consistency did have uses.

"Something to help ours, or - does Germany have land magics the same way? Or France or Belgium?" He considered the way the trenches had felt. "Not like ours, I'm guessing."

"Nah." That was Jenks, picking up. "Though I gather the gasses and all that aren't doing anyone's land - magic or otherwise - much good. Everything ground into mud."

Mud and blood and gruesomeness. Reggie agreed that wouldn't be any good for any kind of generative magic at all. Or protective. Well, not the sort of protection decent folks wanted. Blood made for powerful magic. He suddenly wondered if the grinding line of trench against trench was meant to be some greater plan. It could be some massive blood magic working that was supposed to build to a triumphal climax.

He wasn't sure he wanted to live in that world. Better that the whole awfulness was built of stubbornness and fighting the last war badly. That it was all the other curses he'd heard his fellow officers who'd had actual Army experience mutter when they thought they weren't overheard.

Generals doing this deliberately, wasting lives over and over again, that was unbearable.

Reggie covered the sudden shiver with a gulp of decent brandy. If he were going to be out with these men, at least the drink was good. "And the rest?"

"Oh, we've got a handful of things. Better munitions, bullets that can carry a magical load for tracking, or what have you." Likely that could carry some sort of curse or hex or something of the kind. Or that would be the next step for them, surely. Jenks went on, as if the scope of horrors was simply not a matter of his concern. "Some things for - well. This French mutiny situation, that's a worry. Men up and deciding not to fight. Some things to keep everyone moving forward, ideally. Though it's tricky."

Coercion magics were, as a rule, entirely unreliable at distance or any length of time, or so Reggie had gathered from various discussions during his apprenticeship. Even if someone managed to distil a potion into something that could be added to food or military rations, the effect would still need someone else providing the guidance. That wasn't easy to arrange. "Tricky, mm. And - well, there's self-preservation to consider. As a factor."

He'd offered it automatically, without thinking as much about their reactions, but one of the other men - Kerrad - lit up, as if that had provided some new direction for research. Blast it. Reggie reminded himself to think before he bloody spoke.

Fortunately or unfortunately, Hopkins picked up again. "And of course some things for people going across country for various tasks. Hiding, and what have you. Nothing like a cloak of invisibility out of legend, but some improvements on the charms, for them who can cast them. And I'm working with some chaps on some traps, things you can lay out to keep others out. That might be up your alley, in time."

"Might." It felt like a betrayal of his magic to think of it that way. He'd hated the men in the trench across No-man's-land from him, on the one hand, with the obligatory hatred he'd been told to have. Encouraged into. But at the same time, he still clung to some sense of fair play. Or, if not that, to wanting to be able to look himself in the mirror when the War was over, whenever that was.

He was beginning to suspect he'd be growing a beard and moustache, because shaving wouldn't be any good at all.

CHAPTER 9

FRIDAY, MAY 11TH IN THE WORKSHOP

T he next fortnight went well enough. There had been a pause for the May Day celebrations in Trellech itself, and in London. But it was the Trellech ones that meant they'd not be able to get into the office for the day, since the streets would be blocked off coming from the portal. Then, on Friday morning, one of the undifferentiated posh young men came up, knocking on the door, and entered without waiting for her.

Lynet wheeled. "Back outside, wait until I say enter." The man looked insulted, but Reggie coughed just once, and the man folded and went out. Reggie didn't say anything, and Lynet couldn't decide whether to thank him or tell him never to do that again. He came over to take the piece she'd been balancing. "Shall I set this aside properly, mistress?"

She hated that he could get more courtesy with a cough and perhaps a look than she'd earned in years. But she nodded. There wasn't anything else she could do. "The wax paper in, then into the book press. Check nothing's moved?" Lynet turned away before she could get a look at his expression, to wash her hands thoroughly. Once they were dry, she called out. "Yes? Come in."

The door opened aggressively. "Master Brand wants you for a meeting at ten." It was a quarter to, already, she'd need to find her things and tidy her hair, and that was no time at all.

She swallowed down all the things she might have said that she wanted to say. "Did he ask you to go back down? Let him know, of course, I'll be there on time." Then she turned away, because she didn't want to see this man's expression, that she'd dared to issue an order.

The door closed without the courtesy of a farewell. Reggie was still facing the workbench, carefully finishing his task, but he said, not raising his voice. "Man should have much better manners."

She shrugged, not caring that he couldn't see it. She didn't really want him to. There was nothing she could say, and certainly nothing he could say that she would trust. "Thank you for taking over. Can you cut paper while I'm downstairs? If it's a long meeting, go off to your lunch break, of course."

Lynet heard him shift his weight, the pause as he thought about saying something. In the end, what came out was, "Of course, Lynet. And I'll do some tidying if I'm done with the paper. There are scraps ready to go down. I'll get them all in the same bin." He'd learned properly that those could all go back to be used in other things.

She had no time for that. She washed her hands again for good measure, took off the smock. Her black dress was looking a bit dingy, but what could she do? Perhaps Tressy could sort out something in a dark grey or a deep blue or something of the kind. Something that had started a dark colour, rather than the dye fading.

Precisely at a minute to ten, she was waiting outside Master Brand's office, with a leatherbound portfolio of her notes under her arm. She'd made it herself, five years ago, when she was experimenting with some embossing techniques. It wasn't to her standards now, of course. That was why standards changed as one got better at things, but she found the imperfections reassuring, rather than embarrassing. Also, they were minor, the sort of thing where someone really had to know about leatherwork to spot them without close inspection. She heard the clock strike ten inside the office and knocked, timing it precisely between the chimes.

"Enter."

There were four men inside, Master Brand and three others she'd never seen. Two were in uniform, the third in a dark suit, and all of them were at least in their fifties, even older. "Master Brand, gentlemen." She nodded politely. Master Brand gestured her to the remaining seat, a bit away from the others, as if she were something different.

"Mistress Alder. This is Colonel Henry Howard, Colonel William Attenby, and Master Orion Thorpe. Thorpe's from the Ministry office dealing with communications." Master Brand waved a hand, not really identifying which was which. She tried to memorise their faces. It wasn't even as if the insignia helped, though at least she knew who Thorpe was: the one not in uniform. Perhaps they'd repeat a name usefully. That Ministry office might be the one dealing with censorship, as well as things like the post going along properly, though it wasn't as if anyone explained that, either.

"Of course. What may I do for you today, Master Brand?"

"Tell us about the status of your project. I have your

most recent report, of course, but they would like to hear it from you." That explained the short summons.

"Of course." She opened the portfolio, balancing it in her lap, so she had the dates and numbers, so she wouldn't misspeak. "From the beginning?"

"Yes, please." Master Brand leaned back, his chair creaking slightly.

Lynet took a breath. They'd trained her in that, at Alethorpe, to take her time when people wanted her to be faster, especially in this sort of meeting. Part of the mastery of her arts, whatever they were, was taking up space. Mind, a fair number of her lessons had been that. They hadn't quite been titled "how to have space to breathe in a room full of Schola men" but they might as well have been.

"In November 1914, Master Brand approached my father, Theodore Alder, at his shop in London, asking if he would lend his expertise to the War effort. My father was unable to spend so much time away from London. But he noted that I'd earned my own membership in the Guild, was well on my way to earning my full mastery. And that of course he would be available to consult."

She suspected now that Papa had already felt the early signs of illness then. He hadn't explained it to her, of course he hadn't. He'd just made it clear that he would be spending his time at his worktable in the shop he'd held for forty years. She could go off to Trellech and make sense of their request.

Mind, Papa had also felt that the request would take a miracle.

Master Brand waved a hand for her to go on. Lynet took a breath. "The brief was to take some information from another party working in the department, consulting with a number of specialists. We were told to see if we could create a way not to link two books or a small set, but an unspecified number of them. To permit broad communication. It took a great deal of work, but two years later, this February, we felt we had a successful implementation to work from."

"What did that involve, Miss?" That was one of the Colonels. Who, of course, didn't use her proper title. Not that she could correct him. She knew exactly how badly that would go over.

"It requires my expertise at bookbinding, an equal expert in papermaking." Why wasn't Ellis here, for that matter? At least he was male. Or perhaps that was the problem. "Are you familiar at all with the bookbinding process, sirs?"

"Assume we are not." That was the other colonel, who at least offered a slight smile as he said it. He might not think her anything like his equal, but he was being less deliberately rude.

"The process of making any book has a number of steps, with time between for the paste to dry. The magical journals require additional steps. The paper is made with specific materia in it, to give the enchantments something to hold on to, as one of the consultants put it. Charming the thread, so it will take and anchor further enchantments, then using it to sew the signatures - the folds of paper - together."

She had explained this a number of times now. At least it came out smoothly. "We sew the signatures together, adding linen tapes. We press them, then glue a strip of mull - a sort of open weave fabric - to stabilise the spine. All of these add to the long-term sturdiness of the book. We didn't want to lose papers or signatures with a few weeks' heavy use, especially in field conditions."

"And what do you know of field conditions?" That was the first colonel, quite sharply.

The other snorted, "Presumably she's listened to the brief, Attenby." Right, the first colonel, the one she needed to answer, was Attenby. The other was Howard. She did her best to link the names to the faces.

"Sir, I did listen to the brief, of course. But my father had friends who fought in the Sudan. I heard some of their stories. Dust and mud and spills, even without wounds or injuries. Things getting jammed into a pack, or shoved to the bottom where they get bashed around more than most things. There's only so much a book can take. They are basically paper, after all. But we have built in protective charms as well, of course."

Colonel Howard nodded. "A fair answer." She thought there must be something hidden underneath it, something she wasn't catching, but he waved a hand. "The - mull, you said."

"Sir." She was back on more solid ground again. "Then we assemble the cover. Two book boards, a piece for the spine, the cloth wrapping around it." It was more complicated than that, especially if one wanted a rounded spine or something of the kind. But there was no point in getting into that here. "Then we insert the signature block - that's the paper - and paste it in. There needs to be time for everything to dry at each glueing step, and there's not much we can do to speed that up. Especially in the current facilities."

"The current facilities? I thought you had been granted quite a spacious workroom."

Oh, dear. She'd failed. She could hear that, in Attenby's voice. She dared a glance at Master Brand, who was looking reproving. "The space is lovely, sirs, but we're in spring now, and it's a bit more cool and damp. Warmer and dryer would speed the paste. The papermaker is working on a facility for that, and depending on the space, we might move books down. But it's complicated to get things up the stairs. There's no lift in the building, the hoist outside is exposed to the rain and fog, and of course, books in quantity are heavy. Those that are drying need to be under pressure, in a book press." Neither of which suited two tiny dumbwaiters meant more for food than items, or a hoist where whatever they moved was entirely open to the elements. Of course, these men weren't inclined to think about that problem.

They all murmured, and then Howard asked, "And is that the last step?"

"No, sir. There's a number of additional charm steps, before we glue things together and before we mount the endpapers. Sigils under them, that's part of what makes the enchantments settle and anchor. And we have to do a little work to make the book recognise the user. That's done with a stamp they lick."

"And the - decorative choices, do those play any particular role?" That was the non-Army man, the first time he'd asked anything. Master Thorpe.

"We haven't been able to do a full set of testing, Master Thorpe." Lynet did look up at him. "There are - I don't know your areas of interest, sirs. But dyes are made from plants, or from alchemical processes, and thus have some inclinations of their own, in addition to the material of the paper and such. A lighter influence, but still potentially a meaningful one. To simplify the testing, we've been using one set of bookcloth in blue and endpapers, a simple marbled set in green, blue, white, and a small amount of red. We do hope to expand testing on that. We know people might either prefer variety, or find it useful to avoid mixing up copies."

"Quite." Master Thorpe nodded. "I know your father." It came out of nowhere, and now she'd have to explain. Oh, gods, she had grown to hate this part. It wasn't just having to say it out loud, though that was horrible enough. It was having to hold still through the fumbling condolences, or whatever it was the other person felt they had to say.

"Pardon, sir." She couldn't look at him. "My father died three weeks ago. I'm sorry you hadn't heard."

There was a rattling silence, the sort that meant she could hear every breath, every shift in the chair, few as there were. She could certainly hear her heart pounding.

"My condolences." That was Master Thorpe, and his voice was apologetic. There was a vague mumble from the other two. "We appreciate your dedication to the War effort, being back at it so soon. I think we're done for today. I'm sure you have plenty of work to be doing. Someone may have more questions next week."

As if having that hanging over her was going to improve anything at all. But she could only nod, and stand, glancing from one to the other, refusing to bow or bob or bend before them. "I appreciate your time, sirs. Master Brand, we should have further notes on the next test by Tuesday." When he waved a hand at her, she fled as decorously as she could manage, not breaking into a fast walk until she was past the first floor landing.

CHAPTER 10

FRIDAY, MAY 18TH IN THE WORKSHOP

Reggie came up the last few stairs, listening attentively for any signs of how things were going in the workroom. Ten minutes after Lynet had gone downstairs, Ellis had checked if he could help. They'd spent the two hours to lunchtime setting up the better drying racks for the paper that would allow air flow at multiple levels. Some friend of Ellis's had arranged for it, and Reggie hadn't pressed for details the other man wasn't sharing willingly.

There had been an unsettled feeling below, too, when Reggie had gone to fetch some supplies. No one had been leaning against the wall in the hallway chatting. Usually there'd be a couple, no matter what time of day Reggie went by. Now, every door was properly closed, all appearances of everyone working hard - though it was hard to tell what went on behind those closed doors. Everything felt tight and sharp, though, and Reggie wanted to understand why.

He'd thought about checking if Lynet had lunch. But first, she had brought her own every day so far, and second, he was sure she wouldn't take him checking well. Instead, he'd gone off for a nearby cafe, and come back by the right sort of bakery. Not Patience, the one with the incredibly arcane spun sugar decorations, not Excelsior, who made intricate and very expensive chocolates. Reggie wasn't entirely sure he could carry the first through the streets without breakage, and he was sure Lynet wouldn't permit herself the latter.

Instead, he'd swung by a place on a side street, which still did a steady stream of business. At Ambrosia, he had bought four varieties of biscuit and two scones for their afternoon tea break. The lavender shortbread had smelled amazing, like a breath of summer and warmth. The spice ones were some of his favourites, a mix of creamy vanilla and cardamom, which he felt was a very undervalued flavour.

It wasn't as if he could hear anything meaningful through the door. For all the other limitations of the work-room - the pipes banged, only two of the windows opened, never mind the stairs - the door was quite solid and insulating. But he could sometimes feel when Lynet particularly didn't want to be disturbed. Or at least, all his guesses on that count so far had been accurate, and he could only hope to keep it up.

Now, he wriggled the handle for a second before opening it. "Lynet?"

She was over in the corner of the workbenches, rummaging for some of the marbled end papers, her back turned to him. At least she hadn't felt so startled she'd wheeled around. She'd done that once or twice when he'd surprised her. She reacted the way any man in the trenches had after a few weeks, if they hadn't fled so far away in their heads that they'd forgotten to bring their bodies with them.

"Lynet? I picked up some biscuits and some scones for our afternoon cuppa." It was hard to keep his voice from the false, jarring joviality that would be the worse thing. "I thought you might like to take some home, too?"

"Oh, I'll be in here tomorrow." She sounded - not defeated, not exactly.

"Well, then we can leave a few for that." Reggie left the cardboard box on her desk, carefully away from anything it might damage. "Want me to come in?"

Lynet finally turned around to peer at him. "Why would you?"

"You could need another pair of hands. I'm not bad at that now." It was true, he wasn't. He wasn't at all skilled, he knew that, but he could follow directions, and he'd figured out how to make things easier for her. At least some of the time, he'd sorted out how to anticipate what would be helpful that she wouldn't ask for, not ever. He'd just put himself there, as best he could, so it was natural.

She considered for a long moment, then asked for the first time. "You live in Trellech?" It was, he thought, near the first time she'd made any sort of personal inquiry. He had absolutely no idea what had brought that on, and that unsettled him a little, but he'd give her whatever honesty he could.

"A small flat in a house of them. I'm more often at one of the clubs in the evening, or at the library."

Lynet peered at him, as if that hadn't matched up at all with what she expected. Likely the library.

"It's a good spot to read the papers, and—" He hesitated. "I used to be quite an outdoors sort." In another life,

75

he'd have been out for the pheasant and partridge, perhaps deer, certainly some foxhunting. Food for the pot, a reduction in the losses of chickens and ducks kept by the farmers. A deer could feed poor families in the nearby villages and towns for quite some time. Besides the sport it offered.

Some of that would be going on, War or no. Some of it remained necessary. He added, "There's not much hunting now, of course. Not other than for food. Nor reports from rambles or whatever mountain climbing people are up to. But there's a little, and there are historical stories being run. Previous attempts, patterns. I rather like those."

She tilted her head, bird-like again. "Biscuits? Why did you get biscuits?"

Reggie certainly couldn't tell her the real reason. He wasn't sure exactly how she'd respond, but he was quite sure it wouldn't be positive. He couldn't imagine a world in which he could tell her, and she'd laugh at it, much as he liked the glimmer of the idea of it. After a moment, he offered a different truth. "I thought you might like them. They're from the best bakery I know."

That got a reaction, disbelief. "Why?"

He shrugged. "Because the world is awful, and biscuits won't fix it, but why not have biscuits?" He tried to give it a little amusement. There was something in her face, a particularly wrenching hollowness, and he couldn't have that, so he forged on. "You had a command performance of a meeting, on no notice. That certainly calls for biscuits."

On that inalienable logic, she finally folded, waving a hand. "All right. Pick one out? Let me wash my hands."

It was a minor victory, but he would celebrate it for all it was worth. He went and found one of the plates they kept in case of need, and laid out four biscuits, one of each kind. By the time she came back, he bowed as she took her usual chair. "A selection to choose from. The box has two scones and another four. I like them all. That was part of the point. Lavender shortbread, spice, those have candied orange, and this one has almond."

Having a choice was apparently more than she was up for managing because she just stared at the plate, her hands in her lap, not moving. Reggie hesitated. "Let me make a cup of tea, too. Minute."

That would give her a chance to gather herself, however it was she chose to do that. Making the tea was, he had been finding, excellent for that. Making pauses that were finite, but not over in an instant. He was fairly sure that most men had not yet begun to consider the strategic implications of making tea.

By the time the kettle had sung and he brought the tea back, she was sitting back, having taken the spice biscuit. He snagged the almond for himself and found his own chair. Only once he was sitting, and she had tea in front of her, did she take a bite of it.

Reggie could see the moment when the glory of it hit her. When Lynet looked at him again, he knew he was grinning, the kind of smile he'd ache with in a minute. "Best bakery."

He got a tiny hint of a smile, her eyes crinkling up, before she set the biscuit down to savour her current mouthful properly. Then another small bite, the kind someone took when they didn't want it to end. He took a bit of his own, enjoying the way the almond bit against the sugar, and sang with it. When he wasn't looking at her, she said, quietly, "The meeting."

Just the two words.

"Would it help to talk any of it out? I don't know the bookbinding, of course, not those details, but perhaps

77

there's some other part where sorting out the details could help?"

Of course, there was a long silence. Reggie waited, had another sip of tea, another mouthful of delightful almond.

"You're like them." Lynet's voice was very quiet now. "I don't know if I can explain."

That was the crux of it, really. He was like the men - and women - downstairs in far too many ways. And if she hadn't actually heard their cruelty, she'd certainly felt different every time she was among them. However rare that was, it wasn't like any of them went out of their way to pay her mind. Even Master Brand, who ought to have better care of the projects he managed.

"There is a chance I might be able to help with - with figuring out what they want. How to explain what you're doing in a way they'll listen to. You shouldn't have to do that. I know it. Your work stands on its own. I don't remotely know the details, and even I can see that."

Lynet nodded. When Reggie glanced back at her, ostensibly on his way to pour a bit more tea, she had her hands in her lap. The biscuit sat half-eaten on the plate in front of her. He topped off her tea and his own, and just waited again.

Slowly, hesitantly, she explained the meeting. Or rather, she didn't explain much at all. She certainly didn't share her feelings about it. Just the stark explanation of what happened, point by point. She had, all in all, a remarkably good memory for it, the names, the things they asked. Far better than Reggie's would have been.

When she finished, she looked down at the plate, then deliberately took another nibble of her biscuit.

"Master Thorpe does have his hands in censorship. Not the top man, but high up. I don't know a lot about him."

Reggie considered the rest of it. "They want something specific. Beyond the journals, as well as the journals. I've not the foggiest idea what, but ..." Reggie let his voice trail off. And he rather thought it was more than one thing, something in what she'd said, but they'd been terse with her, too.

She didn't ask. Reggie was beginning to understand that she wouldn't. The world that had encouraged him to ask his questions, to find a mentor, to show how he respected seniority and knowledge, had treated her very differently. Not enough to avoid being awkward, or saying the wrong thing half the time, but he could see where the silences fell better now.

"It doesn't matter."

"It does. They're getting in the way of your work. Work that is - it could change the War. The world. People's lives, in all sorts of ways, small and big."

"Not if we can't get the costs down. It can't." Her voice was hollow again.

"Even the simpler version, the ones where one book talks to a dozen others, same batch of materials. That's a tremendous advance. Imagine that in a family where people travel, or a business that does trade across the world. Even the military, if you distributed them thoughtfully. Or the Guard, anyone who needs coordination. Something that works like the current book, that's a wonder, a miracle. And they don't care."

He was half looking at her, more toward the corner of the room. It was the angle that was less directly threatening, and he caught her shiver, the way her body reacted despite herself. "You think so?"

"That it's a miracle? Yes. That they don't care properly? Yes. That too." He waved a hand. "I could - I'm like them.

You said it yourself. I'm at the right clubs, sometimes. I could do some research in the library. Anything that might give you a better idea how to present things, going forward, in a way they might listen to."

"There won't be much. I mean. Secret research. None of us is supposed to talk about it. Not properly."

Reggie had had that lecture - and that oath - too. On the other hand, it hadn't bit the others much when they were out getting drinks, so clearly some talking was permitted. "Then there's no harm in my looking and finding nothing. I won't do anything foolish. Press forward when I shouldn't. I've had more than enough of that in my life already." Far too recently, too, and now he was the one who had to suppress his feelings.

"I suppose I can't stop you." There, now, she was taking the last bite or two.

"You can't. Do you want to take the rest of the biscuits with you tonight?"

There was a long pause. "My fair share. Split them with you."

Her fair share was all of them. All but the one he'd bought for himself. But there was no way to argue that he wanted to tell her. "Three and three," he agreed.

CHAPTER 11

Friday afternoon, just before the shops closed, Lynet had managed to pick up two new summer-weight dresses, counting out the coins slowly. She needed them; she knew that. But she also knew how scant her savings were and how fast it felt like they were slipping away. One dress was black, one a muted grey. They were at least of decent fabric, nothing at all fancy, but better than she'd had. She wished, painfully, that they'd been ready on Thursday. That she'd been wearing the new black for that awful meeting.

Reggie had been conspicuously helpful all afternoon. And while she'd needed that - the whole thing had thrown her far more than she wanted to admit to anyone, even herself - it also grated. He'd want something for it. People like him always did. Like all the men downstairs, the one whose voices ruled the hallways as easily as their fathers ruled the world.

If Reggie hadn't shown those spots yet, she had to

assume he would. Sometime, sooner than later, he'd find the bookbinding tedious, the repetition of each task to exacting standards, over and over again. Coming up with the underlying charms, that had been exciting, but the rest of this wasn't. It was stodgy. They couldn't even do anything properly artistic with it. Just stitching and measuring and cutting and glueing and waiting for the paste to dry, again and again.

And then there were the biscuits. She had no idea why he'd brought them. Or insisted she take them. She'd had one last night, of course she had, a bit of sweet in a week of sourness, after a bowl of stew in the dining hall. It had been filling, but clearly the sort of stew meat that had needed to be cooked all day to be edible.

Saturday, she rolled out of bed, wincing as her feet hit the chilly floors. The Guard who used the barracks brought things like rugs, she gathered. She hadn't bothered; she hadn't seen the point, even if she'd had a spare rug to bring that wasn't in Papa's room. The biscuits sat there, lurking. Not for breakfast. Besides, she had places to be. She pulled on the new black dress, pinning her hair into a bun with sharp twists of the hairpins.

By half-eight, Lynet was up in the workroom, soothing herself by doing an inventory again. It wasn't that she needed to - Reggie had actually done a decent job with it, consistently, from the second time she'd shown him. But it made her feel better, to brush her fingers over each stack of materials, to count them silently in her head, the way the counting drowned out every other thought for just a little bit. It was almost as good as getting lost in a complicated bit of handwork.

Master Brand had sent a note - privately, in one of the early test journals, at least - last night, as she was leaving.

New quotas for testing, every forward speed. She understood why, she even agreed with why, but he wanted all this speed without giving her any resources to do it. And she wasn't sure she could.

She wasn't sure why he'd sent the message, though. It was the sort of thing that should have waited for Monday, probably. She was glad to have the advance warning, but he certainly hadn't told her just to make her life easier. She wondered, all of a sudden, who he got his orders from.

That thought, the way it swept her feet out from under her, found her bracing her hands on the workbench, awkward. Her knees wouldn't hold, but she couldn't muss the dress. It took her precious minutes to get herself back in working order. By then she had to head out to the Crafting Quarter if she was going to be in good time.

The lines in Portal Square weren't bad when she ducked through, and mercifully she didn't see anyone who wanted to stop and talk to her. Trellech was easier than Southwark that way. Just as the Temple bells rang ten, she was being shown into Master Woolton's office. She'd think it was kind of him to see her on Saturday, but she knew he was often in. It was his chance to get things done when the press wasn't running.

"Mistress Alder, sit, please. Can I offer you some tea? No?" She shook her head, perching on the chair. She'd been here dozens of times over the years, mostly with Papa. They were in different lines of work, but they'd been friends, and Papa had been Master Woolton's choice for anything that needed commercial printing and personal binding.

One of the apprentices showed her in - a young man, must still be seventeen. It was only when he'd closed the door behind him on the way out that Master Woolton cleared his throat. She'd been expecting this, and dreading it, and wanting it, all in a tangle. "May I be informal?"

Lynet nodded. It did and didn't matter to her. "Uncle Matthew." The courtesy title she'd used in private for years felt odd on her tongue now.

"How are things, Lynet, my dear? In general, in London, in …."

Lynet suspected the stillness of her face told him more than enough. One didn't stay long as head of a guild as essential as the Printers Guild if you couldn't manage the politics when half asleep. He tilted his head, considering her. "I'm glad you came by."

He'd been asking her to since before Papa died. She just hadn't been able to. Oh, he'd been at the funeral. He'd come to see Papa several times in those last weeks, too, in kindness and friendship, giving Lynet a chance to go do urgent errands. But she had been sure it was on Papa's account, and that whatever he offered now was because of that. It wasn't a small thing. Lynet knew that. But it wasn't hers, either. It was a borrowed cloak. A slipcover, meant for some other book that more or less fit.

"It's been very busy." And that had come out prim and prissy. That wouldn't do at all.

"They've been working you hard, then? I know you can't talk about most of it. You've been very careful about your agreements. Anything you can that you want to?"

Now, she didn't even know where to begin. Or what was actually an issue, and what was just her. Uncle Matthew leaned back a bit more, his chair creaking. "I've heard a few odd things out of your lot." He opened his mouth, as if to say something more, then reconsidered it. "I'm guessing they don't understand your process. Brand's talented, no one's ever denied that, but he's always been about the flash and the bang and the show, not the steady."

Of course, Uncle Matthew knew him well enough to have that kind of opinion. She'd known that. "He's called me down for meetings several times recently. Assigned me an assistant, but—" She swallowed hard, and Uncle Matthew pushed a waiting cup of tea in front of her. People kept giving her tea, and it helped an unreasonable amount, the kind of thing she wanted to resent and couldn't. Lynet took a sip and forged on. "Reggie Hollis. He knows nothing about the bookbinding, of course, but he's got steady hands, and he doesn't push about doing things he doesn't have the skills for."

"Which is fair praise for an unskilled assistant. I swear, if someone could bottle the undirected energy of someone wanting to help and getting it all wrong, we'd have magic to last for centuries." Uncle Matthew nodded. "And in the meetings?"

"Oh, the predictable. Wanting it faster, sooner. But it's taken ages to get some of the materia we need, and I don't know why. It's rather contradictory. They don't let me do the ordering. It all goes through the central office downstairs, for efficiency. And then, of course, the glueing takes the time it's going to. It's not like you can hurry it much."

"Or that you'd want to. Most of the methods make the paper more brittle. That's a problem too."

Lynet nodded. She considered, then laid out a couple of ideas she'd had about that. It was a neutral enough topic, and she knew Uncle Matthew would either have good ideas or make sure there weren't obvious holes in hers. That took them ten minutes, and by the end of it, she was actually a little relaxed.

Of course, the next question nearly spoiled it. "I could

lend you a couple of apprentices to clean things up in London. Seniors, people who'd take direction. A day or two, if you could get free."

Lynet shook her head. "Thank you, Uncle Matthew, but no." She couldn't bear to have other people in that space, not yet. It still smelled, faintly, like her father. His tea and his pipe and the leather and paper in the workshop. Not the faint decay of a library, but something newer and brighter. Other people would spoil that, in all the worst ways. She wanted to hold on to it as long as she could.

"Are you still staying in the Guard barracks? There might be a room coming free in one of the Guild journeyman houses, if you'd like me to inquire."

That was at least a little tempting. The food would be better, the floors might be warmer, and the journeymen would almost certainly leave her largely alone. She was, after all, not a printer.

"Let me know?" It was tenuous. "I'm going back to London when I can. This afternoon." She'd spend tomorrow going through files and boxes and repackaging all the things Papa hadn't let her sort, so they could go to storage or - or somewhere. Lynet hadn't really figured that part out yet. She could only get as far as needing it if she set up her own workshop or not, and that only on a better day. There hadn't been many of those. Just getting going in the morning was a full day's work, it felt like.

"Of course. And I know you said you can't come to supper, but Thea and I would love to have you." His wife, who would be all comfort and kindness and warmth, and less brash than Tressy at the pub.

Lynet nodded, silently looking away. In the following silence, Uncle Matthew cleared his throat. "Look, Lynet, I keep hearing odd things. Nothing that I can put together properly, it's the sort of copy that makes you think someone jogged the composing stick and didn't notice. Something slightly off."

She trusted his eye. Or his ear, in this case. But at the same time, it wasn't anything she could touch. Certainly nothing she could act on. "It's not as if I can tell them no."

Uncle Matthew's mouth opened and closed again, before he said, carefully. "No. But if you do - would you promise me that if you come across anything that particularly unsettles you, you will come to me? At the very least, I can likely introduce you to the right person to talk to. So long as it's outside that building of yours. Impenetrable. Not the usual Ministry sorts at all." He then leaned back again. "Your Hollis. What's he like? How old? The name's vaguely familiar."

"Bit older than me, but not very much? Invalided out, he's maybe thirty?" Lynet considered, then realised she knew really quite little about him. "Schola man, good family, the sort of voice that goes with that."

"Hmm. I know a few of the Hollises. Mind if I keep an ear out?" Uncle Matthew was looking speculative now.

"I can't stop you, Uncle." She couldn't, and they both knew it.

"Is he being decent?" That was sharper, honing in on the complicated parts.

Reggie had brought biscuits. He made tea. He shut up and didn't bother her. They were all true and saying any of them would give entirely the wrong impression of how things were. "He's not much like the others. I mean, he goes off for drinks with them? Lunch a couple of times. They treat Reggie like—" Her voice caught. Like one of them. "Like they know him. Not well."

"Ah, well, all the Schola sorts do tend to. If they don't

know him, they know a brother or a sister or a cousin or an aunt." He whistled a bit of one of the ridiculous operettas Papa had loved, a song that devolved into patter about the extended relationships of the cast. Then he waved a hand. "If I find out anything you might find useful, I'll let you know."

He was about to say something else when there was a knock on the door, and a "Pardon, Master."

"You've got your work, I've got mine. Thank you, Uncle Matthew, for the tea." And the listening, not that she could say that. He stood, coming around his desk to offer her a hand and a kiss on the cheek.

"You let us know if we can have you for supper. And don't you be a stranger. I'll let you know about the room, too."

CHAPTER 12

SATURDAY, MAY 19TH AT SCHOLA

"Come in, please. Pardon the chaos." Reggie was about to step into Professor Trembley's rooms on Saturday afternoon when two students rushed by, deep in a conversation made of gestures and cryptic words. He hadn't been back to Bear House since he'd left school, but some things apparently never changed. He thanked the boy who'd met him at the entrance to Schola and escorted him to the proper door.

Now, he felt something he knew settle around him. No, rise up under his feet. This was land he knew. It would be wrong to claim he understood it fully, Schola was full of mysteries no student ever plumbed. It did make the contrast to the workshop and offices far more obvious. There it was like walking on a bog or sand, every step shaking his sense of balance, which he was none too certain of these days. Here, there was solid rock. And for all he was nervous about this meeting, it was a comfortable sort of nerves. He didn't know what he'd learn today, but he had a

89

good idea of the possible range, and more importantly, that Professor Trembley would be thoughtful and kind and listen. She always had.

He looked around as he stepped inside, letting out a breath as the chaos behind him went quiet. Professor Trembley looked him up and down. "Ah, pardon. I should have realised they'd be rather much. Can I make you some tea to get started? No alcohol handy at the moment, I'm afraid."

"Tea, please. Can I help with anything?" Reggie offered automatically now.

She shook her head. "Find a chair you like. That one's my usual." She gestured at one rather like a throne, a comfortable blue velvet draped with a blanket of silvers and greys. Professor Trembley herself hadn't changed much either. She had to be in her sixties now, but she barely looked it. Her brown hair was up in a tidy bun, and she wore the academic gown easily over a blue frock. The colour, in fact, caught his eye against the starkness of the workshop. Lynet had an eye for colour, he suspected, from the sample books she'd shown at the beginning. But there was very little of it in the spaces she was in now.

Once the tea kettle had sung, Professor Trembley settled down with the tray between them. She'd laid out the biscuits he'd brought as a thank you, and then snagged one of the almond ones. "Oh, I do love them, you remembered."

Reggie smiled. "Well, and when I was in this week, they remembered you, when I said I was coming out." He gestured at the box of biscuits he'd brought, waiting on the table. "I do appreciate your time. Am I keeping you from anything?"

"Oh, no, you've got an hour or so, assuming there's no imminent crisis, and they usually save those for the evenings. Besides, as I recall, you didn't ask for much of my time as a student. You may certainly call on it now."

Reggie let out a long breath. "It's an odd situation, and I'm hoping you might have some suggestions."

"Not protective magics, or you'd be talking to Dowland." She caught herself and grinned. "Master Trenton. Though he'd be delighted to see you, if he's not busy with something in the Salle when you leave."

Reggie wasn't sure what he thought of that. Certainly, he wasn't sure of going anywhere near the salle. He couldn't do what he had, and he didn't know how to explain it, and he didn't want to. Instead, he reached for his tea to have something to do. "I was invalided out a couple of months ago. When I asked to be useful, somewhere, they assigned me to lend a hand in research and development. I can't talk about the specifics. There are promises and oaths and all that."

"Of course." Professor Trembley looked him up and down, and he was sure she was trying to decide how he'd got hurt badly enough to be sent home. Left home. Then she said, before anything else. "How are you doing now? If there's research or resources, I can see what we can round up. And we do know quite a few Healers."

Reggie shook his head. "Nothing that can be further mended, nothing that should get worse." Well, so long as he avoided having wet feet for an extended period again. Then, unused to saying this, he added, "Thank you for asking."

"Well. You may be long since out in the world, but I still worry a bit about all of you. More at the moment, naturally." Of course, so many from Bear House would be out working their magic in the War, trying to protect others as best they could. That was how the house magics tended.

He nodded and said, after a moment. "I kept a number of my men alive with what I learned here. For a bit longer."

"Ah, there's a thing to hear." She nodded once and focused on her own tea for a moment. He wondered, for a moment, what it was like for her, for the other Professors. What it meant to see the lists as they came back, men and some women who they'd known as bright-hearted unbroken students. He wasn't at all sure he could bear up under that weight. "Your question, then?"

"I'm the unskilled labour, here, but - um. I need to ask this the roundabout way. Much of what we're doing is exploring the interactions of different materia, for a project with far-reaching implications. And I wanted to talk out some of that, the far-reaching part, with someone. But also, the person I'm helping, the one with the skills, has complained about not being able to get enough of what's needed. Or it's slower to get to us. And sh—" He gave up on trying to obfuscate that much. "She doesn't know why."

"Schola trained, or something else?"

"Alethorpe." That wasn't terribly identifying either. He'd basically just said that it was some sort of crafting magic, near enough, but there were dozens of those.

Professor Trembley considered. "That's two topics, then. I can rummage for my lists of what's hard to come by. I keep them, of course, so Dipti and I can stay ahead of the requests, or alter the plans. Some things we need, of course, no matter how difficult they are to come by. The reagents for the salle, for the other protective enchantments. The rare ones are all in short supply, of course, but also most of the midst of the list."

Reggie nodded. "Which is to be expected. If I could get a copy of your list, or whatever parts of it you're willing to share, that would - that would be a help."

"Not brush against your promises and oaths." Of course Professor Trembley would be sharp enough to spot that.

He couldn't help a little smile. "I should know better than to think you'd not be three steps ahead of me."

"It's rather harder, when you're grown up, all of you. Schola is - oh, this is back to Dowland's theories. He argues, when we're having this sort of debate in the staff room, that Schola is a container for magic. That it was designed that way from, if not the beginning, quite early. There's a range of possibilities, but the structure of the place, the buildings, the classes, the way we have staff who are here for decades, the House magics. They all combine to make some more likely than others."

"And then we go off and the world doesn't have those..." Reggie fumbled for a word. "Designed spaces."

"Just so!" She looked very pleased with him. "Have you ever considered the architectural magics? If you're looking to retrain. I could give you an introduction or two, and there's more than one in that set who had some sort of fighting injury."

That definitely wasn't something Reggie was up for, not at the moment. "Not right now, but - whenever this thing ends, maybe. I want to serve, and that's no time for retraining."

Professor Trembley raised an eyebrow. "Even though you're the unskilled labour where you are?"

"I've picked up enough to make myself useful. And enough to wonder about some things. I'm not sure how to handle them. The Materia's a piece of it, and the person in charge, she's - well. Alethorpe, where all those in charge of the project are Schola men and the very occasional woman. All those implications."

He wouldn't have dared to spell it out when he'd been a

student. But to be fair, it's not the sort of thing that would have come up when he was a student. All his fellows had been much like him. He wouldn't have noticed everything that Lynet made visible. That the men in the trenches had made visible.

"You said far-reaching implications, as well. Of the work, not just the people."

"Exactly. And I'm not sure anyone's actually considering them, not properly?"

Professor Trembley leaned back, then she stood up. "Give me a minute. You don't mind me lending you a book?"

"Um. Pardon?" Reggie thought it was usually the other way round, that people minded you borrowing them. She waved a hand at him and disappeared off into the door to her private rooms. She was gone for several minutes, long enough for Reggie to feel decidedly ill at ease, waiting and wondering what had happened.

Finally, she came back out with two. A narrow red-bound book, in bookcloth, and one in what looked like leather, where the headband was coming loose. He could see a few threads against her hand. Then he realised what he'd just thought, how he'd mentally used the proper terms, and he tucked it away to amuse Lynet with sometime soon. And perhaps she'd be willing to do a bit of mending on the headband, if she could.

Once Professor Trembley was settled in her chair again, she held the books out. "You might find both of those of some use. There's a whole field of theory, about coming up with new forms of magic, the - oh, one of those calls it the distance between the idea and the reality. The Penelopes have done a lot with it, unsurprisingly, since they're usually the ones untangling other people's badly considered ideas."

Reggie nodded, following that easily enough. "So there's a body of work about how to think through this. Considerations?"

"Oh, yes. Much like, oh, the ritual preparations you've learned. Best practices, foundational ideas, all that. The problem is - and you might talk to Kelsey Bett about this, too - that war accelerates everything. Good ideas, bad ideas, everything in between. It can bring tremendous swells in new techniques, but they haven't been looked at as carefully, or they're sloppy, technically, or they have long-term implications. Safety, but also, well. If you harvest every blue-blossomed variety of a particular plant, and there's none left, you're going to have a problem if your brilliant new idea relies on it."

Reggie snorted. They'd all had silphium come up in just about every class, one way or another. Well. Nearly all. It hadn't come up in any of the Quadrivium courses, he thought. "Something like that. And the research, it's partly about finding materia that could be sustainable, at quantity."

"Ah, that's always a trick. And not everything in the world runs on dill, much as Linta wouldn't mind that. Or mint. Mint's easy to have in abundance. Or granite or slate, we've plenty of both about."

Reggie wondered, all of a sudden, if the slate might be useful. A lot of it was going to building, of course, but there would be fragments and such. And he half-remembered something about the way it lay in sheets, and of course the use of writing slates. There could be a useful parallel, magically speaking.

"You've just had an idea?" Professor Trembley was smiling at him.

"Maybe." He gestured with the books. "You're sure it's

all right to borrow them? I'm not sure when I'll be able to return them."

"Oh, send them back through the post. Take your time. I won't need them for a few months at the earliest. Not before end of Floralia term." June, then, or near enough. That would give him plenty of time to get through them and take detailed notes.

"Thank you." He hesitated. "If someone's doing really dangerous research, what's the protocol?"

Professor Trembley considered. "Well, it depends rather a lot on the nature of the danger, and how urgent it is. The Guard or Penelopes, if it's putting people in imminent risk. Other than that, you take your chances with the Ministry, and as it's wartime, they have quite a range of additional permissions right now. But oh, poisoning the water table or something is right out."

Reggie winced, thinking about how much water went into the drain from the papermaking. Though at least he didn't know of anything in that which would be terribly harmful to sewer pipes. At least not at the moment. And it's not like it was the tanneries.

"If you're not sure, and you can bring it to me, or let me know the category, I'll see who I can find who might be a help. How's that?" It was a generous offer, and one Reggie felt he didn't deserve. "And right now, how about I make a copy of the materia lists, and we can go through them, see if you have any immediate questions? Or I could just talk through a batch of it."

"I'd appreciate that very much." All of it, not that Reggie would come out and say so. "Shall I pour you more tea, then?"

"That's what I like about you, Hollis. A good sense of priorities."

CHAPTER 13

"It's not working." Lynet was perched on the workbench nearest the desk, with Reggie in his usual chair and Ellis in hers. She wanted to kick at something, but that wouldn't help, and besides, there was nothing to kick. The journal she'd been willing into behaving was on the desk beside her, half-open, the pages slowly fanning.

Nine on Monday morning, and it was only going to go downhill from there. The journals they'd spent all last week making should have been dried and ready this morning, but when she went through the final steps, the magic just had slid off. Or that was what it felt like. The last step, the licked stamp, was supposed to enliven them. That was what the charms experts had said.

These journals, the one by her and the two on the desk, were decidedly not alive. Like a beautifully executed doll, they looked like they should be real, and they weren't. Except, of course, that they were still well-made blank books, waiting for someone's notes or thoughts or shopping lists or whatever other ink and pencil they might hold.

She still wanted to kick something. Or fling herself on the floor and scream like a toddler. She hadn't done herself any favours going back to London, either. There'd been a massive row in the street last night, outside the pub, something about a match or betting that she couldn't follow over the shouts. She'd found four more unpaid bills that added up to a far larger amount than she'd be able to pay in months. Uncle Matthew might be a help at least negotiating terms on those, if she could bring herself to ask him.

Ellis was saying something, and she had to jerk her attention back. "... something in the paper, or something in the book. How do we figure that out?"

Reggie cleared his throat cautiously, and both Lynet and Ellis looked at him. In a way that made him look nervous, suddenly. "Pardon. I did some reading this weekend."

Lynet wasn't sure what to do with that. "Research?"

Now he looked rather abashed. "It, something about the research here has been bothering me. Not yours, mostly. Or at least, not the parts you're doing. But other parts of it."

Ellis coughed. "Start there, please? Fill me in?" He nudged the tea pot a little closer to his own cup and then reached to pour himself more tea.

Reggie glanced up at her, as if deferring. She waved a hand. "We're not going to get anywhere staring at the books. If you think you have something that might help, go ahead." She tucked her ankles together, smoothing her skirts down.

"I went out to Schola on Saturday to see Professor Trembley." He clearly expected the name to mean something to both of them, but Ellis was looking amiably baffled, and Lynet suspected she was a sharper version of the same. "She's the Materia professor, and she was also my Head of House, Bear House. Alethorpe works differently, I gather, but there are house magics, and she's always taken an interest in what we do after leaving school." He took a breath. "Anyway, when I wrote to ask if I could come consult her about something, well, she had me to tea."

It came out of him in a rush, making Lynet wonder what he'd been like at school. She was beginning to think he'd have been one of the lanky and shy ones lurking in corners, up to their own interests. For all he seemed confident and sure of himself most of the time when around the Schola men downstairs. "She must be very busy?" Lynet offered, when Reggie didn't continue.

"Oh, likely. It was very kind of her. She lent me a few books about a different question I had." He didn't expand on that. "But I also asked her what kinds of materia were difficult to get right now, which were all right, things like that. Because she does the ordering for the school, with the deputy headmistress. They go through quite a lot between classes, and upkeep for the salle and ritual room and warding and all that."

Lynet nodded. That much, she understood. She hadn't known how it was organised at Alethorpe until her last year, but they had the same issues with materia and ingredients and dyestuffs and all that.

"That was the easier part. I made clean copies of the list, they're in my bag, in case that helps?" Lynet had swept him up into testing the books as soon as he'd arrived. She hadn't given him a chance for a comment or a bit of small talk, or to take anything out.

"And the other part?" Lynet wanted to come back to that, and she could see Ellis leaning forward.

"Well, Friday, I had drinks with Vance Jessup and

Charlie Pond. They're downstairs, younger, both Schola men. But they're working on a system with a couple of experts for keeping the trench walls steady. Keeping the mud out of the bottom, or keeping people out of the mud without slipping. They had some questions for me." There was a look, briefly, on his face, that she didn't know how to describe, something hollow and awful. But then he went on, as if he weren't feeling a thing. "Anyway, I was thinking about that research."

Ellis frowned. "Why that research in particular?"

"That's the other part of what I wanted to ask Professor Trembley. They talked about creating new kinds of magic in our classes, some, but it wasn't ever an organised class. A lecture or two in any given subject, more in Ritual and Incantation, which is where it comes up the most." Reggie's voice got quieter, as if it were a wind-up toy running down.

"And?" Ellis pressed on, thankfully sparing Lynet from figuring out how to ask. She wasn't sure what was going on here, exactly. Or rather, she understood the words, but there were things underneath, like a grain in the leather, that weren't behaving as she expected.

Reggie reached for his tea, swallowed a couple of times, then set it down, with much more of a clatter than usual. "I've also heard bits and pieces from other people. Out drinking, they'll tell me things they'd never explain to you, I thought..." Again, he stopped.

More quietly, Ellis murmured. "It's useful, all right? They don't talk to us at all. Especially Lynet."

Reggie started at that, as if he'd got lost somewhere along the way, then glanced at Lynet, who tried not to look upset. Given that was how she felt as a general rule these days, it was an effort to veer toward neutral. She offered after a moment. "They don't. So whatever you heard, that might help."

"It's all piecemeal, right?" Reggie paused to figure out how to put this. "We're all competing for things, at some level, right? If a specific materia is scarce, then who gets it? Who sets those priorities? I don't know the answers to that, and I don't know exactly who does. Master Brand, obviously. Lord Carillon, maybe, I think he's also doing something that takes a lot of materia. What Hopkins is doing, maybe."

Lynet frowned at him. "It isn't even clear to me who's doing what, most of the time. I can't keep them straight, but it's not like they talk to me."

Reggie wanted to reach out and touch her, suddenly, but that wouldn't do any good at all. "They're being pricks. Even the women. But it means you're fighting for resources, without it being remotely like a fair fight. They've got better access to Brand, they can coordinate with each other. You're just left hanging out to dry. That's one problem."

"A rather large problem," Ellis agreed, grumbling about it.

Reggie nodded. "And that doesn't even get into other possibilities. The materia's not working right. Is that because there's a substitution, they used the wrong variety, or harvested at the wrong time, or something? Or they're adulterating it? It's hard to tell without specific testing, some of it. If you're looking at a pile of green dried leaf, and it mostly smells right, how do you tell if it's all the same leaf without a lens and some magic?"

Lynet rocked back at that. She hadn't wanted to think about that at all. "Sabotage, or something else?" It came out of her without thinking, and she clapped her hand over her mouth.

Reggie just looked back at her steadily. "Could be. You know we're told to be alert for it. Could be other people's egos, too. They want all the best for themselves, aren't thinking about the consequences." There was a silence, then, until Reggie spread his hands. "You did ask me what I was thinking." It wasn't apologetic at all.

"I asked what might help. That's not exactly a help." Lynet pointed out, her voice sharper than she liked. "Blast. No. Better to know and think about it, though it's not like I can do anything about it."

Reggie blinked, opened his mouth, then closed it again. After a longer silence, he said, "Let me think about something. For a bit." Then he grunted and went on.

"Here's the other thing I was thinking about. There's no sign people have thought about the implications. The journals are one thing, and that's plenty tricky, but they're not directly dangerous in and of themselves. Some people have similar things - a paired notebook, if they can get one made, there are fast messages by various means, there are carrier pigeons and radio and all that."

Lynet nods. "You mentioned that part earlier. And I guess I wasn't thinking much about it." She wasn't sure she wanted to know, but she had to ask. "What kinds of other things?"

"Oh, I'm sure there are people working on gasses and, I don't know, diseases. There's a whole set up on an island off Scotland, doing the kind of thing you'd want to keep on a remote rocky island if something goes wrong. And more on Salisbury Plain somewhere, doing other things. And that's bad enough, but a few other things I've heard, they're worse. More."

There was a long silence, and Lynet finally coughed. "Go on?" She was reasonably sure they were private here, or at least if they weren't, a dozen things would have gone differently so far.

"Coercion magic, maybe. That mutiny in France raised the question. And that's awful, and illegal under Albion's law, but it's wartime, and laws can be changed." He grimaced. "Magical traps, bogging people down. Bullets that could carry a hex or worse. The journal has - the journal has a lot of good uses, outside of the War. Those?"

"How'd you find out about it?" Ellis's voice was a rolling aggravation now. She could hear it if Reggie couldn't.

"They thought I should join one of their projects. Do something better." There was something painfully hollow there, echoing like a bit of the Silence magic pressing on his worst fears. He almost went on and then snapped his mouth shut.

Again, there was a long silence, and Lynet found her thoughts circling one topic, and she knew she shouldn't ask about it. What it had been like to be there. They all sat, like statues, until she thought she might have an idea. And if she didn't ask, no one would.

"When you were in the trenches, what did you want? What magic would have helped?"

CHAPTER 14

Reggie couldn't move for a time. Couldn't breathe, couldn't think. No one had ever actually asked him. They'd given him orders, in the trenches and in the hospital. They'd had expectations, rules he would follow. No one had stopped to ask. He'd not been high enough rank for that.

What kind of magic would have helped? What he'd wanted. If he'd wanted anything other than the formless need for the war to be done and hating himself for his cowardice.

Here, now, he must have kept the show up well enough, because when he could make sense of his eyes again, they were just waiting. An ordinary sort of waiting, not like he'd been stuck there for a minute, gaping like an idiot. "I." He swallowed hard, and at least he didn't taste bile. "No one asked."

Lynet shifted, leaning on one hand. "Well, that's bloody foolish, isn't it? Not even here?"

There was something in her indignation that made it possible for him to think about it. She'd been indignant about plenty of things in his presence before, but this was on his behalf. On a lot of people's behalf, but he was one of them. He looked at her, gaping open-mouthed, before he reached for his tea without looking. His fingers nudged the cup, and he had to look to find the handle.

It gave him enough space, barely, to gather his words. "Not here, either. Master Brand inquired about my mother, my father, my sisters, my aunts and uncles and cousins. Not so much about me." He gave the brief little shrug that should have worked, but it just made Lynet peer at him.

"You have sisters?" They really hadn't talked about his family at all, but he'd wanted to be kind. Well, kind, and he had no idea how to talk about his family here.

"Three, all married with children. Two older, one younger." Reggie shrugged. "We get on fine." That seemed exceedingly faint praise. He loved them, they worried about him, and the weight of the worry was unbearable at the moment. If he'd been able to tolerate it, he'd have gone to one of them for his convalescence. It would have been better than his parents, honestly, now he could think about it with a little bit of hindsight.

Lynet nodded once, briskly. "All right. So no one asked you. Maybe think about that, in case someone does? So you have a ready answer?"

That, now, that was fabulous advice. "I will." He swallowed hard. "The materia, I don't know how to get a handle on it, but I have the lists." Before they could get much further in that, they could hear steps on the stairs below. Louder than they should be, and Reggie suddenly wondered about that, if there was some useful charm in play. He could set up something more palatable, a bell when people started up that last flight of stairs.

Lynet hopped down from the workbench in a flurry of movement, going to stand by one of the other stations, fiddling with paper. Reggie took the hint and started tidying up around the desk. When there was a knock on the door, Lynet called out. "Yes?"

"Master Brand would like to see Stromer in ten." There was a grudge in there. That he'd had to come upstairs, certainly, but something more than that.

Ellis nodded from where he was sitting. "We were just consulting. I'll be down in good time."

The door closed, and they could all hear the footsteps going down again. Reggie coughed, cautiously. "There's someone wishes you ill. Could I have a look at your work-room protections sometime?"

"You think?" Ellis didn't seem surprised by the idea. "I'd not mind, no. They've done nothing more than make mild trouble so far, but..." He gestured. "A couple of the things we want to try, that could get dangerous. As well as wasteful."

Lynet said, without turning around, "I could spare you for the morning, Reggie. I want to get my notes together, lay out charts, all that. And Ellis is right about the trouble." This workroom was warded, and he wasn't sure who'd done it.

"Of course." Reggie stood, clearing off the last of the desk, putting things away, rinsing out the teacups. "Can I go into the workshop, Ellis?"

"Oh, sure. And if you need reagents, anything that's not locked, I've got some spare of."

It was a nice sort of problem to concern himself with. Laying out what he wanted took the length of Ellis's meeting. The other man came back, lips pressed together, and not wanting to talk about it, though he told Reggie, "Nothing new." That would have to do.

By the time it was approaching luncheon, Reggie had laid protections at the doors, the windows, on the storage cupboards. He had to stop to consider what else might be useful without being tedious to work around. "How do you feel about blood locks?"

"Not allowed. Other people have to be able to check the supplies. Some sort of fiscal procedure. The door's less of an issue. Master Brand and a couple of the others can enter the door, but the smaller, tighter locks?" He shrugged. "I asked, a few weeks back. Before you started."

"Huh." Reggie wasn't sure what to make of that. That Ellis had asked, that he'd got the answer he did. "Mind if I see about lunch?"

"Go ahead. I'd not go back up to Lynet until one, mind, if you can avoid it. She needs some time." That was more or less what Reggie had judged, but it was good to have some outside confirmation. He washed up, straightened his clothing in the mirror, and went back to the main building to see who was around. It was a chance to see what other gossip he might catch about other projects.

What he found, surprisingly, was a woman. Not one of the secretaries, either, she was in striking purple working robes, leaning over to scribble something on a notepad. She turned round, and gave him a long look up and down. "You'd be Reggie Hollis, then?" Her dark hair was pulled back into a terrifyingly competent chignon, not a hair out of place, held fast with an equally terrifyingly pointed gleaming hair stick.

She was perhaps five years older, which meant she might well - must have - known his middle sister. He could see the Schola gem at her throat in an ornate bit of silver. A citrine, Salmon, that suggested an inventive mind, as opposed to the Fox her robes suggested.

"Mistress." He made a slight bow. "I beg your pardon."

"Oh, none of that. Take me out for lunch?" It was nominally a question, but really it was an order, and they both knew it. "Unexpected meeting for my usual luncheon partner. We had a table at Vane's. Do come along."

He was not precisely dressed for Vane's, though for luncheon, he wouldn't get turned away. "Um. Yes." He waited while she took the note she'd been writing on, added a sentence that ended with a flourish, and stuck it under the corner of a nameplate. Lord Temple Carillon's nameplate, in fact. Once more, she extended her hand, the sort of movement that demanded he offer his own.

Vane's was at least on this side of Trellech, though he was almost certainly going to be back late to meet Lynet, with no way to tell her. If he had one of the journals, even one of the inferior test options, he could have. Reggie was caught in his thoughts when Mistress - well - spoke. "I'm Margot Williams, of course." It was one of those deceptive last names that sounded ordinary and were anything but.

"Mistress Williams." He inclined his head, trying to do his best to keep his tone light.

"Oh, none of that. We're colleagues, surely. And you've been hiding away, such a pity. I've been wanting to get to know you." She tapped her fingers on his arm. "Now we've got the chance, just the two of us. How lovely."

He was trying to sort through what he knew about any of the Williamses who might be like this. The most notable line of the Williams family had a reputation. Mostly for devastatingly sharp magic, high standards, a comfort with risk that far exceeded his own, and a take-no-prisoners approach to life. He'd have to look her up to be sure, but the present evidence suggested she'd married in, which perhaps explained her excesses that way, if she were needing to prove that she measured up. If only he could remember anything about who was married to who.

"A pleasure, I'm sure." He swallowed. "Margot. I'm rather out of practise with the social scene. Please, pardon me."

"Oh, you poor dear. I heard you'd been at the front, invalided out." She gave him a sideways look. "Doesn't seem to have done you too much harm, but I'm sure we're glad to have you. Alder's been keeping you all to herself, has she?"

Reggie had got used to the casual nastiness of the men, but this was something new and he was not remotely sure how to handle it. This woman could not see Lynet as any sort of threat to her. "I've been learning a great deal. And it's a tremendous project, of course. Um. Not that I'd say more here."

"Military men do have their foibles about that sort of thing." She cheerfully set into a line of gossip and chatter until they were settled in one of the small private rooms at Vane's. Margot had waved her hand, and said, "On the usual tab, Donald." when a waiter had come to take their order. Once he was gone, she leaned forward, focusing all her attention on him. "I am curious, of course."

"You seem like a woman who is interested in a number of things, on brief acquaintance. Which did you have in mind?" Reggie at least vaguely remembered how the game was played, but it had been a long time since he'd had this kind of attention. He'd been engaged, she'd begged off to marry someone she was actually in love with, he'd taken a number of women out, none for more than a few months. There was the War.

"Well, what you think of the journals, for one thing. We're quite private, you can check if you wish. Temple and I come here quite often, a working lunch. Some of our best ideas, darling, you know. We're working on rather a glorious bit, taking a bit of old lore, turning it into something to work on the land. Turn the land against the Germans, wouldn't that be a fine trick?" Margot leaned in again. She was not exactly trying to seduce him, but she was certainly making it clear that she could and would if she exerted herself the slightest bit more, his opinion on the matter certainly not required.

Reggie did take a moment to check, his fingers working through the cantrip that would let him know if any of the common privacy charms were in play. The room glowed briefly in a reassuring gold before it faded again. He took a breath and replied to the actual question about the journals. "They're tremendously clever. Figuring out how to make them at scale is a whole new challenge, of course." That much was public knowledge in the building. He knew that from his other conversations.

"Temple had quite a hand in the original design. Some of his family's magic. So clever, and so portable. Rather a lot of what I do is anything but." Not that she explained that at all, though he was clear she was working on something of her own. "You should see about a consult with him. He's terribly busy with other things now, of course, that meeting today, for one. But I'm sure he'd make time if you asked. We're leading another project, the both of us. He's the one nominally in charge, but he does take suggestions well, at least if they come from me."

Emphasis, notably, on the 'you'. Not if Lynet asked. Not

if Ellis asked. If Reggie asked. Well, he could take that back to Lynet and Ellis, who'd know what questions to ask. They might know who would be willing to coach him, and he would be glad to see if he could get more information. "I'd be grateful for that. I'd need to figure out what to ask, not to waste his time, of course. Mistress Alder's been very good at explaining, but there's still scores of things I don't know."

Margot raised an eyebrow. "And scores you do. You..." She flicked her fingers at his signet ring. "You're a clever boy, I'm sure."

She expected that line to work better than it did. That particular framing, the way it could twist someone up, didn't hold much power for Reggie. It might have, once, but it wasn't a virtue he clung to anymore. It certainly wasn't the one that had kept him alive. In the moment, all he could think of to do was shrug, so he did. "I respect expertise. It always seemed more sensible."

That, for a wonder, made her smile. She didn't press on their work, though he was quite sure she would in the future. Instead, she turned her questions to his family, out to the more distant cousins, a bit of gossip - rather a lot of gossip - about people who'd been between them in school. She had also got him to agree to come out for drinks sometime with the right sort of people.

He suspected he'd regret that one. And regret it more when the others were well into the drinking. But it was just possible it would get him information that would be useful.

CHAPTER 15

Lynet was getting pushed off onto someone else. Again. She had been told the new stores would be delivered on Monday, and asking in the building had got her nowhere. Now they were low on stock for three different materia reagents, and getting there on two others. None of the actual bookmaking supplies, thankfully, but items she would have thought were reasonably abundant, at least given what they were doing.

The thin slivers of wood that went in the spine should have been fine - they didn't need very much of any of them, near enough a thread. But they were low on oak, lower than they should be. She wasn't at all sure why they were low on iris. She'd ordered more before Reggie had shown up. Vervain was perhaps slightly more understandable, it was widely used in materia work, and so was the mistletoe. They couldn't be the only people who needed it in some quantity. And mandrake was always dear, but it was the only thing they'd found that kept the chain of materia that

went into the marbling end papers in the right relationships. They didn't need much, either, not like some uses.
She wasn't at all sure why they were near out of nettle,
though at least that one should be easy to fix.

Master Brand's secretary, a brightly polished woman,
had peered at her from behind her imposing desk, and told
her to go to the Ministry to ask, she had no records about
that. It was not remotely helpful. More to the point, the files
ought to at least have had Lynet's request forms, properly
filled out in septuplicate. Lynet had tried asking if the forms
would have any notations that might be useful or a reference number. Miss Bell had swept off to check on one of her
offices, as she said, leaving Lynet in the hall.

Then she'd gone to the office in the Office of Materia
that she'd gone to before, waited twenty minutes, and been
passed on to another office, down the hall. Then to one
upstairs. After thirty minutes, she'd been sent to one on the
ground floor. None of them could help her. Finally, she'd
been back to the office next to the one she'd started in, with
a slip and a number, the apparent key to some sort of
encoding system.

The last clerk, an older woman, had peered at the
number, then gone away, behind the solid door behind the
counter. Presumably there were files or records or something of the kind, rather than materia. There couldn't be
much storage. She waited for another ten minutes, as
people came and went, leaving papers in a tray.

Finally, the woman came back out, looking irritated. "I
don't know why you're here. Didn't your lot order enough
of the irises already?"

"Pardon, mistress. It's just three of us on my specific
project, and I'm responsible for all the requisitions. We
haven't got our irises yet at all."

The woman looked her up and down, tilting her head and pursing her lips, as if some bit of maths was coming out consistently wrong. "Can you tell me which project?"

"It has to do with bookbinding, mistress. That's all I can say." She gestured at the slip. "I'd really like to find out what happened to the requisitions I made. If there's something I filled out incorrectly, if there's a way to fix them." The forms kept changing every time she did them, but she thought she'd followed all the instructions.

"Sorry, no way for me to know." The older woman had softened, though. "Look, let me rummage a bit, see if I can figure out what happened. I won't know for a bit. Maybe a few days, maybe longer, it depends what else comes in. Is there a way I can reach you?"

Asking her to send a message to the research building wasn't an option. And while Lynet had a couple of the paired notepads on her, where a note on one sheet would appear on the other pad, that was tipping their hand to the research. "If you sent a message to Master Matthew Woolton, at the Printers Guild. He knows how to get hold of me promptly and there's always someone there for messages. I'm Lynet Alder."

"Mistress Alder." There was a little nod. "Here, let me fetch you a copy of the current guide for requisitions. I can't tell if something fouled up your previous ones without seeing the copies, but this will help you put a new one in."

"That's very generous, mistress. I appreciate it a great deal." Five minutes later, Lynet was back outside, without any of the supplies they were going to need, but marginally reassured she wouldn't make that particular set of mistakes again. At least not until someone changed the forms.

By the time she got back to the workroom, it was well past two. She'd circled out to one of the small cafes on the street, picking up an oggie. She ate it standing at the counter along one side, licking the stray bits of lamb and leek off her fingers quickly and wiping them clean. Not too dear, in terms of cost, and it would keep her going the rest of the day.

When she got up the stairs, she paused, listening for sounds. She didn't hear much at all, which meant Reggie was elsewhere, or he was being very quiet. She made sure to make enough noise on the last few steps not to startle him, to rattle the knob just enough. By the time she got the door open, he was turning round to face her. He had a look on his face, for just a moment. It made her sure something awful had happened, and then she couldn't figure out what sort of awful would make him look like that.

Then he pulled himself together. "Is everything all right? You were gone for ages."

"I was doing circles in the materia offices, without much result." She hesitated, then gestured. "Was that sorting out the binding supplies?"

"We're all set, and I tidied up that set of threads, sorted it out properly by material. Did you know you had three rounds that had silk in them, not properly prepared? Not at all useful for the charmwork."

She winced. "No. Anything we'd used?"

"No, all new spools. I'll take them downstairs, to the supplies room, properly labelled." Reggie gestured. "Anything I can help with?"

"Well. No luck on materia. At all. I can try a new set of forms, and I'm going to, but that'll take tomorrow." She frowned. "And I still don't know why the test version we did didn't work. The ones from this morning."

"Would it help to do another test?" Reggie offered it a bit uncertainly.

"It could be any number of causes. We did the charm-work wrong somewhere. The materia wasn't suitable for some reason. I don't know, the planets were in the wrong sequence. It's not as if we've made enough sets to test every possible range."

"It strikes me that Mercury going retrograde would be an issue. But that's not until next month. You made these tests since January, yes?" Reggie came back over to settle down at the desk.

"You were here for all of it, so yes." Lynet rubbed her face. "How are things with Ellis and his workroom?"

"Better than they were. If someone wants to break in, they'll have to be fairly clever about it, or go to a lot of trouble. I'll think about more options. I sort of went for the solid heavy versions."

Lynet frowned at him, peering to take in his general state. "Are you all right? Did you get lunch? That's a lot of magic to be doing, isn't it?"

His reaction was not at all what she expected. He flinched, for a moment, turning his head so she couldn't see his expression. Then he swallowed and turned back, as if it required a bit of force and will. "I went out to lunch with someone downstairs. She rather swept me off." Then he held up his hand. "I learned some interesting things?"

Now Lynet wasn't at all sure what she felt. She swallowed hard, twice. "Who? And did you actually get enough food?"

"It was Vane's, so yes." She must have blinked at him, because he added, "Decent portion sizes there. Not like some places, where it's just a taste or two of each course. A fair number of courses. This was more solid meat and sides, just fancy. Perfectly good bit of chicken, and I'll get a solid supper tonight." Then he cleared his throat. "Mistress Williams. Do you know her?"

Lynet shook her head. "I don't know most of them."

"Dark hair, pulled up in the sort of chignon that makes you suspect it doubles as a sheath for a wicked little dagger. Very fashionable frock, but in that sharp way. Like the dress is carrying the conversation half the time." He didn't sound as if he approved. She suddenly realised she had no idea if he'd had a, well, whatever posh men called the women they were partnered with if it wasn't 'wife'.

"Did you enjoy the lunch?" Oh, that sounded utterly awful.

"To be quite honest, I'd rather have lunch with you. I have a good sense of where I am with you." He paused, as if that had been more revealing than he'd probably intended. "I'm not seeing anyone. She is. He had a meeting."

"Someone downstairs?"

Reggie nodded. "An affair, on his part. I know he's married. I suspect she is too. I don't know what she's got in mind."

Lynet opened her mouth, then closed it. Nothing she could say here would be helpful or kind. Or useful.

"I - look. People like me, a lot of us get married for family reasons. Not for love, or even fondness or affection. A business arrangement, in the long-term sense. A lot of people I know make agreements. Two children, maybe three, and then they can go their separate ways, effectively. Share the house, but certainly not a bedroom, even maybe a wing. Sometimes it's that they're both living at different properties, never together except for the necessary public events. I never much wanted that. I suppose it's better if people in that sort of relationship agreement can find people they actually want to be with. But I don't think a lot of people handle it well. Doing things like that with someone you work with, for one. It upsets a lot of internal balances."

That was rather a lot, all at once, a great deal more than she'd expected. Lynet nodded, hesitantly. "And - um. You don't have anyone like that? An engagement or whatever?"

"I was a while back. Well before the War. She begged off. She actually had fallen in love with someone who she could marry. I don't grudge her that. Never found anyone else I liked enough to have a conversation with, that my parents would also agree about."

Lynet pursed her lips. "Conversations matter to you?"

"Well, yes. I mean, for one thing, if you're going to be around people, sitting in silence is a fine thing, or doing things together in silence. We're quite good at that, actually? Very restful. But you can't have a life like that. Having things to talk about is better. I don't care a lot about the topics, I'm curious about a number of things. But I want someone else who keeps up their end of the conversation."

That left her out. Though then she got caught up for a moment, that he'd appreciated their working silence. But she could at least contemplate something else. "How would you feel about a project? Testing all the materia, to see what meets the quality standards we need. If we've got enough, making another test batch. You making your own journal from scratch, every part of it. You could have two from the batch, one to give to someone else. Whoever you'd like to talk to. When it's just a pair - people have done those before. It's expanding the charms out to infinite volumes that's the trick."

She watched the expressions play over his face. Shock, for a moment, then a wistfulness, before his face settled into a sharp desire, the sort that had him leaning forward.

"You'll show me all of it? Your - you're a mistress of the art. All of that?"

"Well, not everything. We're still doing case binding. But yes. All the steps. Maybe showing you will help me figure out where things are going wrong."

"Right. So the first step is figuring out what materia we can properly use. Need a cuppa, or should I get on that now?"

"You get on that now, and I'll start figuring out the requisition and order forms."

CHAPTER 16

Two days later, Reggie was still puzzling over the questions of the materia. He'd completed a full inventory, both in their workroom and down with Ellis. He'd tested the materia, drawer by drawer, bin by bin. Now, he was staring at the storage, as if staring at it would resolve the problem.

Lynet came back in, carrying a new pile of paper, and stopped. "Did the storage bins offend you?"

Reggie shook his head. "Not the bins. What's in them." He waved a hand. "Four different things aren't responding the way I'd expect. I don't know if the materia's just old, or was harvested improperly, or went bad in storage for some reason. It's just ..." He shrugged again. It felt like he did, honestly, that sense of inertia that could get anything in motion if he could just get it rolling. "Do you mind if I go investigate a bit? It might take a bit. Today, tomorrow."

"Do we have enough for a small batch?" Reggie had been willing to set it aside, much as he was curious about having a journal of his own. But she was leaning forward, her hands on the desk, expectant.

"Yes. We've the least iris - the bit in the main bin's no good, but there was some in the cupboard that's still all right. Enough for maybe ten or fifteen journals. I couldn't remember the proportions you needed."

"It's a fixative, so less than you'd think. One part in thirteen for that. How are we on the amplifiers?"

"We've plenty of the vervain, and we don't need much mandrake at all, right? But we're low on the mistletoe, and also the sardonyx." All of which were used to anchor the charmwork in the journals in different ways. "And I'm entirely dubious about the quality of the lodestone, and that's key to the whole thing, isn't it?"

"One of many keys, but yes. Maybe that's what went wrong with the last batch." Lynet cocked her head, frowning. "If you don't mind waiting on the book, go look at materia first. We know we've got enough good paper. We tested that yesterday."

"We did. So it's something in the marbled sheets for the endpapers, or something in the sigil ink." Lynet shook her head. "Now I'm wondering if we shouldn't revisit putting something in the paste, but that's fiddly."

"Alchemical distillations, a couple of drops?" Reggie had got the impression she didn't care for the more alchemical forms, but he wasn't entirely sure why.

"We tried a few times, it was unreliable, how the paste came together. And even with the magic in play, we still need the paste to work properly as paste. We had to retool it every batch, and that's no good if you're aiming for speed and quantity."

Lynet shrugged and then perched on the desk. "I'll think about the steps again, and if we can swap anything in. The trick's really the marbling. It's one of those horrific sets of astrological magic logic problems. Other people worked it out for me." Her hand flicked downstairs. "But they gave me a couple of alternate lists, and we could try testing those."

Reggie considered that. "Mind telling me what version? I could ask around, see if someone's up for a natter. It'd give me an excuse to see if anyone else here either has a store of something they're not using, or is having the same problems."

Lynet looked at him sharply, her brow furrowed. "Why?"

"Why would I ask? Why would they tell me? Why are we basing our entire system on a series of astronomical and alchemical magical theories that haven't been properly revised in centuries?"

The last one, as he'd half-hoped, made her laugh. "Well, they do, in fact, work. If they didn't, I'm sure even the most traditional sorts would have given up on it a while ago. Probably."

Reggie grinned at her. "The rest of it - well. I can go be charming and inquisitive, and it might get us somewhere, right? It's worth trying. If it doesn't work, no one will tell me anything useful."

Lynet took a breath and let it out. Something about this made her deeply uncomfortable. Reggie could see that. Sense that. Something. But he had no idea how to ask about it, and even if he had, he wasn't sure she'd be able to answer. They'd have to muddle along as they were. "Go ahead. Stop by in the morning, at least. If it's going to take tomorrow too, fill me in."

"Of course." Reggie hesitated. "Let me see if I can wrap up by lunch on Monday, and we can discuss it somewhere?

Maybe talking about it somewhere that isn't here would help."

That was a mistake, and Reggie immediately cursed himself. She froze up, went rigid in all the ways that were about protecting herself, and he immediately held his hands up. "Wherever you'd rather. Pardon, I didn't mean..."

"Didn't mean what?" There was an edge in her voice now, and Reggie couldn't tell what proportion of it was actually aimed at him, and what was about the rest of the situation. That was not one of the charms anyone had ever told him, diagnostically speaking, and he was rapidly considering it a serious flaw in his education.

He straightened up. "It's very clear to me you take this work extremely seriously, as it should be taken. I've been wondering if there's something here, in this space, that is unduly restrictive. Talking about it somewhere else might free something up. One of my professors swore by that, as a good magical practice, as well as a pleasant one. But if you'd rather not over lunch, of course, we don't need to. I'm sorry I made you feel uncomfortable."

She was still for a long moment. Ten heartbeats or so, Reggie could feel them pounding through him. Then she nodded once. "Apology accepted. I'll think about where might work."

Reggie nodded. "That's all I could possibly ask for. Look, I'll be off. I'll report in first thing on Monday, and we can plan more from there."

She nodded once, hopping off the desk and going over to put her smock back on, and over to the paper stores, to put things away. Reggie lingered for just a moment, watching the way her hands moved so decisively and neatly. She didn't waste effort, and he was appreciating that about her more and more.

Then he pulled himself together and wandered down-stairs, doing his best to impersonate a man of some leisure. He spent half an hour chatting with one of the secretaries. He began by complimenting the flowers on her desk - a gift from Master Brand - and then her frock, and then asking what sort of things made her work easier. Once she was chatting away happily, he managed to slip in a few questions about the requisition process. He led by saying that he wanted to make certain they weren't making her job harder. She was clearly a busy woman.

Well, for values of busy that allowed a thirty-minute chat without interruption, though admittedly it was Friday after lunch. Reggie had just inquired about whether he could look at the supplies cupboard, and Miss Cattral had shown him.

He saw Margot Williams sweeping down the hallway, accompanied by another woman who had blonde hair, but who was just as sharply dressed. She looked familiar enough, and after a moment, he placed her as a year behind him, in Salmon House. Her name also began with an M, and she'd married, but he had long since forgot to whom.

"Reggie! Darling. Do you have plans for the next few days? We're just off to a scrumptious house party. I'm sure there's room for one more. The Carillons have oodles of space, and a couple of the usual people can't this time, so tiresome, so I'm sure they could fit you in."

Not what Reggie had expected on any level. He felt like he was already stumbling and falling, metaphorically windmilling his arms in a failed attempt to keep any dignity or balance. He took a breath, counted to three - he'd been taught that looked better. "Oh, I couldn't possibly. I promised I'd call on one of my sisters tomorrow, and stay all day. She's been wanting to show off something for weeks to me." It was not much of an excuse, but it was what he had. And now he'd have to go, in case Margot asked about it later. He was not a skilled liar, and it was not a skill he'd particularly ever wanted to perfect.

"Oh, well. Next party, then. I'll tell Temple properly, ask him to have a word. Such a charming estate, all that land and space, and a folly, and a scrumptious view down to the lake. And there are horses and things if you're that sort of outdoorsy." Margot brushed it off easily.

That sent a pang through Reggie, sharp and painful. He'd been an outdoorsy sort, rambling and a spot of mountain climbing, and certainly riding, when he had a decent mount. But he wasn't at all sure his foot was up to the first two. Most of the decent horses had gone to the War, and at any rate, doing any of it in front of other people couldn't be borne. He swallowed and said, "Not much recently. I beg pardon, you were a year behind me at Schola. I'm having an awful time placing your name. Mostly Alchemy, am I right, but of course with an overlap into Materia."

The second woman took him in, then gave him a smaller, tighter smile. Not nearly as effusive as Margot Williams, but he supposed that was a high bar. "Medea Aylett, these days." Then she softened, visibly, as she went on. "Wallington, my husband, is a genius at it, of course. I'm just glad to be able to assist in whatever way I can. Margot and I were talking about some ideas. The parties really are great fun, and we often find it loosens the inspiration. Not a working gathering, none of that gruelling paperwork, but sometimes ideas just pop into the head."

Reggie nodded his head. "Oh, quite, quite." He often got his best ideas in the bath, personally, but one couldn't say that to women one had a tentative professional relationship with. Certainly not to someone like Margot Williams, who would read ten kinds of innuendo into it. And likely turn up in the bathtub, nude with a cocktail, as promptly as she could arrange. If she'd decided she wanted the entertainment.

"Well. I hope you aren't expected to work until five. Mistress Alder does seem to work you terribly hard, you really must come round and chat sometimes. We know all the best books for things. And other resources."

"I'm actually on a bit of a hunt for some more materials, actually. I was about to go have a rummage in the supply cupboard."

"Oh, indeed? Anything in particular?" Margot leaned forward, just for a moment, the sort of posture that suggested she might blow a kiss.

Reggie contemplated his options. "Owl feather quills, a couple more? The last one broke. I was a bit ham-handed with it. And then there are a few plant things."

"Ah, well. Let me show you that. Did Miss Cattral give you the key?" Margot swept her hand along to the storage cupboard - well, storage room - at the middle of the hall. Reggie held it up and then opened the door. "If I can't find it, I'll get one of the boys on our project to hunt it out, they just leap to do my bidding, of course."

The room was, on the whole, not as fully stocked as he would have expected. The office supplies were all right, plenty of jars of ink and ordinary pens and pencils, though most people had their own they preferred, as far as pens. Stacks of blotting paper, for people who didn't like to use charms or weren't deft with the light touch a drying charm needed. There were plenty of bins of materia, and Reggie now had to figure out how to get these women out of here. He wanted a look at the logs on the bins, for one thing.

Fortunately, he was saved by a voice further along the

hall. "Margot? Medea? Goodness, you do get it into your head to do things. Ready? We'll be late for the portal, and you know they fuss when they have to hold things up. Not at all ship-shape."

"That's Temple. Must go, darling, do say yes next time." Margot did kiss his cheek that time, running her fingers along his arm as she turned to go, Medea Aylett behind her.

CHAPTER 17

Lynet opened up the workroom promptly at quarter to eight, and it was only five minutes later that she heard Reggie on the stairs. She'd learned to identify his step now, the slight, almost inaudible unevenness. Well, that and the fact it wasn't Ellis, and no one else came up here much.

He knocked at the door, and she waved a hand in his direction. "Come in. You up here today, or do you need to finish up?"

"I had some - luck's more or less the word - Friday. I'd like to talk it through, but perhaps not here?"

Lynet wheeled around, peering at him. Hadn't he got the message on Friday that she wasn't going off somewhere with him? It would be the worst sort of gossip, and she didn't know how to do that, anyway. It wasn't anything anyone had taught her.

Going round the pub, yes. Or the Alethorpe club, down on Club Row, she could more or less manage that. Though

128

most of the people there ran to Healers and specialists, rather than crafters. Crafters tended to the pubs in the Crafting quarter. If she didn't quite fit there, at least the Pied Type knew her.

He immediately held out both his hands. "Not for lunch. You were very clear about that. But perhaps helping with an errand? You'd mentioned there might be one today?"

"Taking some of the rag scrap we can't use to the Printer's Guild." They had a number of pieces that weren't suitable, bits of silk scraps that had got mixed in. Or there was a bit of magically woven fabric Ellis had had to pick out of the bin piece by piece. It would spoil the enchantments they wanted to use. "I suppose that would be easier with two. And I don't know. We could talk on the way back."

"Sort of thing that needs a cart?"

Lynet nodded. "If you'd get it ready from Ellis. Would you rather go this morning or after lunch?"

"This morning." He was very prompt about that. "I can tell you a bit about the inventory now?"

"Please." Lynet came back over toward him, and he gestured. "I have some notes?"

She settled at the desk while he rummaged for notes in his satchel. They were very neatly written up, orderly, and she glanced through them, frowning. "This doesn't make sense." Then she put up her hands. "Your notes are excellent. But the information in them, I mean."

When she looked up, Reggie was smiling, the sort of nervous, embarrassed smile she didn't know how to read properly. Certainly not from him. People like him didn't look like that because of something she'd done. Like the praise meant something, like there was more there than excellent notes. She looked away again, quickly. "Let me work through this for a bit. Can you, um? Can you do the maths well enough to figure out what we'd need for each of the test batches we'd want to do? So we can figure out what we can do?"

"Absolutely." He was still smiling when Lynet risked a glance at him again. "You keep the desk. I'll pull a stool up to one of the workbenches. And I do want to see about getting pages ready today, if we get a chance. You have a copy of your most recent parts equations? And can you check the amounts for the paper? Actually, let me run down and check on Ellis's inventory, then I'll come back and do the maths."

Lynet nodded. "I'll have a fresh copy for you by the time you come back, then."

It was almost eleven when they both finished up their parts of it. Lynet wasn't sure what the inventory records meant, but she was at least somewhat more certain of what they could do with what they had on hand. And she was two-thirds of the way to a proposal on how to stack the test batches they wanted to do to make the best use of the supplies. Reggie had worked along steadily and mostly silently, bar a pause to put the kettle on at ten.

Now she looked up at him. "Let's take the cart, shall we?" It was enough before lunch, still. The streets wouldn't be as busy now as they would be in an hour.

"I got it ready when I was downstairs. We just need to roll it out." Reggie waited for her to put her coat on, then added a note to the door saying 'Errand. Back before the end of lunch hour'.

"That's very unspecific." Lynet gestured at the note.

"Those are the best kinds of notes. Not that I expect people will come up so far as to read it. Do you need to sign out or anything?"

Lynet blinked. "No? Should I?"

Reggie hesitated. "Let's talk about that while we walk." Ten minutes later, they were a few blocks from the research building, and Lynet still wasn't sure what she was doing.

"I thought maybe drop off the fabric, and then one of the parks? It's warmer today." Reggie broke in a tad uncertainly. "Maybe pick up something from a bakery for a snack?"

Lynet was about to complain that she didn't need it before she stopped, and Reggie stopped a step ahead. "Are you hungry all the time? Is that why you keep wanting to get food?"

He looked abashed, blushed, and looked away.

"You don't have to tell me." Now it was going to be awful and awkward.

"It's not that. It's a little complicated. Could we - I have money, may I buy something at a bakery, have you join me, my treat? No, no expectations."

Lynet hesitated, then offered. "How far off our route is the one you really like?"

Reggie near lit up at that and something about making him do that made her feel queer inside, a sort of emotion she didn't know how to name. She thought she might like it, though, seeing him look so pleased. "Not far? I don't know exactly where the Printer's Guild is, but it's the shops just north of Portal Square."

She hesitated. "We can circle round there. And then maybe the garden, down where the Ministry quarter starts, you know the little one that goes off toward the meadows?" The meadows were the land that buffered Trellech from being seen from the river. That side park was generally fairly quiet this time of day, though she understood it had something of a reputation as a lover's lane in the dark. But the benches were well-spaced. They couldn't be seen or overheard.

"I was wondering if that would be agreeable." They went on in near silence. Dropping the fabric off only took a minute, and Uncle Matthew wasn't about - she asked. Then they circled about with the empty cart to the bakery, and Lynet waited outside while Reggie went in, coming out with a bakery box he insisted on carrying.

It wasn't until they were in the park, on a bench, with the bakery box balanced on the rim of the cart, that Reggie spoke again. "I am hungry a lot. Still getting over -" He shrugged. "The food was awful, in the trenches. And not a lot better behind the lines most of the time. The Healer I see says it'll take a bit to stop being hungry as much."

Lynet frowned. "You - still see?" The verb tense struck her.

"Not very often now. But I'm still healing a bit, they want to check. He's been willing to see me on Saturdays, or after work hours."

"I - I didn't realise." She hadn't asked. She hadn't remotely thought about it. Not about whether he still needed a Healer's care, not about whether there was something he needed in all his offers of food. Not about a lot of things.

"Hey." His voice was careful now, with just an edge of something she couldn't name. Caution. Fear, maybe. But also with a certainty she hadn't heard much from him, the note that the men downstairs had day in, day out, and she never did. "It's not a problem. But if you'd let me, I'd be glad to bring a bit more for elevenses. And a mid-afternoon tea break. Or for lunch, even."

She shook her head. "I can't..."

"If it's the money, that's not a problem for me. I'm clear

yours is going somewhere that matters to you. Though I'm quite sure they're not paying you remotely what they should."

Uncle Matthew had intimated that to Papa, before - well, before. But it was a Ministry contact, during wartime, she had been told she couldn't negotiate it, or ask someone to review it. They'd implied it was a standard rate, based on her training and years of experience, and she knew that was often how the Ministry worked.

Reggie went on, after a moment, as if he'd read something in her response that made him more comfortable going on. "I know you don't want to go out. But I'd be glad to bring two solid box lunches for us. I know some places. And—" He hesitated. "Food matters. Not to my family much, but I learned, my apprentice master felt very strongly about properly feeding mind and body and magic whenever we were doing significant work. Especially day in, day out, like we're doing right now."

Lynet blinked. She hadn't entirely thought of it that way. Oh, she'd known she wasn't eating well enough, she'd put it up to limited options, and the fact most things she ate still tasted wrong. Too salty, too bland, too something she couldn't name. Though the scone in her hands tasted like sunlight, the lemon and the orange and the sugar of the glaze coming together beautifully.

The silence stretched on until she cleared her throat. "Oh." Then she nodded. "We can try it? See how it goes?"

Reggie smiled at her, like he'd just got the sort of gift an eight-year-old hoped for and didn't expect to ever get. That optimism, unbent and unbroken. "I'll find a place and what they're likely to have for tomorrow, then, after work tonight."

"And give up your library time?" She said it, not meaning to tease quite that much, but he just grinned.

"I have a bit to spare." Then he sobered. "We should talk about the supplies. I don't know how much made sense to you from my notes?"

"That someone's been ordering massive amounts of iris, and vervain, and mandrake, and leaving us the - I don't know. Chaff from the floor? Like cheap tea."

Reggie nodded. "And I'm none too sure about the sardonyx, and Solomon's Seal, or the mistletoe, either. Though some of that might be seasonal. I couldn't check everything. I was focused on what we cared about, but several of those need to be harvested at Midsummer."

Lynet frowned. "True. So if we were low on stocks, it might be seasonal. Do we know anything about - I mean? Could we request specific batches be harvested for us? Or even do some of it ourselves?"

"I don't know, but that's definitely something I can ask people. Professor Trembley, for one, she must know who'd know." He looked very pleased with the suggestion. "That's clever. If we can't requisition it through the ordinary channels, could we go around? It might take some money, but there's probably some way to solve that. Or a way to make out that we need to be absolutely sure about the preparation chain. Can we commission the harvesting directly? It might even work out cheaper for the Ministry." He gestured with one hand. "I'll find out more."

"Not that any of that helps us now." Lynet pointed out. "It's near a month to Midsummer. And longer before anything would be dried and usable."

Reggie nodded. "So - one thing we could do, by which I mean I, here, is see if we can figure out who has some. And if they're using it or just hoarding it."

Lynet shivered. "I don't - I." She hesitated. "I can't make trouble like that."

"Would you trust me to ask, carefully?"

She couldn't answer for a good minute. Or even really breathe. Finally, though, she said, without looking up at him. "I want to know why it isn't working. What, what broke."

She meant in her, as well as in the magic that she thought they'd figured out. Reggie cleared his throat. "Of course you do. That's because you care about what we're doing. Here, there's one of the biscuits you liked." He pressed it into her hand, and then let her eat in quiet, not saying anything else as they headed back to the workroom.

CHAPTER 18

FRIDAY, JUNE 1ST IN THE WORKSHOP AND A
MEETING

The week had - nominally - gone smoothly enough.
She had permitted him to go out and bring back
luncheon for both of them, and indicate what
she'd like for the rest of the week. Reggie considered that a
major victory, to be celebrated with scones and a bit of
good tea from the tin he'd brought in.

By Thursday afternoon, they'd put together a journal
for Reggie's use. He'd greatly enjoyed sewing the signatures, much more than he'd expected. Better yet - at least in
terms of producing more journals promptly - he'd turned
out to have a steady hand for the paste. Steady enough it
got a moment of praise from Lynet, a comment that few
people managed to do it cleanly the first few times.

It was a bit like folding Ordnance Survey maps up properly, really. Feeling how the cloth and paper ought to fold,
how much space there was for things to move, how tightly
it should clasp the book boards. He found the whole

process satisfying. Work of his hands, making a thing that was real in the world. It was what he had loved best about Materia work, before the War. Doing something that had weight as well as meaning that couldn't be ignored.

Friday morning, they'd breathed magic into it. Or, technically, licked magic into it, or rather, he had. But also a bit of breath. Lynet had gestured when they were settled in front of the workbench. "The licking is because it's a concrete act. We know it works. But if you'd rather do something else, or as well. What matters is the stamp knows it's you, that there is a brush of yourself, your magic, so it responds to you the way it ought."

Reggie tilted his head. "Like a duck imprinting on the first thing it sees?" he asked.

"I'm a London girl. I don't know about ducks, unless it's eating them. Or I suppose feeding them bread." She smiled as she said it, though, and Reggie filed it away as a form of humour that she was comfortable with. "Go on then, whatever you're going to do to breathe life into her."

"Her?" Then he bent forward, breathing on the stamp, then licking it. It was an oddly intimate act to do in front of someone else. But as he placed the stamp on the back cover, centred on the endpaper, he could feel the book pulse under his fingers. It was alive, in a subtle but very real way, and he almost dropped it.

"Most people can't feel it that clearly. Or at least - the ones we've made as tests. Master Brand has one. There's a couple of dozen now. They—" She waved a hand. "Yours isn't. You haven't made hundreds of books. But it's very good for a first time." She seemed about to say something more, then changed her mind. He could see it, her setting something aside.

"All because of your excellent teaching. And seeing how

you do it, the way you position things. I have been trying to pay attention." Reggie felt at least that was a good reason to be watching her. A suitable professional one.

She half-smiled, then made a visible decision about something. "Would you test it out? I suppose with me. Or Ellis."

"With you, certainly." He said. "Anything else?"

Lynet took a half step back, pivoting on her heel to look at him. "Would you come to my weekly meeting with Master Brand? I want to make it clear that we can't proceed without either more materia or time to completely revamp and test our plans. And maybe, well, maybe he'll listen better if you're there."

"Do you want me to say anything, or just sit and take notes? You're the expert, I'm quite clear on that. I've only begun to get a grip on the theory behind the things, all the layers of it." Reggie spread his hands. "Whatever you'd find helpful."

Lynet chewed on her lip, then turned away to tidy something up. He didn't rush her. There was no need to. Without turning back, she spoke clearly enough he could hear her. "You don't take over. Thank you."

"Of course not. You're the one with skills. I'm strictly a novice." Reggie shrugged, even if she couldn't see it. "But you're right, Master Brand will probably treat you better if I'm there. And I might spot something in what he says that could help. We won't know until we try."

They went downstairs, timing it to be precisely a minute early. When Lynet entered, she gestured. "May Reggie join us? He's been helping keep the inventory straight. I'd like to know how you want us to proceed."

She did, Reggie thought, an entirely reasonable job of laying out the issues. It wasn't the polished perfection Pater would have done in a boardroom, but she had her own style about it. She spoke plainly and clearly. She added in little phrases to make sure Master Brand had the context for each issue.

Lynet, in fact, talked about the connections between materia choices. She'd chosen the magical amplifiers as a focus, since they were low on stocks of two of the three, the mistletoe, vervain, and mandrake. Master Brand wasn't visibly rude or dismissive, not exactly, but he was also not helpful.

And he should have been more helpful. That was what kept nagging at Reggie, as he kept up with the notes of examples Lynet was laying out. Even if he couldn't fix the supply issues himself, Master Brand wasn't - well. He wasn't leading.

A proper leader, the kind Lynet deserved, would have offered some administrative support for the supplies. Maybe seen if someone could go round with the revised forms. He had the rank and status to insist on a meeting with the Ministry of Materia, someone high up in it. Or Master Brand could help arrange a consult with someone who could help with alternatives.

He did none of that. Instead, he heard Lynet out, nodded once, and said. "Carry on as best you can with what you have." Which didn't even answer the question about whether they should take the time to revamp the entire process. "Good day, Mistress Alder. Hollis, stay a moment, would you?"

Lynet gathered herself. "I should check on something with Ellis." Which meant he could find her there, after.

Once the door had closed behind her, Master Brand leaned back and lit a cigarette. He didn't quite put his feet up on the table. He wasn't as casual as all that, but Reggie was honestly a little shocked he hadn't been offered a drink and a bit of ribaldry. It was as if the office had gone from a place of work to the middle of a country house shooting party with a spot of business in the interstitials as the door closed.

"We could find you something else in a week or two. Margot tells me you were intelligent enough to keep up, over lunch."

"I'm quite happy where I am, sir. It's an important project once we figure out the practicalities." Even if Reggie was still dubious about people having thought through the implications. "It could change the War in so many ways."

"Or it could sputter into failure in a month or two. It would be harder to get you onto anything suitable after." Master Brand let that settle, a general threat. "You have a great deal of promise, Hollis. Don't waste it."

Reggie considered, then pulled out his own pack of cigarettes. He barely smoked now, it reminded him entirely of the trenches, when it kept hunger and terror and misery at bay for just a touch longer. "Can I get a light?" It did, however, give him a few moments to gather himself. "Can't smoke up there, it's bad for the materia."

"Ah, yes, of course. That's true for a number of projects." He leaned over and flicked his lighter. Magical, naturally, the spark was nicely stable.

Reggie leaned forward to light it, across the desk, and then back in his chair. Inhaling and exhaling gave him a few more moments. "To be honest, I don't know that I'd do well right now in a crowd. I'm still healing a bit. Mistress Alder's pace suits mine. The way she breaks down the work, it's very orderly, well-sequenced. Something more chaotic, ideas being flung around, I suspect I need a few more months to be up for that day to day.

Much as I like going out for a drink or supper with the chaps."

"Or luncheon with our Margot." Master Brand leaned back himself, chuckling. "She's curious about you. Several of them are, of course. It would do you no harm to spend a little time with them. A few hours a week. I'm sure Alder can spare you."

Reggie inclined his head. "Is that - pardon, sir, I'm still used to military hierarchy. Is that an order, a suggestion, an offer, or something else?" He thought again how he'd never have said that, certainly not that way, a few years ago. Before. Now, he had no qualms about saying it, about using every tool he had in pursuit of his particular goals.

"Something for you to consider." That was deliberately unhelpful.

"I'll certainly give it the proper amount of thought, sir. Is there anything else I should know? About the materia, or other projects, or anything of the kind?"

"Not at the moment. Possibly in the future." If he were obedient to the proper patterns. "And I suppose you're making yourself useful upstairs. Before you go up, how is your aunt? I had the most delightful letter, full of gossip from her."

That sort of thing ran out Reggie's cigarette and then some, but he eventually managed to make a retreat in good order. Not until they'd talked about his aunt, a second cousin, Master Brand's grandmother who had been at school with a different relative, and the expected complaints about the lack of the bohort league. Also Master Brand's thoughts on the Schola end-of-year matches. It was meaningless, that was the thing, except that it was all about Reggie continuing to demonstrate that he was the right sort. That Master Brand could trust him to behave in the known, approved ways. It wasn't as if Brand cared about the answers, so long as they fit those narrow slots.

When he knocked on the door of the paper workroom, he could hear low voices, the sort of fierce consonants that weren't fighting, but were certainly not happy. "It's Reggie?"

The door was flung open. "Oh, you're back. Coming?" Lynet went charging off, back across the courtyard and up the stairs, without waiting. Ellis caught Reggie's glance. "She's frustrated. With good reason. Go on."

Reggie didn't manage to catch up to her - his foot cramped on the second flight. By the time he made it into the workroom, she'd put the kettle on, and flung herself into the chair behind the desk. "Well?"

"There's something decidedly queer. I don't know what. He offered to take me off the project, give me something he thought was better. I declined, before you say anything. Made a noise that I might be more interested in a few months, not up for noise and chaos yet, all that. Which is true, but I'd rather be here. And I expect that will be true months down the road."

She looked up at him, rather pale all of a sudden. "Oh." It was as if something had deflated her head of steam utterly. "You said that? To him?"

"I did. I mean, I had to say it the right way?" Reggie shrugged. "I thought you handled yourself well in the meeting. Not how I'd go about it, but that's only to be expected. What you did should have worked better. And it didn't."

"Which - well. Bloody hell."

He answered the question she hadn't asked in words. "Which means there's something going on. I can't see what it is. We'll keep working, right? Best thing we can do." The thought caught him again, the way the very ground felt unsettled. "You're not making it up. How he's treating you. What it might mean. There's something wrong here, I see it too. Especially after this meeting. And you're not alone with it. You and Ellis. Whatever I can do to help, I'm here for."

Lynet let out a little puff of breath. "Suppose so. All right." She ran her hand through her hair, catching at the back by her bun. "I'll have to look at trying to redo the calculations again."

"Let me know if you want me to have a look at the options, too. Right now, going to pour you some tea when the kettle sings, and I wanted to have a look at that reference, about distillates, whether that might work."

Having something practical clearly settled Lynet a bit, and Reggie let out a breath. He could spend the afternoon being reliable. Or at least doing his best to be. He just hoped it was enough.

CHAPTER 19

FRIDAY, JUNE 8TH NEAR PORTAL SQUARE AND IN
LONDON

Lynet had kept working well past the bells striking six. And then seven. By the time she wrapped up, it was getting on for sunset, edging into twilight. It was quieter, at least. She was thinking she might make it all the way through the portal without running into someone. Then she came up toward Portal Square to find Uncle Matthew waiting for her.

He was clearly not in his most professional mode; he must have changed his suit since finishing work for the day. "Lynet!"

"You haven't been waiting for me, surely?" Lynet was horrified at the idea he'd been sitting there for hours.

"Oh, no. Checked that you hadn't gone through yet, but I've only been waiting half an hour or so."

She frowned. "How did you—" She knew he had an infinite number of connections in all sorts of places. He must have had some idea if she'd left the workroom. Or hadn't gone back to her room in the Guard barracks.

He raised a hand. "You're listed for a portal token, of course, and you haven't used it yet tonight. And I thought you might go back. How are things on your project?"

She couldn't say anything about that. Both because she'd promised, and because even if she'd been entirely free to speak, she wouldn't know what to say, how to put it into words. Some fraction of it must have shown on her face.

Uncle Matthew held up his hand. "I know you can't give me details. But I had two things for you, one better not written down. Three. Come sit for a minute?" He gestured at a bench on a quieter side street. Well-lit, she was certainly safe with him. And honestly, quite safe in general in Trellech, especially this close to the Guard Hall.

Lynet nodded and held her tongue until they were both sitting in the glow of the streetlight. Uncle Matthew spoke carefully. "Three things. There's a room coming free in one of the Journeyman houses. Sink in your room, shared bath with two others, they're quiet and not likely to be a bother to you any more than you are with them. I gather one's only there half the time, anyway."

"The rent?"

"About what you're paying now, I think. Two meals a day, the option to have bread and cheese and such, maybe a bit of leftover roast, for a packed lunch." He named the number.

Lynet ducked her chin, remembering how insistent Reggie had been about the lunches - and how good they'd tasted. It had been good food, well-made, tasty. But it was also food she hadn't had to think about at all, beyond sharing what she did and didn't like, and that had somehow been even better.

"A little more dear, but not by much." She could handle it, probably.

"I'm still glad to look at your contract for you. Or get someone from the Bookbinders to do it. I know you didn't want to ask, when they hired you."

"I was told negotiation wasn't an option, Uncle. And you know what Guildmaster Thorpe thought of Papa." They'd had a longstanding feud, carried out in snubs and silence.

Uncle Matthew nodded. "As you wish. Second, then. I've heard a few more odd things out of your building. Large requests for some materia. Vervain, which isn't in shortage, but also a couple of things that are." He hesitated, not listing them.

That, though, was information Lynet needed. She rummaged in her pocket for the small notebook she kept, and the stub of pencil. "It'd help to know, please."

He silently reached into his own jacket and passed over a small list. "Copy that out in your own hand, would you, and give me the original back? I'll use it for a firestarter later."

She glanced at the names - the proper Latinate ones - and scribbled them down. Solomon's Seal. Vervain. Mandrake. Foxglove, though too, not that she did anything with that. Thornapple. Henbane. And then the others she'd expected. Iris. Mistletoe. And onyx, which was curious.

Lynet checked the list twice and then handed the original back. "That matches up with some of my sources. And a few things I don't know about, but I can ask someone else." She hesitated. "Thank you, uncle. It's a help."

It didn't tell her anything she didn't already know, or at least suspect, but it was good to get confirmation from someone else. Somewhere else. She had been beginning to wonder if she was losing her mind, or if she'd been told something and remembered the opposite. It was part of why, truth be told, she'd asked Reggie to come sit in the meeting today.

Only then she'd been sent off, like an assistant, and he'd been kept behind, and she had all sorts of feelings about that. A roiling anger that she didn't know what to do with, for one. Like she was only good for the physical labour, that she'd had nothing to do with pulling things together to make the journals work. Certainly other people had designed the charmwork, and she respected that.

But she'd been the one to figure out how to put it together, stable and steady, in a book. And in a way that didn't rely on each person making their own book. Lord Carillon, the bit he'd consulted, had gone on and on about the individuality of the process. Which was fine for his family traditions, and honestly, a tradition of making books was far better than what most posh families got up to. But his book wasn't particularly well made. The spine was beginning to crack, which suggested uneven use and care, and one of the signatures was visibly looser than the others, which suggested he'd sewed them too loosely.

Not that she'd said anything. Even to offer to lend her skills to mending and strengthening what she could. She knew better than to suggest something like that. It had, however, made her cautious of his other suggestions. And while the foundational ideas had been solid, she'd had to work up different ways to anchor most of the charms.

She was called back to the moment by Uncle Matthew clearing his throat. "The last thing was I got a bit more about your Hollis. Posted in Belgium, in the trenches. Invalided out about four months ago, no chance of him being sent back into combat settings, whatever the cause is.

It wasn't a long rehabilitation though, so not gas, nor a prosthetic."

Lynet nodded, slowly. "Anything else about him?"

"Things you probably know, at least in outline? He's a Schola man, his family all are. Bear House. He apprenticed in Protective magics. The person I talked to - friend of the family - expected he'd likely get scooped up for some sort of warding work here in a bit. When there's a need for someone else. Generally considered easy to get along with, but the family's known for having a bit of a temper when roused."

Lynet couldn't imagine Reggie actually angry, now she thought about it. He'd always been very careful with her, in fact, even when he got frustrated. And it wasn't as if she weren't familiar with a bit of roughness. But Reggie had avoided all of that, even when a bit of irritation would be entirely normal. Much better than she had, to be honest.

Uncle Matthew went on. "He's from a good family, fair bit of money, the sorts who work but live comfortably. I gather he was engaged, before the War, a few years ago, and it didn't - well. I heard several bits of gossip, mostly about her breaking it off. Sometimes it's that the girl has some particular reason to."

"I haven't seen anything like that." The words bubbled out of Lynet instantly. It wasn't as if Lynet hadn't seen people being awful. The way men, specifically, could be awful. Or the after-effects, bruises and worse. She'd heard the screaming arguments from a house nearby. She swallowed. He'd told her why the engagement ended, and it wasn't about that, but she didn't know how to explain it to Uncle Matthew. "He's been very considerate, all the way through. More so than I expected."

Right. Now she was defending him, like she had opinions about him, beyond the scope of his work. Which, to be fair, kept rapidly improving. He was quick to pick things up, and he understood which bits needed to be done precisely, and which were tolerant of a certain amount of artistic vision. And that was something you couldn't teach properly, she thought. And that thing he'd said about working quietly together, that was true, and she'd kept noticing how much she enjoyed it, all this week.

"I'm glad." Uncle Matthew hesitated for a moment. "I should let you get on. You've had a long day. Do let me know if you could come for supper. You could - if you'd like to invite him along, you'd be welcome."

Like she'd do that. She wouldn't even know how to ask him, what to expect. She shook her head minutely. "I'll be in touch. When I can. It's still a lot of working. And Papa's workshop." Now she'd walked right into Uncle Matthew volunteering people to help again.

To her great relief, he didn't press the point. "I know you know what I've offered. That you remember it. If you need a hand, you let us know, both me and Thea. Let me walk you up to the portal?" That, she could accept, and they talked of smaller things, a recent pamphlet and the complexities of laying the tables out sensibly, mostly.

By that point in the evening, the traffic through the portals had settled down significantly. She made it through the queue for the Southwark portal in only one cycle, barely ten minutes wait. She took a right down the street, back toward Papa's workshop and the flat above.

Lynet passed a few people in the street on their way to the pub. Or, judging from the way they were walking, migrating to a second pub. She ducked in at the Tipsy Book, and waved at Tressy, who was serving up a plate of food, to pick up her supper. Well, and at least one of her meals tomorrow, too.

Tressy held up a hand, asking her to wait, rather than just handing over her food. Lynet did, shifting from foot to foot. Her feet were a bit sore, and so were her shoulders, and there wasn't much she could do about either. She only had to wait a minute or two, while Tressy was efficiently cajoling one of the men along into a bit of food as well as his beer.

"Ed noticed someone lurking about in the afternoon, when sensible people would be working. You want he should go over with you?"

"Someone lurking? What sort of lurking?" Lynet didn't know what to make of that.

Tressy shrugged. "Lurking. You know Ed. Man of few words." He was their general man of all work, doing a spot of cleaning, a spot of cooking. A spot of pitching people who caused trouble out into the street to have their fights there.

"I'm sure it'll be fine. I'll come straight back if I'm worried."

"You see you do." Tressy patted her on the cheek. "Two pies in there, and a bit of bread and cheese. You come by sometime tomorrow. We'll give you some stew or somewhat. Not eels, we have the leftovers from a nice roast."

"I will." Lynet suddenly wanted nothing more than to go home and put her feet up. She ducked out of the pub just as another knot of people were coming in, calling out for celebratory drinks for some reason. She went across the street, unlocking the door from the stairs to the second-floor workshop. The landlord had rented out the shop below, quick as could be.

She opened the door on chaos. Not an obvious sort of

chaos, with everything pulled out of place. But Lynet could instantly see the disorder, the way things had been moved and put back carelessly. The stack of books there, to the left, had had a red kid leather binding on top, and now it was blue cloth. The three books on the side table had all been turned around, resting precariously on the edge where they might fall and get bent corners or worse. The books on the shelf, to the right, were upside down.

Lynet froze, first of all. She ought to go back to Tressy, no matter how busy the pub was. She ought to see about the Guard. He'd been in the portal courtyard when she came through, he wouldn't have gone far. But all of that would mean admitting it was real. And they might not believe her. It didn't look like anything had been taken. She'd taken the valuables to the bank, long since, and she had her current wages and coin on her.

She shivered, suddenly and inexplicably cold. Then, slowly, tenuously, as if every movement might collapse the whole room on top of her, she slid to the ground, and pulled out her journal. Reggie had a journal now. He knew protective magical... things. He didn't think she was making everything else up. Maybe he'd know what to do.

The pen nib scratched, several times, and there was a blob of ink at the end of the line she couldn't manage to blot in time. But then there was the note, in plain ink. Before she could reconsider, she pressed her thumb to the paper, willing it to appear somewhere else, miles and worlds away.

CHAPTER 20

Reggie felt restless. He'd gone out for drinks at the Bear's Cave, and it had been a perfectly reasonable night. He'd spoken to a few people he'd known at school, a couple of men and a larger knot of women. No one had pressed him on why he wasn't at the front, not after his brief explanation that he'd been invalided out. No one had pried into his research and development work.

Mostly, they'd chatted on about what was up with people they knew in common. Reggie had asked a question or two, and he'd stood for two rounds out of the six, which was also fine. It wasn't like he was spending the coin he had in other places. Eventually, though, the group had split up. Half of them had early duty on the Saturday, with the Guard or other projects, and the rest were going on to drink somewhere a bit louder.

Reggie had come back to his rooms. He'd settled down to read, but when it came down to it, he couldn't focus.

Then his satchel made a noise, not so loud it actually startled him. It was quiet enough, in fact, he had to peer around, wondering if a bird had got in the fireplace or something of the kind. The noise sounded like a chirp, but it kept repeating, seven times, and then it stopped. By the time it went quiet, though, he'd realised it was coming from his bag. And then, that it must be the journal.

He knew it could only be Lynet or Ellis writing him. They were the only two who even knew he had one. Or at least, Ellis knew he'd been making one, and how long that would take. Reggie fumbled with the book, almost dropping it, then spreading it open on the table. There, under the message Lynet had sent to him to test it worked, so he could see for himself how the charms made the words appear, were a few sentences with a visible ink blot.

She hadn't said much. "Someone broke into the workroom." Just that, and an address in London, a note that it was closest to the Southwark portal, and a brief sketched map that suggested the proper route. No actual request for his presence, but everything else sounded like she wanted him there.

Reggie rummaged for a pen, checked his watch, and managed a brief reply. "Coming. Currently 8:05. Should be there in 20-30, depending on the portal. Stay put or go somewhere it's safer if you need to." Then he wheeled around, almost catching himself wrong when his foot didn't react like it should, like it always had before the War. He caught himself on the chair back, jarring his hand, then ignored it as he rummaged for his working stones and a case of materia that might be helpful. His cloak. The journal, of course. He felt like he was missing something, but that would do.

Twenty-five minutes later, he was walking down the last street on the map. There was a bit of chaos from the pub on the right. Then he saw the dark shop and the staircase beside it, going up the side of the building. He made his way up carefully, calling a charm light as he got into the shadows, to find Lynet sitting on the top step, shivering. She peered up at him, and he couldn't make sense of her expression. To be honest, he suspected she couldn't either. She looked completely overwhelmed, for one thing, as well as cold.

"Hey, it's— thank you for writing." He wanted to ask what he could do to help, but he could see that she wasn't in any fit state to answer that. She'd gone shocky, the way people had at the front, when all the decisions were too many. Hopefully, they weren't as awful as that. "Can you tell me what happened?"

"Came home. Late. Quarter to eight. Stopped at the pub." She gestured vaguely across the street. "Got supper. Came up and - someone had moved things. Nothing big, but."

"All right. First thing is to figure out if someone's still there. Is there a Guard somewhere near?"

"Not close. Not close enough if I yelled."

Reggie sucked in a breath. "All right. Is it all right if I suggest some things to try?"

She hesitated for just a moment, then nodded twice. It was a little jerky motion, not like her usual efficiency.

"First step, see if there's anyone still here. That's why you're out here, yes? You weren't sure?" He got another of those jerky redundant nods. "If there's no one there - and I should be able to figure that out in a couple of minutes - we get you warmed up. Tea and soup and— whatever your supper was meant to be?"

She nodded again. "Meat pies. Bottle of beer. Bread for the morning."

"That should do. Once we've done that, and got you sorted better, then we can, we can figure out what we've learned." Reggie swallowed. "I don't want to overstep."

Lynet went very still for a moment, then she looked away, over his shoulder, out into the dark. "What do you mean, overstep?" There was an awful echo in her voice, something distant and harsh, like she'd pulled a cloak of thorns around her.

"Do something that would make you uncomfortable. But I want to help." He kept his voice as even as he could. "Thank you for asking me." He'd said that already, fool that he was. Coming over all over-eager wouldn't help. She wouldn't trust it, it would worry her. She'd never asked for help with anything more complicated than carrying that needed more than two hands, not directly. Just assigned him tasks. "What I'd—" He swallowed hard. "To figure out what's happened, magically, I need to go in. By myself, to start."

She curled her arms around her knees. "Can't stop you."

It wasn't good enough. Reggie closed his eyes for a long moment, trying to remember all the advice he'd got when it came to taking care of his men. "Tell me about the space, a bit? I'll touch as little as I can."

Something in that made her let out a sigh. "My - my father's workshop to the left. Benches and such. A sitting space. Flat above, the stairs are in the back right. Pull cord for the charm lights by the door to each room. Upstairs is a sitting room, two bedrooms, kitchen. Do you - do you have to see it all?"

"Maybe. It depends what the charms tell me about if

anyone went upstairs. When's the last time someone should have, when you would have?"

"Monday morning. I sleep in Trellech, mostly."

He wondered about that, why, but he certainly wasn't going to ask. "All right. The charm I know gives the past forty-eight hours, fairly reliably. Any unusually strong magic I ought to know about? I don't know, warded safes, or blood locks or tools in the workroom?"

"There's a letterpress to the left. It's - it's imbued, I guess, is the term? You can't unenchant it, but it's like cast-iron pots. It picks up seasoning."

That was a line of magical theory he would very much like to learn more about. "Most of what I expect to be doing is diagnostic. Seeing what magic was cast, maybe tracking someone through the space. How far in did you go? Did you look around? It's fine if you did, just want to be clear what was you."

"Just a few steps. There wasn't anything obviously wrong, but things had been put back differently than I'd left them. Subtle things, the order of books." Lynet was settling a bit now he'd asked her more concrete questions.

"Do you have any idea when? Or - just sometime this week?" This was more delicate, because she'd been gone.

"Tressy said Ed - he does their heavy work, the Thirsty Book." She gestured at the pub across the street. "He saw someone this afternoon. I said I'd be fine." She shivered again.

"Do you want to go back over there to wait? It'd be warmer?" Reggie was not at all sure how to handle that part.

"No." The single word came out, as sharp as a shot. Well, right. No pub for her.

"All right." Reggie took a long breath, convincing his

heart to stop racing. "Take my cloak then, if you're sitting out here." He took it off as he spoke, and she didn't argue when he moved to drape it over her shoulders. It was properly dense wool, and the charms woven into it should help warm her as much as the fabric itself. "May I go have a look? I'll be as quick as I can, but I'm going to be thorough, it will take me a few minutes at least."

She just nodded, curling a little tighter around her legs and looking out across the street into the dark. Reggie squared his shoulders and prepared to go into the unknown. He eased the door open as gently as he could, and then looked around. He could cast one of the charms he had in mind without any tools. For the other two, he'd want a clear space where he could spread things out, a counter or table or something like that. He closed the door, making sure it didn't fully lock in case Lynet wanted to come inside, then looked around.

It was a large room, taking up the entire floor, he suspected, or nearly so. There was a wall full of bookshelves, but not books laid out for reading. Instead, it was some sort of other system. There were neat little labels under each. Similar sizes or colours in some of the sections, others that held a single book, or only two. There was a side table, a pair of comfortable and well-worn leather chairs. And then to the left was much more of a workshop. The letterpress, it had to be. He'd seen pictures of them, and it was in pride of place in the centre, ringed by workbenches and countertops.

If this was what Lynet was used to as a workspace, it explained a lot about how she'd laid out their shared workroom. No, more than that. It explained how she moved around the space so easily and efficiently. If you had the letterpress in the place where they had extra work benches, you'd move around the edge just the same way. You'd step from station to station, with all the supplies for that step right at hand.

He could ask her about that later. The first step was to see if anyone was here. If there was any immediate threat. And that would, he was almost certain, mean searching the entire space to make sure no one was hiding. He cast the first charm, Ptolemy's Third Schema, the one that showed him where people had been.

He saw a figure - male, almost certainly - move in, then begin to deliberately search the space. He opened the books, as if looking for a piece of paper that might be slipped into one of them, as well as the desk in the far corner of the workspace. The drawers and cupboards, though he didn't actually rifle through the stacks of paper. Nothing that was waiting to be used, just anything that might have notes.

Reggie held his breath, watching the figure. It wasn't a clear image. The charm he was using was like looking through clouded glass. He had a sense of the shape and height, but it wasn't acute enough to see someone's features, or even be entirely sure of the hair colour. Darker rather than lighter, but probably more in the mousy brown indistinguishable range. The man carried no light with him. There must have been enough from the afternoon sun, which meant he could use that line of charms to investigate.

Then the figure turned to go search a small room down at the end, by the stairs, and Reggie followed cautiously. A storeroom of some kind, but the figure didn't linger beyond poking at a couple of specific boxes. Then he turned and went upstairs. Reggie would have to follow.

The upstairs was, at least, simpler. The man made a

cursory search of the sitting room, the kitchen, the bathing room. Then he went into both bedrooms. Reggie trailed along, standing in the doorway to watch. The figure pulled drawers open, peered, but didn't do as much rifling through as any proper search would suggest. The smaller room first, and Reggie was sure it was Lynet's. Even before the figure opened the wardrobe, and he saw a glimpse of simple frocks, in shades of heathery blues and greens.

Those were the sort of colours that came out of plant dyes, rather than the newer alchemical and chemical ones. He remembered Professor Trembley talking about that at one point. And that the newer dye methods sometimes had unexpected interactions with other materia, especially if you were working closely with other dyed items.

Reggie held his breath, stepping back as the shadow figure stepped into the larger bedroom. Everything was perfectly cleaned and tidied, but it felt very much as if it were full of loss. Or maybe it was that it felt hollow some-how. The figure rummaged under the pillow, then under the mattress, and it felt like sacrilege to Reggie. Then the figure retreated, searching the sitting room, riffling through anywhere that might have papers again, before disap-pearing down the stairs and then out the door.

Reggie retreated back upstairs, first casting a charm that would help him identify a stray hair, or anything else that might help later, for identification or tracking. He got lucky, with a soft glow from a hair, a leaf left from a shoe, and what looked like a cuff link. Reggie picked them up carefully, tucking them into a precisely folded silk handker-chief from his kit.

He took a long breath, considering, then went to tidy that larger bedroom. He smoothed the sheets out again, gently nudged the pillow so it was as plump and inviting as it had been before. There was a little fold of a blanket that had got pushed in under the mattress, and he pulled that even. And the drawer, there, stuck a little open. Then he went and did the same in Lynet's room, trying not to look at anything there, just tend it as best he could.

Then he turned to go back downstairs and let her in.

CHAPTER 21

L ynet jumped when the door opened. "I have more I want to check, but you can be here for it. Come in, where it's warmer?"

He was silhouetted against the light of the room behind him. She couldn't see his face. She thought he sounded gruff, even upset, and she wasn't sure what to do. Then he held out a hand and she could see it in the light that spilled past him. "Please. Come in?"

Something about the gesture caught at her again, and she found herself standing up and moving forward, into that light, because he was there and she knew it would be the right thing.

Once she was inside, he closed the door behind her. "Sit here, wherever you'd prefer? Can I put on tea? I saw the kettle on the counter."

Lynet nodded, hesitantly. "The food. I can't eat, but." She held out the bundle of newsprint and string holding everything together.

161

"Should I take them up to your kitchen?" He'd been upstairs, then. A moment later, he caught that. "There was someone here. He was looking for something, searching for it. I had to follow upstairs to see what he did. I don't think he found what he was looking for, but I want to do some more checking. There's no need for you to sit out in the cold for that, though. Kitchen?"

She nodded once. "Kitchen. There's nothing in the cold box." She'd finished out the last bit of the milk on Monday and left the bottle with Tressy for the milkman. Reggie nodded, turning away. She heard the distinct sounds of the kettle going on, then his footsteps receding to the stairs and going up. She shivered again, pulling the cloak around her, for all it mostly wasn't a physical cold she felt.

He was gone slightly longer than it should have taken to put something in the cold box. When he came back down, he sat in the chair facing her, leaning forward. "I'd like to check to make certain he didn't leave anything. I don't believe he did. I can check magically, but I might need your help to figure out what should be here, what's ordinary. Some of the books you make, they have magic in them, right? Not just the journals?"

"Papa did more with it." Lynet swallowed. "He—"

"Ellis told me." Reggie's voice was very gentle now. "He wanted to make sure I knew."

It wasn't like she'd told him much of anything, except about the journals and their work. Only then, she'd asked him for help, and he'd come. Nearly right away, even. "Oh." Lynet swallowed once. "Did I take you, I mean, away from something?"

"I'd just got back to my rooms when you wrote. I had supper at the Bear's Cave. None of the lordly lot from work, decent people doing their bit."

Something in the tone confused her, and she set it aside to deal with later. "I've been sorting out Papa's projects. Which still need finishing, which he was intending to sell. I thought I knew more of it than I did, it turns out." She gestured at the shelves. "There are a lot more in the storeroom and in the cabinets."

Reggie glanced to the side at the shelves. "Is that what you've been doing when we're not working? But not sleeping here?"

"During the week, I've got a room in the Guard barracks. Safe, I can eat in their hall. They name their barracks for virtues, and I'm in *Fortitudo*. Perseverance in the face of difficulty."

Reggie half-snorted. "Also courage. Which you have quite a lot of." He might have said something more, but the kettle sang at that point, and Lynet wasn't sure if she was pleased or infuriated by the interruption. He went back to the kettle, bringing back the mug that had been left out to dry, her favourite, and a smaller mug for himself. "Drink that. You want the warm. And tea's good for many things."

Lynet nodded, drinking it. He wasn't wrong. She felt better once she'd had a quarter of it, and cupping her hands around it felt good too. "Does it help you?" She wasn't entirely sure what she was asking now.

He nodded. "It does. It's reassuring. Steady. A thing that didn't change." He glanced down at the floor, near his feet.

"Can I—" Somehow, it popped into her head, as a thing she needed to know now. And she didn't have her defences up, she couldn't manage it, couldn't keep the wrong questions behind her teeth and away from her tongue. "How did you get hurt?"

There was a long silence, neither of them moving, just the ticking of the clock on the shelf. Then he swallowed.

"It's embarrassing, honestly." He paused for a sip of his tea, as if that would make it easier to answer. "Trench foot. Too long in the trenches with wet socks and wet boots. A bad case of it, usually they heal you up and send you back out."

"What - why was…" She wasn't sure what she was asking. Why his was worse. Why he hadn't caught it sooner. What it meant.

He shrugged, a little uneven twitch of a movement. "I lost three toes, and the side of my right foot doesn't - it aches, sometimes. Not badly, but it affects my gait." Lynet suddenly expected that 'not badly' was something of an understatement. He usually stood while working, rather than finding a stool, and she wondered how deliberate that was.

"Thank you for telling me." She glanced over at the stairs. "Someone went upstairs?"

"And then back out again. There's no one lurking in the closets or that storeroom or anything. But I would like to check." He seemed relieved to be back on somewhat safer ground, conversationally speaking. "Do you have somewhere else you can stay tonight? Just in case?"

She shook her head. "Not without going back to Trellech." Which she could do, she supposed, though there'd be all the evening traffic now. People who still managed to go to social outings, no matter about the War. "If it's - you could stay? Would you stay?" She wasn't sure if he thought she wouldn't be safe, or whether he didn't think she should be alone. "The sofa in the sitting room makes a decent bed. It folds out. Or Papa slept on the one down here, sometimes." Mostly when he was drunk enough not to manage the stairs.

Reggie hesitated. "Are you…" He stopped and tried again. "Would it be a help? Not an intrusion?"

"A help." She didn't want to go anywhere else. She didn't want someone to drive her out of her home, no matter how rarely she was here. And having him here almost felt all right. Not like when Uncle Matthew had offered help. Reggie wasn't intrusive.

"Right. I'll stay." He considered. "Let me do the checks I was planning to do. You sit right here, drink tea, and I'll see what questions I have." The next two hours were full of him going back and forth, casting a charm, then another, testing things, checking with her. Halfway through, he asked her to move upstairs, to the sitting room up there. She didn't like the idea of him being in the bedrooms, but she liked the idea of something lurking there even less.

"Did he - do you know, did he do anything in the bedrooms?" She finally got up the courage to ask when Reggie came out again.

"He searched. I - um. I tidied a little. Put things back straight in both rooms. He didn't turn all your things out. He must have been searching magically, as well, now I think about it. He didn't have to go through every drawer, just use a charm. You can't see whether it's caught anything, if the drawer or cupboard is closed."

Lynet considered that. She'd made another cup of tea, this time with the upstairs kettle, and she gestured at the one she'd made for him. "Oh." Then she looked up and realised he was looking nervous about something. "Is there a problem?"

"I wasn't sure what you'd think about me tidying. Another invasion." He glanced away, then grimaced. "You should eat something."

It made her remember his comments about food. He'd had supper, he'd said that, but he'd just done an awful lot of magic. "You too. I have two meat pies, we can get something for tomorrow - well. Later." Then she went still. She'd said 'we' like it was an entirely natural way to say something.

Reggie, though, looked pleased. "Good, I don't have to talk you into eating. And I am - that was a lot of work. So I will not turn you down. The beer, too?"

"There's two, you should have one. And then - is it safe?"

Reggie nodded. "Best I can tell, he - I'm fairly sure it was a he - was looking for something specific. Something magical, because he was using charms for it. I was wondering if he was going to try to leave some sort of eavesdropping charm, or something to alert him when you came home, but I can't find anything." He pushed himself upright, going to rummage in the kitchen for the food from the cold box and plates. She thought about explaining where things were, but he was doing a fine job. Probably he'd looked in the drawers when he was checking everything out.

"So you didn't find anything?"

Reggie turned around, a tray in his hands, grinning. "I didn't say that. I've got a hair, a leaf from a shoe, and I think it's the top of a cufflink, maybe a tiepin. They're wrapped up safe. The Guard can do more with them than I can, but you'll have to make a report."

She grimaced. "Here?"

"You could do it in Trellech. You're staying in their barracks. You must have met a couple of them, right? The way to play it is to find someone you know who's on duty tomorrow, and ask what you should do. That you're concerned he was looking for something. In the meantime, I'll go do some warding and protections once I've eaten, and then we can get some rest. I can sleep downstairs if you'd rather."

"An alarm on the door and windows is probably enough? Maybe? I ..." She'd rather know he was closer. That was the thing.

He lit up. "I can do that." Reggie spread his hands. "I hadn't exactly wanted to keep my skills up this way, but I have the skill, and I'm glad to be whatever help you'd like. Do, um. Tell me if it's too much? The thing about protective magics is that they can get a little pushy. All-encompassing. A tad thinking everyone is out to get you?"

"It is not exactly wrong in this case? Or if not everyone, certainly more than one someone?" Lynet accepted her plate and bottle, as well as a fork, and began digging through the pastry shell. Once she managed to take a bite, the hunger washed over her and she sighed.

"There you go. Food's good for the soul. All right. You tell me if something's more than you're comfortable with, and I'll keep asking. What I intend to do for the night is something rather blunt. It'll keep everyone out. It won't do long-term, it takes a lot to keep it up, and it - well. You'd not get your post. People would forget where you were, if I do it properly."

"That seems a rather awkward side effect." She felt a lot better, actually, to be able to tease him a little.

He grinned, pleased at it, as he devoured a bit of his own pie. "I can do something more subtle in the morning. Or after we've talked to the Guard, maybe. There are a couple of variations they really would rather people got permission for first."

"Permission?"

"Think of it a bit like a flytrap. Someone gets too close who's not allowed, they get stuck in the ward. Quite widely used at Schola, to keep students out of places they shouldn't be, but of course you want someone to know they need to fish a miscreant out."

"Which the Guard would want to know." She wrinkled her nose. "The local doesn't think much of me, I'm pretty sure."

"We can see how to work that. Right. I'd like to wash up, if I can. Not a bath or anything, I don't know how you're set for that, but ..."

"I can find a washcloth and a towel. I—" Lynet hesitated. "I'm sorry to put you out."

"I have slept in far worse places for much less important reasons. It's a perfectly fine sofa. I'm sure I'll be quite comfortable."

And, of course, she couldn't argue with that. Whatever the sitting room was, whatever threat was possibly lurking outside, it wasn't a trench facing imminent bombardment. That must have changed his standards for discomfort rather a lot.

CHAPTER 22

TUESDAY, JUNE 12TH

Reggie didn't know what to do with himself. Sunday morning he had woken up, and he and Lynet had seen to the necessary reports to the Guard. He had laid out additional warding.

Lynet had turned to him, when he was done, entirely wrapped up in herself now. Not quite thorns, but intricate lattice work that was part armour, part external skeleton holding up a crumbling wall. "Thank you for coming last night. I need - I need some time now. See you tomorrow."

It wasn't a question, and it wasn't an order. It was a statement of fact. But it was a rather isolating one.

Reggie, of course, had nodded and murmured his good-byes, like a gentleman. Grandmama would have been pleased at that part, even if the rest of this situation was, he expected, rather outside her experience. Though now he came to think of it, she'd been reputed to have a wilder youth than one might think, looking at her now. It had left Reggie alone with his thoughts.

What bothered him was why someone would go to the trouble of searching Lynet's home. It could, arguably, have been someone looking for something her father had done. But if that were the case, he'd have expected more signs of the search in among the books and the workshop. It could possibly have been meant to upset her, and distract her from her work. Though he wasn't sure who'd have wanted it enough. Or why they hadn't focused on the workshop proper. None of it had answers, and that was deeply annoying. It was damnably personal, and he thought she was not the sort of person who drew that sort of attention.

Monday, Lynet had been entirely agreeable getting on with the necessary work. She'd spent most of her time working out alternate calculations for the materia they couldn't get, getting him to check the maths and figures. They were flawless. She knew the theory and what was needed well, but they couldn't make something out of nothing.

"Do you know anyone who could help?" Reggie had just put another cup of tea down. "Anyone who might know what's going on?"

"That's the thing, isn't it? We don't." She blew a wisp of hair out of her face, and rubbed her hands on her smock again, as if something were making her hands clammy. "Maybe. I knew someone at school who's working in the Materia office. Maybe she can get free for a cuppa. I want to know - I guess I want to know if it's us, this workroom. Or us, this building." In so far as that included them in any meaningful way. "Or if it's a general thing."

"That would be a help." Reggie nodded. "I'll go round a club or two, see if I can find anyone who might know. I can't think of anyone specific, but sometimes going fishing turns up something useful." He shrugged. "Sometimes an old shoe."

"Do you fish?" Lynet looked up at him, blinking a little.

"I went in for country sports. Before." He turned away, more to hide his face than because he really needed to tidy up the tea things just then. "Rambling. Riding. Hunting, shooting, fishing. For the food we ate, mind, I never saw the point in killing solely for sport. Even less so now."

"Go fish, then. Maybe you'll have some luck." Reggie wasn't at all sure what to make of that note in her voice, something almost wistful, but when he turned back, her face was composed and still. "See if Ellis needs a hand this afternoon?"

"Sure." Reggie tidied up. Ellis did need a hand. But it was all shredding cloth to more or less even sizes and then breaking it down in the vat. That didn't allow for much talking. It suited Reggie just fine.

Bourne's was the usual crowd, more or less. Reggie ordered a brandy, and positioned himself in the conversation room, in a chair by one of the windows a third of the way down the room. He could see people come in if he turned over his shoulder, and the chair next to him was invitingly left open. Then he settled in to wait. A lot of fishing was in the waiting. People had opinions about the bait or the lure or the hook or the timing, but there was nothing quite like good old-fashioned, stubborn patience.

Besides, where else would he be? The library had an evening program on. He didn't want to sit in his flat. Lynet certainly didn't want more of his company, and sitting here might just do something useful. Mind, by the time the clock chimed half-seven, he was beginning to give it up as a bad idea.

Then, however, a few people came down, in a little

knot, from one of the rooms upstairs. One of them caught sight of him and waved the others on. "I'll catch you up. Tell Delphie I'm coming."

He stepped forward again, out of the shadow that had obscured his face, and Reggie realised it was Temple Carillon. Lord Carillon. Coming right for him. Well. That was an interesting sort of fish. Was the brandy the lure, then, or was it the way Reggie was sitting, appearing to be entirely at home with himself? Rather than, of course, the reality that it made his foot ache slightly less. And if he had to stand up, it would be obvious his other foot had gone to sleep.

"Hollis, isn't it?" Carillon nodded.

"Lord Carillon. We've not met, but I've seen you in passing."

"Just the man I wanted to see. Thank you for squiring Margot around the other week. She thought you were delightful. And not one to roll over for her charms, either." Clearly, that amused him, more than offended him. Curious, actually.

Reggie took the opportunity to get a good, solid look at a man who did roll over for her charms. He looked like what he might expect of a lord of middle age. He was well built, with the sort of shoulders regularly seen in illustrations of brave soldiers at the front. Blond hair, worn on the long side for a man, no beard or moustache, going a little thin on top, but impeccably maintained. He wore a suit of wool silk, and Reggie was sure it had several charms sewn in to make it drape perfectly, to go with the impeccable tailoring. Reggie didn't match up to most of that, though he was dressed properly for an evening at Bourne's.

Reggie just nodded. "She isn't the sort to do well eating

alone, clearly." He made himself offer a smile. "And she's charming, though I'm not remotely in her league."

"Oh, is that what you think?" Temple snorted. "Look, that's just the thing. Clearly you need some people, a circle to spend time with. I gathered you don't want to shift your work, and I suppose that's understandable." There was a little hint there that whatever Master Brand had shared, it had included that Reggie wasn't up for the far more rowdy sorts downstairs.

"But do come out, we're having a Friday to Sunday - have to be back at work on Monday, of course - next week. Bring your case in Friday morning, my man will collect them before lunch, and everything will be unpacked and ready when we turn up at quarter past five. Do say you'll come. All sorts of delightful girls, you know. A few from work, a few from other places."

Reggie hesitated. For one thing, he wasn't at all sure he could manage it, that he remembered how to keep up the right show for that long at a time. It had been years, lifetimes, since he'd been at a house party.

"It's not hunting season, old chap. No guns, if that's what you're worried about. We might take the hawks out, depends on the weather. More likely to be a spot of bohort, a pleasure ride down near the lake and back. Gorgeous countryside, you know we're out in Cumbria, yes? Grand view down to Lake Windemere." Lord Carillon waved a hand. "And of course, excellent food. Our cook's grand, and the old place is quite comfortable. Plenty of room. All the usual conveniences."

He sounded like he was trying to sell Reggie on the place. Though, honestly, some of the older houses had their challenges. Sometimes it was draughts, sometimes swallows or even bats in the chimneys, or leaks from the roof or interesting new species of mould. Interesting for the protective magic specialist in him, but not comfortable.

Reggie nodded once. "May I let you know in a day or so? My sister said something about wanting me to come stay and I can't remember if she had a specific day in mind for some reason. You know how it is, some particular reason to have me come down."

"You're of the Buckinghamshire Hollises, yes? My wife knows your people, I believe. Anyway, you really must join us. If not this time, the next. And perhaps I can find a time to consult with you. I gather your work's hit a snag?"

"More with supplies than the working model, but we're looking at some alternatives. I'd not mind a word if time allows, of course. The more heads the wiser, isn't that how it often goes?"

"Sensible man." Lord Carillon leaned forward and clapped him hard on the shoulder. Hearty was the word. Yes, it nearly rattled Reggie's teeth. "Come round and knock when you know, or leave a note if I'm not in for visitors. Either way."

Then he backed up a step. "Grand I ran into you, and really, we want to make sure you can do well for yourself, don't we?" Lord Carillon made one of those little gestures that pretended at being a nod at a salute, and had nothing of a real one in it. "Now I really must catch up and see to my wife."

"Evening, and my best wishes." Reggie was still speaking when Lord Carillon strode off. He watched him go, the easy rolling stride of a man who had everything, and had lost nothing to the War. Or not yet, anyway.

He was still watching, though he'd picked up his brandy again, when there was a soft cough to his right. "A rather fast crowd, as I understand it."

Reggie did not drop his glass, nor did he actually flinch. He turned to peer at the man over his shoulder. "Beg pardon?"

"Lord Carillon." The man gestured, more with his chin than anything else. The other man was the sort of man Reggie would have assumed a better fit for Oxford or Cambridge than anywhere else. Well turned out, but there was a sense of underlying tweed and the scent of a library. Not that Reggie objected to either.

"Do you know him, then? Reggie Hollis. Captain Hollis, I suppose, but no longer in active service."

"Hollis." The man offered his own hand. "Lapidoth Manse. Ridiculous name, my friends call me Lap."

Reggie would not walk into that, so he just nodded. "You know Lord and Lady Carillon, then?"

It got him a sharp bark of laughter. "Not very well. I know his younger brother better. I was up at Oxford with him, stayed on, assigned to the Ministry for the duration." Which suggested Intelligence work of some kind, though what sort Reggie had no idea. "They're a fast crowd." The other man considered his words visibly, but that was a second iteration and Reggie was sure it was deliberate. "The sort the War's touched more lightly."

"Someone close?" It was in his eyes. Reggie knew that look.

"My younger brother." Manse shrugged, slightly. "Quite early. Carillon's brother was in the trenches, to start." He said it conversationally, and Reggie put together that the man wasn't now, whatever he was up to.

"If you know the family, can I ask what you know about their training? Magically speaking?"

"Ah, I knew you looked a likely sort. Nothing you couldn't track down, if you had a rummage, but I'll spare you the trouble. Lord Carillon inherited last year. You know that part, yes? He trained up in Incantation and Materia, but if you ask me, not entirely disciplined about either. No mastery, but he didn't expect to go into either field."

"And his brother?" Reggie was beginning to think it might be informative, at least by contrast.

"Geoffrey?" There was a moment of consideration, as if he was deciding what to say - and what not to. "Mastery in Ritual. A steady sort, mostly. He read History, and he's got quite a fondness for the proper traditions. Early books." Manse waved a hand at where Temple had gone. "The elder's the sort to go charging off on the hunt, for the thrill of it. Geoffrey's the sort to train up horse and hound and hawk, and it's the harmony coming together that he's after."

That was an exceedingly telling comment, but Reggie nodded. "Would you advise I accept the invitation, then?"

Manse chuckled. "Oh, you're sharper than you look, aren't you? You might learn a lot. Keep your wits about you if you do." He then rummaged in his jacket, pulling out a card. "Keep that somewhere safe. You might want to find me for a chat later."

"Later, sir?" The man wasn't more than a year or two older than Reggie, but he instinctively straightened up a bit. There was a weight here, a sense of gravity and rank that he recognised and wanted to respect.

"You'll know when." With that, Manse nodded once and strolled off, leaving Reggie peering at an entirely uninformative card, with an address in London.

CHAPTER 23

Lynet was trying and failing to lose herself in her work when she heard Reggie on the stairs. She'd woken at half-five and hadn't been able to get back to sleep. By seven, she'd been in the workroom, because she couldn't think where else to be.

He was also early, nearly half an hour, which was not like him. He was far more often precisely five minutes early, or he'd be clear he might be late. Especially after that time he'd come back from lunch much later than expected, and apologetic, like he'd done something wrong. Rude, but wrong in other ways, too.

And then he'd come out on Friday, without hesitation, and he'd stayed. She should have offered him Papa's bed, but she hadn't been able to. The smell would change, and she could still smell Papa's aftershave, the potion he'd preferred, on the sheets, and the way leather oil for the books permeated everything in the flat.

And yet, knowing he was down there on the sofa, that had been a comfort, and in a way she wasn't sure what to do with. She'd wanted to come down, and watch him, but that had seemed quite rude. Besides, Reggie would have woken, likely, his instincts were like that.

Lynet hadn't even been able to tell him any of that. She'd thought about trying, and it had all got crumpled up inside her head in the morning. The evening before, for all the terror and the cold, had somehow been simpler and less tangled. And Monday and Tuesday, she'd just felt awkward.

Now, though, she pivoted on the stool she was sitting on, as he let himself in. The expression on his face was odd, like he was worrying over something. She'd begun to be able to tell. The moments of discomfort he had looked different, or at least the ones that showed did. Worrying and perhaps a bit embarrassed. "May I check no one's over-hearing?"

Lynet blinked, but nodded. "Yes?" Not could he, but did he have permission. "I don't generally like that sort of thing, for the record."

"Also, it's early enough. It's probably not a problem." Reggie set a small container, tied up with string, on the counter by the kettle. "That's for elevenses. Lunch boxes are in my bag."

"You - you don't have to, you know." She heard her voice catch. "I mean. I've been—"

Reggie turned around and held up one finger. "Moment." He went through three different charms in quick succession, comfortably assertive with them. "Quite private. You were saying, Lynet?"

"I was rude, Saturday. Telling you to go away."

"Were you?" He blinked at her, as if the thought hadn't

even occurred to him. "I thought you had good reason. I was glad to help, please do call on me again if I can. But you didn't expect to have me in your space."

"Most people don't understand that. Most people think it's ridiculous I'm keeping it when there's just me and I'm not even working there."

"Most people do not have a rather large and heavy letterpress in the middle of the workshop, nor all the type that goes with it. It's not a thing you could just pack up in a few days. Or any of the rest of it."

Lynet half turned away, shaking her head. "That's what I do on Saturday and Sunday. Go through things." She almost wanted to ask him to come, to at least keep her company, but she couldn't do that.

When she looked back, there was an expression on his face she couldn't make sense of at all. She'd have thought humour, somehow, the way his lips were pressed together to keep from laughing, but that wasn't quite right either. "I'd be glad to lend a hand sometime. My hands, still good, even if my feet are a bit shaky, remember?" Then he added, quickly. "Not this week, though. That's the thing I wanted to talk to you about. Sit, maybe, if you would?"

She perched on the workbench again, feeling her feet swing. That seemed a somewhat ominous way to begin. When she was settled, he went on.

"Lord Carillon invited me to a Friday to Sunday. Leave from here, Friday afternoon, there through Sunday afternoon, I presume. As he said, we do need to be at work on the Monday."

"When?" She lifted her hand. When it was clear the question was confusing. "I mean, when did you talk to him?"

"At Bourne's last night. He seemed quite eager about it." Lynet was managing to watch him closely again, and she thought that there was something else too. "That there were people I might want to meet. He implied, rather strongly, that if I were obliging, he might lend a hand with our current problems. I don't know that we want that, but I do think making nice might be worth doing."

"What does it involve for you?" It wasn't like Lynet could tell him not to go. Even if something about this made her feel uncomfortable, deep down. The sort of feeling she tried not to think about, that lump of fear and worry and nameless dread.

"A lot of extravagant food. I suspect a lot of drink, possibly some reckless sport. No shooting, it's out of season except for rabbits and hares. He made sure to be clear about that. Possibly some falconry. I might get in a ramble or something of the kind. A lot of people who'll want things I don't care about, I'm sure, but I know how to make the right noises and which fork to use."

"Which fork." Lynet grimaced. "Oh."

Reggie looked up at her, half-frowning now. "Would you rather I didn't go?"

"It's your time to do what you want with." That was true, so why did it come out like ashes and awfulness?

Reggie tilted his head. "I think I might have to decorously handle some propositions. House parties are notorious for bed-hopping, and even if there's a war on, I get the impression that's not going to stop some of this lot." He glanced away, sharply, as if he couldn't let her see something.

"How - um." She had no idea how to ask this. Not something covered in the Alethorpe curriculum, when it came to dealing with Schola men. Her housemistress had certainly had opinions on the matter of discouraging men in a professional setting from taking liberties. That was not nearly as much help here as it should be. "If there weren't a War, um."

He turned back, and now he was half smiling. "I would much rather be with you, sorting through books, lending a hand, than in bed with anyone likely to be at that party. I could - might I invite myself to stop by on Sunday, when I get back to Trellech? Or come straight through with my case?"

Lynet looked down at the floor, past her dangling feet. The offer did make her feel better. "I'd, I'd like that. I could get something in for tea."

"You needn't, if it's a bother. But I'd like that too. It'd make it easier to get through the party, knowing I'd be able to sort through it with you right after." He gestured. "I'm sure they're not horrid people. Or at least, that there's the same range of horrid and not horrid in them that there is in most people? But I don't fit there anymore. And I'm not going to again, not the way they think I do."

She snuck a glance at him before looking back at the ground. "Can I ask why?"

"I left a lot of things that mattered before in Belgium. With my toes and all. The things that used to shame me, that used to be a lever to get me to do things a certain way, most of them don't work the same way." He spread his hands out and she caught a bit of the gesture. "But I think I should go."

"Why?" That was what she wanted to get at. She wanted to know why there was this lump in her stomach at the idea of him somewhere beautiful. Probably with a gorgeous library. Weren't country houses supposed to have that sort of thing? And land and hills and not smog and mucky streets and wondering about making the rent or who was having a screaming fight next door down. If people fought in such places, she rather thought it wasn't like that.

"The chaps downstairs, they're very eager to make me one of them. I don't want that. I want to keep helping you. You're doing something complex, important. I'm not sure about implementation yet, but the idea of it? We've been trying to send better messages between fighting forces since before Marathon. There's a long line of people, down to Barbier and all that, and people now. It could save lives. Or - I was thinking last night about an emergency. What it would be like if you could get the Guard out somewhere on short notice, to a small village when they needed more hands. Or an outbreak of disease."

"I - I'd only thought of some of that." It was true enough. All her thoughts, what she had other than thinking about Papa, had been about making them work. Not what to do with them after. Only then, she'd done just that sort of thing on Friday, used it to get help she'd have had a hard time summoning any other way. And it had felt almost entirely natural. "Friday, I wrote to you, and it felt - ordinary. Like leaving a note in someone's letterbox."

"Just like that." Reggie shrugged once. "I think going to the party is a good idea because we might figure out what's going on. Why we can't get the materials we need. If there might be something we could do differently, so we got them. Maybe even if there's some reason someone searched your place. I don't know that I'll get an answer, of course. But I can manage the party, and we might learn something. Who knows what they say when they've had too much to drink."

"And if you have too much to drink?"

"I won't." His tone was absolute. "For one thing, I don't. Can't really. I don't like who I am when I've had more than a bit these days." Reggie grimaced. "Makes me stroppy, I think is how you'd likely put it? Not my best look. But I've a contact for a decent hangover potion. A few drops help clear the head. You can't use it over and over again, not good for the blood or something like that. But to get me through a party?"

Lynet tried to put all of that together. "There are things like that?"

"There are. Not inexpensive. And it's rather a waste to pay money to drink and more money not to feel it, isn't it? But when all around you are drinking and you want to keep your head." He hesitated. "Besides. I ran into someone else at Bourne's. Chap gave me his card, but I couldn't find out much about him so far. He knew Lord Carillon a bit. He didn't warn me off, but he made it clear it's a fast crowd. I'm half-wondering what would happen if I chatted with him again with a little more to talk about."

This was too rich for Lynet, on several levels. "Why?" She kept coming back to that question.

"There's something foul going on. I don't know what, I don't know where, or how big it is. But there's a thread of something. I want to track that down. I wasn't sure until someone was in your flat. Why would they bother you at home?"

It was the question Lynet had been trying not to think about, in all honesty. "What if they try again? While you're - wherever it is."

"Cumbria. For one, they do have a portal. I could come back if I had to. But your warding is excellent, if I do say so myself. If you hear anything, you give a shout in the journal and I'll come back. Did you talk to your friend at the pub?"

Lynet nodded. "Not the details, but asking if they could keep an eye out. Nothing so far."

"Well, then. We'll muddle on for now, and see if we can't figure out more of what's going on. Why things are odd. It's the oddness that bothers me. The unnecessary secrecy, as opposed to the parts that actually need to be."

CHAPTER 24

FRIDAY, JUNE 15TH

Friday evening, Reggie tried to figure out what was going on. He had, as instructed, brought a suitcase with him, leaving it downstairs to be collected before luncheon. He went down again just before five, to meet Lord Carillon and the others. They hadn't welcomed him effusively, certainly, but they'd been cordial enough. Naturally, they didn't explain all the little in-jokes or nicknames, but they used them freely, enough he could begin to pick up which went with whom.

Hawk's Breath was stunning, in fact. Lord Carillon had rather understated it. The house was large, mostly Georgian, but Reggie thought the wings were a bit later. He was no expert in architecture, but he'd picked up a fair bit during his apprenticeship. It was relevant to warding, quite often, or at least the part of it that was knowing which materials were likely used. He could almost see why Professor Trembley had suggested a shift to this sort of work.

He could see the hints of a layout of an earlier house. He'd done his research on Thursday, about the land and the family. This was not the landed estate, that was down somewhere in the New Forest, and a rather smaller house if he'd got the details right. This estate had been in the family since the Tudors, granted in the late 1480s, a few years after the Pact. It had that layout to it, and he was sure there must be some expansive gardens on the far side, nearer the lake.

As the group walked up from the portal, Reggie could feel the layerings of the wards. Established, though there was something nagging at him, like a tiny stone in a well-fitting shoe. It wasn't his place to poke at that, certainly not as a guest here on sufferance. Or at least, a guest here for whatever reason Temple Carillon found amusing.

One of the maids had shown him up to a pleasant bedroom. She'd bobbed an apology as soon as they were in the room. "Pardon, sir, that we've not so many footmen. If it's a bother I can let one of them know."

That only made sense, and Reggie had waved it off. "I don't need much of a hand, other than the ordinary house-keeping things." A fire in the morning, whatever one did for breakfast here. "I'm used to doing for myself these days." And he could take his shirts and suits back to the couple who saw to things for all the flats in his building. "Anything I should know about the house?"

He asked it off-handedly, as he turned to check how things had been unpacked. He caught another bob from the maid, then she cleared her throat. "This is the quieter wing, sir. If you wish to add any sound muffling charms, you're welcome to. Lady Delphina made that clear. Or one of the staff can see to it, sir, over supper."

That was interesting. Both that they'd placed him here, presumably deliberately, and that someone - Lady

Delphina, perhaps - had wanted to be explicit about the permission. Reggie reached out his hand, brushing his fingers against the wall, which was papered in a slightly out of fashion flocked print in a soothing blue-purple. He suddenly wondered if he'd been given a room decorated in the shades someone from Bear House might find particularly appealing.

The question was, would taking them up on the offer suggest something? There were plenty who'd consider it a weakness. He gave it a moment's further thought. "I'll see how the noise carries this evening. How do you do things for breakfast?" That line of questions was far more ordinary. Chafing dishes downstairs. She'd be glad to show him when she showed him the way down to supper. Then, at his nod, she disappeared to whatever other duties called, and Reggie settled in to change for supper.

That evening passed more or less the way he'd expected. The party itself seemed to have an ever-changing number of guests. He suspected that he couldn't keep count because they kept disappearing in varying combinations, and returning in different ones. Decidedly a fast crowd, and familiar with each other's tastes.

Lady Delphina herself stood out, dressing in the current mode but without the glitter and glamour of some of the other women in attendance. She had the sort of classic English beauty that poets opined about endlessly, almost effortless. More helpfully, she also seemed quite kind, and took care at making sure he was introduced to people properly. She included all the relevant names, and a bit about what they did with themselves or who their people were. Reggie picked up, part way through those introductions, that she was choosing the information most flattering to the person she was talking about. She had a gift for seamlessly shifting to avoid a few touchy topics Reggie had heard gossip about.

As the evening wore on, people disappeared and reappeared, and several of the women seemed to be eyeing him thoughtfully, as if considering an invitation. Reggie got himself thoroughly ensconced in a game of billiards and dodged the whole thing until most people had retired to whatever bed suited them.

He had not been opposed to a tumble with someone willing before. But, as with so many other things, he seemed to have left all that behind. He was old enough now to prefer the comfort of bed, and that meant taking one's shoes off, and that had a number of complications. Both what someone might say, and the chance that she might hit the tender scar tissue. He'd done it to himself often enough in bed, without extra feet in the mix.

The next day, there were a wide variety of opportunities for fun on offer. Reggie had gone out for a long ride, complete with a picnic luncheon, with half a dozen others. The horses were older, spared from the War by their age, but they were gallant well-trained hunters who knew their work and the local landscape. As they came back across the fields, Reggie fell into quite an ordinary and pleasant conversation with two of the others before it was time to change for the evening.

If the afternoon had been calm, the evening had a frenetic energy to it. People made bright and chirpy comments, as if their lives depended on it. As if a quip or a laugh or the perfect bon mot was a protection, warding off a coming doom. Margot Williams kept catching his eye, and not just because she was wearing the most shockingly bright coral frock. Not just the frock, either, her hair was up and drawing attention to a shimmering deeply toned aquamarine at her throat, and matching earbobs. She flitted here and there, through the party.

It was partway through the evening that Reggie found himself sitting on his own, after a round of cards. The betting had got too rich for his blood, and he'd bowed out, taking the chance to go gather up another drink to nurse. Everyone there was at least two drinks ahead of him, and he wanted to keep it that way, which meant making sure no one would insist he top up his own.

He wandered from there into the library. The lights were dim, and he almost wondered if he'd wandered into one of the quieter assignation spots. Then he heard a cough from one of the chairs near the fire. It wasn't lit, not at the height of summer. "That you, Alton?"

"Hollis. Didn't mean to be a bother."

The figure turned, peering. "Oh, Hollis. Come sit. Have a smoke?" That was Lord Carillon, but it took Reggie a moment to realise it. The man was leaning, all of the sharp intensity transformed into something languid.

Reggie came over, he couldn't not. He was trying to understand what was going on here, what was so queer about the situation. Besides, well, near everything. "Went off it, most of the time, after the trenches." He wasn't sure what made him say it, not that way.

"You mind if I do?"

"Course not. And it's your house." Something in his tone made Lord Carillon snort, and he spent a few moments lighting his own pipe.

"Hope you're having a pleasant time, old chap." There was a hesitation there, like it mattered to this man that Reggie enjoy himself. Reggie considered. It wasn't a bad party, of its sort. The food had been excellent, the amusements well-planned. The beds were comfortable, and the roof didn't leak, nor the windows. He had not been obliged to make much of small children, nor beloved but now decrepit dogs. Actually, the house was rather lacking in both, now he thought about it. He was fairly sure that was against some ancient country custom.

"Takes a bit of getting used to, honestly." Reggie spread his hands. "But you've been generous hosts, you and Lady Delphina. She was very kind about making sure I could sort out who's who. No one I knew well, but overlap at school. You know how it is. Or I know their brother or sister."

"Alton was telling me. And Margot thought you were doing well." He hesitated, as if trying to decide between two paths, both dangerous. "Do you mind speaking about the War? The trenches?"

Reggie did, and he didn't, and he wasn't at all sure which applied here. He went, in the end, with honesty. "Depends on the topic, really." He waved a hand. "Glad to give it a try?" There. That should be an amiable sort of propping the door ajar.

"My brother was there. Younger brother, you know. He's doing other things now. Probably safer." Lord Carillon looked away. "Earned a few medals." Lord Carillon was clearly proud of that, but there was that odd note again, something deeply unsettled underneath, as if the whole enterprise were built on a crumbling foundation.

It made him think back suddenly to the comment Professor Trembley had made about Professor Bett, about war accelerating everything. This had that feel to it, that something had gone from a scattered pebble to an avalanche, with almost no warning. Whatever Lord Carillon was gnawing on had weight behind it, the dangerous sort of weight. Possibly it was a weight that had come on him unexpected, leaving him on unsteady ground.

Reggie nodded at that. "You must worry about him." He wasn't sure about putting it into words, especially as he saw Lord Carillon straighten, the sort of instinctive pose men of their class took at an insult. Then the other man let out a breath.

"I do. Perfectly competent, but he's my little brother. Looks up to me no end, always has. And he's there, and I'm here." Another man might have said more, and Lord Carillon cut off sharply. "That's - well. I couldn't go over, not both of us. He's my Heir, you see."

Reggie was fairly sure he didn't see several parts of it, but he had the running theory. It strongly implied there were no little Carillons up in the nursery, and no older children where they were sure of the strength of their magic. "Indeed."

"It's why the work we're doing is so important. Coming up with something that might keep them safe." That, that was some of the echo Reggie kept hearing. A chasm of it, of needing to fill it, to be certain. All the charms and talismans of safety either of them had ever learned at Schola, or in all the places they'd learned things since. And for all that natural impulse, there was something fractured there, something not entirely hinged. It made him think of the echo in the wards, the echo was the same there, and that made him wonder what had caused it. Not that he could remotely ask about anything like that.

"I'd appreciate your thoughts next week. And perhaps you might have some ideas about the materia. Rather an interest of yours, as I understand it?"

The moment passed, and Lord Carillon waved a hand, amiably. He had been about to say something else, but then there was a voice from the doorway. "Temple?"

"Alton." Alton was greeted with a sudden warmth,

different from the tenuous thread of conversation Reggie had kept up. Reggie stood, a little wobble as he caught his shoe on the rug. "Take this chair, Alton. I should go see if there's a refill for my glass."

Twenty minutes later, he was on the sofa again, with an increasingly tipsy girl leaning on him, then taking over his lap. In a cat, it would have been adorable, but she had elbows in unfortunate places. And more to the point, he wasn't remotely interested in someone who barely knew where she was.

It did occur to him that he could use that as something of an excuse, at least in public. He got her upright, then upstairs, before calling the maid to see her and perhaps sit with her until some of the drink wore off. Drink, drugs, potions — it was possibly all three. Reggie himself fell into bed after a brief wash at the basin.

CHAPTER 25

L ynet had entirely lost track of time when she heard the knock on the door. To be honest, she hadn't been sure Reggie would come by. But he'd written, at half-six, to see if she was at home, and still wanted him to come to London.

She had. It had been a long weekend, a tiring one. While she'd made a fair bit of progress in going through the bound books, there was so much more to do. She'd found another five that needed finishing to varying degrees, and she had two whole shelves she hadn't checked against the records yet. She'd taken half an hour to sweep and tidy, and somehow that had just made her feel worse, like it was endless and would always be endless.

And now there was Reggie, who'd want to talk. And who had things to talk about. His note had suggested that, and that he'd rather talk somewhere outside of the work-room, or even the garden bench.

Lynet opened the door. "Reggie. Come in?" She had at

least managed to go across to the pub and pick up some meat pies and beer. "I have something for supper, if you want?"

He held up a small box. "Pastries. Been in stasis since Thursday, mind."

Lynet took a couple of steps back, peering at it. Specifically, what it meant that he'd thought that far ahead, for something that he surely didn't need. He'd just come from a party full of fabulous food. At least that's what the stories Lynet had heard suggested.

"Since Thursday?" Now she sounded daft. He came in, closing the door behind him, and smoothing the warding back into place. She gestured at the workbench by the teakettle, where the other food was waiting, with a couple of chipped plates and a pair of glasses.

"Well, yes. They aren't open on Sundays, of course. No reason you should go without a pastry. It's far less logistical planning than the materia involves, mind. Are you ready to eat? I can bring things over. You look done in."

She felt done in, and it wasn't solely physical. When she hesitated, he waved a hand. "I've had people waiting on me. I can bring things over. Just a minute."

His mood was confusing, too. Reggie seemed like he'd relaxed as soon as he walked in the door. Like it was easier for him being out here, easier than being in Trellech, or wherever he'd been in Cumbria. Lynet tucked a foot up under her, propping the other on a footstool, and watched him.

"I hope nothing terribly exciting happened? How are the wards holding?"

"Ed's not seen anyone around. The postman left the mail downstairs, but that's easy enough to manage. Like people just look right by the steps."

"Excellent. It might not hold someone truly determined, but that's why there are multiple wards. I'll check them before I go, if you like, just to adjust. Sometimes they need a touch of encouragement once they've settled into place. My apprentice mistress always thought it was sweeping all the way into the corners, catching the little spots where things don't quite flow until you know the space."

Lynet nodded silently, not sure what to do with her hands until Reggie brought a plate and glass over to her. He went back for his own, then made one more trip to put the biscuits on the table between them, where both of them could reach. Finally, he sat down and stretched his legs out. "Oh, I'm glad to be here and not there."

She didn't know what to make of that, either. "It. Um. How was it?"

"Beautiful countryside, lovely vistas. The people weren't..." He stopped. "They were what I expected. A lot of drinking, a fair few trying potions or drugs. I didn't inquire about the specifics. A lot of people pairing off, some more privately than others." He didn't notice her sudden near inhale of her beer, or if he did, he didn't react to it.

He did go on, smoothly. "I didn't, mind. For several reasons, but I didn't feel entirely steady on my metaphorical feet, there. And I always wonder about things like talking in my sleep."

"Why would you worry about what you might say?"

"Oh, plenty of reasons. That we're worried about the materia. That we have reason to think other people in the building are doing something queer. That all the secrecy is simultaneously understandable and deeply frustrating." He counted them off on his fingers. "That Lord Carillon keeps offering to help, and what do you think about that? I couldn't decide. That how they treat each other is baffling me, and I'm used to that set, or near enough."

Lynet frowned, with a forkful of meat pie almost in her mouth. "What do you mean, that last one?" It would give her time to think about the question before that, too.

"I'm used to the posh, First Families types. Being one myself, of course." Reggie leaned back, then hooked one of the footstools carefully to nudge it closer to his feet and let out a little sigh. She wondered all of a sudden if the visit had been hard on his foot. Feet. Injuries. "This was different. I don't know if you had much literature at school?"

"I've heard a fair bit of it. Alethorpe has a custom of someone reading aloud during practical work periods. We went through dozens of books every year, and there was a fair bit of that sort of thing in the mix. It's a help, with people doing artistic designs, to know the stories and the tellings."

Reggie cocked his head, blinking, then he grinned broadly. "Oh, that's clever, isn't it? Right. Do you know the *Decameron*? People locked up to avoid the plague?"

"I do. There's quite a range of different stories." Lynet wasn't sure, however, where this was going.

"It felt like that. People pressed up against something, in extremity, doing their best to drive the gloom and risk away with anything that came to hand. Even if it perhaps wasn't actually a good idea. False brightness, that's the phrase I want." He took a sip of his own beer. "Not to my taste now, if it ever was."

Lynet wasn't sure how to take that, but she could only assume it was something about his War. It must be odd to be around so many men who hadn't served somewhere that had the risk of being shot at or worse, waking and sleeping. She suddenly wondered if Reggie felt like she did, never fitting in, never trusting that they weren't out to make things difficult. Not that Lynet could figure out how to ask about it. "I can see how that wouldn't be restful."

She hadn't meant it as a joke, exactly, but he broke into a broad smile, as if she'd said something that mattered. "What about you? Besides sorting through the books."

"I had to go down to one of the booksellers near the portal to check on something I found, an order, and I ran into someone. She wasn't exactly a friend, but we got on fine. From school. She works in the Ministry of Materia now."

"Did she have any advice on our problem?" Reggie leaned forward, visibly interested.

"We went for a drink, and talked around it, more than anything? She's frustrated, because she keeps seeing odd patterns in the orders, and she can't get anyone to take it seriously."

"What sort of odd? Our kind of thing, where they think we've ordered things we never got?"

"That. Orders out of proportion for what they know about the work. Some very specific requests. You must know how it is, how some things need to be harvested at particular points, but other things, the timing isn't that relevant? A lot more of the 'must have been harvested under the first full moon after the summer solstice' type. Which is quite tricky, really."

"Also complicated on the record keeping front, I'm sure. I've heard a few comments about that over the years." Reggie shook his head. "Did she have any advice?"

"Not really. She's not very senior, I mean, it's the kind of place where the senior people have been there fifty years, or sixty or seventy. And we're in our twenties. Well, later twenties, now, but that's barely knowing where things are, in her department."

"When's your birthday?" The question came out of the blue.

"Next month." She hesitated. "Why?"

"So I can do something nice for you." He shrugged. "Someone should. I volunteer." It came out sounding remarkably cheerful, and Lynet truly wasn't sure what to do with that.

"The eighth." He blinked at her, taking that in, then beamed, as if she'd just given him a gift.

"Mine's in early October. The tenth." He offered the information back just as cheerfully, and Lynet nodded. And made a note of it, tucking it into her head. If he was going to be like that about it, she'd have to figure out some sort of plan. Assuming both of them were working together then, which she wasn't actually assuming.

The silence must have dragged on longer than she'd realised, because Reggie set down his plate. "Can I ask you a question about the books? How much consulting did other people actually do? And how much is you and Ellis?"

"That's hard to measure, isn't it? The idea of anchoring charms in a book - some of that came from Lord Carillon. But not a lot of the details. He only spent a couple of hours consulting. And of course, it's not as if we don't make charmed books, or that people haven't for centuries. Not like his, but not that different."

"So what's the new element here, then? Connecting them together?"

Lynet nodded. "We've been able to do a small set of shared books for a while. They have some limitations, like distance, but they work well enough within Albion. But the ones we're working on now, first, you want a lot of distance, unknown distances. And second, you want to be able to add books to the system over time, because there's no way to, oh, make paper for thousands of books at once. Or even hundreds."

"The materials vary, batch to batch, the paper and all that. Even if you have good controls on the quality." She did like how Reggie picked things up. "And that was all you and Ellis?"

"Pretty much. We both did quite a bit of research in the guild libraries, and he consulted a couple of people. I asked a couple of my teachers at Alethorpe. And Papa, of course, quite a lot."

"And could anyone else learn the methods you've been doing?"

Lynet frowned at him. She could feel her forehead furrowing. "Why do you ask?"

"I'm trying to figure out how unique the process is. How much it relies on you and Ellis, in particular. Did the people in charge want your father, especially, for it?"

"Yes." Lynet thought back to it. "Papa was ill already, I think. Or at least feeling something off. And he helped me sort things out, it was the two of us talking about it."

"So we have a method that quite possibly can't be fully duplicated. You've said yourself, you've taught me more of it than anyone else has seen." He paused, tapping his fingers on the chair. "I think I want to find out more about the landscape. Talk to that man who gave me his card, maybe."

"Why?" Lynet wasn't sure now what he was on about.

"There's something off about the whole situation. There has been for a while. They should be supporting you. Giving you someone proper to train up, if they want more journals. More materials. So why don't they? Do you know someone who could talk about it?"

"Not really." She hesitated. "The head of the Printer's Guild is a family friend. He's offered to help a few times, but I don't know what to tell him. I don't want to be in debt to him, either." Before Reggie could say anything, she added, "Owe him anything. Even being grateful."

Reggie opened his mouth, then closed it. "All right. And I assume you've got a reason you don't want to talk to the Bookbinders Guild."

Several, in fact, though it wasn't like she could explain all of them. That feud between Papa and Master Thorpe. The fact she didn't trust the foundational skills of a couple of his recent apprentices. The fact she still worried someone might take this project away from her and do something wrong with it. More wrong. Differently wrong. Maybe that was the word. "I don't want to lose control." Her voice caught. That had come out wrong. "Lose control of it, I mean."

"We're back to it being a thing with risks, aren't we? All right. May I see about an appointment with this man with the card? I'll have to go to London, but I can send a message to go through tonight. Maybe I'll hear back tomorrow."

"It's not as if I can stop you." Lynet pointed it out as evenly as she could.

"I won't if you say no." He was just as insistent. "It's your project."

Lynet closed her eyes, utterly unsure what to do with this responsibility. Finally, carefully, she nodded. "Write to him." She couldn't say why she did, just that it was the direction she felt they must go.

CHAPTER 26

On Thursday afternoon, Reggie came through the Bedford Square portal. It was a clear day, but decidedly on the warm side, especially given Reggie was in a full suit and hat, dressed the way his mother would approve of. He made his way down toward the Thames, glancing at a shop window or two. It had been an age since he'd been in this part of London, and seeing how it had been dimmed by the War set him back a bit.

His goal was a set of offices in Whitehall. The note he'd received back from Lapidoth Manse had given him the name to give - James Manse. And precisely what he should say at the front desk when he arrived for a four o'clock appointment. The whole thing was entirely mysterious. The fact this was London, too, was puzzling. He'd met the man in Trellech. But Reggie could get to London easily enough. He walked with enough of a limp he'd probably dodge women with white feathers or insults. And he was still more than enough of a military man to give precedence to a senior officer's orders.

He had left himself plenty of time, so he had ten minutes to spend in the nearest park with a book and a close eye on his watch. At five minutes to four, he walked the last half block from the river to the entrance he needed and presented himself. He gave his name, then presented his other bonafides. The man at the desk nodded, and passed him off to someone just inside, who escorted him up the stairs and down a long hallway to an office, before knocking.

"Yes?" The voice inside sounded tired, perhaps. Or maybe it was just that Reggie felt tired. He'd see about taking a cab back to near one of the portals when he was done. Whenever that was.

"Your four o'clock, sir."

"Excellent. We'll be a bit, likely. I'll ring. Oh, and can you take something down to C?"

The man with Reggie opened the door, going in ahead of Reggie and taking a large envelope, big enough for writing paper. "Sir, of course."

"Door and all that on your way out, thank you." Lapidoth Manse leaned back in his chair, but he didn't say anything else until the door had closed firmly. Reggie could feel the brush of magic, and wards coming back into place. Curiously, he'd not felt them elsewhere in the building, or at least not more than something quite general.

He must have glanced at the door, because he looked back to find Manse grinning. "Just so. I, obviously, am magical. So is Phipps, who brought you up. Most of our lot aren't. I'm assuming you don't have any particular solstice obligations, yes?"

Reggie nodded, slowly. "Nothing today, sir, no. A few

family things tomorrow. May I ask what you can tell me about what you do? Government work, clearly, but..." His voice trailed off.

"International information, by and large, though of course at the moment, international affairs cross over into national, and vice versa."

Reggie wasn't entirely sure what to do with that, and on the whole thought it better not to bluff his way through that. "If you're concerned with international affairs, sir, why did you speak with me? Or give me this particular card."

Manse leaned back a little further, a sharp grin now entirely plain. "You intrigue me, Hollis. And I have a certain amount of leniency to pursue people who intrigue me." He flicked his fingers. "I was actually keeping an eye on Lord Carillon, of course."

Reggie frowned. "A - um." He didn't know how to ask about this. "May I ask why, in particular?"

"His brother, as I said. Currently in the midst of something tricky, and if there's a problem here at home, knowing what's up would be a help."

"And do you know what's up? Or is that why you approached me?" Reggie was thinking out loud now, which surely wasn't the way to do this. Whatever else this place was, whoever these people were, they kept their thoughts well hidden. Reggie wasn't well made for that, and especially not these days. He did have a thing he could share, that was the difficulty of it.

Manse shrugged, spreading his hands out. "I know a few things. You might know a few others. What brought you here today?"

There was the rub. Reggie had talked this out with Lynet, cautiously. They were stymied, in several directions, and Reggie had advised seeing what happened here. There wasn't a great deal of risk for him. They might not get information, but he hadn't thought it would lead to trouble. Reggie was beginning to reconsider that notion.

Now, though, he did his best. "Without details I've sworn to keep private, sir?"

"Whatever you feel you can share. I may ask questions, but I won't press on your oaths. You're not in trouble with me, and I think it unlikely, shall we say, that something you will say today will change that." It was measured and precise, a scholar's answer who'd seen all the citations laid out already.

"I served in the trenches, sir, and an injury invalided me out. My foot." Obvious enough to anyone paying attention. He was sure Manse hadn't needed more than the half-dozen steps from the door to the chair in front of his desk to spot some of that. "I was assigned to assist in a research and development project." This was the trick. "Related to rapid communication. I am decidedly junior there, able to help with the physical labour, set things up, but not the person doing the magical work. That's a skilled specialist."

"Schola?"

"Alethorpe." It was a detail someone with resources could track down, but either this man had access to records at a high level or he didn't. And it wasn't like that was identifying a single individual.

"Rather more on the practical end, then." Manse steepled his fingers. "How's your project going, in the main?"

"Initial prototypes were successful. The next goal is for manufacture at greater speed and scale, and lower cost. The usual sort of thing, I gather. Only, the project hasn't had the practical support I would ordinarily expect."

Manse frowned. "Do you - tell me what you suspect. Fraud, ego, foolishness, sabotage, short-sightedness, bias, something else?"

Reggie looked down, away. He'd considered sabotage. He'd seen no direct sign of it, but now he came back to it, the best sabotage would be indirect. Reggie hadn't wanted to think of it from men he more or less knew, men like him, but of course that was where the danger was. Part of his training in protective magics had been about figuring out what he was actually protecting from. He didn't know much about sabotage, not directly. It was a specialised form of protection, after all. But he knew that the pieces fit, at least so far.

He kept circling the question of the intruder. The man had not even snagged some valuables to cover his intrusion, though Reggie supposed he had been trying to make it look like he had not been there at all. None of the ordinary explanations seemed to apply, which meant the project, and that meant someone who knew about the project. Which would be doing perfectly well if it were getting the support that Brand should have been giving it, he reminded himself, to get his mind back on the current conversation.

"I am honestly not sure, sir. We've had difficulty getting the materia we need." He caught himself before he began to say Lynet's name. "The person in charge has put in the proper orders, but we've been told that some of it was delivered, only not to us. Some of it is spoiled, or not of high enough potency for what we need. It's no one thing, there's more than a dozen materia types in play, as well as charms and other materials."

"How much of what you need is affected, then?" Manse made a few notes with a flick of a fountain pen on his desk.

Though they couldn't possibly be English words, the strokes were sharp and too quick and short for that.

Reggie counted it up. "Six items we're short on, or don't have an adequate supply of. And we've enough quills to be going on with, but not indefinitely." He added after a moment. "We were able to confirm the forms have been filed properly. Not that that seems to have done much good. All the Ministry of Materia says is that there's a war on."

"True, and yet entirely unhelpful. I'm not going to ask what the items are. For one thing, not my area, and for another, you sensibly realise I might make some guesses about what you're up to from that. And we barely know each other."

"Sir." Honestly, it was the only thing Reggie could say to that, the neutral to a superior.

"I can have a look at a few things, see if I can figure out why you're having difficulties. Or what category of difficulties they might be. Some things falling under our purview, some under a brother department's. And some being - well, people will make fool decisions."

"I appreciate that, sir. And I realise the limitations and your numerous other priorities." Reggie ventured a little editorialising there and got another sharp grin for it. Not a bad call, then.

Manse nodded, his attention sharply on something on his desk for a moment. "Do you have concerns about sabotage in any form then? Even, perhaps, something you would not have labelled that way previously?"

Reggie was about to say that wasn't the worry at all, of course it wasn't. Only he took a breath and then he knew better. It snapped into place, like he was hearing the shelling from across No Man's Land all over again, making the count so he knew how close his imminent death might be. "I hadn't thought that, sir." He felt himself retreating to careful politeness. "But now." He swallowed hard. "Now I'm not sure."

Master Brand had assumed the project would fail. That in six weeks, Reggie would need something new, and he wouldn't want a bad mark on his record. Only, Reggie knew that was wrong. The journals worked, they had proof. Certainly, there were improvements that could likely be made, but their problems had to do with materia and with labour. That was maths, not prophecy or prognostication or whatever term applied.

He'd been assuming that Brand was professional. That whatever the man had felt about this particular project, he was handling the work properly. His apprentice mistress had commented on that, more than once, that Reggie assumed good intentions more often than he should. When he'd been helping Lynet with the wards, it had been clear. There were people who wanted to be somewhere they weren't allowed. But this kind of thing, where Brand should have acted better, and didn't, that had caught him up.

All of it could only mean Brand knew they were going to fail, because he intended them to fail. That he had his thumb on the scales, so there was no way they could win. Maybe he was even the one who'd sent someone to Lynet's home. Maybe Brand was hoping to scare her into giving up, maybe he was hoping for something to use against her. It didn't really matter, because all of it was rotten to the core.

Reggie was sure this must have shown on his face, as easy to read as a child's book with large friendly lettering. To his surprise, though, Manse didn't press him on it, just nodded once, before changing the subject. "I gather - from his conversation - that Temple Carillon's working in the same building. Do you have any idea what category of thing he's up to, by chance?"

Reggie hesitated, but then realised that he honestly didn't, and could say as much without trouble. "Very little, sir. Even after being off at Hawk's Breath for a few days. Something to do with the land magic, I believe, but I don't know any details."

"Beautiful estate." Manse said it almost fondly. "Though it's been ages since I was out there. My university years. I remember the light, though, on the lake." He flicked his fingers. "Any sense of what sort of people are working on it?"

"There are several projects going, and I believe some overlapping. Again, no one's told me details. I got a bit of a sense that one of them's on the newer side. A bit before when I started, perhaps." Reggie frowned. "A mix of skills. I know Lord Carillon has a reputation for Materia as a field, but also some Incantation work. And several of the others have a background in Incantation, I think." He paused, then added, "I don't think Lord Carillon is doing terribly well, sir. Not seeing a few glimpses at the party. But I couldn't ask, and I'm certain he'd not tell me if I did."

Now that he said it, Reggie wondered if they were working on something that needed some kind of more immediate trigger. Incantation was used for that, quite often, though it could also be used for the longer, slower, steadier work of something like the journals.

Manse let him think for a moment, making a few more mysterious notes. "Had you thought about going back into service? Not field work."

"Yes and no, sir." Which was also the truth. "I like what I'm doing now. It could be a real help, and I think the mechanism's more - individual than people are thinking right now. I'd like to help sort that out, how to make it more efficient and all. If we can get the materials."

"Very loyal. And you're not comfortable dissembling. Definitely not field work."

Reggie grimaced and looked down again before he cleared his throat. "My time in the trenches changed things for me, sir. If you're dealing with other men with that sort of background, it might be worth knowing."

Manse's head came up sharply, then, like a great cat with an eye for new prey, the dangerous stillness that came before a pounce. "Thank you, Hollis." It was surprisingly warm, actively grateful. "You've just more than repaid the time for your visit, for the record."

Reggie was utterly baffled, and retreated to another mild "Sir."

There was another lengthy silence, a few more scratched notes, then Manse cleared his throat. "How's this? I'll have a look round into some of the materia matters. By which I mean I'll turn it over to a counterpart who might shake something loose. If there's a way to get materials to you, we'll see about making that happen. If you decide you'd rather take up a role with us, at any point, you have my card. And if you come across anything notable that should be reported my way, I know you'll do that. Signs of more direct enemy action or sabotage, for example."

It had an absoluteness to it, like a magnet pulling north. Reggie had no idea what to make of this man, how he was so confident and sure of himself, and not much older than Reggie himself. All the same, he found himself nodding. "All of that, sir." Then, he swallowed. The only way out was through. "There was an intruder, in Mistress Alder's flat. The one in London. I think someone might have been trying to scare her off." He hadn't previously given her name, but now it slipped out, and he didn't try to claw it back.

"Same person as the one interfering in your materials?" Reggie blinked. Manse obviously had some idea who, even though Reggie had never said. Though, admittedly, the cast of characters was somewhat limited in direct access.

"Logic suggests, sir. Occam's razor and all that, isn't that what we learned in our Trivium classes?"

Manse nodded once, looking almost amused, and then touched something on his desk, well out of the way of an ordinary gesture. Almost immediately after, there was a knock on the door, and the same man, and that shift of the warding.

"Captain Hollis has been most helpful. Show him out and get him a cab where he chooses."

Reggie stood. "I appreciate your time, sir." There seemed nothing else he could say.

CHAPTER 27

MONDAY JUNE 25TH

The office had been closed on the 22nd for the solstice. There was still nominally a Solstice faire - agriculture still mattered, even with a war on. But Lynet hadn't been able to face the idea of going without Papa, or dealing with crowds, or who she might run into.

Reggie had written a quick note, Thursday evening, in the journal, saying that the conversation in London had gone well enough. They'd talk about it soon. No details, though she supposed that made sense. He'd already mentioned, rather apologetically, that he had family obligations for the solstice. He hadn't mentioned what they were, but of course he'd be there.

She had spent the three days in the workshop, going through books again, and finding another dozen where Papa had made a mess of things. In half of them, he'd missed key details in the order. Those would have to be remade, at some cost of time and money, neither of which she had. The other half, there was no way to put it except that he'd made them badly, resulting in books that wouldn't hold up as they should, where any use would quickly show the flaws. A bad batch of paste, in two cases.

She didn't know how she was going to fix those. Or rather, she knew what needed to be done, but she'd need time and focus and materials she didn't have. She might be able to manage bringing them to the workroom in Trellech, Then she could at least work on them while waiting for other things to dry, but that felt dangerous, too. Someone might inspect the workroom, or claim she was using materials from the project. Even if these were an utterly different paper weight, and bound in leather rather than in bookcloth.

Lynet didn't blame her father, not exactly. Certainly, it would have helped if he'd been more honest with her. He'd said more than once he didn't want his illness to be a burden to her, but it was definitely a burden now. Trying to pick up the pieces was harder than doing it right the first time. That was one of the earliest things she'd learned from him, and to have its truth be here, in shards and scraps, just hurt more.

Being angry with him didn't make things any simpler, either. She wished she could talk to him about what to do about the project. She needed to pick his brains about what else to try. Lynet was proud of how she'd taken the fragments of ideas she'd been given, and what she knew about books and magic, and pulled them together into something that had worked. That kept working. And now they wanted her to do it again. She didn't have that sort of brilliance in her twice. Certainly, she didn't have it the way her life was now.

She finished up Sunday evening by making a handful of notes about what she wanted to try that week, given their limited stores. When she arrived Monday morning, the secretary was waiting in the entry hall, looking immensely put out. "Master Brand wishes to see you as soon as you get in."

No time to go upstairs and leave her bag or things, apparently. Lynet ducked her chin. "Of course?" All she could do was follow along obediently, feeling as if she were fifteen minutes late, rather than near twenty minutes early.

Master Brand was behind his desk, frowning. "Sit."

Lynet sat. Arguing about it, disagreeing, wasn't going to be any help.

"I understand you've been talking about your work."

She froze. "Sir?"

"I have a notification about irregularities in the materia here. You must have been talking to someone. Who?"

Lynet was caught. She didn't want to get Mairwen in trouble. If it were Mairwen who'd talked, which now she thought about it, seemed a tad unlikely. Mairwen had agreed that what she was seeing was odd, but that talking to people more would not get anywhere. She'd already tried.

"Sir?" Not that it had worked the first time. Then she swallowed. "I made oath, sir, on the Silence, about the project. You'd know if I'd broken it."

Master Brand pushed back from his desk suddenly, violently. It was the sort of force and repressed fury that came before a pub brawl. Lynet knew the signs perfectly well. This time, she couldn't duck behind the bar with Tressy and get out of the way. She had to sit here and pretend everything was all right, when it was all wrong.

He wheeled around, staring out the window, refusing to acknowledge her. She could see the tightness of his shoulders and back, the way nothing moved except for a small jerk as he inhaled. The way another man would have struck out by now, at her, at a wall. How others would have swept the crystal and finely carved wood off his desk, sent his ink bottle flying.

She didn't move. She felt like a songbird who knew a falcon was watching, or a man with a long hunting rifle. Both, perhaps, because she could feel the door behind her. She knew at any moment someone might knock or there might be a noise in the hall that changed things.

Finally, Master Brand turned around. His voice was tight and hard, like his shoulders. "I would. What did you talk about with others?"

That was going to be difficult to answer. Because, of course, she'd talked with Reggie. "I've talked with Reggie and Ellis, sir."

"Not that." He almost spat it out brusquely.

"I've been investigating our materia problems, sir. With the Ministry offices, I reported that. And last week, I ran into a friend from school who works in the offices there. She has been frustrated, sir, with some patterns in materia. I didn't specify which materials we had requested, but I believe she's able to look up the requests. I did mention we'd had trouble ourselves, and I wasn't sure why."

It was more or less an accurate retelling of the conversation. A lot of it had been Mairwen complaining, honestly, and that condensed quite a lot.

"Nothing about what you were doing or making?"

"I assume, sir, that she'd realise it had something to do with books. That is my expertise, sir." Honestly, if he hadn't figured that out, he was a great deal more dense than his reputation suggested. "But I didn't say anything about what sort of books, or even directly where I was working, just that it was a research project."

"Have you seen this girl again?"

Mairwen was a full-grown woman. By many standards, more grown than Lynet, because she had three children at home and a husband off fighting in France. Certainly not something Lynet was going to get into right now. "No, sir. It was only chance we ran into each other."

"And you haven't talked to the Ministry folks about your materia needs again?"

"No, sir. As I told you in the last meeting, it makes sense to wait until they've had a chance to dry and process the several items that can only be harvested on the summer solstice. I put in the proper request forms, of course, a fortnight ago, and checked with the clerk that they were correctly filled out and filed."

Master Brand didn't have much to say to that. He turned round again and braced his hands on the desk. "I don't think you realise how delicate your position here is. You are here on sufferance, because we don't have people who can be spared from other parts of the War effort to do what you're doing."

"Sir?" She wasn't sure where he was going, though she was sure she wasn't going to like it.

Lynet lost track of the words shortly thereafter. He took that as a reason to tear into her. Everything about her. That she was a woman, for one thing, and therefore clearly less worthy than a man. That she was obliged to do her part for the War. That he'd taken her on because her father had refused to do the work, and was this how she repaid him for that favour? For giving her a chance, when no one else would?

Then he got onto how she was uncollegial with the others. How they had complained to him of how standoffish she was, how she kept to herself. That they'd complained about how she was limiting Reggie - he said Hollis - from doing his part. Making him weak and cowardly, and they couldn't have that.

It left her quivering and shaking, unable to defend herself. By the end, she wasn't even able to look up, just stare at bit of a knot in the grain of the wood desk in front of her. There was silence, as if he'd said something. When she didn't answer, he barked one more word. "Go."

Lynet went, barely managing to avoid knocking over the chair as she bolted from the room, out into the hallway, brushing past someone without seeing them. She turned up the stairs, on pure instinct, taking them quickly. Wanting to be as far away from that awful office as she could, but not daring to flee the building.

She heard someone behind her, a sound she couldn't understand, but it fell away as she ran.

CHAPTER 28

Reggie had been puzzled when he got in, and found that not only was Lynet not in the workroom, but she hadn't apparently unlocked it yet. He did so, setting the wrapped lunches out by the teakettle and the little box of biscuits. Then he went downstairs to see what he could find out.

Ellis was in his own workroom, but he hadn't seen hide nor hair of Lynet either. Reggie nodded, said he'd go have a look round. Maybe she'd sorted out something about the materia. When he came back into the main building, he could hear some movement from the far end of the hallway. As he was about to turn down to see who was about, an arm snaked out from one of the offices.

"Say, Hollis, you're just the right man to help with this. Just the right height. Stand here, would you? We're trying to mark a model." One of the men working on trench supports gestured at the wall. "Back against the boards there." They had a large piece of thin wood pressed up against the wall.

Reggie sighed. "This going to take long?" On the other hand, it was a way to show he was helping out, and it seemed harmless enough.

"Just a minute, just a minute." Of course, it took longer than a minute, and by the time they were almost done, Margot had come along, looking sleek and entirely at ease.

She was about to say something, her fingers brushing Reggie's arm. There was a louder sound from the other hall, a chair clattering, a door opening too fast, hard-soled shoes on stone floors. Lynet came rushing by, not looking at all where she was going, so fast and fierce that even Margot backed up. Reggie spun, trying to catch her, and she just blew past.

Someone called after Reggie, but he was already halfway up the first flight of stairs, a flight behind Lynet. He didn't call out. He needed all his breath to try to catch up to her. He managed to almost catch her at the door. She swung it behind her, hard, so that it hit the side of his bad foot, catching it between the door and the frame. He felt the burst of pain, and shoved it down, feeling all the coiled magic in him wanting to do something.

He didn't know what had happened, but he knew it was something deeply wrong. He pushed the door open again, turning to close it behind him firmly, and forced himself to take a step. "Lynet?"

"Don't." Her voice was jagged now, like broken slate, something dark and opaque and full of sharp edges.

"What happened?"

She swung around, slapping her hands, them coming down flat on the worktable, making a loud echoing sound that filled the room. Not at all like her, either the anger or the noise, and it put Reggie's back up. Not at Lynet, but at whatever brought her to this place.

"Brand." There was no title there, absolutely no deference. Then she turned her back on him again, mumbling something he couldn't hear.

Reggie found a place where he could lean against another of the workbenches and take the weight off his foot. He was refusing to acknowledge it, at least for right now, but he wouldn't be running any races for a bit.

"How may I help?" Reggie tried to keep his voice even, not to let his own growing frustration show. For one thing, while it would be useful if she communicated a bit more, he could understand why she wasn't. And it wasn't Lynet he was upset with.

She wheeled around, hair coming out of the bun at the back of her head in wisps that moved as she turned. "Why do you care? You're just like the rest of them."

He spread his hands, then regretted the way it shifted his body and put them back for balance. "That's not fair." He didn't argue, he didn't raise his voice, beyond the three words. "Something's wrong. Was Master Brand angry at you? At the project? Something else?" He knew Brand wanted them to fail. This could only be one more attempt at it, but he didn't dare say that out loud now. He thought his wards and charms would hold, but he wasn't absolutely certain. And he wouldn't trust anything other than certainty.

Lynet turned away again, and Reggie thought she might honestly be crying now. He didn't move toward her. That would be seven kinds of horrible mess, and not a help to either of them. Again, there was that mumble that he couldn't make out.

"I'd like to know when you can. Make some tea? Tea's a help."

She shook her head, but she waved at him. "Chair. Whatever." She went off to the far end of the workroom, leaning her elbows on the workbench. He let her have what privacy he could give her. He limped back to the desk and a chair, before managing to prop his bad foot under the desk, which eased the throbbing slightly.

It took quite a while for her to gather herself again. The bells rang twice, making it somewhere between fifteen and twenty-nine minutes, before she turned back, circling the room, and putting the kettle on to boil. Then she came back to lean against the workbench facing the desk. "Master Brand was—" She cut off. "I can't talk about this here."

That was a sensible thing, and possibly the most sensible one she'd said so far. "This evening, your place?"

She hesitated. "It's Tuesday."

"The London route'll be quiet still. Everyone going out to the Solstice faire if they're going anywhere." He had some inarguable logic there, and she nodded once, after a moment.

"All right. I'll." She shrugged, not really looking at him. "I can get something from the pub for supper."

Reggie was deeply relieved that she was being reasonable about this. On the other hand, he was beginning to worry about how bad it was that she'd been so visibly upset. He took a breath and let it out. "And today?"

"Today, we do our work." Her chin had come up, stubbornly, now. "As much as we can. Can you work on cutting this batch of paper and laying it out for signatures once we've had a cuppa?"

Reggie considered, but that should be fine. He was trying to figure out what else to say still when the kettle sang. Once they'd both had their tea - still in silence - she rinsed out her cup. "Ready?"

He'd thought he was, but he was two steps from the desk when his foot came down wrong. He landed hard on his right knee, grunting with the pain of it.

Before he could say anything, she was bending down, peering at his face. "You - you're all white."

Reggie gave up any pretence of dignity, and let himself settle on the floor, sitting. She half offered him a hand, and he shook his head.

"What happened?" His foolishness at least had her out of her own worry a bit, so maybe it'd do a little good. Enough to hold them both for the afternoon.

"Banged up my foot, coming up here." He grimaced. "I —" Then he wasn't sure what to say, not at all.

"You should go, um. Do you go to the Temple of Healing?" She was leaning forward now, solicitous.

He probably should. It wasn't getting better. He could feel the throbbing more. They'd at least be able to do something for the pain, and check he'd not set one of the scars bleeding again. It was a damnably bad spot to check for himself.

"I don't want to leave you alone." He didn't, either. He had no idea who'd come up and bother her. That hit home with her as well.

"Oh." Lynet reached to rub her face. "I can ask Ellis to come up? Write to him? And he had an idea that could do with some library research. We could do that today. They're open."

Her being out of the building was both reassuring and worrisome. If Brand came looking for her and didn't find her, he'd be furious. And who knew who else he might send to look who'd make their own trouble. On the other hand, if she were safely out of the building, he could set the strongest wards he'd laid in to the workroom. They could feel confident nothing would be messed with, that there would be no sabotage when they'd been driven out. More than anything else, he wanted to know she was safe, if he couldn't be right there.

It struck him, then, how much he was thinking like one of Bear House. That burning desire to put himself between danger and what he cared about. It was something Professor Trembley had talked with them about often. It could be a glorious, necessary, life-changing thing, to let all those instincts and all the training he'd had come out. And it could also be incredibly dangerous, for him and for others around, if he didn't keep his control.

Put in that light, an afternoon with a Healer seemed like a sensible move. It'd let him settle. Reggie was quite sure he wasn't going to like whatever Lynet told him this evening, as necessary as it was. But it would be best if he could come into the conversation in a better frame of mind.

"Do you need a hand down the stairs? I can pack things up here and get Ellis to come up, and we can lock up here. Maybe if you made noises about the research, they'd take it better from you."

That was the rub of it. They would. And it might protect her a little more. Her, and their work, both. He was feeling very possessive about this workroom, really, for all none of it had been his idea, nor his plan. But the journals, they were an amazing bit of magic, even as limited as they were right now. He wanted to see what Lynet could do if she had the chance.

Which just brought him back to the choices Master Brand kept making, the ones that kept suggesting that he wanted to see them fail. Now that he had seen it in the conversation with Manse, he was stuck with the thought. Reggie realised then he'd been quiet, that he hadn't answered Lynet. "I could use a hand," he admitted. "And you should go with Ellis. We'll set the warding here."

Lynet hesitated, then she nodded. "Let me write him. And make notes of what we need to research."

Reggie leaned back on his hand. "Ask for Madam Thornton. She's the head librarian. She looks stern, but she knows exactly where everything is. Tell her I told you to ask for her?"

That got him a half-smile from Lynet. "All your evening reading. All right. Do you need a hand up?"

Reggie wasn't entirely sure he did, but he also - well, he wanted to touch her. Get a sense of how she was really doing, now that she'd had a chance to put a few of her own walls up again. He held up his hand. "If you don't mind?"

The contact was enough that he got a sense of things. She was pretending to be better off than she was, he thought, and he could understand that. Also, he was doing the exact same thing, and being a hypocrite seemed wrongheaded for a number of reasons. At the same time, he didn't want to drop her hand, and she wasn't being quick about doing so either.

By the time Ellis got up the stairs, they were both ready to go, with the workroom solidly locked and warded. Reggie had enough presence of mind to add a bit of a sting to them if someone tried to force the issue. Nothing that would cause real problems, but that would be a lingering discomfort. He'd developed it back in school, when people snuck into his trunk or his room.

He made it half a block, out to the main road and out of sight. Then he stopped and flagged down a cab to take him up to the Temple of Healing. He was surprised when someone could see him quite promptly. They tutted over his foot, did a charm that eased the pain dramatically, and then settled in to figure out what he'd done to himself.

It might well bring up a nasty bruise, from what they could tell in the moment. So he was sent off to soak in the baths under the temple for as long as he could stand it. They were good for healing, good for circulation, good for a dozen other conditions. And, well, they were a vastly more pleasant form of treatment than most he'd been given.

By the time he was done soaking, they'd rounded up a cane for him to use, a rather nicely carved bit of wood, smooth and polished. It was just the right length, and meant he could take himself the short distance to the portals, and then through to Southwark, only a little later than he'd hoped. Lynet should have been back for a good half hour by the time he turned up, if he had the times right.

CHAPTER 29

THAT EVENING

Lynet had been back in the workroom for an hour by the time she heard Reggie's steps on the stairs. Ellis had offered to come back with her, but by the time the two of them were done in the library, she was wrung out. She'd come back, pausing by the pub to let Tressy know she was around and get supper.

And then she'd taken a bath. It wasn't a luxury she indulged in very often, for time reasons as much as anything else. The water took magic to heat, though, and she often didn't have it to spare at the end of a long day of work and a dozen different complex charms. At the barracks housing, there was a very pragmatic sort of bath, not meant for soaking. She wasn't sure the Guard permitted themselves that kind of loafing around, especially right now.

It had still left her with a good hour before Reggie arrived. She'd have worried he was late, but he'd sent a note with his expected arrival time. The sound on the stairs was odd, though, three sounds, not two. It wasn't until she opened the door - after checking it was in fact Reggie - that she realised why. He was leaning on a cane and looking rather drawn.

"Come, sit. Please. Are you - um? Your foot?"

"It'll be fine." Reggie shrugged. He was wearing the same clothes he'd worn that morning, she thought, not that she'd really noticed it then, with his jacket over the top, despite the warm weather. Of course, a man of his background didn't go about in shirt sleeves, and he must have cooling charms or something like that. People could.

Lynet wasn't sure what to do now he was here, but she nodded. "Chair? Um. Would a footstool help?" She'd pushed Papa's off into the corner. She'd kept tripping over it as she went back and forth to the shelves.

Reggie hesitated for a moment, then nodded. "If it's not a bother."

"Sit, it's not." She felt there was something off here, a nagging little strip of paper that needed trimming or tending to. A thread that wasn't bound off neatly. "And I've got food. D'you want that now?"

Reggie nodded at that. "Not putting you out?"

She hesitated. The money was a factor, but he'd been buying her lunch. She had a little to spare. "We can talk about it for next time." Admitting that there would be a next time, that felt decidedly queer. But he'd been here twice now. You didn't stop at two. No sensible tale had two of a thing. It was always ones or threes or sevens. She thought about it and then corralled her mind back onto her actual tasks.

Lynet pushed the footstool over, glancing at him to see where he wanted it, then turned to go fetch the food. No sense in making him move. The beer had been in the cold box, and was pleasantly cool, and she'd got four bottles, just in case the conversation went longer. Reggie leaned back in the chair. She could see the angle of his head and hear the way he let out a slightly uneven breath.

There was pain there. She knew the way that sounded. Papa had sounded like that, more and more, at the end. When he couldn't pretend he didn't, when even his breathing showed how much work it was to manage what his body was shouting at him. But he'd said - oh. He'd said it would be fine. Not that it was. Not that Lynet had the faintest idea how to bring that up with him. She wanted to offer him something more, to put a hand on his arm, some sort of something she didn't know how to describe, and she couldn't do any of that.

What she could do was feed him. They'd agreed that was a good thing, the food, and right now in particular. She brought Reggie's pie and beer over first, then her own, pulling her chair forward a bit so they could share a table between them. "I don't know where to start." That was true enough, and it was fair, too.

"What happened this morning?" Reggie hesitated. "Or should I start with Thursday?"

"Was it any good, Thursday?" She hadn't really expected it to be, but Reggie had wanted to make the attempt, and it wasn't as if Lynet had had a better idea. She wondered, now, if that was what had got Master Brand so upset, but she didn't think so. It would have come out differently if he'd worried about - well. Whoever it was.

"It was a very cordial meeting. Not many details, but I didn't expect that, and I didn't share many myself. That I was working on a research project related to rapid communication, that we were stymied by materia shortages." Reggie still hadn't touched his food yet. "He didn't press me for anything secret, though he did ask about my interactions with Lord Carillon. And I said something he found very helpful, but it doesn't seem related at all." Reggie hesitated. "Offered to look into it, see what he could shake loose, but without any commitment, of course. And that if I wanted something in that line of work, to let him know, though apparently I'd be a poor field agent." Then he took a deep breath. "And I realised something, but we'll come back to that." She didn't know what to make of those hesitations.

"You?" Lynet leaned forward. All of that wasn't as helpful as they'd hoped, but it was something.

"Bad at dissembling, apparently. Which I knew." Reggie shrugged and tugged his plate over. Lynet let him have a few bites. It wasn't as if she wanted to talk about this morning, even though she knew she'd have to. She poked at her own food, feeling her appetite disappear.

He must have caught something in her expression. "I want to help, as much as I can. But I can't do that without some idea of what happened. Do you - did he stop you on the way in?"

The question, oddly, helped. "I was stopped on the way in, his secretary saying I was wanted. And then he just..." She shivered again, and Reggie reached out a hand. His fingers hovered over hers for a moment before he withdrew, though he didn't pick up his fork again.

"What - pardon, I'm sure it's painful to revisit, but I'm trying to understand. You were very upset." His voice had an odd note to it, a quiet ferocity, that reminded her of the thing Uncle Matthew had said about his family having a temper.

"It doesn't make sense!" It burst out of her. "You've said, before. You'd think they'd want us to make progress, and instead, there's nothing. I can't get the materia we need. I can't even get anyone to explain why we can't. And then maybe we did get it, but someone else has it, and Master Brand should be sorting that out, and I don't know why he isn't."

It wasn't that she expected the world to be fair, she bloody well knew it wasn't. In a fairer world, both her parents would be alive and here. Her skills and knowledge would be respected, and her hard work. Instead, it was like being a mill horse, at some of the flour mills she'd seen when she and Mama and Papa had gone out to help with the hops picking when she was young. Always walking in a circle, never getting anywhere new, just grinding out the same thing over and over again.

There was a clink of fork on the plate, and Reggie set his to one side again. "I was thinking about that." He let out a breath. "You said you had colonels talking to you, at one point? What were they like about the project in general?"

"They asked questions, some of them a bit foolish, but they ..." Now she thought back, they'd been reasonably encouraging. And she thought Master Brand had been a bit disapproving, actually. She said as much, adding, "Master Brand's been queer about it. All through. I just, I've been assuming he'd much rather have had Papa."

"And they got you instead." Reggie frowned, furrowing up his forehead, visibly thinking. "Here's the thing. I realised, while talking to Manse, that Brand doesn't want you - us, if you permit - to succeed. I don't know why, but it's the only thing that makes sense in the context. I don't know if he'd rather support some other project, or if he's..." He grimaced. "I suppose he could be a spy. Or suborned in some way. It happens. And I just handed Manse a whole set of possibilities there."

"It doesn't make sense that he would. I mean, he could have hired someone else if he didn't want it to go anywhere." Lynet was finding that saying it out loud helped. Not that it helped it make sense, but it was helping her think through the different parts of it. Then it hit her, that Master Brand coming after her today, that must have been deliberate. Not incompetence, not poshness overwhelming everything else, not anything she'd done or not done, except make the journals work. Which was bad enough, if he wanted them to fail. But she wasn't wrong, she was right. "He wants someone he knows will fail." Saying it out loud suddenly made it sharply real, like the slice of a paper cut that stung all the way down.

"Instead, he has you and Ellis. And you're both past your apprenticeships, but you're not established masters in your fields, not yet. Brilliant." He looked up at her with a quick grin. "But they don't know that. Or at least don't appreciate it properly."

Something in that grin freed Lynet a bit. As if all the things Brand had said that morning might possibly not be entirely right. "You really think so?"

Reggie nodded, now very earnest about it. "It could change the War, like I said at the beginning. A lot of other things, too. That doesn't mean I'm not still worried about the ways it could be abused. I'm sure there's some people who know about the idea who'd worry about morale. Bad news from the front is awful for morale. It's bad enough when it's newspapers and censored letters. This would be unfiltered."

Then he stopped, as if he'd had some sudden realisation. "Though there's got to be a way to get people to make oath on it, that would work. I don't know how, but that's why there are ritual experts in the world, now, isn't it?"

He stopped and swallowed some of his beer, as if he were a rock rolling downhill that couldn't stop. "More to the point, these journals, they could save lives. Directly in combat, but - oh, think about what it would mean if a Healer at the front could consult an expert back in Trellech. Or get information quickly to people trying to help with a new gas or weapon." There was a growing fierceness in him, coming out in his voice, but she wasn't scared of him. He was on the side of right here, and Lynet knew it.

She hadn't thought about that in that context, and her hand went to her mouth. "Oh. All right. So. Is it Master Brand himself? Or do you think someone is making Master Brand block it? Me? Us?"

Reggie nodded. "I don't know who's pulling the strings. Just, the evidence fits the circumstances." He let out a slow breath. "I can't tell what it would change, not entirely? Just that it would be so many things." He hesitated. "The generals are throwing away men, left and right. What would it change if they couldn't do that, not without people knowing? It's one thing to go over the top with some hope of success. It's another to know it won't change anything at all."

Lynet hadn't known it was like that. She'd assumed - everyone she knew assumed - that those heroic charges, the stories they did hear, they made a difference. Won back ground, changed the War. And everything about Reggie, right now, made it clear that was a lie.

She couldn't begin to get her head around it. Or that someone - Master Brand - would willingly help that continue. That people would interfere in anything that might help shorten the War or save people's lives. Or the dozen other things the journals might mean, even if they also had a risk. Her head was spinning now, so she retreated to something she almost understood.

"If it had been Papa..." She hesitated. "Would it have been different?"

"Could your father have done the work? I know he did excellent work. I can see that in you. But you're not the same person." Reggie was leaning forward now, intent on the conversation.

Lynet thought about that, really thought about it, for the first time in more than a year. "They'd have done the same thing to him. Wouldn't they?"

"More than likely. It would come out differently. An older man, his own allies. But Master Brand is posh, and - I know how they play the games." He shifted and brought his foot down on the floor. She saw the wince, almost before he reacted, the way his entire body curled up against the pain.

Her fingernails were digging into her palms now. She could feel them, as much as she could feel anything. Lynet took an uneven breath, another one, until Reggie had straightened up a bit, and taking a long drink from his beer.

"Your foot. What happened?"

There was an absolute silence in the room, so quiet she could hear people out in the street, outside the pub, clearly. He didn't answer for what felt like hours, then he cleared his throat. "The door, this morning. Should have picked the other foot. But." He stalled there.

"But?" Something in her had to know, wanted to know.

He looked away, off toward the bookshelves. "I wanted to put myself between you and whatever had hurt you."

CHAPTER 30

Reggie found himself free for what felt like the first time in his life. He hadn't intended to say that, hadn't even intended to bring up his foot, but here he was.

And he wouldn't run from it, he couldn't. So here he was, cut loose from all the expectations he'd felt, all the ways he'd felt he'd failed, and all the weight that had settled on him. He didn't know what Lynet might be willing for, but he wanted to stand between her and the world. He wanted to let her brilliance shine out, and do some good, in a way he couldn't dream of doing himself. Most of all, he wanted her to have space to be herself.

Now she was leaning forward, peering at him. "You did?"

"I wanted to put myself between you and whatever had hurt you." Reggie repeated it, in hopes that would help.

She blinked. "Why me?"

This was the harder question. He'd come to respect her

quite early, as he looked back on it. She knew her work. She had high standards, but she'd been remarkably patient with him, considering the circumstances. Even when she'd had an awful time of it, she didn't blame him. The few times she'd been snappish, she'd had excellent reason.

She was herself, good and bad. Reggie realised now he'd been following her, tracking her like the sun and the shadow, always circling her. He'd snatched up the tiny crumbs she'd offered of what she preferred, and he'd wanted to bring those things to her. And he'd brought them, whether they were biscuits or sandwiches or little tidbits from his reading.

Someone else might have waved a hand and made a comment about knights and their ladies in a tower. It wasn't like that. For one thing, Lynet would refuse to be a demure maiden locked up in a tower, or only seen from a distance, decorous and ornamental. She would have her hands right in the work, whatever needed to be done, and there would be skill there. She brought that to everything she did, skill and deliberate decisions and knowing what she did today affected tomorrow's choices.

He wanted more of that for himself. Selfishly, yes, he had to admit that, at least deep in his heart. But he wanted more of that for everyone. The world would be better with more of her practical stubbornness and fierce commitment to solving the problems in her path.

None of that answered her question, though. "Because you're doing something important. That matters. Because you're doing it whole-heartedly, even though..." He waved a hand. "Grief and a whole mess of things you didn't expect to have to deal with. And you should have someone else on your side beside Ellis."

Lynet sucked in a breath and looked away. "I don't

know what you mean by that. Being on my side." Then she twisted. "If you wanted to get me into bed, I'd understand that."

Well. That too, really. Not that he'd been going to bring it up. Certainly not right now. Her bluntness left him spinning, scrambling for traction. "What would you understand?"

She shrugged, a twitch of her shoulder, sharp like percussion in an orchestra or the click of the scissors. "People being nice, because they want that. You haven't, but."

Now Reggie wanted to go fight a number of other people, up close and personal. He wanted the sort of fight that involved punches and bloody noses and leaving them writhing on the ground in pain. "Did anyone hurt you? Threaten you? Anything like that?" His voice had gone into a low growl. He could hear it. She could too, and her eyes went wide. She didn't back up, or tell him to stop, rather she looked honestly surprised.

"Oh, I agreed. It wasn't unpleasant. Crafters, there's the line about them being good with their hands." There was no hint of passion there, of the sort of pleasure Reggie had tried to reach for, even if he'd known they'd only be together for a tryst or two. He forced himself to take a breath or two.

"Well. I'm no crafter, but I've reliably given my partners more than just being good with my hands. A man should have pride in his skills. That one in particular, really."

"Because it's all about your manly pride?" In another time and place, it could have been sharp and edged. This wasn't, though, this was more teasing. The tone he'd heard from her when she was relaxed and comfortable, the one she saved for him and Ellis.

"Bloody well not." He wanted to match that, and it came out in a rolling half-laugh. "No. I always thought it's about the intimacy. If we're going to let someone close, even just for a little while, it - " His voice trailed off. It sounded foolish now.

"Yes?"

Reggie pressed himself to the words. "If we're going to be close, it's an insult not to give it my best. I'm not perfect. Merlin knows that. But I want to give it my all." He looked down and away, across the room. When he looked back, after an uncertain silence, she was watching him, her head tilted.

"I believe you." Lynet said it like it was a surprise to her, too. "I didn't know you..." She cut herself off abruptly. "I don't know what you're saying."

Reggie turned, ignoring the way his foot registered a complaint. "I want to fight the world, if it would help you. I want you to have space to think and to put things together. To make a difference." He swallowed. "And if I thought you'd be willing, I'd take you to bed in a heartbeat."

"Tonight?"

Reggie's breath caught, and then he was nodding before he could even form words. It was going to shatter everything into bits, but he couldn't lie to her. He couldn't lie to himself. "If you wanted. Only if you wanted."

Her mouth quirked up. "And what would all the men on the ground floor think?"

Reggie shrugged. "They don't know what they're missing." Honesty compelled him to continue. "About that."

Lynet's eyebrow arched. "Yes?"

"You know they're - let's say unpleasant, shall we? About you? They call you nasty names. Every time they've done that, when I was around, when I couldn't stop them, I decided you should have something nice. A biscuit. Me picking up lunch, or running downstairs so you didn't have to. It wasn't the only reason I did nice things for you. I mean, I liked doing them? But you should - you should have good things."

That sounded even more awful, now it was out of his mouth. He turned away, mumbling. "I'll go."

He heard something he couldn't make sense of, and then she was touching him, her hand cupping his cheek. He could feel the callouses and texture of her fingers, the way they'd worked needle and thread and book cloth, over and over again. The little bump where the brush rested. "Don't."

Reggie looked up to find her peering at him. She'd bent, so she was near enough on his level.

"We'll likely regret it in the morning. But I suppose we'll muddle on. Show me. Are you up to the challenge?"

Then she stepped back. Reggie - well, part of him was definitely rising to the moment. He closed his eyes for a long moment. "I, yes. Oh, please." That came out like a schoolboy, offered some unfathomable delight. "Give me, let me. I need a moment to think about how."

"Surely you don't need an instructional diagram." Now she was arch, and she was definitely teasing. Her eyes were dancing, gleaming. He hadn't expected that from her, not at all, as if something had opened and he could see everything clearly. There was a light there that he'd seen flickers of, but now he saw what she'd been like before, without all the weight bearing down on her. He might not give her anything that lasted until morning, but he could encourage that light for a little while.

"Tab A inserted in slot B is so simplistic, isn't it? Not like your instructions about folding the book cloth." Which involved nine diagrams, sixteen arrows, and a certain amount of mind reading to fully decipher. "Not that. The practical parts."

"I've a potion." She held up her hand. "Recent enough make it'll still be good, even if I didn't think I'd need it any time soon."

"That." He agreed there. She couldn't risk a child, not now. It would mark her as only good for that, and in all the wrong ways. And a couple of the techniques used to make the journal, he was sure no one had actually evaluated them fully to be safe in pregnancy. "Also my foot. Need a moment or two to think about positions and all that." The risk of bumping it in a moment of ecstasy was far more likely than he wanted.

"Ah." She let out a breath. "If you'd rather not?"

"Oh, I want." He hesitated for a fraction of a second, and then reached for her hand, tugging it so the back of it pressed against him and the entirely tangible desire. "You can feel that. I want to show you what it's like when someone wants you to have the best of times."

She rolled the back of her hand against his hardness for a moment, then twisted her fingers in his to cup him, watching his face. He let the sensations roll through him, let her see how good that felt.

"Mmm." Lynet pulled her hand away slowly. "Let me take my potion. Come up when you've had your moment." She took a couple of steps toward the stairs, then turned back toward him. "Don't take too long."

Reggie, a lifetime ago, would have read it as a challenge. The man he was now knew it was more complicated than that. Not to keep her waiting, certainly. That was rude. But that they both might lose their courage about it, if there was too much space.

"A minute or two." He let her get up the stairs, then levered himself up, cleaning up the plates and bottles as best he could with one hand. The purely physical actions helped get his mind unstuck from the flashes he saw now, of what she'd look like in the moment of her greatest pleasure. What it would be like if she fully gave herself over to that, even just for a fleeting second.

He tugged his mind back to the question of position. He couldn't stand - for one thing, he wanted to touch her more than that. Kneeling between her legs, that had too much chance of knocking his foot into her calf. Side by side had some possibilities, but he wanted to see her, and he wanted to be more active, or let her be. She might straddle him with his back against the headboard. That might do nicely, if she were inclined. She'd be free to move against him, his hands could touch and stroke and encourage.

As soon as that had settled out in his mind, he checked the warding one last time, and went upstairs, steady as he could. She'd dimmed the lights in the rest of the flat, except for the one in her room. She must have heard him coming, because she was standing in the middle of the room, her fingers brushing at the buttons of her frock.

"You can tell me to stop, any time. You know I will."

Lynet tilted her head. "I - you know, I am sure you would." She glanced over her shoulder at the bed. "It's not much. Not what you're used to." As if she was suddenly afraid he'd find it old and shabby, and think her the same.

"It's fine. Honest. Far better than I had for years. Less mud, many fewer rats. Far more pleasant company. May I touch you? Help you off with your dress?"

The touch helped. Quite a lot, it turned out. She was nervous, at first, and he set himself to touching her like she touched books. Any book he'd ever seen her touch, revelling in the sensation of this particular moment, the way it lay under the fingers. He began by undoing a button on her frock, then another, letting his fingers draw outline after outline until she was leaning into the strokes.

It took them quite a few minutes, but finally he was steering her toward the bed. All of their clothes lay discarded in a pile on the floor, bar his right sock, to help keep the bandages in place. "Eventually." he said, "I'd like you to straddle me in my lap, facing whichever way you like. You have your choice of how to move. My foot's out of the way. Everything we want, mm?"

"Eventually?" She frowned at the bed. "You aren't - um. Right now?"

"Good grief, who have you been with? Oh, I have quite a few things in mind, first. Fingers and my mouth, and I'm fairly sure I still remember a few sensation charms for your pleasure. Though you've by far the best sense of touch."

"And do I - do I touch you, in this?"

"If you like. And I hope you will like." He felt, fundamentally, his pleasure would be fine. On the other hand, making it entirely his to manage wasn't fair to her. It wasn't equitable. That was the proper word. He wanted her to find her pleasure, and he had to hope that she felt the same.

"What do I do, then?"

"Stretch out on the bed. Now, if I'd actually planned this properly, I'd have a few oils and ointments and such. We'll have to make do with our own personal production. Let's see what might encourage that." He was teasing now, and she blinked at him wide-eyed. That was just proof that he should spend quite some time teasing her.

He gave it his best, first with his fingers against her soft skin, then his mouth against her breast. When his fingers dipped between her legs, she made the first entirely uncontrolled noise he'd ever heard from her. He pursued that like a hunting hound who had the scent. When she convulsed, crying out, with his fingers deep in her, he let her come down from it, grinned, and said, "More of that, then?"

"Oh, oh, yes." She was panting now, and Reggie shifted on the bed, careful of his feet, to lower his mouth to her. Her hands caught in his hair, and he went gently here, not sure if she'd like it. Her thigh pressed against his ear, the other against his side, before she shuddered again, letting him tip her into an endless circle of touch and reaction.

When she was recovering from that, he pushed himself up on his arms, then settled beside her on the bed. "If your knees still work...."

Lynet twisted to peer at him, and then leaned in to kiss him. It was fierce, a kind of kiss he'd never had from a woman before, not like that. It wasn't possessive; it wasn't claiming him. The kiss was all about flinging herself into the pleasure, taking what she could from the moment. He entirely approved. A moment later, she was kneeling, then trying to figure out how this worked.

He held still, one hand keeping himself in place, so that all she had to do was settle on top of him. Reggie was watching her, the way her eyes widened and her head rocked back, as she felt him, as she pushed down on him. He thought, for just an instant, how this had been the perfect choice. Then she slipped down on him, taking him in so smoothly that it flooded every other thought out of his head.

Everything came apart, then, into flashes and moments. The grin on her face, as she found her own rhythm. How her eyes lit up, even more, as she realised what it was doing to him. How he was barely holding back - well, with a bit of help from a charm - from his own explosion. And then she figured out how to shimmy her hips, how to make them as clever and dancing as her fingers. He bucked up into her, again and again, pressing up on his good foot, groaning with it.

When she finally clenched around him again, brought to a scream of pleasure by his fingers, he let the charm fall away. He gave himself over to the moment, utterly, and lost at least a few seconds to the velvet blackness. When he could focus again, she was still in his lap. Her head was resting on his shoulder, and he curled his arms around her, just holding and not ever wanting the moment to end.

CHAPTER 31

L ynet woke the next morning, confused. Then the bed shifted and there was a soft cough. "Should I clear out, give you some time?"

Reggie was stretched out on his side, giving her most of the bed, as if he'd migrated himself to the edge as soon as he reasonably could. She shook her head, rubbing her eyes to get the sleep out. "No, don't. Not on my account."

Then, Lynet couldn't figure out what to do with herself. Should she thank him? Feed him breakfast? Coordinate how not to be terribly obvious when they walked into work? Was it going to be a problem, for that matter? The silence dragged on, until she finally decided to start somewhere. "Last night, erm. You didn't need the diagrams, no."

It made him snort and push up on one elbow. "Glad my skills meet your high standards." He was utterly in earnest about it, too, not being cruel about it.

She hesitated, then reached out to touch his shoulder. "Your foot?"

243

Reggie considered. "Haven't tried standing on it, so I'm not entirely sure yet. Doesn't feel worse, though. Having it elevated, good circulation going, that usually helps." He grinned, a rather boyish expression. "And I did both."

"We did both." Somehow, making that clear was important now. "Um. How do we do things now? Today, I mean."

"That is up to you. I'll follow your lead, of course."

"There's no 'of course' about it, you realise. Most people wouldn't." Lynet wasn't at all sure how he could be so agreeable about that. He didn't have any of his ego tied up in being the one in charge, and it was simultaneously refreshing and deeply confusing.

He shrugged again. "I'm not most people. You're in charge of the project. You still get my best work, as much as I can give it. If you decide you need me off the project, I can get myself reassigned. If you don't want to see me ever again, just tell me."

"No. I don't want that." She hesitated. It was true, though. She'd slept well last night, and not just because of the exertion itself. There were flickers of sleepy memory there, of his warmth against her and of not feeling alone in the world. "You'd go away, if I said so?"

"Well, I'd rather not." Again, that slight amusement, then went on, making what he felt more clear. "I very much enjoyed last night. Generally do enjoy time with you, in whatever form. I'd be delighted with more of it." That felt like a vast new territory that Lynet didn't know how to navigate. Some of it must have shown on her face, because he reached to touch her hand. "We don't need to decide that now. Just what we're doing this morning."

"I don't know how to think through it. Would it cause trouble if people realised we had?"

"Master Brand would probably be glad you're

distracted, honestly. And me. If it gets back to my family, they'll have opinions, but they have opinions about lots of things. With the bright young men downstairs, it might humanise you. I'll get teased about my taste, so it'd be good to know how far I may compliment you to others."

"You'd do that?"

"Tell the truth? Oh, definitely. Shame them into decency? I certainly hope so." Reggie was just so even-handedly pleased about the whole thing, and Lynet didn't have the strength of will to squash that hope. When they gossiped, the bright young men, it would be awful, but it probably wouldn't be more awful than they'd already been. She'd managed so far.

"Work through what you'd say if you could." That conversation took them through getting ready for the day. At least Reggie's clothes weren't in bad shape. Also, no one would notice he'd worn the same thing twice in a row once she used a few cleaning charms to refresh them.

Precisely on time, they walked into the building together. Reggie solicitously juggled his cane to hold the door for her. She was smiling, she couldn't help it. He looked so pleased with himself and with her. She half-turned, as she went up the stairs, adding a "What was it you were saying last night about having an idea?"

She knew a few people heard it. There was a buzz behind them as Reggie came up the stairs behind them. She was terrified of the gossip, but Reggie had argued, persua-sively, that it could shake things loose. And at least it would be different. He understood how the bright young men thought. She had to trust that.

Just before eleven, he went down to get tea, and Lynet came down the stairs with him to check on something with

Ellis. When she came back inside, she stopped just inside the door, where they couldn't see her.

"Come on, Hollis, she's so grim. Why would you?"

Reggie's voice came across clear as day. "Her father died in March. I was helping her sort out some things from his workshop. Big strong muscles, good for something." Someone must have said something, because Reggie's voice turned more pointed. "She actually loved him. People do sometimes." Reggie's comment got a bit of a murmur, how they hadn't known.

"Well, you didn't ask, either, did you? And she's been wearing black, straight through. Honestly. Good thing none of you went into signals work." Reggie snorted. "Miss the nose on your face, you would."

The murmured comments went on again. She couldn't quite hear them. Then she caught a bit of "Who'd go to bed with her, anyway?"

"I've a fair idea what you all get up to, and some of who. And I've got to say, your tastes are questionable. Me, I've found a good time with a number of people. It's all about their attitude and interest if you don't have a specific thing that gets you going." He then hesitated, just a beat. "Besides, I've heard the stories about crafters being good with their hands. Must be some truth there." It was ambiguous, but cheerfully so.

The conversation turned sideways from there. One of the bright young men asked a question about something work related. That turned into a laugh, a round of it, and Lynet took the cover of the sound to go back upstairs.

Reggie didn't come back for another ten minutes, at which point Lynet was pacing back and forth along the length of the workroom. He nudged the door open.

"Needed a basket. Got one of the errand boys to run out for our lunch."

"You were - downstairs." Lynet turned and faced him.

"I think that went really rather well." Reggie said, entirely cheerful. "We'll have to see how it plays out. And you let me know, or do what you need to, if any of them give you trouble. Think you're fair game. I can be your knight in somewhat battered armour without admitting to what we might have done in private, and I think I made that clear. How much did you hear?"

"From you telling them about Papa to the bit about crafters and their hands." Her voice cracked just for a moment at that, and she turned away.

"Hey. Your hands were most excellent. And I hope to explore that more sometime. When we get a chance in private."

Lynet nodded, feeling herself flushing now. "So, what do we do now?"

"Now, we let them gossip. We get on with our work, and we let them pass the word over luncheon. And about, oh, two in the afternoon, how about you go down and see if you can get anywhere on the requisition forms, and I'll go chat with Ellis and lurk if you need to yell about anything."

She peered at him, then moved to perch on the work-bench again, her feet swinging. It at least gave her a slight height advantage. "You think that will work?"

"I think it will be informative. And we can use that to make more decisions."

Lynet frowned, leaning forward to peer at him. Reggie shifted, so he was standing, waiting. Not quite like a soldier in whatever formal posture they used, but something like that. "You're different."

He nodded. "I am."

"Because we...." Lynet let her voice trail off.

"That helped." Reggie considered. "You know I'll be honest with you, as much as I can be? As much as I know how to be?"

She did, and she nodded. He had been all along, even when she hadn't been able to trust any of it.

"I feel like I was drowning, and now I have my feet under me. I can make a plan, and think about seeing it through. It's - last night was a great help. Feeling like we were doing it together. And downstairs, that's more of it. I want to find out what's going on, and how we can fix it. I want to make sure you have what you need to do something brilliant. I want - well. I want things again. Like someone had turned on a light."

"I'm not your salvation." She wanted no part of that. It seemed like a tremendous amount of effort, and too much weight to carry. She was done with that, she'd been done with that before Papa had died, if she were honest with herself.

He took a half-step back, grimacing as he caught his foot wrong. "Not like that." He turned and found a stool to perch on himself. "You're not responsible for me. Except in whatever ways you might direct an assistant. We both have some idea how apprenticeship goes, and this isn't that, but it's not as far off as all that."

Lynet nodded judiciously.

"But I felt like myself, last night, for the first time since..." His hand swept down to his foot, then back up. "And I still do. It shook something loose. And I'll be grateful for that, whatever else happens. Honesty, again."

She found it uncomfortable, the gratitude. But she couldn't actually argue with it. She looked off, toward the door, beyond his shoulder, trying to figure out what to say. "I feel different, too. I'm not sure what to do with that."

"How about we see about binding some books, and you can investigate later, see how things are?"

It did, in fact, keep them busy until she needed more beeswax. Properly prepared beeswax. "Suppose I'd best see what happens."

Reggie nodded. "I'll go see if there's anything for a mid-afternoon tea break."

Lynet went down, step by step, doing her best to be calm and confident. It was all an act, but if they couldn't read her well before, maybe that much would still be true. She turned right to check with Master Brand's secretary. "Can I get the key for the supplies room?"

Miss Bell looked up, then glanced at the office. "Master Brand is out for the rest of the afternoon. A meeting some-where." She gestured. "Let me."

Lynet wasn't sure what to do with this, but she nodded, waiting for the door to be unlocked. Somewhat to her surprise, Miss Bell closed the door. "They were, pardon, mistress, talking earlier. The men."

"They often are?" Lynet wasn't sure how one responded to that. "About what Reggie said earlier?"

"Ma'am." It was very polite. "Captain Hollis was very clear about some things." She hesitated. "No one's been sure what to make of you, mistress. But I realised no one's actually asked you, either."

That was accurate enough. Lynet shrugged. "No. And no one has yet, either. Not to me."

That made Miss Bell half-laugh, awkwardly. "Um. Yes. Pardon. First, I'm sorry I wasn't more help earlier. I was taking my cues from..." She gestured at the hallway.

Really, Lynet understood how that went. "They're the

ones you report to. That only makes sense." It would be foolish for her to blame someone else for doing what Lynet had been doing, trying to keep her head down and get her work done. "It has to be a challenge, balancing all the different things people need."

Miss Bell bobbed her head. "Exactly. And Master Brand is very demanding. It's an honour to be working here, to be helping with the war effort like this, something that matters. But he's not very good at explaining things, sometimes. You wanted the beeswax, right?"

"I did. And I wanted to check about the requisition orders for the herbs."

"Oh, I have that list. I was going through it just now, checking everything is in order." She glanced up. "It's - the problem, Mistress, is that some of the other projects need the same things. Only they're not nearly as well-organised about their requests, and he's given their projects priority." It came out quickly, as if she were nervous about something, or felt she was giving away a secret Brand would not want shared. "I'm not always sure why."

Lynet nodded. "I wouldn't ask you to tell me things I'm not supposed to know, anyway." For one thing, it wasn't like Lynet could trust that information. Everything Miss Bell said was supporting Reggie's theories, but that didn't mean it was entirely accurate. "But could you tell me, in the future, if there's anything I need, different forms, or if I need to do something different for your records?"

"Oh, I can manage that. Your forms really are quite good. Most people I have to fix a lot of things before they go off." Something in that had relaxed her. "Um. First, I'm sorry about your father. I knew, and I didn't say anything. Because I processed the leave paperwork. It must be hard."

That had a note of honesty to it, at least. "Thank you. It

is, even if he'd been ill for a while, we had some warning." There were other things she might have said, but not to someone who was still, fundamentally, a stranger.

"And do you mind a question? About Captain Hollis?"

"Reggie? Go ahead and ask?"

"Is, pardon, do you know if Captain Hollis is seeing anyone?"

Lynet felt as if this conversation were getting away from her, faster by the minute. She took a breath, trying to think about how Reggie would go at it. Then she hit on something that should do.

"I'd not want to speak for him, but I believe he'd say so." At least if their conversation this morning continued along similar lines next time they got a chance to talk. "But I know he knows some other people stationed here. Wasn't there a dance on Friday, keeping up morale, and all that? You could ask if he knows anyone who's going."

"Oh! That's very kind. Do you think he'd mind me asking?" That line of conversation kept on while Lynet got her beeswax and a few other small things. When she retreated back upstairs, Miss Bell was looking rather pleased with her corner of the world.

CHAPTER 32

The world went along, more or less, for more than a fortnight. Which was to say, the news reported on a number of items. The first American troops began fighting in France, the German chancellor was forced to resign, and the British royal family changed their last name. There was a significant win in battle against the Ottomans, and a significant loss.

Someone in America somehow had the wherewithal to launch a new set of prizes in journalism, arts, and letters. One of the first had gone to three daughters writing about their mother. None of that particularly interested Reggie, except in the hopes it might bring an end to the War. That seemed more plausibly possible about the American army and the change in chancellor, rather than the other two, particularly seeing as how the battles probably came out at neutral.

Reggie had spent two more nights with Lynet in the flat in London, and two days there, helping her sort through the books. It went faster with two people. She sorted through the books, and he took down notes, so she didn't have to flip back and forth between the book and her notepad. The first Sunday, he'd helped her move her things from the Guard barracks into a room in a boarding house. Smaller than his own, but it was pleasantly managed, and he thought she looked happier there.

The time with her, helping, had been a pleasure. It had been a lot of companionable working in tandem, in a way Reggie was growing to love. The evenings, once they went to bed, had been even better. He'd had a long dry spell of it, and hers had almost certainly been longer. Now they were getting past the first urgent rush of exploration, and just beginning to settle into learning more about what the other liked.

The project, though, that was near enough in stasis for the moment. The materia they needed was still working its way through the drying process, or being made into tinctures. They couldn't make much forward progress without it. Or rather, they tried, but all the alternative combinations they attempted failed miserably. Lynet made her reports, Reggie went with her, and Master Brand didn't yell at her more.

Reggie had gone out for drinks with several of the chaps downstairs one night, and he'd been pleasant. One of them, Madsen, had asked him about why Lynet was in a better mood these days. Reggie had thought about that in advance, both what was helping and what he wanted to say about it. Privately, he thought bedding her - or rather them bedding each other, which was much more how it was - hadn't hurt. It had certainly been good for him. But it wasn't what had changed.

"Feeling as if I'm on side with her." He shrugged. "That

I take her work seriously, that someone does. Which I do, and Ellis does. And she wasn't eating well for a bit in there. Grief does that." Grief, and not nearly enough money, and worries over debts, but he could at least keep showing up with food, and did. He shrugged. "I'm not from a crafting family, you all know that. But I understand enough of what they need to do what they do, right? The supports."

He'd hoped to work it around to a conversation about the materia, but Madsen wasn't biting, and neither were the others. "And she's not awful to you?"

"Some of us pay attention to what we're told and do good work." Reggie flicked a finger at that. "I know what you were like in school, trying to find the easy way out." It made the others laugh. When that quieted down, Reggie shrugged. "We get on well together. People do, sometimes. And it's easier here than in the trenches. My standards changed a fair bit, y'know?"

That got the lot of them onto some cautious questions about that, what Reggie's experiences had been like. It still wasn't clear to them why most of this lot weren't there. Ellis had a reason, Reggie did now, and probably a few of the men at this table did as well. But all of them? There was likely some bribery in there, or something of the kind. Reggie did not approve.

Talking about it was easier, though. His foot had healed up well enough. It hadn't hurt much since the third day after the door. Something about dealing with it, about having it be a thing he had to pay active attention to again, had eased up a clenching Reggie hadn't realised he was doing.

Something about telling Lynet was probably it. He'd been protecting himself from the pain of talking about his foolishness, perhaps, when he hadn't been able to protect himself from harm in the first place. He still wasn't going to tell anyone else what he'd done, how it was quite arguably his own fault. But it didn't ache in the pit of his stomach as much.

All in all, he was feeling pretty good about how things were going when he went down to get something from the mail room on Wednesday afternoon. He was there sorting through notices in their cubby - he was looking for the requisition forms - when he heard, "There you are, Reggie!"

Margot, naturally, this time dressed in an entirely sunny golden yellow dress. "Come out to supper with me tonight, do? My plans cancelled on me, and I'll be so bored."

Reggie hesitated. He did not, in fact, have plans other than the library, but he'd been looking forward to that, and a bit of quiet to get his head around things. He hoped to see Lynet on Saturday, but she'd not been decisive about it, and he didn't want to press her. That wouldn't do at all.

"Come on, do you have somewhere you need to be? A demanding aunt or something of the kind?" Margot tapped the toe of her shoe, and it echoed a bit on the floor, a thump against the boards.

"Not on a Wednesday, no." He tilted his head. "Where did you have in mind? I'm not dressed for Vane's in the evening hours."

She twitched a shoulder up. "The Stream, if you like. Or I suppose I could go slum at your Cave." Clearly she was required by some personal code of honour to have an opinion about the relative merits of their respective house clubs. "Or I could put in for a private room at Wishton's." None of those were precisely ideal choices, but Wishton's was probably the best of the lot, considering.

"Wishton's. I might wander home and change, mind, a tidier jacket. Six? Or do you prefer a little later?"

"Let's say seven, darling. Still a trifle early, but we do have to keep working hours, don't we. I should slip into something for the evening."

Reggie nodded, and she at least released him from that conversation. He went back upstairs, and half-confessed to Lynet that he apparently was going out to supper with Margot. Lynet blinked at him several times.

"Don't you want to go? You could have said no."

"Society women don't work like that." Reggie held up his hands. "I don't know. Maybe she'll say something useful. Walk you back to your room? I said I'd go change first." He hesitated. "I could take you out somewhere, in London, or here. If you liked."

That was too much, and he realised it as soon as the words were out of his mouth. He coughed. "I'll go check on things with Ellis." By the time he'd gone and done that, and come back an hour later, she'd gathered herself again. Lynet was entirely pleasant, even teasing him, as he walked her out, but Reggie wasn't at all sure how she actually felt about it.

He was unsurprised, however, when Margot came up to the private room she'd arranged, wearing a stunningly modish frock. It was not actually scandalously short, if he counted the layer of largely opaque whatever-you-called-it that ran from knees to ankles, and down to the middle of the forearms. But it was a bright teal, with bands of golden yellow. He found it garishly bright, really, but Margot was at least consistent about such things.

"There we are, such a delight. And I do find this room charming. Have you been before?"

"My father's a member here, as well as Bourne's." Reggie shrugged. "I haven't kept it up, during the War, of course."

"Do you go to the Arthur, then?" Margot settled in her chair, sipping a cocktail.

The ensuing small talk kept them going through a cocktail, through ordering their meals, and through the first course. It was only when they got into the second that Margot turned the subject. "Mistress Alder seems in rather better spirits. You do know there's a pool about it. Whether you've been showing her a good time."

Reggie had also prepared for this. "Not something I'd talk about if I were." He shrugged. "Pater's a bit of an old-fashioned gentleman, and Mater's, well, I'm sure she's been bedded at least five times, but she'd never admit it. Children are properly found under cabbage leaves, and all that."

"Four siblings, then?" Margot leaned back, not focused on eating now.

"Three sisters living, a brother who died just after he was born." Reggie didn't usually get into that. How in a different world he'd have had an older brother, who - who might have several things. It was at least a diversion from Lynet, or so he thought.

Margot, of course, had a different idea. "It was good to see you enjoying Hawk's Breath. And we didn't have any time to chat, did we? So many people there last time, really quite grand, and you see how well they do the thing. Do you think Mistress Alder would come next time? August third through the fifth, go up Friday after work, come back to town Sunday evening."

Reggie blinked. Not at all what he'd expected, and he was immediately suspicious about why they were inviting her now. "I can't speak for her, of course. I'd be glad to see what she thinks? She's still seeing to various matters relating to her father's death, of course. It's hard when she's working in Trellech all week."

"It might do her some good to, well, have a bit of fun. And we can help that along, certainly. Besides, I gather she's been a little less..." Margot made a face, pinched and sour. She had, in fact, a certain gift for it, the sort that couldn't ever come with kindness, but which made him appreciate the raw skill, just a little.

"She has had fair reason. Her father, dealing with his business, setting aside all her own work there for the project. And we've had such a time with the materia requests. Not a lot of reason for her to be in a good mood."

"But she clearly responds to you. Or something you're doing. And I find that fascinating, honestly. For several reasons." Margot traced a finger along the table for a moment, the sort of touch that might just as easily be applied to a body. "And you're not particularly interested in me, are you? I find that even more intriguing."

Reggie spread his hands. "You are stunning, Margot, and you know it." No reason not to be honest. "But I'm also quite clear who you're in bed with on the regular, and I'm not in that league at all. I'll talk to Lynet about the invitation, though it would help to hear it from Lord Carillon."

"Oh, Temple would be glad. He's interested in you, as well. And he does take an interest in the books. So much of that was his idea, the underlying what do you call it, schema."

Reggie was entirely sure Margot had the proper terminology ready to deploy, and that she'd known it since she was a child. But he didn't press the point. "I'll ask. I'm sure she doesn't have the right sort of frocks and things, though. I might need to see if I could borrow a few things from my sisters."

"Oh, I'm sure we can sort something out. Delphina has some things she doesn't wear, not bright colours. The poor dear is in mourning, I suppose. Lavenders and mauves and all that, or there's a silvery grey, a muted one, that might do well." Margot clearly had an answer to all problems of that kind. Reggie had no idea what Lynet would think of that kind of clothing, but he could only put the question to her.

"And, of course, it's such a good opportunity for informal collaboration. There are a few things we'd like to ask you about. Over drinkies. Or out on the lawn, or perhaps a little boat on the lake. Quite private, intimate... And of course, maybe you'll change your mind and join us on our little project, sooner than later." She ran her finger along the glass now, against the rim, and Reggie almost expected it to sing out, though it didn't quite.

"If that's how the game is played." He hadn't planned to say that, but it made Margot grin broadly, a satisfied smile, and that was information he definitely wanted to take back to Lynet.

CHAPTER 33

"An invitation to what?" Lynet managed not to shout it - that would have not done anyone any good. Reggie had waited until they were out on the bench at lunch. It was at least a pleasant day, but there was no one very near them in the small park.

"Lord Carillon left a note in my box. I checked on the way out. One for you too, I assume it says much the same?" Reggie handed over a square envelope, the size that would hold a card. It was sealed with a bit of deep purple wax and what must be some sort of heraldry, but had mostly come across as smudged dots on a shield. Four somethings.

Reggie silently handed over a penknife, and she worked the wax loose, handing it back without looking at him as she worked the card loose. Inside was a beautifully written invitation, in a woman's hand. It invited her to join Reggie at a gathering from the third through the fifth, and noting that they'd be glad to arrange suitable clothing. That they understood she was still in mourning, and of course her work for the war effort meant she wouldn't have put together a suitable wardrobe. It was signed Delphina Carillon, with a signature below from Temple Carillon, in a much bolder nibbed pen.

She silently handed it over to Reggie, who skimmed through it. "Fast work." His voice was carefully neutral. "I mentioned I wasn't sure if you had the right sort of frocks and things. Between being in mourning and being busy dealing with your father's affairs when you're not here."

"That's why the loan." Lynet wasn't sure what she felt about that. "And she just offered?"

"Well, I said my sisters might have something, which they likely do. And Margot thought Lady Delphina would have something." He added after a moment. "She's about your size, and I'm sure they have a maid who's good with fitting charms, a place that big. With that many parties, they must have someone on staff."

"Staff." Lynet felt like she'd bit into a lemon, all sour. "I don't even know how to be somewhere with staff."

Reggie leaned back. "You do, actually. Not somewhere with that many. But when you were in the Guard barracks, there's someone cooking, and someone cleaning the halls, and seeing to your laundry, right? And now you've got the landlady, and she makes the meals and sends the laundry out, I suspect, and so on? A big house, one of the stately homes, it has more people, and the food's certainly fussier and fancier, and the rooms are bigger."

Lynet wanted to argue with that, rather a lot, but the logic was sound. "But that's different from a maid."

"You go to a dressmaker, yes?" Reggie leaned back.

"You think we should go. Both of us. Me." Lynet still wasn't at all sure what she thought.

"They'll likely be sure we're - well. Seeing each other. If

we do. But you'd save me from having to duck out of things with other women there. I'd have an excuse to keep an eye out for you. And who knows, someone might share something useful."

Lynet hesitated. "What, are there implications, if they think we are?"

"There's already a betting pool, I gather. Margot said as much last night. And that you're clearly in a much better mood. I pointed out you had been quite busy, and she didn't argue, mind."

She looked off across the grass without saying anything. She could hear Reggie unwrapping the lunch boxes, setting one on the bench beside her. "Eat while you're thinking?"

Lynet snorted, but reached for her sandwich, which was a pleasantly solid ham and sharp cheddar, with a mustard that held up its end of the flavour. He somehow always knew what she was likely to want, something more potent or something lighter.

"What happens at these parties? Or rather, why on earth would I want to go? You know they'll just point out all the ways I'm not like them."

"Good thing, too. I certainly don't want to go to bed with any of that lot. Even if Margot's made it very clear she'd be willing."

Lynet twisted quickly to peer at him. "And you turned her down?"

"First, she's not you. Second through, oh, at least a thousand, she's still not you. Whatever number after that, she wants things, and I think not getting them is probably good for her. Builds character. And also, not sure where this one actually falls, but I'm not actually a fan of adultery, even if it's technically within agreements."

There was quite a lot in those sentences to contend with. The idea that he thought her better than Margot, in any dimension, was baffling. But he was entirely in earnest about it. She knew what honesty looked like on him. She knew that quite well by now. And here he was, looking at her with steady eyes, not quite touching her. He wouldn't, unless she were clear it was welcome.

"How do you expect me to know where to start with that?" It came out edged, and she regretted that. He didn't deserve it, not really. He'd been trying to figure out a solution to their problems. Some of that involved figuring out what all these people, far more like him in some ways, were up to.

"Pick a bit, and we'll work our way through?" Reggie wasn't teasing, not exactly, but he wasn't anxious about this. He was at ease with whatever she wanted to ask, clearly.

"The adultery?" Lynet hesitated, but that seemed a logical place to start.

"Well, Lord Temple is married to Lady Delphina. And they get on reasonably well, from what I've seen. She's beautiful, the sort of English rose beauty, that's the phrase for it? Dresses well, moves like she's sure of her place. Her health's a little delicate, I gather, though not because of children, at least not any living ones."

"How do you know that?"

"I checked the Gold Book, of course. It's Geoffrey Carillon who's Lord Temple's Heir, at the moment, as the younger brother. Lord Temple and Lady Delphina have been married, fifteen years or so?" He shrugged once. "Anyway. Margot's married, too. Her husband's off in France. I gather they were an arranged match, amiable enough. I found some news pieces about them, before the War, the

263

usual sort of philanthropic things. Temple of Healing, some other fundraising for Ministry projects. He's got a reputation for being harsh."

"But you just don't care for adultery." Lynet frowned. "But you're talking like it's not that uncommon."

"It's not. I mean, it's not uncommon in Southwark, either. Just less of it happening at house parties where people sneak into other people's bedrooms in the night, and back out before the maid comes to light the fires. The trick is not running into the wrong people in the hall."

Lynet found the image hilarious, actually, all those posh men and women scurrying about in the early dawn light. "There are music hall songs about that kind of thing. The ways it can go wrong, and be funny."

He nodded. "It's a bit like that, when it's going well enough. Sometimes people are awful. And - there's a chance the invitation's so they can, y'know. See if they can get you to talk. But I know the ways to check drinks for potions. I can teach you. And..."

"And you think we should do this." She realised after she said it that she'd said 'we'. Though admittedly, the invitation was for both of them.

He half-smiled. "I like being we. For the record. Even if it's a bit wrong, with me working for you."

"Well, it's not as if there's several of you helping, and I could be accused of favouritism, is it? That was always the trick with apprenticing. And it's not as if I'm the one who actually hired you, or keeps you on. Seeing as it was made very clear to me I didn't have a lot of say in that."

"You don't mind?" Reggie looked uncertain for a moment, and she wanted to kiss him and reassure him. Where that had come from, she wasn't sure, but she was certain of what she felt.

Lynet compromised by reaching for his hand and squeezing it. "I'm very glad of you. And your help. But that it's you, in particular." She coughed. "And on the more personal side, even if I suspect I'm being difficult sometimes."

"Whatever time I might get is delightful, and you have, as I've already said once this lunch, have plenty of things that are keeping you quite busy. I'd be a lousy friend, whatever else, if I made that worse, wouldn't I?"

"Most people wouldn't think about it like that." The comment popped out of her without her thinking about it.

He shrugged, still looking at her. "I keep telling you, I left things with my toes. I want to be better than that." He let out a puff of breath. "I admit, I want to show them all what it looks like, to be with someone you care about, to be attentive to someone else, those ways."

"I suspect it's going to make Margot even more interested in you, not less." Lynet wasn't entirely sure what she thought about that, but she had to assume Reggie was up to dealing with it. He'd done well enough so far.

"She'll have to live with disappointment." Reggie seemed entirely comfortable with that. What it meant.

Lynet hesitated. "You really aren't interested in her?"

"Not one bit. I mean, aesthetically, she's a type, certainly. And I'm sure she knows a number of erotically charged things to do in bed. But that is not what I'm looking for. I love your stubbornness. Your determination to keep going, even when things are hard and heavy. I'm not sure what I'd do with someone who didn't understand that. I think she folds, most of the time, when something is too much, and she finds some other target. You don't."

It was the first time he'd said that word; she was sure of it. Love. It spun out through Lynet's head for a moment.

The rest of it, she wanted to argue about, and she couldn't. At least, she couldn't think of anything at the moment. "But she's - she's fashionable, and rich, and..."

"And married." Reggie shrugged. "I'm being flip, but the clothes come off. The money doesn't matter much to me, I have money. I don't need more." He must have caught something in her expression, because he went on quickly. "And I know that's very different for you, and sometime we should probably talk about that. But I've got plenty for my needs and wants, and for your needs and wants too, if you're willing to let me help with that at any point. Beyond sandwiches."

Lynet glanced at the boxes. "That's - nothing for you?"

"Think of it like a cup of tea is for you, maybe. There's a finite number you're going to drink in a day, but you're probably not limiting it too much by cost, if you're not drinking fancy tea. You just go make tea." His voice trailed off. "Or maybe having pen and paper. You might count it up, you might use up what you have as scrap paper, but you always have enough around in some form."

"Pen and paper." She echoed him, then nodded. "I don't know how that works when it's money. We always had to count our coins, even when Papa was doing well. You've, well. You've seen."

"Enough, yes." His voice was very gentle now. "Anyway. I'm not looking for money. I'm looking for decency and caring about the work, and being an expert at what you do. And also, because it is also true, and it also matters, how much I enjoy time with you. In bed, and out of bed, like this, and when we're more private, or when we're working together. I hope that's clear?"

He fell silent then, and Lynet couldn't look at him for a long moment. Finally, she met his eyes and cleared her throat. "I don't know what I'd do without you now. Not anymore. I don't know what to do with that." She couldn't say she loved him back, not right in the moment, but she could be clear about that much.

His eyes lit up. "That's quite a lot to be going on with. Gives me a great deal of hope, you know. What do we do now? Besides accept the invitation? We might learn something. And who knows, you might enjoy some of it, and then I could see about arranging more of the things you like."

That made her laugh, the hopefulness in his voice. He seemed certain he wanted her to have good things, to shower her with gifts, if she only permitted. She couldn't tell him yes, yet. Not about that. But she could smile and nod. "Accept the invitation. Help me sort out clothing, and what to expect." She swallowed. "And come spend Friday and Saturday night with me this week?"

"Of course." He leaned over and kissed her on the cheek, before settling into a far less provocative conversation about something he'd read last night, after his supper out.

CHAPTER 34

"Goodness, are you working all alone up here? How diligent of you. It's a beautiful afternoon. Half of them are gone off for the day already downstairs." Lynet wheeled around to see Mistress Williams leaning against the door frame. Lynet had been working on cutting bookcloth, and she carefully set the knife and carpenter's square she'd been using aside, where she couldn't knock into it immediately.

"Pardon, let me wash my hands first." It would give Lynet a moment to catch up. She had never expected to see someone like Mistress Williams up here. Lynet washed her hands carefully. She didn't want to transfer any dye to clean paper. Or anything else. "May I help you, Mistress Williams?"

"Oh, pish, none of that. Margot, please. And you shall be Lynet to me, of course." That last was an unalterable fact of the universe, apparently, not something Lynet got any say in. She took a step in, then stopped, almost like a villain in a melodrama, though those were generally men. Lynet was baffled, utterly unsure what to do with this. And Reggie would not be any help, he'd gone off to sort through materia with Ellis. "A chair?"

"We're not much for chairs here, more stools." Well, now Lynet was babbling, that was no good, but she came around to grab the chair from the desk, then leaned against the worktable behind her. "Can I help you with something?"

"You can, yes." Margot said it with a purr in her voice. Lynet wondered, suddenly, if she sounded like that all the time. When she was, oh, jostled in the line for the portals, or buying a pastry, or paying a porter. Whatever it was she did when she wasn't lurking in hallways being a fashion plate. "I'm just so intrigued that you're coming along to Hawk's Breath in a week. You must be full of questions about what to expect. And we're quite a fast set, honestly."

Lynet felt that 'full of questions' was entirely the wrong phrase. Full of dread was closer, not that she was going to admit that. She considered her words carefully. "It's rather new to me, I admit. I went straight from Alethorpe to apprenticing and helping my father. And unlike some apprenticeships, bookbinding isn't really seasonal, though of course there were things like a holiday rush. Six days a week in the shop, the seventh getting ready for the next week. Not a lot of time for parties, really."

Margot shook her head just enough to make her earrings dance. "Oh. My." It sounded, for a moment, almost unsettled. "Quite unlike anything I know, really." She cocked her head sideways, uncomfortably like a bird of prey considering a field. "How quaint."

Quaint wasn't the word. It was how most people lived, day in, day out. Lynet just shrugged. "It's very kind of the Carillons to invite me." That should be a safe enough statement, surely.

"Oh, darling." Margot laughed, the sound echoing in the room. "That was my doing. Or at least my thumb on the scale."

Lynet blinked several times, unable to hide her confusion. "Beg pardon?" Margot surely couldn't read minds, but Lynet could only assume she'd see Lynet's reactions laid something like Great Primer or even Paragon, eighteen or twenty point, or more. Easily read, quite some distance away. Though maybe she wasn't shouting it like a headline in seventy-two point.

"Well, darling." Margot looked her up and down. "Reggie's quite taken with you. However did you do it?"

It wasn't as if Lynet had any idea how she'd done anything here. With Reggie. Or, rather, she had been there for it. Of course she had some clue. But it wasn't at all clear what had led to what, and certainly she wasn't going to lay it out for Margot. The young men of the first floor had called Lynet names. What had Margot done, when she thought it didn't matter, except for her own amusement?

Something must have caught Margot's attention in Lynet's expression, because Margot laughed. "My, you do have some fire to you. None of the men saw it, you know. You do know…" Her voice trailed off delicately.

"I'm clear I'm not their sort of person." Lynet managed to say it without gritting her teeth, and counted that a victory.

"Darling, men have the oddest ideas about who their sort of person is." Margot glanced behind her, at the door open to the hallway, then flicked her fingers, and the door closed with an audible click. "There, nicely private. Men, dearest sweet child, want to be told things. They want someone else to decide things for them, but you simply must let it look like they made all the choices. But when you do that?" She snapped her fingers. "Everything you might want, on a plate."

Lynet was entirely sure that wasn't on offer to her, and she was equally sure she didn't want it to be. It sounded awful, frankly. From both sides, though worse for the men. She glanced away, unable to hide her discomfort. "Oh?"

"You are such an innocent, aren't you? How novel! Well, the party will give you a grand chance to see how good it can be. Now, Temple, ridiculous fool he can be, he is actually fond of Delphina. It's very sweet of them, really. And she dotes on him. That's not good for him, of course."

Lynet couldn't begin to untangle that, and gave up trying. "Beg pardon?"

Margot laughed. "Ah, well. Whatever it is you're doing, you've got Reggie wound round your little finger. Quite compelling, really. He wouldn't even look at me, darling, and there aren't so many men who manage that. But being doted on spoils a man terribly."

It was an interesting question. Lynet was clear, at this point, that Margot was having an affair with Lord Carillon. But surely, one did not bring that up in conversation. Not that it made it easier to say anything now. "What makes you say that? I appreciate his work."

"I hope you appreciate quite a lot else about him. Though I suppose all these - bits of paper and things you have." She waved a hand, her rings glittering in the light. "You'd get to see him using those scrumptious shoulders over and over again. I could watch that all day."

Lynet had a burst of what must be jealousy. It certainly

fit every description she'd ever read, but she'd only felt it professionally before. People who had opportunities she wasn't offered. And that felt different, somehow. Less personal. "He's turned out to be quite good at the work."

"And so dedicated. We've tried to lure him away, several times, to other projects. We could use his gift with materia, honestly. Temple's quite good, really, far better than I'd expected, but he can't be everywhere. He does have other things he needs to be doing." Lynet had a sudden flash of certainty that some of that doing involved keeping Margot happy in specific ways, details she did not want to think about.

Margot sailed on, ignoring the implications entirely. "And he doesn't gape. So tedious, being gaped at." Margot's fingers flicked up. "Though I suppose you might not be bored by it." There, that was the sort of insult Lynet had expected out of this woman. What was more startling was that there were, so far, few of those. Considering.

Lynet shrugged. "He's said he likes the work here. And he's glad to be helping." She heard the steps on the stair, then raised her chin slightly. "He'll be back in a minute."

"Ah, well. I would be glad to give you a teensy bit of advice here or there once you're at Hawk's Breath. So you don't pick up any - hmm. Any habits that would limit your options." That, now, wasn't an insult. It sounded more like a threat. Margot stood in a sweep of skirts that were ostentatious in their amount of fabric, given the War, and opened the door, right as Reggie tried the door.

When the door opened, Lynet caught his look of surprise, which was quickly muted. "Margot. Did you need something from up here?"

"Just a tiny little chat with Lynet. So charming." Then Margot was gone, her heels clicking down the stairs.

Lynet waited until they had entirely faded, counted another ten seconds out, then cleared her throat. "Would you close the door behind you? We don't want a draught."

Reggie did as she'd asked, then came over. "Are you all right? Was she - well, no. She was rude. Was she rude in particularly painful ways?"

"She was actually rather less rude than I expected, actually?" Lynet considered the conversation. "But she made it clear that it was - what was it she said? Her thumb on the scale, for me to be invited. And that Lord Carillon is very much inclined to do as she asks."

"Margot's got him entirely wrapped up in her. Whatever she'd like." Reggie hesitated. "I'm sorry I was so long. I wanted to take the chance to look at the supplies room again. They're low on half a dozen things I was sure we had plenty of, just earlier this week. And what's there is the worse quality stuff."

"How are we on it?"

"I had the good sense to take what we'd requisitioned to Ellis when it came in. Or up here." But they'd talked about that. The storage up here was a little more precarious, both in terms of possible access, and in terms of the preservation charms. Ellis's building, between having its own walls and being on the ground floor, took some of the preservations better, as well as the protections.

Lynet let out a long breath. "All right. That's what matters. Not the ..." She grimaced. "She scares me. Margot."

"Well, she should. She's terrifying. Competent, sharp, up to at least six things before breakfast she shouldn't be. Well, except that I'm fairly sure she doesn't actually rise early, or at least admit to it. That kind of cosmetics takes time to apply. And she's never less than perfect when she might be seen." Reggie leaned against the wall. "Whatever she gets up to with Temple, it's either entirely private, or designed so that not a hair on her head gets out of place."

"Reggie!" Lynet couldn't decide whether she should be scandalised. "Really?"

"I gather there are quite a few options, but I admit, that sort of arm's length business has never appealed. If you're going to be close to someone, be close."

"She wants the - I don't know if it's power or manipulation or to get her own way or what." Lynet said. "She doesn't want close. She likes playing with him. Maybe even because he's a Lord."

"More fool her." Reggie then grinned broadly. "I am not that kind of fool. May I come by tomorrow?"

Lynet considered. "You had something tonight?" She felt, all of a sudden, like she could rather use the company, but she wasn't going to press.

"I was going to get drinks with someone. Maybe get a bit of information about the materia, I don't know. What else it might be used for, a couple of things. I don't expect much to come of it, but I'd like to try." Reggie spread his hands, and Lynet was taken, suddenly, with his openness about it. Entirely unlike Margot and the rest of the downstairs mysteries and snares.

"Would you come to London after that? Whatever time you're done?" She hadn't asked before, not with that sense of need, but that's what she felt.

"Of course. I'll write in the journal when I'm on the way, so you have an idea when to expect me." He hesitated. "You might work on one of your own projects, for a bit? It would do you good. A bit of colour."

Lynet shrugged. "Margot took up all the colour in the room. It'll take me a bit."

"Well, that's no good. You definitely should. Marbled papers, leather tooling, gorgeous inks. All three, if you like."

His indignation made her smile. "I'll see."

CHAPTER 35

Reggie was not at all sure this house party was a good idea. He'd arranged to borrow a few frocks from his sister, in case whatever Lady Delphina came up with was too much. And some light shawls and such that might give a bit more coverage, if the frocks on offer were the sort that bared a lot of skin. Also four pairs of shoes, after Reggie had sorted out what might fit from his knowledge of Lynet's feet. He'd given her a foot rub last week, after their long Friday. It had given him a chance to get a sense of how her feet measured against his hands, at least.

Edith had also suggested - and provided - a number of other small items. Hair combs and a couple of simple semi-precious stones in settings, and some cosmetics, all without commentary. He had rather flung himself on Edith's sympathies. She'd taken his explanation as true - well, it was. That he and Lynet, the woman in charge of the project he was working on, were invited to a house party. And that she was from an established crafting family, not kitted out for that sort of thing.

"You could always claim a horrible headache and take to your room for the duration." He offered it carefully. Lynet was walking beside him as they walked from the portal to the house. They were a bit back from most of the others who were getting into the spirit of the party already. Or rather, had probably started drinking by three, the way the tipsiness was coming through.

"After all the bother? No. I'll muddle through." Lynet seemed resolute, with no sign of nerves, though Reggie wasn't at all sure what she actually felt about the thing. Except that she was here.

Lady Delphina was waiting just inside in the foyer. She'd smiled and waved the others through, with staff to take the cases up, but she was clearly waiting for them. "Mistress Alder. So good to have you join us. And Reggie, so good to see you again. Mistress Alder - may we be informal? Only if you'd prefer, of course, I'm Delphina, or use the title if you'd rather. My lady's maid, Rodworth, is waiting for us upstairs. Do, please, come along." She offered her arm to Lynet, who glanced at Reggie.

"I'm sure Lady Delphina has things well in hand, but if you need my opinion on anything, I'm sure someone can come fetch me." Reggie did not precisely want to let Lynet go, but it was the done thing, and Lynet nodded. They'd talked a little about this, about what parts she'd have to put a brave face on.

One of the footmen escorted him upstairs. Lynet and Lady Delphina were ahead of them, turning into a room further down the hall as the footman opened the door. Not too far away, then, and he could go lurk in the hallway when he'd seen to his own things.

"Unpack for you, sir?"

"Please, yes, the larger case. I'll see to the smaller one myself." It had his writing materials, the journal - at least he and Lynet could write, and that seemed quite a lifeline at the moment. He spent a few minutes setting his personals out on the desk and the dresser. He dropped the cuff links for the evening into a small dish to keep them from rolling around. "Dressing gong at six again?"

"As usual, sir, yes. Supper at half-seven. The weather's fine, her ladyship suggested dining on the terrace. You're welcome to go out any time after the gong for a cocktail." It was half-five now, Lord Carillon had made a reservation in advance, though he hadn't been at work the past three days. Something to do with the land obligations. There had been no wait at Portal Square, of course. Had to spare everyone the tedium of waiting for even a second.

"Thank you. If someone could come by in an hour or so, for a hand with my cufflinks, that's likely all I need tonight."

"Sir, of course."

Reggie thought that, given the opportunity, he'd suggest he and Lynet go down early, and get the lay of the land. She'd like the garden, he thought, and the view, and they were far less complicated to deal with than the people. Most of all, he didn't want her navigating the space by herself. He didn't quite think Lady Carillon, in particular, would tolerate outright nastiness to a guest, but people could be unpleasant in so many ways.

He took his time changing into a clean shirt, then his waistcoat, tailcoat, and all the fittings. He was just finishing up when there was a knock on the door. "Sir?" The footman was back, with a small covered tray.

"Just ready for you." They went through the fuss of

getting the cufflinks settled, and the footman adjusting his tie, then proferring a flower from the tray. "From the garden, sir, for your lapel?" It was a rather charming single white rosebud, trimmed of its thorns.

"Thank you. Anything else to know?"

"I believe her ladyship has arranged Mistress Alder's clothing to mutual satisfaction, and Mistress Alder asked if you could go along when you were ready."

"Appreciated. I'll see Mistress Alder downstairs. We'll ring if there's anything needed."

"Sir." The footman disappeared with his tray, presumably to deliver flowers elsewhere. Reggie wondered, for a moment, if all of them were the same, if there were a variety, and if so, if there were any meaning in it. He shrugged, and went along to Lynet's room, which had her name in elegant calligraphy on a card on the door.

He knocked twice, adding, "It's Reggie."

"Come in." He opened the door to find her in a rather pleasant room, all calming shades of medium blue, without too many fripperies. There were summer flowers in a vase on the desk, the scent of them filling the room but not overwhelming the senses. Lynet was dressed to match, in a silvery blue-grey frock, darker in colour. Not black mourning dress, but on the conservative side, and a couple of years out of fashion.

She looked stunning in it, and the more so as she turned to face Reggie from where she was perched on a chair in the corner. Someone had done up her hair in a loose roll at the base of her neck, adding a couple of the silver combs Edith had sent along. She wore one of the pendants, with a pale blue stone, at her throat, and it brought out the colour of her eyes.

"I - I must look a fool."

279

Reggie made sure the door was properly closed, and took several strides across the room to go to one knee by her. "You look beautiful. Very put together, not frivolous. I wasn't sure the frocks would be right."

"The maid suggested one of the shawls and did you know your sister wrote a note about that? About how if you don't trust the company, it's safer. There's a lovely one, a pale grey, that goes wonderfully. Did you really ask her to help?"

"I did. Edith came through in spades, then?" He recognised the shoes, too.

"They fit better than the ones they had. But they did have shoes. And a dressing gown, and some night things, and day dresses. People go through a ridiculous amount of clothing, don't they?"

"Edith swears there are days she spends half her time changing clothing." He held out his hand. "I thought you might like a genteel walk in the garden before supper. We're apparently dining on the terrace, so more informally, but it would give you a chance to scout out places to escape to."

Lynet raised an eyebrow. "Do you think that's likely?"

"I think good strategy takes it into account. Shall we?" They went off, downstairs, and through the house to the terrace. No one was out there yet, other than the staff making the final arrangements. Reggie nodded and gestured. "Just taking a walk in the gardens. We'll be back in good time for drinks."

A circuit of the garden - a small one, given Lynet's shoes - took them a pleasant half hour or so. When Reggie checked his pocket watch, it was perhaps quarter after seven. As they came up the path, they heard two people on the terrace, two male voices.

"You have people here?" That was the one he didn't know.

"People from our project, a few related ones." That was Lord Temple, and Reggie gestured with his chin. Lynet nodded back, and they moved to where they could get a better view from one end of the garden hedge. That was indeed Lord Temple, his back to them, talking to another man, who looked very like him.

"His brother, must be?" Reggie leaned over to whisper it in Lynet's ear. The second man was younger, five or ten years, and he did not look well. His left arm was bound up in a sling, tightly against his chest so the shoulder wouldn't move, with his jacket draped over that arm. Behind him stood a man about the same age, but not at all related, sturdily built but not handsome, holding a suitcase. He was standing, Reggie realised, where he could offer a supportive arm if needed.

No wonder. Geoffrey Carillon looked like he was near out on his feet. He had that worrisome paleness of a man who'd had an injury far worse than he admitted to. It was the kind of pallor that made Reggie want to escort him right back to the Temple of Healing. As Reggie watched, he swayed slightly on his feet, as if gathering his thoughts meant he couldn't focus on staying upright.

A moment later, a gaggle of people burst out of the house onto the terrace, and a champagne bottle popped as someone got the cork out. Geoffrey Carillon didn't jump - not enough energy in him to do so - but he jerked and moved just in front of the man with him. It was the bone-deep flinch of someone who'd known the trenches far too well, and found the sound still made him wonder who the snipers had got now. And he'd put himself in harm's way, automatically, even when he could barely keep his own feet, for a man who was clearly not of his class.

The man behind him stepped a little closer, bringing his hand up to steady without quite touching. A curious dance, and one where the man - a valet, a batman, something of the kind - was focused solely on the younger brother.

"I see you are busy." There was something utterly defeated in that, in the younger man's words. The group of guests had spilled over onto the other end of the terrace, and Lady Delphina came out behind them. There was an expression on her face, as she closed the gap, that he was sure no one else could see, an instant worry. She immediately came to her husband's side, but she paused to kiss her brother-in-law's cheek, saying something too quiet for Reggie and Lynet to hear.

"You can stay, of course. If I'd known..." That was Lord Temple, a bit louder.

"If you'd known I'd been shot. Sorry the letter didn't make it." Geoffrey Carillon almost shrugged and stopped himself at the last moment. He'd already learned, then, just how much was attached to his shoulder, even on the other side. "I won't keep you." That was sharp.

"Ytene?" It took Reggie a moment to parse that as a name. Lord Temple's voice had a very queer tone in it now. In Latin, it would have had the enclitic, that was the word, indicating that he expected yes, for the answer, the "nonne" at the beginning of the sentence. And yet, there was something fearful in it, like he wanted any other answer.

"Yes." Just that one flat word. "Temple. Delphina, you look lovely, of course. Evening." Geoffrey Carillon didn't quite nod, but there was a jerk of his chin. He turned away, with his man following close behind him, around the side of the house, not even going back through the building.

Lord Temple held up a hand, then dropped it, before turning to speak quietly to his wife. Reggie couldn't really see either of their faces, to see what they might be feeling. If they'd let him see, which he was sure they wouldn't. As he expected, a moment later, Lord Temple turned to the party, striding over and claiming a glass and some champagne. Lady Delphina hesitated, going so far as to take a few steps as if to follow them, then catching one of the footmen and sending him on instead.

"What was that all about?" Lynet spoke quietly, against his ear.

"Nothing good. If that's Geoffrey Carillon, he looks - well, like he's been to the underworld and back, dragged through the seven hells. I suppose there's not much we can do." Reggie could write to Lapidoth Manse, he supposed, and he wished the man had a journal. He'd have to see about dropping a note to the man at his club in Trellech, and hope it would be forwarded on, in an enclosing envelope. He had no idea how much the staff here might report to their employers, and he knew someone in Manse's position wouldn't appreciate having any attention drawn to him.

"Shall we find a place down at the end of the table? Begin introducing you to a few folks?"

"We must, mustn't we?" Lynet took a deep breath and let it out. "You're sure I can do this?"

"I'm certain it's easier than going to war."

CHAPTER 36

SATURDAY, AT HAWK'S BREATH

Lynet was not at all sure what she thought of house parties, either in general or in specific. Friday evening had seemed to involve a fair bit of drinking for most, as well as people passing around little potion vials or tiny pill cases full of unnamed substances. Reggie had refused everything but a few glasses of wine and champagne, about as much as he'd drink in beer, the nights he'd stayed with her. Lynet drank less than that. She needed her wits about her.

The other women were not exactly welcoming, but they were not as nasty as Lynet had feared. Mostly, they talked over her, about people and places she knew nothing about. This modiste, that jeweller, this perfumer, how of course the War limited things, but not as much as all that. A few of the crafters were people Lynet knew. Two directly, half a dozen by reputation. She tucked the commentary away, in case it would be useful later.

All in all, the War seemed to have touched all of them

lightly. Most of the women had some man in their lives serving overseas, whether it was a husband or fiancé or brother or cousin. But the way they talked, the men might have been on some Grand Tour. Not nearby, not convenient, not amenable to pleasures, but merely distant for a little.

And of course, the men here hadn't served. Not except for Reggie. He was being more than a touch stoic. Oh, he'd joined in the commentary a few places, mostly when the talk had settled onto notable bohort matches, or school reminiscences for a few minutes. But mostly he let the conversation roll over him. None of them asked about his experiences, of course. That wouldn't be festive at all.

He'd seen her up to her room, and then asked if he might add a bit of warding. Just something that would wear off by the time the maid came by to bring a tray. He'd earnestly explained that, before they came, how there would be someone in and out of the space, morning and night.

Lynet had pointed out that whatever she lived with, they'd had housekeepers when she was at school. She'd manage, but she'd accepted the warding gratefully. He'd taken himself back to his own room, showing no sign of wanting to linger in hers. It made sense, she couldn't have begun to relax enough to enjoy any of it. Even if she'd wanted him to stay, as the person who made sense in this mess.

On Saturday morning, Reggie asked if she'd like a ramble in the countryside. There were some rather nice views, within an hour or two's walk. She'd accepted, and they'd been joined by two other couples and brought a picnic lunch with them. It meant Lynet wasn't able to ask anything in private, but the views were indeed glorious.

Lynet almost thought the country might have some decided virtues if the landscape kept doing that. There was something about being surrounded by living things, plants, a clear sky above that felt gloriously different from London or Trellech. And the ground under her feet was soft, springy, not hard pavement or cobblestones.

When they stopped for lunch, the other two couples swapped little powdery pills and pulled out flasks, clearly intending to enhance their day. When they settled back in a tumbled pile of bodies, languid with the effects, Reggie had murmured, "We'll go back the long way round. Shall I leave the basket?"

One of the men had waved a lazy hand, and Reggie had taken that as agreement. It wasn't until they were well up on the next rise that Reggie spoke again. "How much walking are you up for?"

"Does it come with conversation?" Lynet considered the state of her shoes. And the state of his feet. He'd borrowed a walking stick, and she hadn't been able to decide if that was promising or worrying.

"We can go the long way back - about two miles. No stone circles, but a good bit of view and a nicely venerable tree? Or we can go back and find somewhere to sit, but there's more chance of someone else spotting us."

"Are you up for the longer way?" Lynet gestured. "I'm not exactly in a rush to get back into it. What were the afternoon plans?"

"Pickup bohort - I can play, you can watch and tell me I'm clever even if I'm not." Reggie seemed to take it as the natural way of things. "Or you could play, if you wanted, but..."

"The women don't usually?" Lynet had been noticing that, the rather stark divisions that seemed to play out.

"Some of them do. But it's a tad more aggressive in terms of personality. And I don't know what your actual skills are there."

"I played pickup games, our house tourneys, when I was at school. Nothing serious though, nothing like you all were talking about last night. Long way or short way?"

"Long." Reggie made the decision she had hoped he would. "And we'll find a stone wall or something on the way." They walked along in companionable conversation about the others at the party. Reggie made sure she'd put two and two together about who was theoretically paired up with whom, and who had famous relatives. Which was a surprising number of them, or perhaps she should recalibrate about that.

It did remind her of last night. "What did you make of Lord Carillon last night? And his brother?"

"It must be his brother. I was at school with Geoffrey, though I didn't know him to talk to. And they looked decidedly alike." Reggie hesitated. "I really hope his man got a Healer out promptly. He didn't look well at all."

"Even though he wasn't in the Temple of Healing? Did you catch anything about what was going on there?"

Reggie paused, stopping in the ramble. "Near as I can tell, he'd been shot, something rather bad. They'd treated it, sent him off to recover, and - this isn't quiet. You saw how he was with the champagne cork."

"I saw how you jerked, too." Lynet wasn't sure naming it was the right thing, and she watched Reggie closely.

His shoulders slumped for just a moment. "Did I?"

"You saw him clearly. Is - is he going to be all right?" Lynet frowned. "He looked quite ill."

"I'd be worrying about an infection or something of the kind. I'm sure he had a fever, or was about to start on one.

It's unmistakable, once you've seen it a few times. I'm glad he had someone with him. His man, I think." He grimaced. "It's a whole mess. And it makes me wonder, again, why these parties? If they just needed a pause from the labour of the week, it wouldn't need to be like this. Noise and drink and drugs." He waved a hand back where they'd come from. "And frivolity all the time."

"Does it bother you to be here?" Lynet wasn't sure what Reggie thought of it. He'd been stoic throughout.

"Not exactly. Not if we figure out what's going on. Or if it means they lay off you a bit, and we can get our work done better. That's worthwhile." He let out a sigh. "I was thinking, last night, how amazing it would be if Lapidoth Manse had a journal, you know? And I could let him know about Geoffrey promptly. I did send a note this morning to his club, with an enclosure for them to pass on, and I hope that reaches him quickly."

Lynet stood on her toes and kissed his cheek. "You think about things like that." She approved. She didn't know how he did it, but she approved. Then she slipped her hand into his, and they continued walking, talking through various pieces. The afternoon was indeed full of bohort. Reggie played a fair bit of the time, being steady and reliable, and making the others on his team look better as a result. In the end, they pulled out a win unexpectedly.

Then, of course, there was the fuss of changing again. That made three outfits in the day, as well as her sleeping things and the dressing gown for going down the hall to the bath. Which was just ridiculous. Even if she rather liked the frock she was borrowing for the evening, deep in her heart of hearts. It was a richly heathered purple, a shade she'd never have thought to wear herself, but which somehow made her hair shimmer and brought out her eyes. The maid had been very pleased with the effect, and Reggie had lit up when he saw her.

The supper itself was more or less the same as the previous night, but Reggie asked her to take a walk through the garden. As they came halfway back, they found Lord Temple sitting on a bench, staring off down at the lake.

"Have a minute, Hollis? Do you mind, Lynet, if I borrow him for a few?"

Lynet thought she did mind, except that perhaps there was some reason. Reggie turned to her, and rummaged for something, then pressed a small object into her palm. He bent to her ear. "Hold that near your head. You should hear what I hear. Thirty feet or so, find a bench a bit closer to the party."

That was startling, but remarkably prescient of him. She nodded, kissed his cheek, and left him to the conversation. When she turned back, Reggie was sitting next to Lord Temple. She hurried to find a bench about twenty feet away, behind them both, and managed to tuck the object - a cufflink - into her hair by her ear. It took her a moment to get used to the queerness of it, a voice in her ear, but it worked well enough.

"I'd like your opinion, Hollis. Someone who knows what it's like over there." She could hear the strain in Lord Temple's voice as clear as the words.

"Of course, if I can help." Reggie's back stiffened, and she knew this was difficult for him, but the sort of difficult he'd forge ahead with.

There was a pause. "Before that. My brother was shot. Recuperating at another of the family properties. This week." There was a terseness now, not Lord Temple's smooth geniality. "Do you think the Healers are up to the thing?"

"Every Healer I've met this past year has been working themselves to the bone. Over and over again." That wasn't terse, exactly. Reggie sounded almost gentle. "But they have a lot of experience with injuries now. Much more than previous wars. Saving more lives. If your brother's back here, not in a hospital or the Temple of Healing, that suggests he's recovering, right?"

There was a long pause, a murmured something Lynet couldn't hear entirely, but that might have been a prayer. "And you, did they take - sufficient care of you?" That just came out awkwardly, and she was sure that was not an emotion Lord Temple normally let people hear. Now she'd heard a bit, she was sure he was rather drunk, verging on maudlin. She'd certainly spent enough time in the pub to spot that quickly.

"Some things can't be mended. I hope your brother has better luck there than I did." Reggie shrugged one shoulder. "You worry a lot about him, then?"

"I'd do anything to - he's out fighting, risking himself. I'd do anything to..." Lord Temple paused. "Before the War, he travelled. He'd bring back materia, plants and animals that might be helpful. To the Healers, in different kinds of magic. He had such stories. Not that we'd see each other often, but when we did." His voice trailed off. "Listen to me, I'm an old fool. Just. He's been over there, somewhere awful, it's changed him, and I'm not there, doing the same. I have to do my bit, here, whatever it takes."

Lynet frowned. There was a thread there, the way Papa had sounded, especially toward the end, of a particular kind of martyrdom that did no one any good in the long run. She couldn't understand why Lord Carillon would sound like that, not really. He seemed to think he had a way to do something about it, about his brother or the War or something. Before either of them could say more, there were people coming down the path, a gaggle of them. "Temple! Come back up, we've got a treat. You too, Hollis, and bring your girl."

They did not have good timing, any of that lot. Ever.

CHAPTER 37

SUNDAY MORNING

Things were quiet on the Sunday morning. In many households, even after a party, some people would go off to the local church or whatever, make a show of it, but that wasn't likely here. They were quite a bit from any village, and very few of these folk seemed the sort to have a steady religious practice.

Reggie and Lynet had a pleasant walk around the gardens, with enough of a hill to it that they both wanted to wash up before luncheon. Once they were back inside the house, Reggie was guiding her toward the main stairs when he heard a sound from one of the side rooms.

It wasn't a sob, not exactly, but it was something made out of distress and discomfort. Reggie hesitated, and Lynet squeezed his arm. That was enough to let Reggie turn and knock lightly on the door. "Beg pardon, can I lend a hand?" That sounded terribly stilted, but it wasn't as if he knew anything better to say.

From inside, there was a muffled sound. "Who is it?" He

couldn't quite make out who it was, but he was fairly certain it wasn't Margot.

"Reggie and Lynet. We were just going up to change."

"Oh." That sounded a little startled. "Is it that near luncheon? I didn't hear the gong." Then she caught herself, whoever the woman was. "Come in, please, if you don't mind?"

Reggie eased the door open to find a small sitting room, not one that had been opened up for the party in general. It was decorated in a remarkably soothing colour scheme, all deeper purples and lavenders, with bits of golden yellow. A reasonably comfortable looking sofa and chairs looked out the window, with a large desk at the far end, where Delphina was sitting. She put down her hand, still holding a handkerchief, and more or less shook herself back into place without actually moving a muscle.

"I do hope you're enjoying yourself, Lynet?" That sounded entirely in earnest.

"We had a lovely walk this yesterday, up by that ancient oak. Reggie showed me the way? I've spent all my life in London, other than when I was at Alethorpe. Getting to see the countryside here is a pleasure." Lynet picked up easily enough, and Reggie shifted his arm a little so he could squeeze her hand. He was glad they'd done the long walk, and given her something she could talk about without worry.

"Oh, I am glad." Delphina hesitated. "I hope no one's been awful to you? Sometimes, people are drinking and..." Her voice trailed off.

Lynet shook her head. "More pleasant than I expected, honestly." She paused, then added, "Were you worried about anyone in particular?"

That made Delphina fall quiet. Reggie waited to see if

she was going to say anything. When she didn't, he cleared his throat. "It's clear to me you've got your own worries, Delphina. Is there anything we might be a help with? Even just a listening ear?"

For one thing, he rather liked the woman. Not that he wanted to bed her. She was entirely outside his scope for that, even if he hadn't fallen for Lynet along the way. One of the finest flowers of the Great Families wouldn't have that sort of time for him. Not unless he had something very particular on offer. Or unless she was only looking for a pleasurable moment or a bit of spite against her husband. Neither of those appealed, any more than Margot had appealed.

She considered, tilting her head, the first truly unmeasured movement he'd seen her make. "If you have a few moments." She gestured at the door, and it swung fully shut with a little click of the latch, and then she did something from her desk that called up warding. Reggie expected it was highly skilled consultants who'd set both bits of that up, rather than Delphina's own work, but he could still appreciate the expertise involved. At her next gesture, Reggie guided Lynet to the sofa while Delphina took the single chair.

There was a long and rather painful silence. Reggie had no idea where to begin, though he certainly had a few possible guesses about why she was upset. But one couldn't ask about whether a woman's husband was off doing whatever it was he did with Margot.

Rather to Reggie's surprise, Lynet cleared her throat. "I'm sure I don't understand many things about how matters are handled in a house like this, but you have been so kind to me. As Reggie said, if we can be any help. Perhaps an outside perspective?" Lynet waved a hand. "I mean, all of this is unusual to me."

Delphina managed a weak smile. "Well." She let out a breath. "You know, I'm sure, anyone with eyes does, that my husband has a particular interest in Margot at the moment. Has for a while, rather honestly. That's not a particular problem. I understood when we married it was likely."

Reggie noted, in the part of his mind that was analysing this conversation, which was most of it, that this didn't say anything about what Delphina thought about it.

"Margot is not terribly subtle about it, no. Not, um." He coughed. "Not blatant at work, except that anyone who can read the more subtle signs is quite aware."

Delphina nodded once. "Like that. Here, as well. I'm sure they're off in the folly, or perhaps one of the less used rooms." She hesitated. "I do have questions, though, and I do not know if you can answer any of them for me."

"We do not work on the same project as the others here." Reggie pointed out. "And I've only heard scraps of information, here and there." A fair few of them last night, when people were more in their cups. He hadn't had a chance to work through the implications of those tiny pieces of knowledge, yet.

Delphina twisted her wrist slightly. "Just so." She was not, Reggie realised, a foolish woman. She knew her role in this particular dance - the party, as well as this conversation - and she was doing her part. But it wasn't just rote steps, she was thinking through each piece of it. "You have some expertise with materia, yes?"

Reggie nodded. "I do. I was Bear House at school, and I liked Professor Trembley's courses. My specialty's in Warding, or it was."

Delphina inclined her head, as if that kind of thing was entirely ordinary, though in her circles it probably was. "I am worried that there is something in the research that is..." She hesitated. "A blight, is that the word I want?"

"Possibly." Reggie cleared his throat, cautiously. "I don't know much about what they're working on." He glanced at Lynet, unsure if he should mention what they did know.

Lynet hesitated. "We've had some difficulties getting the materia we needed. Or it hasn't been of good quality. But we're not sure why."

Delphina half-turned, looking out the window, which also rather obscured her expression without being too obvious about it. Reggie waited until she turned back to say, "It's all rather a mystery. And for our part, we'd like very much to get Lynet's work moving forward." He considered, then added, "I'm sure it would be a relief to your husband to be able to write directly to his brother, for example. The comfort of that."

Her face changed in a moment, like that was a rope thrown to someone drowning off the side of a boat, a faint hope, but just enough of one. Then her expression smoothed over. "Oh, yes. He does worry. He thought there was less to worry about, now Geoffrey's out of the trenches." That made her tilt her head. "You were there, weren't you?"

"Invalided out. And not the same trenches, I assume. Or at least we didn't run into each other. Though the mud does make it hard to spot people, a fair bit of the time." The mud, everything mixed in with the mud that he tried not to think about. Reggie coughed, hoping for something to change the subject. Then he offered, a little uncertainly, "Most of the people here, they're contacts through Temple, yes?"

"Oh, yes. Mostly people he's been doing research with, or that he knows from various projects. Who's been brought in on a project. That's a thing. My own set of friends, we see them other times. Everyone here, you've made your own oaths about things not going any further."

Reggie felt Lynet squeeze his arm. It explained why they'd been willing to invite her, in part. Even if she wasn't at all like the other guests in terms of background or class, she'd made sufficient oaths. Though now that he thought about it, Reggie's oaths had been fascinatingly non-specific on the topic. More a wisp and a trust that he'd keep his mouth shut, rather than anything truly binding. He wasn't enough of a ritual magic specialist, certainly not a judicial one, to figure out the details by himself, though.

There was something terribly wrong here, and he didn't even know how to ask about it, even when given the opportunity. The silence drew out longer, and then the gong sounded in the foyer. Delphina twitched, she didn't quite jump. "My, is that the time? I mustn't keep you." With that, she stood, waving her hand at the door, and that required that Reggie stand and offer his arm to Lynet.

A minute later, they were on the stairs. Then Reggie was walking her down to her room. "May I come in, for a moment?"

Lynet nodded. "I don't think anyone's going to comment about propriety." She let out a long breath as soon as the door closed behind Reggie. "That wasn't much help. Except that I'm sure there's something odd."

"And that Delphina is worried about Temple. And whatever he's got into." Reggie shook his head. "I wish I knew more about Margot's training and skills, honestly, but I don't. Other than the obvious."

"There is a woman who has honed her social prowess to

a fine point. Sharp enough to cut, whatever way you hold her." Lynet said it with what Reggie thought was a mix of exasperation and wistfulness.

"Give me a nice solid book, any day. Meant to be held and used, not a weapon. I've had more than enough of those." He hadn't been quite sure what he was going to say until it was out of his mouth. Lynet visibly relaxed, then twined her arms round his shoulders to kiss him gently.

"You always know the right thing to say, somehow. Is it going to be awful, do you think? Luncheon?"

Reggie shrugged. "Not worse than last night? More drinking, probably. Or rather, they've certainly already started. They'll just keep going. The one thing I am sure of is that if you make an excuse - a headache, or whatever - Delphina will understand. Or perhaps you could have a quiet conversation with her, somewhere, if it gets rowdy? Sometimes things get a bit rough, on the last day."

"That would be a kindness on both ends. And you?" Lynet drew back, her fingers just brushing his arm now.

"I'd like it if you were visible enough that no one else went on the prowl at me. But I'm a grown man. I can take care of myself."

Lynet snorted at that. "You could have any of them, likely. Why do you stick to me?"

"That would take longer to explain than we have. But - we're back to being solid, real, doing something that matters. And besides, you took pity on my fumbling."

"You are, in fact, learning how to do the basics remark- ably quickly. I—" Her voice caught. "I don't want you to be doing something else, it turns out."

Reggie could feel his smile growing and growing, fit to crack his face open. "I'll do my best to stick around. Can't make you and Ellis carry all your own paper, can I?" That was a right thing to say, it made her laugh.

Then there was a knock on the door. "Ma'am, do you need a hand with your dressing?"

Lynet sighed and nodded. "Come in, please. Reggie was just going to wash up and change his cuffs, perhaps you could help with the cuff links when I'm in my frock?"

CHAPTER 38

SUNDAY, RETURNING TO LONDON

Naturally, Reggie escorted Lynet back through the portal to London on Sunday evening. He hesitated on the steps. She opened the door and peered at him. "Of course you're coming in. I need to give you back the things your sister loaned, for one. Also, there's a letter here, addressed to you, care of me."

That made him smile. She was wearing one of them now, a quite pleasant day dress in a twilight blue, which was still in keeping with mourning, but fit her well. And showed off her ankles to some advantage. "As you wish." He followed her in, then up the interior stairs to the sitting room, where she handed him the letter and took both suitcases in hand.

"Are you staying tonight?" She tilted her head.

He hadn't entirely expected to. "Isn't that for you to say?"

"Please, do. We need to talk about things. Let me change into something of my own, pop across the street for

300

something to eat, and come back. Who'd be writing to you here? I'll put your sister's things in the case. You can take them both with you when you go." She swept on back to the bedroom, and Reggie turned the letter over in his hands.

Lapidoth Manse. He'd mentioned in the note that a letter to Lynet's would likely get to him faster than to his rooms until Monday evening. The landlady liked to bring the mail round personally, to make it absolutely clear nothing had been lost or misplaced. Reggie flicked the letter over, skimming it, then reading it more thoroughly. He barely heard Lynet go by, or down and out the door, but he had somewhat surfaced when she came back in, five minutes later, with supper.

"What's that, then?"

"I wrote Lapidoth Manse, about seeing Geoffrey Carillon." He tapped the edge of the envelope on the arm of the chair. "He thanked me for the information, said he'd see to something. I feel rather like I've been thanked by someone out of a Fatae tale, and there's an obligation owed now. But I can't put my thumb on which direction."

"That's how you know it's a Fatae tale. The ambiguity. What else did he say?"

"He wants to know if we have anything we'd like to report about the materia. Did you hear anything? We've not had a chance to talk privately since our walk yesterday."

"Our extensive ramble, across hill and over dale. My blisters may not forgive me, though the maid was helpful." Lynet put the food down on the table between their chairs and sank onto the sofa. "Blast, the bottle opener."

Reggie waved a hand. "Have a pocket knife. And a bit of magic. Hand yours over." He cast the charm, then twisted the cap off neatly, then opened his own, offering his bottle to clink. "Cheers on surviving the house party in glorious style."

She blushed very charmingly. "I wasn't."

"You were one of the best-looking girls there, I think is my expected phrase. Not that you're a girl at all, mind. I will say Delphina did right by you. You looked like you fit in."

"I had no idea what to say to most of it." Lynet cleared her throat.

"You had a mysterious and fascinating air about you. Half the men wanted to find out why. Mind, the other half were pining after Margot."

Lynet tilted her head. "You weren't."

"No. For several reasons." Reggie considered how to talk about some of this and then decided he'd let Lynet ask about what she thought mattered. "Go ahead and ask?"

"Why aren't you interested in her? You were very polite, but she's stunning."

"Like you said, she's sharp enough to cut yourself on. All the time. You, Lynet, are sharp - a paper-cut's a nasty thing, isn't it? But with you, it'd be because I was rude or careless or dismissive. With Margot, I have the sense that she'd take advantage of any sign of weakness. Not just in the moment, but she'd file it away and pull it out six months later, two years. That she'd keep that sort of thing far longer than she'd keep a frock in her wardrobe."

Lynet blinked at him and then leaned forward to snag her supper. "I don't know what to do with that. With any of the excess. Only, it's an excess in other things, too." She gestured with her fork. "You men got plenty of hearty food, but most of the women just picked at theirs. All that waste, from the suppers."

"Not just there." Reggie nodded.

"The frocks. All of them having three or four changes a

day, plus whatever they wore to bed. And clearly dozens of outfits, at least the showy pieces, because apparently one can't wear the same things to two house parties in a row. That's before we get into the jewellery."

"Not everyone in the posh set is like that. My sisters, for example. Much more likely to have a small set of smart clothing, fit for the current mode, and classic jewellery. Margot really is on the outside of things that way. Not just the frocks - the orange one Saturday was rather a lot - but the brightness of them. That kind of shade either takes some particular dyes or a touch of magic, and the magic's tricky with silk."

"I went to Alethorpe. You needn't tell me about that. I spent years with a couple of people in my house complaining about it. Endlessly."

"What happened? What was it like? Tell me all!" Reggie leaned forward. He'd been curious for some time about what the differences were like, but Lynet hadn't seemed inclined to talk about her education.

She snorted. "Eat your supper. You must be hungry. You were busy talking to, who was it, Alton, during luncheon?"

"I was. And we should talk about that. School first." Reggie did pick up his plate. Lynet eyed him, amused, and then settled into a comfortable explanation of what Alethorpe was like, what the houses were like. They sorted out compatible groups to live together, which is where she'd got to know Ellis and trust his work. But also, there had been people learning to work with leather and inks, and all sorts of other items. It sounded like the other half of her house had been interested in herbs and materia, and that's where she'd picked up some knowledge.

"And then apprenticeship." Reggie said, in a pause. "Was that always going to be with your father?"

Lynet nodded. "Mama had died years ago by then. I'd been worried about leaving him on his own, you know?" She waved a hand back toward the bedrooms. "And so I wanted to come back here. Besides, he made some of the best books by a long shot."

Reggie finished up the last of his pie. "I envy that, really. I didn't have a focus for my apprenticeship for a long time, I just knew I was supposed to have one. And warding's a field where having a strong sense of what you're doing is key to the whole thing." He hesitated. "I suppose that's what brings me to - well. What we do now."

"Go on?" Lynet set her own plate back on the table.

"Did you hear them talking yesterday evening? After the bit I had with Lord Temple. And I'm assuming you heard most of that?"

"The cufflinks are very clever." She'd handed it promptly back, or rather reattached it for him. "Don't people check with charms for that sort of thing?"

"For one thing, the range isn't terribly good, and if there's other conversation around, it's almost impossible to make sense of it. For another, the charm on it's a particular twist on sympathetic magic, and a lot of people just think it's something to make sure you never lose a pair. Have one, find the other, that sort of thing. And third, among that crowd, most people are wearing half a dozen talismans or enchanted pieces, so any ordinary detection of magic won't stand out."

"Half a dozen?"

"Head to toe, mm. Earrings or tie pin. A necklace or pendant or something on a chain around the neck, that's classic. Perhaps something in the flower in the lapel, or tucked behind the pocket square. Then there's a belt buckle, a watch, a bracelet, cuff links, of course. Maybe something in the shoelaces, or around an ankle, especially for men. If I'm doing warding work, something on the ankle for protection is quite handy. Most of the charms are the ordinary sort of protection. For this set, maybe something more. I don't entirely know what they're afraid of."

"Lord Carillon was clear about that, though." Lynet shifted, leaning forward to rest her fingers on Reggie's arm. "I felt rather sorry for him."

"Curious, wasn't it? That mix of guilt and worry. Feeling like he wasn't doing his part, desperately wanting things to be all right. And yet, he didn't really beg his brother to try to stay. I'm sure the family wing was a bit quieter. They could have tucked someone up there without too much fuss. A bit hard on the staff, maybe, but the staff are devoted. I suspect even you could see that."

"More or less. They were very present. They seemed honestly quite happy with the work - well, except for cleaning up the mess, when people had too much to drink last night."

"I was always taught that it's a waste of good alcohol to have it come up the wrong way after. And that was some quite fine liquor once we got into it. The house cellars must be overflowing, if that's the ordinary run of things." Reggie said it off-handedly.

"I wouldn't know how to judge. It was?" Lynet's question caught at something he'd been chewing on.

"Let me talk this out for a minute? You might spot something I'm missing." When Lynet nodded, Reggie went on. "So, we have Temple and Delphina, hosting, quite regularly." He contemplated. "There's something odd in the wards there, though, but I don't know what it is. Maybe Delphina's right about something he's doing harming him. And it's not the sort of thing one asks about."

"Rude, then?" Lynet offered.

"More like offensive." Reggie shrugged. "Then there's the people, leaving aside the wards. These are people he works with. He doesn't need them at a party to get their ear. They all look to him, anyway. Or if they're not looking to him, they're looking at him, and crooking their fingers. Margot, for example."

"She's, I don't know the right words." Lynet frowned. "Like something out of the theatre or the moving pictures, bigger than life. Brash, eye-catching."

"I'm wondering, honestly - and this is my warding training, talking, paying attention to the landscape - what she's hiding. Or rather, you see her when she's a bright butterfly or hummingbird, flitting around. But when she's not doing that? What's she up to? She was rather invisible most of Saturday afternoon, and it wasn't just because she was bedding Lord Temple somewhere."

"That was at least part of it." Lynet said. "He had more than a whiff of her perfume on him, when he came around at tea time. Just before the gong went to dress."

"Good timing for it, at least, Delphina having gone to lie down. I can't even tell if she particularly objects, though they do seem to get on well, overall. I mean, they probably don't share a bed, but I might be wrong."

"You posh people are very confusing." Lynet said.

Reggie spread out his hands. "I think I am perfectly sensible. I wish to share your bed whenever you decide I may, and otherwise I will find somewhere that suits for the night." Then he brought himself back. "What I heard last night makes me think there's something going on with their research and the land magic. I don't know for sure. It was that reference to Hetheringstone that did it. There's only a few things that might suggest, in terms of text. It's a particular theorem, the one I'm thinking of, about affecting a whole slew of space at once. Wide-ranging, affecting the land and the water and the air, all three of them."

"What do you want to do about that? What does one do?"

Reggie let out a breath. "I think I take it to Lapidoth Manse and see if he knows who we should talk to. Both of us."

CHAPTER 39

Lynet took her seat in a comfortable enough chair and looked around the room as Reggie sat down beside her. She hadn't been sure what to make of the address. They were in a flat in one of the rows of posh townhouses in Trellech, one of the neighbourhoods she knew very little about. Reggie's sort of people, not hers. They'd been met at the door by Lapidoth Manse, who had bowed over her hand like she was someone to be respected, then shown them up to the second floor.

The flat belonged to the third man, now settled behind his desk. It was his office, and Lynet wasn't sure what to do with that. He'd introduced himself to her, amiably, as Cyrus Smythe-Clive. Reggie, mind, had explained beforehand that he was a Council Member, and Lynet had no idea what to do with that. She'd never met one before. She wasn't the sort of person who did. Though Uncle Matthew probably had, now she thought about it. Council Member Smythe-Clive had dark curly hair with sharp features, and he was beginning to go a bit silver at the temples. He waved his hand. "Tea? A drink?"

"Clear heads for this, but you might want a drink after." Manse inclined his head. "I am here to facilitate, as I mentioned, being more aware of some of the pieces in play."

"Quite so." Council Member Smythe-Clive leaned back. "I trust Lap when he says this is worth a bit of my attention. I am a member of the Council, naturally, but I am currently serving in overseeing logistics in London. Both magical and non-magical. Would you please tell me what brings you here, and how that might overlap? I am broadly familiar with the nature of your project, in the sense that I knew someone was making the attempt, but not about any of the details."

Lynet glanced at Reggie, and he squeezed her hand. They'd talked about this, that it was her project. "I am trained as a bookbinder, both in terms of the physical process and the magical applications. I attended Alethorpe, then apprenticed with my father, who was a master of the art. He was approached in late 1915 with the idea of creating a magical system of journals that could intercommunicate. He was - he died earlier this year, sir."

"I am very sorry to hear that." Smythe-Clive's manner was remarkably gentle. A moment later, he added, "I have a daughter a few years older than you. Her mother died when she was born. I've worried a fair bit about what she might do if something happened to me."

That was oddly personal, and somehow also reassuring. He clearly didn't mean in a purely financial sense, not with a flat like this. But that larger question, of what it meant to live up to your father, seen from the other side. The other end of the book, as it were. "Sir." She swallowed. "He consulted, of course, a great deal. And some others in the research group did as well."

"Do you feel you can name names?" She had to admit, he had a knack for asking questions without pressing. It made her want to answer.

Manse commented, almost idly, "Your oaths don't prohibit it. I did check the contracts on file, and the notes on the ritual. It turns out Cyrus helped write out the language for the department. He's a ritualist, by preference."

That was a form of magic Lynet didn't have much experience with, though it was certainly a help with the oaths. Smythe-Clive lifted a hand, gestured lightly with it. "I can hold my own in discussions about Alchemy and Materia, and a fair swath of Incantation. I'll ask for an explanation if I need one."

Lynet nodded. Reggie squeezed her hand, and she gave the explanation that now felt almost comfortable, the one that went a little into the complications of the materia.

Smythe-Clive nodded several times as she went along, but he didn't interrupt her, even when she paused. She wasn't sure what to do with that, either. When she came to the end, explaining the challenges of the materia, he said, "I should be able to shake something loose there. Do you have theories on what's going on? It might help me figure out what approach to take."

Reggie cleared his throat. "Are you familiar with other projects in the building, sir?"

"To varying degrees. Some are being kept quite mysterious. You understand, of course, that the Council doesn't have direct approval of that sort of thing. We know about the journals because, truth be told, every single one of us wants one, as soon as they can be made ready. Sufficiently so that if you've got the other materials, I think we could likely round up sufficient materia for that purpose by the end of the week."

He leaned forward, as he said it, and Lynet saw how much he meant it. That he understood what it would change. Certainly, how it would make the Council's coordination vastly easier. And she saw, too, glancing at Reggie, that he realised the impact that would have, for good and ill.

"We've talked, sir, about the way this sort of research changes things dramatically. You can see it yourself, yes?" Reggie was right on that point.

"Oh, rather, yes." Smythe-Clive gestured at his bookshelf. "We have some rudimentary versions, but they have to be individually charmed, so each of us has three or four volumes, and we pass along messages through a chain. But keeping up with that many volumes is tedious, and then, of course, someone's always sleeping and not looking when you have something urgent. Then the message gets stalled."

He shrugged and went on. "It works well enough for, say, coordinating about ritual language between meetings, but not for anything that requires prompt action. What you suggest, though - it would shave a dozen hours of work off my life, every week. Sometimes more. And it would, I suspect, change how I thought through some things. Likely incline me to be more systematic, though obviously that's a guess. Do you have working copies?" So that success hadn't been reported upwards. That was curious.

Reggie nodded. "Lynet helped walk me through the steps of making my own. Not as beautifully bound as her usual work, of course, but I'm proud of it. And it's been exceedingly useful several times. She mentioned that someone broke in. It meant I could come out and be a help right after she discovered it."

"And that's something that mattered to you." That wasn't phrased as a question. "And the difficulty is something about the materia?"

"Yes, sir." Lynet cleared her throat. "The magical amplifiers, in particular. I know they're in high demand overall, but our orders seem to be going into a pit in the larger department. We weren't sure why."

Smythe-Clive caught the verb, like he was snatching it out of the air like a hawk took a bird in flight. "Weren't?"

"We were invited out to Hawk's Breath, sir, the Carillon estate in Cumbria, the past few days. Various other people working on projects." Reggie took over, smoothly. "And we heard a few tidbits that made me wonder what they're doing. There was a reference to Hetheringstone, combined with the idea of affecting quite a lot of material. Something sprayed or spread, somehow, that took a tremendous amount of sheer substance."

"And that's when Hollis wrote to me." Manse leaned forward.

"What did you make of the references you heard? And what do you know of Hetheringstone?" Smythe-Clive glanced first at Reggie, then back at Lynet.

"Reggie explained the theory last night, sir. At least briefly." Lynet swallowed. "Large scale magic, beyond a local area, beyond the size someone could walk. How that has implications for the land magic, among other things. But also, oh, different kinds of crops, or waterways, coastlines."

"There's a theory that some of what he talks about is what weakened the coastline at Dunwich. They're a bit more sure about Ravenser Odd." Lynet knew that there had been issues with both towns falling into the sea, at different points, in the thirteenth and fourteenth centuries or so. Before the Pact, that's all she really remembered. Smythe-Clive waited a moment, as if checking their faces for comprehension, and then went on. "I'd like to go through what you have, as far as evidence. And then I can see if I can shake loose some materia for your uses. Which really should be a priority all round."

Reggie hesitated. "That's the thing that's been bothering me all along, sir. Not just the way they've treated Lynet, though that's certainly part of it, but also that there's been no support. Master Brand seems to be saying the right things, on one level. But he's had chance after chance to at least do more to find a resolution, or get us materia we need, and there was none of that. Even before he got rather nasty with Lynet." Reggie paused, for the weight of it. "We suspect, sir, that he wants the project to fail, and is making sure it will. Passively, more than directly destroying the work."

Lynet did her best not to flinch at either the memory or the fact Reggie was laying it out so boldly. A moment later, he leaned to rest his hand on hers.

"Mistress Alder, may I be of assistance with any of that?" She realised, all of a sudden, that he'd avoided using any name for her, and now he'd been formal. She looked up, meeting his eyes, and she could see a slight smile. He'd been very deliberate. She'd noticed it and he'd acknowledged it.

Of course, that didn't make it easy to figure out what to say. She swallowed, taking her time and feeling Reggie squeeze her hand. "Council Member, I would like to move forward on our project and produce a substantial number of prototypes for ongoing testing. Your fellow Council

Members would be an excellent test case, if we are permitted, or perhaps Master Manse and some colleagues or associates. My own journal has been working smoothly for nearly six months, but it's possible there's a decay in the enchantments or some such that happens over time."

Reggie cleared his throat and added, "I had a thought, sir, about the issues of security and information getting out. It's the kind of thing that might be solved by an oath, for those serving in sensitive positions. With your interest in ritual language, perhaps you might have some thoughts about the construction that would be helpful as part of the ongoing development?"

Smythe-Clive nodded, looking very pleased at something. "I will be glad to look into this for you, without bringing your names directly into it. Yes, and to consult on some sort of ritual oath, I quite see the point about security." He tapped his fingers on the desk. "From the notes Lap has given me, I should have plenty to work with. The amounts that have gone into your building are rather notable, as well as the fact you've made multiple requisition requests, due to not receiving previous ones. Two of the other projects, too, have been stymied on necessary supplies."

He tapped his fingers. "Which does suggest some sort of influence of the more political sort. Untangling that will take some time. I will be in touch. How's that? Lap, would you stay." That last part wasn't a question. "Mistress Alder, Captain Hollis, thank you for bringing this to my attention. Please let me know if you get any additional information, a letter here will reach me quickly."

With that, they found themselves fairly quickly outside in the evening air. Reggie offered his arm. "Walk you back to your room?"

"Please." Lynet didn't want to talk about anything delicate while they were out in public, but once they were back in the rooming house garden, she cleared her throat. "Do you think he can do anything to help?"

"Chances are good. I don't - my family aren't close in with the Council either, or at least not for a couple of generations. But this seems very relevant to their interests. And he asked the right sorts of questions, didn't he?"

"He." She stopped and started again. "He just believed me. Us. I'm not sure how I feel about that." Lynet turned to face Reggie. "Thank you for being there with me. For being brave enough to write. Putting it all together. Just - all of it."

Reggie cupped her cheek. "It matters what you're doing. What we're doing, since you permit me to help. We'll see what happens, all right?" He hesitated. "I think I'd rather know there was someone else around - as a witness - when you're in the building. May I meet you tomorrow to walk over?"

Lynet hesitated. She'd have thought, in the past, that someone offering that sort of thing had some other reason. Wanting to claim her work as his own, or get something from her. Here, though, she looked up at him, then nodded. "Eight, if you don't mind? We'll be there at quarter past."

"Pausing to pick up lunch on the way. Excellent. I'll be here right on time." Then he hesitated, before leaning in to kiss her. It was a decorous kiss. He was clearly well aware that there was someone peering out the door by now. "Tomorrow."

She waited until she couldn't see him past the turn in the road, before going in to take her things upstairs and wash up for supper.

CHAPTER 40

They didn't hear anything all that week, or the next. By the following Friday, Reggie had had plenty of time to think through the implications. While Lynet went across to the pub, he unpacked some of the groceries he'd brought along for their other meals, eggs and milk and toast and such. Lynet was a good plain cook, even though Reggie still found the process more than a tad mysterious, at least when it involved a proper kitchen and not field rations.

They had, however, made some progress. On the Thursday after they'd met with Smythe-Clive, they heard the dumbwaiter creaking not long after their morning tea break. It had been followed by one of the bright young men, younger version, coming up to tell them that some of their requisition had been delivered.

It had taken the three of them - Ellis had come up to help - a good hour to unload everything and put it away.

Ellis had gone off with stocks of mistletoe and Solomon's Seal, and he'd apparently worked through Saturday, to make sure there would be more than enough paper.

They'd had enough to do a large batch, with the components they knew worked, producing a hundred copies by the end of the following week. Reggie's thumbs were still a tad sore from the sewing and cutting involved, but he felt he had earned every bit of the pride he felt.

Lynet had been delighted, too. She'd been a symphony of movement, near spinning from workspace to workspace. She was always aware of what stage the paste was at, where Reggie was, or what could be worked on next, like a most glorious dance. When they'd finished the last of the volumes this afternoon, she'd looked at the stacks and brushed her hands off on her smock.

"Do you think they'll help more now?"

"That's a topic for tonight, I think. Do we have somewhere safe to put these?" Reggie had a thought, but he didn't want to express it just yet.

"The locked cupboards for now? Stack them flat. I'd like to give the spines a bit more chance to dry."

Reggie had done as he was told, and that, well, brought them to this evening. Reggie had just finished putting things away when Lynet came up the stairs. "Why didn't you want to talk about things in the workroom?"

"Caution. I trust my warding, honestly, but the best precaution is doing your talking somewhere the people who might want to overhear don't have access to." He had, in fact, checked the flat here while Lynet was across the street, and he wasn't sure if mentioning it would reassure her or worry her. He hadn't found anything, anyway, or any sign anyone had been inside since they'd left Monday morning. On the other hand, he still checked.

The Guard hadn't found anything either, he'd seen the report. Nothing that linked to anyone they knew to be of concern. From Reggie's point of view, that suggested that it was Master Brand, or someone acting for him. Probably to see if they could find a lever to shake Lynet's determination, or plant something suspicious, and they hadn't been able to do either.

Lynet let herself settle onto the sofa, then patted the seat next to her. "Beer? To go with the conversation? It's cold pies tonight, it's warm enough I didn't want anything hot, and I don't think Tressy's had the oven going for hours, anyway."

"No, that's fair." Reggie opened two of the bottles of beer and handed her one as he sat down. "How do you feel, getting all of that done?"

"Excellent. Really pleased. Frustrated that it took this long. And I don't know what we do now."

"That's the thing I was thinking about. Well, one of them." Reggie took a long sip of his beer. "It comes down to strategy now, I think."

Lynet shifted on the sofa to peer at him. "What do you mean?"

"We have a bit of leverage now that we didn't have a fortnight ago." Reggie twisted his hand over and back. "I'm not entirely sure how to play that, though. Especially since we haven't heard much of anything. Just that note from Manse confirming he was following up."

"I hate the feeling all these people are talking about our project, and we have no idea what they're doing." Lynet let out a long sigh. "It feels, what's the word. Infantilising."

"They're doing it to me, too. And they're likely going around everyone in our building, at the moment. If that's any help at all." Reggie didn't much like it either, but at least they were together in that.

Lynet tilted her head. "Does it bother you, or are you just used to it?"

"More the second. No one is actively trying to kill me at the moment. It makes it easier to be patient. No, that's not quite the right word. Knowing there are things I can't change, and storming and raging won't help. I'm too tired for that." Reggie shrugged again and took a long sip from his beer.

Lynet was quiet for a good minute before she cleared her throat. "Can I ask what you see happening next? As the choices?"

"Sure." Reggie gathered his thoughts. "First, perhaps the Council comes through and makes a formal order, or something of the kind. Shakes loose reliable amounts of what we need, makes sure it's not diverted. In that case, you make journals, and I hope I get to continue to lend a hand." He held up a finger, then added a second. "Second, the Council doesn't do anything, or can't. I'm not sure how we'd tell the difference. In that case, we have a couple of choices. We have more leverage now." Lynet opened her mouth. "I'll come back to that."

She nodded and let him continue.

"Third, the Council doesn't act, and someone else notices we're making progress and tries to stop us. Master Brand, whoever Master Brand is reporting to."

"You think he's the one making materials get stuck, I don't know..." Lynet chewed on that. "I still can't understand that."

Reggie swallowed hard. "I - you know I got a bit of bad news last Friday? Two people I knew at school, both dead." He hadn't been close to them, exactly, but you couldn't share a house common room with people for four out of five years, and not know them. They'd been decent men, who should have had much longer lives to be decent in.

Lynet nodded, cautiously. "Yes? You went off to the Arthur for the night, and I'm glad it helped."

"Memorial services, always a curious kind of helping." But he'd been able to go, at least. Reggie swallowed, considered the bottle, and drank the last of his current beer. "But it got me thinking. There must be people - a number of them - who wouldn't want others, even other generals or others back here, in London or Trellech, to know how awful things are. How brutally awful, wasteful, and ineffective the current approach is. How people are dying because people at the front keep trying the same thing, even though it doesn't work."

"And the journal would change that." Lynet nodded. "And you think someone has Master Brand's ear and wants to stop us. But..." She was reasoning it out quite well, really. "But can't just order that the project stop."

"No. For one thing, now you know how to do it. And other people know the basics of it. That it's possible, the general line of theory. You couldn't remove everyone who knows now. And you've documented some of it, not the exact process, but enough people might recreate it."

Lynet considered. "I've been thinking about that. Even when I explain it to people - you're the first person who's managed most of it, even with me coaching. Ellis couldn't." She flicked her fingers. "What does that do for your logic?"

"Well, for the people who very much want the journals, it makes you priceless." Reggie said. "At least until you figure out how to teach it. Really, I've got further than anyone else?"

"Ellis admits this isn't really his style of doing things?

That's part of it. And it's not as if I've tried to teach dozens of people. But even just talking about some of the theory, you picked it up much more quickly."

"I did have a certain incentive." Reggie shifted and took her hand. "I wanted to prove myself. And I wanted to be useful, more than anything else. Feel like there was some good I could do, somewhere."

Lynet squeezed his hand in turn. "We're back to the awfulness over there, aren't we?" She hesitated. "You feel - I don't have the words for it - about being invalided out."

"Shame, mostly." He could name it now, at least here with her. "It was stupid, getting trench foot. And now I can't do what I'm trained for, keeping the warding and protections up. I keep wondering if there are trenches that caved in, because I couldn't help. Or something that exploded."

"Would you go back, if you could?" Lynet was very careful now.

Reggie took a long breath and let it out slowly. "I'd like to say yes. I want to be the sort of person who'd say yes. But I also saw how badly things were going. And I'd not want to go back and be stuck like that, knowing it was going wrong and not being able to change it."

Lynet nodded and looked down at their hands. "If you went, I don't know what I'd do with myself. I don't - I'd carry on, I suppose. People do. But I'd, I don't know what I'd do. Times like tonight, but also the work. You help more than you think you do. How you paid attention to how I wanted things done. Even when I'm demanding."

Reggie went still. He hadn't expected her to say anything of the kind. He swallowed. "You - I hadn't wanted to assume." Then he cleared his throat. "So you want me to stay on as your assistant? For as long as there's something to assist at?"

"More than that. I mean." She went quiet for a painfully long pause. "There's a war on. And you want to help with the war effort, whatever else happens. Need to. But sometimes, I think about what it could be like after. You helping, here. Doing private binding for people. You could set up consulting for warding, I suppose, as well. But I like how you cut things, how careful you are. And you know when the paste's ready, or needs a little more heat."

"I don't have nearly your deftness with most of it. Or with the charmwork. But I do like..." Reggie considered, turning his free hand so he could look at his fingers. "I like the physicality of it. That's what I like about the protective magic work, actually. It's very tactile, much of the time. Books are different, but they're still the same category of things."

Lynet nodded. "I can see that. I like the textures, the way the different paper weights feel, or how the needle goes through them. Book cloth is different from leather, of course, or all the different kinds of leather. The smell of the oil, oh, that's lovely."

"I have noticed you just standing and breathing in the workroom downstairs." There were rolls of leather there, and they'd spent some time last week making sure they were all in good order and updating inventory. One of them had picked up a bit of mould, and Lynet had some thoughts about doing something useful with it if the cleaning charms took well enough. "All right. I hadn't wanted to assume." He'd said that before, but it was worth saying again.

"That is why I'm telling you, Reggie. I want you around, please. In a range of ways. We work well together. And other things together." That had a shy little crack to her voice. The only thing to do with that was to kiss her, and kiss her he did.

It wasn't until she pulled back a few minutes later that he had one more thing to say. "We do have some leverage. Especially if it's the two of us - and Ellis - working together."

"Can't forget Ellis, no. He's essential to the whole thing. So we wait a little longer and see what they come up with? And keep making journals."

"Yes. Let them ask for the finished copies, or at least..." Reggie considered. "If we don't hear anything by Monday week, then we can make it clear we have some available. If they can clear up these problems we've been having. I don't expect the wheels of change to be instant. Even for a Council Member. But near three weeks should be enough for something."

Lynet leaned over, then cupped his cheek so she could kiss him again. That was answer enough.

CHAPTER 41

They arrived at their building on time. There was someone out front, a middle-aged woman in the unofficial uniform of the Ministry, a dark skirt suit. A couple of people were helping move things out, people in basic khaki uniforms. "Mistress Alder? And you'd be Captain Hollis?"

Lynet blinked. "Yes? Is there a problem?"

"You're welcome to go right up, but if you could come down to the back courtyard, where it's a bit more private, at half-nine. There are some changes in the projects here. Someone from the Ministry will be here to explain, but we'd prefer to do it once." She sounded a bit harried, honestly. "I gather most of the others here don't get here as early."

"Generally, no, ma'am." Reggie nodded. "I'll open a window. If you get people together earlier than you expect, just give a shout or send someone up."

She just nodded and braced herself to address the next

person in. Reggie peered down both hallways, but all he could see was some bustle from where Lord Temple and Margot and that lot had been working. People were coming and going from the offices, and one of the doors open at the other end, down by Master Brand. Neither of them said anything until they were upstairs. Lynet took her usual perch on the workbench and waited until Reggie closed the door and called the warding in.

"That wasn't what I expected."

Reggie shook his head. "Me either. And it looked far-reaching." He moved to glance out to the courtyard. "It looks like they're piling up boxes to move somewhere there. Not that there are that many yet, a dozen or so? So they can't have started since we left Friday, just this morning. That's an hour's work, maybe."

Lynet frowned. "Moving things without people being here?" That bothered her, more than a bit, the idea of other people moving her things.

"Well, not most of them. I'm sure there was some other party. Everyone's sleeping off the hangover before they take up drinking again. Do we want to do anything while we're waiting?"

"Inventory check, just to make sure? You wanted to test a little of the vervain for potency, didn't you? I can help. I think I've got the knack this time." It took a delicate touch with a pipette, the way Reggie had been testing it. They should have plenty of time for it. Lynet thought she was up for the challenge, though.

"Let's do that." The process occupied them agreeably for most of the hour they had to wait. By that point, about half the staff seemed to be downstairs. "Shall we go down?" Reggie gestured.

Lynet nodded and they both quietly tidied up. No one

had implied they needed to be doing anything differently, so they left things neat, and that was it. By the time they got down to the courtyard, Ellis had come out. "You know what this is about?"

Reggie shook his head. Lynet stood between them, somehow wanting the protection of people she trusted on either side. Right at half-nine, someone came out of the building, formally dressed, in a posh suit. "Thank you, all. As you are aware, we are making some changes to the research being done here, and we also have some other announcements of changes."

"What's going on?" That was one of the bright young men, looking unsettled. It was not a flattering look on him.

"Give us a moment, and we'll explain. A review of the records for this building indicates some ongoing issues with materia use and distribution. One of the projects that has been using materials heavily is moving to another site, where there can be more support for their needs. And of course a dedicated staff to manage the requests. Two other projects are moving out and under new sub-departments of the Ministry. Those of you affected by this have already been informed."

There was a round of nods. Lynet saw most of Lord Carillon's people nodding, the ones who'd been at the party. Margot held her chin up, aloof, and Lord Carillon himself was leaning against a wall, looking steadily at the speaker.

"For the rest of you, we are releasing Master Brand to other duties. We'll be speaking individually with the projects affected today, and we'd ask you to wait in your usual workrooms and to take your luncheon in the building. One of the Guard will be around to take requests for food from the Ministry canteen with today's menu."

That, now, made Lynet very glad they'd paused to pick up their box lunches on the way in. The Ministry canteen wasn't bad, exactly, but it was stodgy and beige and boring. There were a handful of other questions about who was doing the moving, where they were moving to, but that wound down very quickly.

"Come up with us, Ellis? Bring your lunch up?" Lynet felt it was better to have them all together. She hadn't explained the visit to the Council Member to Ellis, she hadn't been sure what she could talk about. She'd said nothing more than that she and Reggie had had a meeting with someone who might be able to help.

Ellis nodded agreeably and ducked into his own workroom. He stuck a note on the door on the way back out. "Saying I'm upstairs."

In the end, they didn't have to wait terribly long. Lynet had told Ellis about their conversation with Smythe-Clive, and the three of them could only assume this was related, but it wasn't as if they had more information to work with. Lynet spent most of the waiting time perched on the workbench facing the door, with Reggie leaning beside her, his back against it. He let his fingers rest against her leg, and she didn't stop him. Ellis had figured it out, and some time ago now.

Right at ten-fifteen, there was a knock on the door and a polite, "Mistress Alder?" Reggie immediately turned his hand to offer his arm as she hopped down. He waited until she'd brushed out her skirts, before moving to get the door.

"Come in." He sounded entirely in control of the world, and Lynet envied that rather a lot. She stayed back against the workbench, and Ellis and Reggie came around beside her.

It was the man they'd seen outside, as well as Smythe-

Clive, who nodded agreeably at all of them. It was the Council Member who spoke first, with the other man standing respectfully. "Mistress Alder, Captain Hollis. And you must be Master Stromer." He took in something about Ellis's expression. "Mistress Alder and Captain Hollis were kind enough to be of some assistance a fortnight ago, when I had some questions about how things were going here."

He glanced around, taking in the space. "How have things been going since?"

Lynet glanced at the other man, who cleared his throat. "Pardon. I should introduce myself. Master Hodge. I'm a senior departmental secretary in the Ministry of Materia, currently charged with making sure the projects housed here are properly supported. It's a shame you've had such problems, and that no one brought it to our attention as they should." That had a scolding note to it, but something in his tone made it clear that he disapproved of the junior staff who hadn't brought the issue up. Not of Lynet and Reggie.

That answered some of the question, but not all of it. Lynet waited a little more. After a good twenty seconds, Smythe-Clive snorted. "Like that, of course it is. Master Brand is being moved to somewhere he can be, shall we say, less obstreperous? We would very much like to have a meeting later this week. Perhaps Thursday, where you can update us on what you need, where you are, and when we might have steady journal production. I do hope shaking the materia loose was some help."

Lynet considered. She could tell him, of course, that they had near a hundred journals ready to go, or would, as soon as they'd tested. They'd lose a handful, probably. Some the magic just hadn't taken quite right for some reason. She glanced over her shoulder at Reggie, and he nodded, just once.

Lynet turned back. "We need to do the final testing, but I expect we'll have close to a hundred from last week's work. We can't keep up that pace for long, some of why we could was because we'd prepared stocks of materials as we could while waiting for materia in previous weeks. I can confirm the final number by noon tomorrow, if it would assist with your planning."

"And begin making more?" Master Hodge leaned forward.

"Another twenty-five this week, if the materia isn't diverted, and Reggie is able to help me. And we don't have too many meetings."

She tacked the last one on and watched as Smythe-Clive grinned suddenly. "We were wondering if Reggie might like an additional task. Or a new one. But I gather he's of great help?"

"I certainly couldn't work as quickly without him. He's picked it up remarkably well, and he knows his limits. Why?" She risked making it a challenge.

"We were wondering if he'd oversee checks on materia for the building. Not inventory, we can assign one of the office staff for that, but making sure that the materia is still effective. You could hire your own staff, Hollis. There's room in the offices down the hall on this floor."

Reggie's hand brushed hers for just an instant, the sort of thing covered by her skirt and his jacket, the way they were standing. Then he nodded. "I do want to continue working with the books. But there's time to oversee something like that. I'd want much better controls on the materia itself, both checking the storage and how people are signed in and out of the room. Perhaps a double key method." He waved a hand. "For Thursday?"

"Thursday." Both the other men nodded. "Think about what you'd need to do it properly. We'll get a precis of the projects to you sometime tomorrow once we've gone through the immediate needs. Master Stromer, is that agreeable to you as well?"

Ellis chuckled softly. "I trust Reggie's touch with the materia, so yes. I just want to make the paper properly. We do have some capacity, if paper's needed for other projects. And I'd not mind an assistant. It seems to have done Lynet all the good in the world."

"We can see about that, certainly." Master Hodge wasn't committing, Lynet could see the calculations about budgets in his eyes.

Reggie cleared his throat. "I assume that some of this will involve a new contract, seeing as how Lynet's and mine were both with Master Brand as signatory. And of course, I'm sure you'll be making certain Lynet's getting her due in her crafting rank. I've heard a few comments here and there that made me think she wasn't. I'll have a look at the standard scales by Thursday, of course." He hesitated just a beat, and then added, "And of course, this is in the standard contract, I understand. But clear provisions for her continued development of the method, after the War ends."

Smythe-Clive looked deeply amused, while Master Hodge grimaced for an instant, then straightened out his face. "I'll add that to my list, of course. I hadn't realised it might be a concern."

Reggie just shrugged once. "I'm sure you want Lynet to be able to focus on her work here rather than worry about other matters." Which was entirely true, even if Lynet would never have dared bring it up herself.

"If there's anything else before Thursday, I'll be working out of the office across from Master Brand's former office for the time being. Until the new administrator is able to move in. If that's all, we have a number of others to talk to."

Lynet nodded as politely as she could. "Master Hodge, much appreciated." He went out, and Smythe-Clive turned and offered a quick smile, before following him out, closing the door behind them both.

"Well. That's a cat among the pigeons." Ellis shook his head. "I'll go back down to my workroom, then. Unless there's anything to talk about."

"I think you should have an assistant." Lynet said. "And Reggie, asking about the pay."

Reggie grinned. "I'm quite sure you're underpaid. I just don't know by how much. I will have a look at the scales. And we can work up a list of ongoing supplies, and all that."

Ellis nodded. "Catch up at the end of the day, about where we are? I'll write if there's anything else." He went out, barely waiting for an acknowledgement.

Lynet didn't press on it. Reggie would make this thing happen, clearly, and she wasn't going to say no. For one thing, she could, in fact, use the money. And for another, well. She wanted it to be fair, somehow. And he wanted to make it fair. She wasn't going to turn that down.

Before she could say anything else, though, he was pulling her closer. It was an embrace, a hug, that was all about company and being together, and she wanted to lean into that particular reassurance for days. Not that she could.

Instead, she let herself have five breaths of inhaling his scent and feeling his warmth and just being in the moment. "Right. We have work to do and reports to prepare."

"And tonight?" Reggie was teasing. "We should celebrate our change in circumstances, just a little."

"Tonight, we will wrap up, check in with Ellis." Lynet let out a puff of breath. She knew Reggie had wanted something particular. "And you may take me out to supper, if you like. Somewhere people can see us."

EPILOGUE

R eggie was nervous about today. Not as nervous as Lynet almost certainly was, he at least had a pretty good idea what to expect. But his eldest sister, Edith, had indicated that if Reggie knew what was good for him, he should bring Lynet with him for an afternoon's visit. Sooner than later was the implication, or else.

And so here they were. They had Michaelmas Day as a holiday, the building was going to be closed up. And it was, admittedly, a pleasant enough day to be in the country rather than the city. Reggie usually felt that, of course, but even Lynet had agreed it was good to get some fresh air. Now they were strolling up from the portal nearer the village, along the long row of oaks.

Edith had married into a good country family, exactly the sort of match Pater had wanted for her, from everything Reggie understood. Her husband was well on track to being appointed as a magistrate in due course and already had taken on various positions of responsibility in the local area. Edith herself hadn't formally apprenticed - it wasn't the done thing in a woman who didn't have obvious talents and who intended to marry promptly. But she had a knack for the stillroom sorts of things, and for an abundance in the garden. He could see the autumn flowers doing well, even as the leaves were turning colours around them. The house looked well; the ivy was green, the stonework in good shape.

He'd expected one of the staff, but Edith was there, standing at the door, wearing one of her less formal dresses. Reggie was sure immediately she'd chosen it to make Lynet feel more comfortable. It was a dark green linen, the sort that had been worn and washed enough to be soft to the touch.

"Edith, this is Lynet. Lynet, my oldest sister, Edith." Reggie had offered his arm to Lynet as they came up the path from the village portal. The gardens were even fading attractively into autumn.

"Come in, come in, you're just perfectly on time. Frederick's gone for most of the day. It's the quarter day, and he has to see to various things at the local magistrate's. He's not the magistrate, of course, he just runs the records. One of these days, though. Do come through to the drawing room, here on the left."

Lynet glanced around, and Reggie wondered what she made of the place. The books in the drawing room were far more for show than any actual reading. Or even any demonstration of the book-binder's art. They were mostly in matching brown leather, which he knew these days was a deeply unimaginative choice. On the other hand, Edith's husband Frederick, for all his other virtues, was deeply unimaginative.

Edith beamed. "I thought a very informal lunch. Now,

tell me, is Reggie actually eating properly? He's not at all good at being reassuring about that, and I do fuss."

"He makes a point of picking up lunches for us, some-where better than the canteen." Lynet settled on one of the sofas, and Reggie joined her immediately. "And the flat and workshop is opposite a pub - well, it's London. Half the shops are within a block of a pub, really."

Edith chuckled. "Well. Not that I've been that sort, but I'm told there's something about it as a gathering place? There are two in the village. I just don't make it down there often. It makes them a tad uncomfortable, most of the time, like we're going to be telling tales. Please, do sit down, luncheon will be ready in half an hour or so. Reggie's told me a little about you, your skill with books, of course. But we're dreadfully curious about everything."

"May I ask who's included in 'we', please?" Lynet settled on the sofa, and Reggie promptly sat next to her. He, on the other hand, knew exactly what Edith would read from that, and correctly. He didn't touch her. He wasn't sure how Lynet would take that right now, but he could be right there, and would be.

"I am, more or less, the representative of the family here. Our mother will listen to me on this point. And our father - well, he'll have opinions, but Mother will talk him round given a bit of time."

Reggie cleared his throat. "You're making assumptions, Edie."

"I am not." She sounded highly amused now. "You've been frittering around, and everyone's been worried you wouldn't ever settle down. Especially not after, well." She flicked her fingers at his legs. "You seem much happier. You enjoy what you're doing. How is that going, anything you can talk about?"

Reggie felt that on that front things were going perhaps a tad too smoothly for comfort. The new contracts had been signed, with a decidedly better rate of pay for Lynet. She'd been getting paid an apprentice's wages, when all was said and done, rather than the rank she had every right to. They'd even come through with a lump sum to make up some of the difference, and that had gone a long way to paying off her father's debts.

Reggie was getting apprentice wages for his work with the books. That was right and proper. But he was also getting journeyman wages for his work managing the materia, which was running to five or ten hours a week at the moment. And besides, he wasn't relying on the income.

Better, though, was the codicil in the contract that made it clear that when the War ended, Lynet had the right to produce the journals on her own. Or, for that matter, if the Ministry ended the project sooner. She was obliged to fully document her methods, but she, Reggie, and Ellis were now fairly sure it would be tricky to find someone to simply pick up the process. He'd got the impression that the folks overseeing them now had realised the same thing. They'd been quite eager to keep Lynet happy when it came to her work.

"We're making much better progress now there's more support for the administrative side." That, Lynet clearly felt entirely able to answer. "But we're going to be kept busy with it. Getting today off was easy partly because we're waiting on two new staff and some supplies. Apprentices. Reggie's managing the administration." She didn't touch on what they were doing, but Lynet had checked earlier, and it wasn't like Edith didn't know that books were involved somehow.

"Not a talent we'd entirely known about in him, but I'm

glad it's being put to good use. And other things are well?"
Edith was prying.

Lynet tilted her head. "Would you please just ask straight out?"

Reggie snorted. "Edith, you are being entirely too polite and also obscure."

His sister spread her hands. "I am a creature of my upbringing, Reggie. We do worry about the difference in backgrounds, Lynet, and if that's going to cause problems. But also, wanting to know if you're doing well enough with, I don't know, the practical things."

Those, at least to Reggie's way of thinking, were going rather well. He was reliably spending Friday and Saturday night in London and in Lynet's bed. The weeknights, they stayed in Trellech. But if things went on as they were, Reggie rather hoped he might propose sometime in the first half of the coming year. He was already on the lookout for a pleasant flat large enough for both of them and a modest workroom. Or perhaps a larger one. He wasn't at all sure whether Lynet would choose to move all her working space to Trellech or not. They'd have to discuss it sometime, but not just yet. For now, he would make sure she ate well, had all sorts of amusements when she wasn't working, and generally keep an eye out for her well-being and happiness.

It wouldn't replace her father, nothing could. But he found the way she grieved mattered, too. She'd begun talking about him more, the last few weeks, and the way she talked about him made Reggie ache. He had been raised largely by Nanny, and somewhat by his elder sisters - especially Edie, before her marriage. His parents had been distant but pleasant.

Lynet loved her father closely and deeply. In fact, she loved him enough to be angry with him about his choices.

Reggie didn't ever want Lynet angry like that with him - or, he hoped, not whatever children might be, in a world where that was a thing that happened. But that fierce loyalty and love, that was something he wanted to learn more about, until it felt as comfortable under his fingers as sewing a signature together did.

He'd been woolgathering. By the time he realised it, Lynet was watching him, her head tilted. He felt her fingers slip into his hand. "Reggie is very determined about making sure we're both well fed. I'm sorting out some of my father's workshop and finishing up a few of his commissions that were outstanding. And starting a few new pieces, though not generally on commission, since I can't guarantee a timeline." She'd finished the first of them, from Reggie himself, last week. "Would you?"

That was his cue. He needed both his hands for this, to reach down into the bag he'd brought with them. Inside was a volume, wrapped up in a neat square of linen. He stood, bringing it over to Edith and presenting it with a bow. "For you and the children."

Edith blinked at him, but waved him to his seat while she worked on undoing the ribbon that held it in place. He waited while she unfolded the fabric to reveal a beautiful bit of green leather. He'd helped prepare it, after Lynet had got the printed pages all properly arranged. Edith opened the book, and then her smile grew. "You knew we were looking for a new copy. Ours is near in pieces." It was a book on the lore of Buckinghamshire, one that Reggie had loved in his own childhood, with lovely engraved illustrations.

"I'd be glad to rebind that for you, too, if you liked. If the pages aren't in too bad of a shape." Lynet gestured. "Reggie explained, you particularly like that telling of the local stories."

"A bit dated now, I suppose. But this is lovely. Reggie, did you help?"

"Sewing the signatures, some of the glue work. It's all Lynet's work in the design and the details, and the marbling for the endpapers." She'd chosen beautiful shades of green that reflected the meadows and hills and woodlands of the stories, with just a touch of brown and golden yellow. "And the embossing work's all Lynet. I'm clumsy with it yet."

"Thank you, then, Lynet. For the time and the attention. I'm quite sure we'll treasure this. And my, it's something to have a gift that's meant to be used, isn't it? Not something to be put up on the mantle and admired."

"That's what a book is for. If you don't read it, touch it, what good is it?" Lynet shifted to take Reggie's hand again, and he squeezed back once.

From there, the conversation got rather easier. Edith settled in to giving Lynet a summary of everyone in the family, complete with amusing stories. Half their relatives would complain about those getting shared, but Edith had a knack for choosing the illuminating ones. Along the way, she was making it quite clear which of the family would support Reggie's choices in the matter, and which would be difficult. But she was also nearly as clear about what she intended to do about that, firmly on Reggie's side.

The rest of the day went quite well, with a walk in the garden and a look at some of the family's art. Lynet had an eye for the design of the things, even if the artists themselves weren't something she was terribly familiar with. Reggie made a mental note to see about taking her to the museum at some point whenever they could find the time.

And she was natural and easy with with Edith's little ones, they properly thought Lynet was wonderful.

As they made their way down to the portal to go back to London, Reggie cleared his throat.

Lynet snorted. "You're trying to figure out how to ask? I had a remarkably good time, and I'm aware Edith was doing her best to make it easy on me. Will you help me write a proper note, to go in the post tomorrow?"

"Absolutely." That was easy, gathering up all the proper etiquette he'd learned and sharing it, so she made the kind of impression she ought to. "And tonight?"

"Tonight, you can come up with something we'll both enjoy."

If you enjoyed *Bound For Perdition* and would like to read more of this series, please sign up for my mailing list to get all the latest news and fun extras.

Your reviews (on whatever review site you use) are much appreciated, too!

Read on for more historical details about this book and more about Albion!

Author's Notes

Welcome to *Bound for Perdition*! Thank you for taking this journey with me into the origins of the magical journals, a glimpse into more of what happened with Temple Carillon, and a great deal of pleasure rolling around in the beauty of bookbinding.

My thanks as always to Kiya Nicoll, both for editing and for helping me sort out the different aspects of Temple's arc in particular. And as always, so much gratitude to early readers for making sure everything made sense.

The question of what Temple is up to - and what happens to him in 1922 - is a long arc through my books. This is only one piece of the puzzle! More will be revealed (including a reappearance of Margot Williams) in *Three Graces*, set in early 1945 and coming out in early 2024.

If you'd like more of the Carillon arc, in chronological order, they are: *Bound For Perdition* (1917), *Ancient Trust* (1922, available free by signing up for my newsletter), *Goblin Fruit* (Geoffrey's romance with Lizzie in 1924), *On The Bias* (1925), *Best Foot Forward* (1935), and *Nocturnal*

Quarry (1938), with some additional relevant references to Temple and his fate in *Upon A Summer's Day* (1940).

That's rather a lot, but I do love Geoffrey and the nest of people and experts he collects around him. You can learn more on my public wiki at bit.ly/celia-lake-wiki.

Onward to the notes about this book. Bookbinding notes in general first, and then we'll get into the other details.

Bookbinding is, of course, an incredibly complex art. I have done my best here to present the sort of choices that would be practical for the goal - something sturdy, that could be packed into kit bags, carried around, be taken out and put away dozens of times a day. As Lynet explains, case binding (where the book is mounted onto book boards, a protective spine, and so on) is the optimal choice here.

As part of the research for this book, I tried my hand at a bookbinding kit, and discovered I enjoyed sewing the signatures rather a lot, but I was not nearly as good at the glue parts. (I am not the most dexterous human on the planet...) Figuring out how to take something from a stack of pages and parts to a real book was delightful, however, and I can see just how Reggie came to the same conclusion.

The **journals** themselves, of course, have a number of magical aspects. Some of this, as Lynet mentions, has to do with numbers in the design features. After some considera-tion, I decided that a "Council octavo" (a designation that doesn't exist in our world) is a 6x9" book. Octavo means that you get 8 pages to the sheet.

To make the magic work smoothly, and keep in lines with Albion's commitment to the number 7, they use groups of 7 cut sheets to the signature, or 14 pages. This comes out to 196 pages, total (though you will lose a few of those pages to the end pages, securing the book to the bookboards, and to things like an index or owner's information.)

As noted in the text, each page is a separate conversation, and the magic allows you to more or less scroll (as you would on a scroll of parchment, or these days on our phones) where you can see comments back and forth. At this point in time, you can only do single person conversations. By the mid-1920s, the journals will work with established shared contact points, and by the Second World War, there are options for information transmission to a large group of people with permission to read that information.

My 1920s books make the point that journals are not inexpensive. For much of the early 1920s, they're about the cost of a car. Certainly something people might well own - but in that period, not a thing a lot of people owned. The cost comes down slowly in the middle of the decade, so by the late 20s it's more like the cost of a higher end computer. (Still out of reach of many people, or a cost they might not chose to make, but within the realm that employers might provide one to certain staff, and where many people might consider the cost worthwhile.)

The **actual magic of the journal** is in multiple parts.

The **paper** relies on a chain of astrological magical and alchemical relationships, a sort of circle of planets. You move from Mistletoe (associated with Sun in Leo) to Quartz (Moon in Cancer) to Sardonyx (Mercury in Virgo), to Rose (Venus in Taurus), to Nettle (Mars in Aries), to Amethyst (Jupiter in Sagittarius), ending with Solomon's Seal (Saturn in Capricorn). Each of these brings its own properties to the paper, from being a magical amplifier (the mistletoe) to providing clarity (the amethyst), to anchoring and making something lasting (Solomon's Seal).

Then the book is bound with slivers of three woods in the **spine**. Apple for connection and many other aspects of lore, hazel for conducting the magical energies cleanly, and oak for stability and managing high levels of magic. Sigils are drawn with ink made from cedar (attainment of magical power), lodestone (connecting natural realms and pointing in a direction), and with an owl quill - rather finicky - for clarity, insight, magic, and secrets.

Finally, the **paste** plays a part: this is where Dill (clarity of thought), Iris (a fixative, protection as well), Rue (finding a mark, making that connection to another journal), Mandrake, and Vervain (both magical amplifiers) play a role. As you can see, having one ingredient missing might involve reworking the entire process, because it's building a complex net of interlocking magical tendencies that all need to work together. Not unlike a computer, indeed! (You can also see why I didn't try to explain all the mechanics in the text of the book: it's unwieldy to lay out!)

Onto the rest of the notes, in order as we go through the book.

Trench foot was, in fact, about as Reggie describes it: unpleasant, vaguely shameful, and not talked about much. There's still some question about what exactly caused it, but it ran rampant in cold wet environs like the trenches. It can come on quite quickly, causes swelling and damage due to poor blood supply, and can lead to decay, infections, and other related harm. As Reggie implies, his case is worse than most: beside the amputation of three toes, he also has some ongoing infection damage to his foot, and will be susceptible to similar conditions for the rest of his life.

The **Wain** mentioned is Orcus Wain, Seth and Thesan's oldest brother and second oldest sibling. (He's mentioned briefly elsewhere as having worked for some rather secretive position during the War for the Ministry, and he's quite obviously exactly the sort the second floor swots are made of.)

There were a series of **mutinies** among the French army from April through June 1917, involving ultimately almost half the French infantry divisions on the Western Front. The soldiers remained in the trenches and were willing to defend the line but not attack. They were protesting - not unreasonably - the massive shock and loss of life from the Nivelle Offensive, the non-arrival of American troops, and enflamed by a growing movement toward pacifism. The French army leadership responded with mass arrests and mass trials, but also took steps (like longer leaves, and a promise to end grand offensives "until the arrival of tanks and Americans on the front.")

The reference in chapter 11 to "they know **a brother or a sister or a cousin or an aunt**" is the Gilbert and Sullivan reference you might expect, from *H.M.S. Pinafore*.

An oggie is the Welsh version of "let us wrap some filling in some dough and eat it with our hands" (similar to a Cornish pasty). Traditionally, they're larger than a pasty, sometimes called a giant oggie, and most often feature lamb and leeks (both common and widely used Welsh foods).

If you're trying to place the name **Medea Aylett,** you've read *On The Bias* (she's also referred to briefly in *Best Foot Forward*). A resolution to the question of what happens to her can be found in *Nocturnal Quarry*, set in 1938 (out in

March 2023). **Margot** will be making an appearance in the future, too, as part of the tale in *Three Graces*, book 6 in the Land Mysteries series (out in early 2024).

Reggie refers to both **Marathon** and **Charles Barbier** as methods of rapid communication in battle conditions. Marathon, of course, is the famous battle where a soldier ran 26 miles to bring a message without stopping (leading to the modern sport). Charles Barbier was working on a method of passing messages that could be read by touch (without needing a light that might give away information to a nearby enemy), which led to Louis Braille developing his method of reading and writing for the blind.

The *Decameron* is a series of Italian tales, where the framing story is a group of nobles shutting themselves up in remote country estate to avoid the plague sweeping through Italy in 1348. Because of the setting and period, there's a certain underlying 'everything is going to be all right, yes?' driving through the stories.

The first **Pulitzer Prizes** were awarded in 1917, established in the will of Joseph Pulitzer as an award for achievements in various kinds of writing and musical composition. The first award for literature went to three daughters of Julia Ward Howe, a Boston suffragette, poet, and author, for a biography of their mother.

Latin has a number of ways to ask questions. The enclitic **nonne** is the form used if you're asking a question that assumes a 'yes' answer, as described in the text. There are other places Geoffrey Carillon could have gone, but if he'd wanted to stay in the Trellech townhouses, he'd likely not have come out to Cumbria in the first place.

Ravenser Odd was a port built on the sandbanks of the river Humber in Yorkshire. The sandbank and the buildings on it were destroyed in a massive storm in the 1350s, similar to the storm that destroyed the village of Dunwich the previous century.

That's it for our author's notes! We have a lot more to come in this series, exploring the various arts and magics of Albion. The next book in the series will be out in August 2023, *Shoemaker's Wife*. It's set in 1920, with a "we got married quickly during the War, and now we have to figure out what it means to be married" romance with a lot of theatre and holiday pantomime fun, a theatre ghost, and a mystery to solve.

Again, if you'd like more about the arc of what happens with Temple and Geoffrey, all the books dealing with them are listed on the Carillon arc family page on my authorial wiki. (You can also find it under Series and Arcs in the sidebar.)

You can get *Ancient Trust*, a novella in 1922, for free by signing up for my mailing list and learn a little more about Temple's (tragic) outcome and about what happens with his brother Geoffrey. I hope you'll come join us there - or on my Discord or Patreon (https://celialake.com/contact to learn more) - to hear more about my books, get access to extras, and other delightful things.

ALSO BY CELIA LAKE

The Mysterious Arts Series

Bound for Perdition

The Mysterious Charm Series

Outcrossing

Goblin Fruit

Magician's Hoard

Wards of the Roses

In The Cards

On The Bias

Seven Sisters

The Mysterious Powers Series

Carry On

The Fossil Door

Eclipse

Fool's Gold

The Hare and the Oak

Point By Point

Mistress of Birds

Charms of Albion

Pastiche

Sailor's Jewel

Land Mysteries

Best Foot Forward

Other stories

Complementary

Winter's Charms

Forged in Combat

Learn more about the world of Albion and future books at my website, celialake.com. Additional information linking characters, places, and timelines is available at bit.ly/celia-lake-wiki

Sign up for my newsletter to be the first to hear about future books and learn about fascinating bits of research. Happy reading!